Falling Stars

Julie Rogers

56 MOUNTAIN PRESS

Falling Stars
Copyright © 2023 by Julie Rogers
Printed in the United States of America.

All rights reserved.

No portion of this book may be reproduced, stored in any retrieval system, or transmitted in any form or by any means (electronic, mechanical, photocopying, recording, scanning, or otherwise) except in brief quotations for critical reviews or articles, without prior written permission from the author. This is a work of fiction. Some variations and inconsistencies in linguistic usage and style, particularly between historic and contemporary accounts, are intentional. While the story does employ *factasy*—an incidental integration of fact and fantasy—all names, characters, places, and other references herein are used fictitiously. As in all fiction, the literary perceptions and insights may be based upon experience. A few well-known people (Jonathon Frid and Norman G. Baker) appear in these pages, but this remains a work of fiction, and the usual rules apply. Some works of art described in this novel are fictional references to the cult classic *Dark Shadows,* first created and produced by Dan Curtis in 1966.

FIRST EDITION
First Printing, 2023
Falling Stars/Julie Rogers. — 1st ed.

ISBN
978-0-9971074-7-0 (sc)
978-0-9971074-6-3 (e)

www.julierogersbooks.com

For Lois

In manus tuas, Domine

Prologue

𝒟isappointment is frequently my inevitable companion while I hack my way toward the truth, not in so much I go scouting assignments that turn out to be hoaxes, but because oversights, misinformation, lies—and the mental tides which shore them—are intrinsic to us all.
We all lie to ourselves some of the time.
Every effort to editorialize therefore entails a shirking off, a surrendering of childhood fantasies held close to the vest. The dastardly deed of finding objectivity can lay bare even the best memories under a different light, it seems—sitting ducks for harsher scrutiny.
After all, what is truth?
One such aboriginal concoction from my formative years was the extraordinary concept of a falling star, straight from summers-long investigations of vast Montana skies alongside my maternal grandmother. We'd drive out from Helena in her Olds Custom Cruiser to the Boulder Batholith, sit shoulder-to-shoulder on the hood, and stare up into the night. When I was knee-high, Gram would spot them first, those streaking fireballs she called *shooting stars*. Internet access to wiki engines, NASA, and Google didn't alter our tradition or what we continued calling them, either.
With the help of her astronomy binoculars, I sighted my first falling star when I was six. And for the next twelve years, I dutifully cataloged these appearances in my officially waterproof steno pad while ignoring mounting evidence that what we were really viewing was the atmospheric entry of meteoroids and reentry of space junk. Serious student, I was. I kept astronomical charts and grids about every single sighting with tiny notes-to-self bordered by tangled curlicues and mod flowers little girls are so fond of including.
Our night sky observations yielded some recurrent backyard

Falling Stars

conjuring as well—such that many of those *shooting stars* had wholehearted wishes attached to them. Over the years, these evolved from pleading for my first puppy to yammering for a stud-of-a-guy I thought I wanted, to longing for an acceptance letter to Syracuse and trying to forget the selfsame guy who casually suggested we call it quits when I got into Syracuse. At some point, my young adult version realized, too, that my dear, sweet Gram had an expiration date—and I recall one star-studded night wishing that she would never leave me.

When Gram developed Parkinson's in the fall of 2021, I was in the thick of spearheading *Philly's Argosy*, an all-consuming, online pulp fiction magazine I'd dreamed up with fellow alum and squibbler, Percy McWatters, straight out of college. He'd taken his rightful place as editor in chief after front-loading the enterprise with every penny of his inheritance, in addition to collecting any and all pulp comic magazines he could buy from Jim Hanley's in Midtown Manhattan before he turned twenty.

I assumed second-from-top nerd on the masthead with an equally audacious goal of outsourcing ten more contributing writers besides yours truly. I didn't know it at the time but securing that kind of talent would require nothing less than a five-year endeavor.

Though McWatters never actually *left* work when he vacated the office, he'd opted from the beginning (in the middle of a worldwide pandemic) to lease a brick-and-mortar storefront. I think he liked the rabid climate of the CNN effect and shouting out word choices across the bullpen. He also expected our central location to draw a good amount of walk-in talent or benefactors regardless. Which happened—eventually. Airs of professionalism, with rent.

By July, Gram had observed an ever-so-slight distension of my jugular vein during our weekly FaceTime. I'd just carved up another very bad first draft of my *Philly's Starscape* column.

"Geez Louise, baby girl," she'd said, her mouth altering into a junket of tremors over and around and between almost every word. "I think you could use a few nights under the stars again." Freeze, long tremor. "Don't you?"

As I'd watched each twitch rudely captured in 326 PPI, I saw only Gram's resolve to live out her remaining days unmedicated, and the uneasy spasm expanding in my throat (better known as grief) overrode everything else. I couldn't—*wouldn't*—let her see me cry, because I understood: none of the prodrugs or central nervous system agents, COMT, MAO-B, or decarboxylase inhibitors, dopamine agonists, anticholinergics, or deep brain stimulation would do. With medication therapy she might get ten more years, but she didn't want them. I thought I knew her reason. I assumed I understood why.

So, aside from what contributed to my daily, stress-induced JVD, my grandmother's rapid deterioration—from the first stiffening facial postures to a freeze-fall that claimed her life—summarized year one with *Philly's Argosy*.

Mom didn't deal well with Gram's illness from the get-go, and her sudden passing from a fall-induced brain bleed polished off any remaining reserves for arranging a *splendid* funeral and interment. When Mom called me late one night from a hospital in Helena, I sensed the news wasn't good.

"Your Grammy didn't leave me much to go on," she kept saying over and over. By the end of that conversation, I'd talked her down to a quiet memorial service (at a church Gram had formerly attended) and begged off a transcontinental flight to Montana in one sentence. *Philly's Argosy* was cranking out weekly cyberspace copies at a screeching pace, and besides, Gram and anyone else who knew her understood about the lifetime of affection we'd shared. As far as Gram was concerned, I'd always been off the hook. I smoothed out things with Mom by volunteering to manage the interment, saying I'd have Gram's ashes shipped with a biodegradable urn to my apartment in Philly. A Yucca, or a bonsai. At the time, Mom seemed all right with that.

Like many of the need-to-know arrangements I made with my mother (including the reason I lived 2,222 miles away), I had no intention of confining my grandmother's remains to any variety of urn. To keep the peace, however, I'd learned over the years just what, when, and how to say it.

Eleven months passed with Gram on hold inside a sift-proof cardboard box, top shelf of my clothes closet, before I came up for air at work—a small, but doable window for spreading her remains where I knew she'd prefer to rest. In the middle of October, I traveled 2,612 miles to Death Valley.

Death Valley National Park in California is renowned as one of ten federal parks in North America where stargazers can view the night skies without light pollution—even after an addition of 40,000 orbiting satellites added by SpaceX in 2020 and 2021. The valley's 3.3 million acres contain virtually every possible terrain-with-a-view: mountain-size sand dunes, salt flats, sailing stones, and sandstone canyons.

On clear nights like ones in the middle of October, it's possible to see 4.5 million light-years away with the naked eye. Gram and I made our first real stargazing trip beyond the outskirts of Helena to Death Valley when I was thirteen, middle of October. We carefully picked a night forecast to have the least cloud cover and, under one very thin crescent moon, set out to see what we could see.

Only the phenomenon of sailing stones wasn't observable on that trip, due in part to the weather. The sailing stones seem to slide across the desert quite literally on their own, leaving trails in their wake at Racetrack Playa. The playa is actually a dry lake bed where locals first observed these rocks in the early 1900s. Some claimed strong winds or magnetic fields moved them. Others claimed aliens did.

The long-standing mystery was solved in 2014 with the discovery that the stones are nudged into motion where they lay upon melting panels of thin, floating ice driven by light winds—and only in winter. This rare combination of weather conditions involving just-freezing temperatures only seems to occur every two-to-three years, and the daylight hours following those freezes must bring enough sunlight to melt the ice in the playa into large sheaths. Slabs of dolomite and syenite—all different sizes and weights, are then free to move.

I returned to Death Valley ten years later to, in a sense, recreate those nights we'd shared together, plus escape the damning confines of caustic city life under costly artificial lighting. Given what was happening in Death Valley (and worldwide), I had some things to work around. A 1,000-year flood in the summer of 2022 marked historic records, a year's worth of rainfall in three hours that blew out water systems, park facilities, and miles of roadway. All courtesy of climate change in an environment of extremes already, Death Valley had a bullseye on its back.

I was determined to re-encounter its wonder regardless. From the moment I disembarked my rental car I began retracing our original visit meticulously, step for step—obsessively so—drawn and compelled like a madwoman. Immediately I walked to the edge of the hotel's parking lot like I had so many years before, closed my eyes, and breathed in the desert's upcoming twilight.

October in Death Valley is the perfect time to avoid its atmospheric extremes: summer temperatures that can reach excesses of 130 degrees Fahrenheit and winter nights that frequently dip below freezing. The valley's shape—a long, narrow basin 282 feet below sea level walled by steep mountain ranges—determines much of its meteorological highs and lows. I'd heard Gram furtively call it The Death Trench a couple of times, a colloquial slur that goes in lockstep with all the others like the iconic Funeral Mountains, Last Chance Range, Coffin Canyon, and Deadman Pass. A tough place to survive anytime, yet life finds a way.

One location where life teems *in spite of* is Death Valley's badlands, cited as North America's lowest topography. It's also on record the salt flats were a terrible disappointment to thirsty nineteenth-century settlers who crossed the open plains in search of a better life. The salty puddles—sometimes morphing into surprisingly sizable ponds following rainstorms—are what remain of a freshwater lake that could've been close to 600 feet deep about 10,000 years ago. Mostly all that's left today are large tracts of salt crystals.

In the puddles, however, live rare pupfish, two-inch mud minnows that can tolerate water temperatures from near freezing to almost 108 degrees Fahrenheit. Supposedly they evolved to survive these extremes by going dormant.

Although panoramic star viewing is blocked somewhat by mountain ranges surrounding Badwater Basin, I knew how Gram felt about sharing life among the living. This was her favorite location. She'd marveled aloud at the amazing creatures inhabiting this place: the pupfish, the blue herons, the chuckwallas.

"What's not to love, Ellie?" she'd quipped as she bent to gather a fistful of salt. "I'd like a tiny house"—pointing—"right over there."

I immediately went to work on our itinerary after checking into Scotty's Castle, a 1920s Spanish mansion, the pomp and circumstance of Death Valley. Just for the task I'd made a list using my cell's Evernote during the flight, ordering and reordering everything until my memory coughed up all the details. I booked a ranger-led paleontology tour, which explores the secret maze and tunnel system beneath the castle, for the following day. And, if hindsight served me, next on the agenda was a stroll around our accommodations.

Thirty minutes had already clicked by before I left our room—the original room—overlooking the mansion's swimming pool, and a preregistration hustle requiring several months' advance notice. Since our last visit, Scotty's had closed, renovated, and reopened. While I could appreciate its overhauled courtliness and frequent reminders of old-world charm in the middle of a largely uninhabitable place, I found myself looking for what had remained the same, hell-bent on preserving progressively unraveling memories of my first experiences here with Gram. Perhaps even then a part of me couldn't believe she was gone.

I walked toward the lobby and mentally picked apart the milieu. Hand-forged wrought iron, buffed Spanish tile, encased antiques and gilded tapestries were familiar. The Chimes Tower, a keynote feature with its twenty-five carillons set to play every quarter-hour, would execute a series of hyperactive sonatinas just before dusk. I arrived at the south portico in time for its quarter-past-five reveille like before, my elbows draped over the balustrade, eyelids lowered to half-mast as I scanned the desert valley three stories below.

Well before dark (determined to miss the pink Jeep parties rumbling across the desert highways toward Dante's View), I headed out to the badlands. For the next two days I'd planned to explore the sights of Golden Canyon's Zabriskie Point, Ubehebe Crater, and Mesquite Flat.

Thus began my Spruce Goose demands and mission to return to each spot we'd visited ten years previously. I stood surrounded by every imaginable shade of aurum in the wrinkled cliffs of Golden Canyon; I hiked the trail to Ubehebe Crater's southwest rim to snap photos of red-ochres and palatinates in the sedimentary folds of Last Chance Range; I waded ankle deep into the sands of steep, rippled dunes where the setting sun casts long shadows. I surveyed the blackest of nights overrun with heavenly bodies appearing close enough to dust my cheeks and thumbed my nose at a couple of stray streaks from—yes—orbiting Starlink satellites.

As hours tumbled into days, a part of me sensed all those carefully selected points of interest were under equal observation by invisible company just beyond my left shoulder, where Gram had frequently tarried over a decade ago while we inspected the night skies. That much became clear. I wasn't sure what to make of it, for my interest in paranormal phenomena was at its best a hobby, sidelined since middle school. Even all the obscene overproduction of spectral John Travolta for *Philly's Argosy* hadn't rekindled any interest in ectoplasm or The Grinning Man . . . yet.

I missed Gram, but certainly hadn't returned to Death Valley expecting to reunite with her ghost. Even if she'd been at my side the whole time during the past eleven months, I guess I'd been too busy or distracted to notice. Not that I hadn't thought about making an exception for her; on some days, I longed to see her smile again. When that didn't happen during waking hours, I'd halfway expected Gram to visit me in my dreams. She hadn't.

This was different. With each passing day in Death Valley, the movements in my periphery grew sharper. A spray of freckles across her right hand, the toe caps of her favorite hiking boots. Still, they were glimpses only. *Here, not here.* By the third evening, however, her fly-by presence was frequent enough to leave me imploring her to stay in Death Valley. Though I could certifiably use her input inside my everyday steamroll back in Philly, at that juncture I believed her time here was done. I urged her—all four pounds I'd deposited in a heap between two dormant salt pools—all the way back from the flats to remain behind and watch the stars for me.

I still felt a distinct impression of Gram hovering around me when I sat down three days later to interview Miles Cochran at Con Murphy's Irish Pub in Philadelphia.

But what did I know?

As confident as I'd been in my own cockamamie plan to lay Gram to rest, I'd started to worry I hadn't. After exploring Scotty's underground tunnels and availing ourselves of every nook and cranny the canyons' marbled surfaces offered, she'd followed me back to Filthadelphia as sure as Easter eggs in April. And here we sat.

So, during the first thirty seconds of that conversation, I was still trying to convince myself the week-long trek to Eastern California hadn't been a fortuitous disservice—and for the next, that the interview with Miles Cochran wouldn't go to bust as well.

The inner-office moniker *Cockroach* silently skittered off the top of my head as I occupied the streetside half-booth across from him, for the

Falling Stars

Cochrans of this world are best described as inevitable infestations that can ride home in our grocery sacks and survive more than one nuclear blast. I hadn't seen him in nearly a year, and another year hadn't done him any favors. Not so difficult at the moment to regurgitate all the other reasons why McWatters had nommed him so *and* pawned off the interview on me, either.

At times like these, the ugly and inevitable truths dawned on me that, *a*, I was still and perhaps forever a yes-man, and *b*, I'd been duped once again into scrubbing the toilet. As I squirmed to find a better vantage point of our frenemy, only then did I integrate the finer details of a previous conversation, McWatters and me, yesterday in his office, upon my reentry into our pulp fiction diorama:

"How's the trip?" McWatters, bent forty-five degrees over an L-shaped laminate desk, his spindling frame surviving largely on Slurpees and licorice, had pushed up his pair of wire frames, flash-in-the-pan grin aimed in my general direction.

"Good, good," I'd lied, eyeing the papers stacked in the inbox on my adjoining desk and reminding myself I was in for a seventy-two-hour sprint just to undo *that*. We'd talked about going paperless, but it never seemed to work. Besides, defining one's productivity by how the mound shrinks—however illusory it may be—can be quite satisfying.

McWatters ducked behind his computer screen again, back on task. I rolled out my chair and sat.

The long and short of it was routinely enough for McWatters, cursory casts for two- and three-word summaries about life experiences that probably deserve far more attention. In the jet-fueled plume of launching *Philly's Argosy*, I must admit I'd slipped into similar habits.

I thumbed through the mail first, including the park service's Special Use and CalTrans permits required for burials in national parks, which (yes) I was signing and sending in after the fact. Such was life these days.

"Came in yesterday," McWatters added over the nonstop clickety-clack at his computer keyboard. He'd watched me sweat over the documents' arrival as the sixty-day window narrowed to nil, and I'd had to pinky swear I wouldn't perform any ceremonial *boomshakalaka* out West. He'd also warned me to scatter Gram leeward to the Black Mountains, away from satellite surveillance. I think he was genuinely

concerned I'd get arrested. We couldn't afford that—not then, anyway.
"On it," I answered.
"Your two tomorrow," McWatters began—
clickety-clickety-clack-clickety
"Rescheduled. Four-thirty."
"The Cockroach?"
"Happy Hour."
"Figures."
McWatters siphoned the last of his forty-four-ounce Sour Patch Watermelon and continued typing zero-to-sixty. "Isn't his, anyhow."
That got my attention. I stopped what I was doing and walked over to the water tower behind McWatters's desk. "Really? You know that for sure?
"Yup." He coughed. "Old journal."
"Ancestral?"
"Great-uncle's."
Visions of picking through a long and tedious memoir danced in my head. "Should I reschedule?"
clickety-clickety-clack
"Up to you."
Yes, it was—and no, it wasn't, really. I thought about it for the better half of a minute while I filled my Eagles tumbler. *Both of us had waltzed around this one long enough already, hadn't we?* And though I never liked to go into any interview with too many preconceptions, I had to ask. "Subject matter?"
McWatters was headlong into a line of scrawled notes at the bottom of a legal tablet directly in front of him. When I glanced up from the water tower, it looked like *clickety-clack-clickety* he had no head. Sometimes the presence of *simply wrong* alongside our everyday normal can be the most unnerving; I mentally swore at my eyes for playing tricks on me.
"Vampires," he replied.

For the most part, I liked people more than McWatters did, and certainly handled the lion's share of interviews for *Philly's*. Typically, I wasn't openly disparaging, either, but Cochran had a history with us, starting as one of *the older students* in our COMM 177 class, Multimedia

Storytelling, freshman year. After that class, we (swamped and distracted undergraduates that we were) lost track of Cochran, the unspoken assumption that he, like most 50-plus students, had either discontinued his studies or dropped dead. In our third semester at Syracuse, however, Cochran had resurfaced, dumpster diving in plain sight again for ideas from classmates, fronting the same dark comic he'd announced as *the next great thing* the previous year in class. Three years later he was still broadcasting his brainchild but had yet to write a single word.

Our first month into *Philly's Argosy*, Cochran showed up without a mask at the office, primed to write the same said *next great thing* for our publication. McWatters had flatly turned him down.

When he showed up again six months later, McWatters rightfully requested (for the second time) a completed first draft of his story. Cochran declared he wouldn't hand over anything without a contract and a sizable advance.

"Screw our budget and submission guidelines," McWatters shared with me later. (Yes, six complete words.) I'd missed the hapless meeting somehow.

"He said that?"

"Yup."

"What'd you say?"

"Called security."

A couple of security guards we shared with a cell phone repair service next door had arrived, pried Cochran's fingers off the door frame, and dragged him off the premises.

Once I'd mentally constructed that gouache—Cochran gripping our unceremonious, prehung door with his portly mauling irons—I couldn't unsee it, even as he (tight-fisting his pint of beer and one very old Moleskine ledger) sat across from me now. Impervious to correction, alarmingly alert, and hideously hulky, Cochran also adequately met every medically predisposed category for high-risk obesity. His jowls doubled over into dewlaps, his complexion, anemic—*not* the Pillsbury Doughboy. He was wound way too tight for any kinship with that lovable Poppin' Fresh; I decided at once Cochran's lifelong plus-size had never been cute.

Something had convinced McWatters, however, that Cochran

possessed viable material, although we were pretty sure it wasn't his own. I was therefore assigned the task of optioning the journal for ghosting it . . . if I could pry it from those beer-bellied fingers. *If* the alleged scribe of the journal in Cockroach's keep hadn't previously submitted a copyright claim, either. A precious hour of trouble for me, Kevlar twine attached. Still jet-lagged and grouchy, I wondered *what in the holy thunder* McWatters thought we were smoking.

I extended the olive branch, neither too cleverly nor imaginatively. "Tell me about your story."

A sidelong grin. "Obviously, he sent you." A wet chuckle. "I'm afraid I can't do that."

Although I had equal authority to accept or reject any material, I decided to take a swing at self-preservation and offload this one back onto McWatters. "*He's* not going to consider your idea unless it's in written form, you know."

Cochran thoughtfully nursed his beer. Finally, "I've held onto this too long to see it dismantled."

What in the ever-living—I mentally reordered and censored my next question. "What makes you think we're in the business of dismantling?"

Cochran laughed, a thick, slurpy one that threatened to lapse into a jag requiring a Heimlich. After a fit of coughing and sputtering, he contained a bit of phlegm politely in the folds of his elbow, leaned forward, and muttered, "I've seen what McWatters does to postmodern literature. He *butchers* it."

I clicked through some of our recent headline stories at lightning speed, including those with a handful of thumbs-down reviews. McWatters hadn't bombed even *once,* though. Certainly not with *Gigantic Wings*, his Gabriel Garcia Márquez spin-off about a winged vagrant who slept in the city's subways, or his other hybrid brainchild where *The Third Policeman* meets *A Confederacy of Dunces.* If McWatters was butchering anything, it was the laser-ablated letters on his computer keyboard.

I held my tongue by stating the obvious. "We're not a literary magazine."

"I know."

Slap me. My carotid artery danced a polka. At my left, Gram shook

Falling Stars

her head. I was being too nice, and Cochran was boxing me in. *And pissing her off. Who had time for this?* Although I'd put in several hours proofing copy while on vacation, I was still looking at my next column and one week in the hole back at *Philly's*.

I flagged the waiter for the check. "Your apprehension about the readable health of postmodern literature makes me think you'd be happier placing your story elsewhere."

McWatters was going to skin me alive.

Cochran's flattened expression, though, belied his hops-succulent composure; I'd hit a nerve.

"I can email you a list of suggestions for submitting your literary material elsewhere," I added, driving the curve ball over home plate. Or so I'd hoped.

"Who said this was literary?" Cochran snorted.

Hard to tell without seeing a single effing word, I thought. Our waiter had just snagged a large table of happy hour regulars behind us. I stuffed my debit card back inside my briefcase and began searching for cash.

"Here's the deal," I charged. "*Philly's* is willing to option your *unwritten* material to be ghosted for three-point-five percent royalties on all final sales, all printable rights to us."

A slack-jawed Cochran looked over the table at me. "That's pretty stiff," he backpedaled.

"We offer six percent royalties for completed submissions only," I punched.

His eyes narrowed. "No seed money? No purchase options?"

Unbelievable. Our offer was generous, and Cochran knew it. "We rarely work that way—and for completed submissions only," I repeated.

Gram nodded.

Cochran straightened, looked away briefly, then back at me. "I want rights to *review* and *refuse* publication," he said.

I cringed. McWatters had expected this as well. Which meant weeks crafting something for *Philly's* rightful ownership that might never see the light of day. The only alternative I had was to chase his prerequisite with one of my own.

"You won't have any rights to revise our copy or submit it elsewhere."

Cochran grinned through my tit for tat. "Oh, that's just my standard precaution," he sallied. "I wouldn't want a byline for something that's rubbish, would I?"

I allowed myself the better of three seconds to think. "We... could offer you four percent, if we byline the story to McWatters." *Epiphany, life story rights acquisition.* In my game-changing quiver of options to offer, this had worked well for us in the past. "You'd get more money without the risk of smearing your—artistic reputation." Perhaps Cochran didn't really want a byline. *Or did he?*

Gram passed her hand over her mouth to stifle a giggle.

"Oh. No, no," Cochran blurted, a bit unnerved. "I want *you* to write this, not McWatters."

Didn't see that coming, either.

"The initial arrangement was good," he muttered. "Just promise me you'll write it."

In all fairness, with a week's backlog on my desk, my column, and the rapid turnaround requirements looming for the next issue, I wasn't sure I could. "Okay," I said, anyway.

"All righty, then. Give me something to sign." His eyes darted toward the party commencing behind us, then back at me.

Gram gave the friezed edge of our table a congratulatory fist-bump. I lowered my head to conceal my victory grin and rifled through my briefcase for the overly complicated legalese McWatters had our attorneys prepare.

"Better yet, I'll just drop by your office tomorrow," he said, and pressed a ten under his beer mug.

Cochran, suddenly all in a rush? I wondered—

The chair groaned under his weight as he scooped up the ledger and pushed away from the table.

Sure thing, I thought bitterly. The contract went back into my briefcase. I also noticed Gram was gone.

"I'll get over there, no worries," Cochran insisted. "It's just that—" He glanced at the empty seat beside me and leaned forward. "She was beginning to get on my nerves."

Of all the—I sat back. "You mean, you could see her too?"

Cochran nodded pensively, his former bluster and yap completely absent. "Where did you pick her up?"

Falling Stars

For real? My blood boiled, and once again I managed somehow to hold my tongue. In order to seal the deal, I couldn't allow myself to get sidetracked by his rudeness. *Just chalk up the majority of his back and fill as unintentional social awkwardness and pay your tab,* I warned myself. For *Philly's,* for McWatters—I had to. After all, how could Cochran know who Gram was, or how precious she'd been to me?

He quickly added something else under his breath; I almost missed it. "After you read this, you'll understand why she follows you." And quieter still, "Why her soul can't leave."

All of us are fabricated from stardust and we have fallen here.

When the story lead hit me (possibly yet another childhood contrivance borrowed from a Carl Sagan documentary, which originally aired on PBS), I scribbled it in my tablet's left margin and concurrently dismissed it. Not the way to begin Cochran's fare. I continued poring over his great-uncle's old ledger and decided after the second pass that star stuff really didn't belong in Cochran's ball of twine, anyway. The idea belonged somewhere else.

I've always been a sucker for retrofitting bits of truth with magic, just as I found myself tempted to do here. Some ancient cultures believed falling stars were falling souls—special ones spewed from purgatory, finally freed to ascend. Others claimed falling stars were consciences of new babies catapulting toward Earth at 45,000 miles per hour, ready to be born. And it just so happened that the stardust component *was* one of those level balances on my seesaw of knowledge, lore that retained an essentially magical element while successfully buoying all the data-to-date I'd acquired regarding goings-on in outer space. Magic—*and* truth.

A good bit of the astrochemical intelligence I'd mustered during my childhood regarding stardust, it turns out, was correct. Carbon, nitrogen, and oxygen, as well as atoms of several other heavy elements extant in our bodies *can* date back to generations of stars over 4.5 billion years old. Which means our average 71.5-year lifespan and the give-or-take eighty breaths we'll have in the next five minutes were created in furnaces of long-dead stars that never fell.

They exploded.
We fell.

Withstanding our atmosphere's fiery ablation at those kinds of speeds remains the primary reason why Earth isn't mercilessly pummeled by every meteoroid within range. Only a tiny percentage of incoming material survives long enough to land. An even smaller percentage, one in forty, can be followed with the naked eye to its collision location and recovered. These meteorites are upgraded in their classification from *falls* to *finds*.

Gram and I hadn't watched any gas giants taking nosedives into Earth's atmosphere, I'd learned. In high school I studied main-sequence stages of lower mass stars, those which take much longer to burn up their hydrogen stores and implode. I remember feeling relieved our Sun was one such gas giant on slow burn. So, with the stars in the heavens and the sun still smiling down upon us for many more millennia, what else was there?

I'd hoped the magical moments in Death Valley would carry me through the high tide and shitstorm awaiting my return to Philadelphia, but I hadn't planned for Miles Cochran or the story he peddled to *Philly's Argosy*. McWatters hadn't, either. True to form, he had only two words for our impending dilemma.

Holy Cow.

—Elise Anderson, November 2023

Chapter One

Tommy Lucas said nothing during the four-hour drive from Chicago to Bloomington. Despite his terminal illness, his black, bowl-cut shag cast a rich, essentially synthetic sheen in sunlight. People who presumed Tommy was having chemotherapy also presumed he wore a wig. He didn't.

Today his color was off, June noted. From the minute he'd curled up on the U-Haul's passenger seat under his favorite super shag blanket (black, of course), June had counted the miles necessary to blue-pencil those motherly worries, those warning her that even a healthy uptick in his most recent blood work—the reduced clone size and lowered lactate dehydrogenase (LDH) levels—might mean only a temporary reprieve. As a doctor, she believed in the numbers, especially when these offered hope—but as a mother, she took account of everything else.

By Springfield, she'd settled upon a moderately comfortable stance that any pallor she thought she witnessed was more about overcast skies, a black Sherpa backdrop bunched under his cheeks, and the polarized, atomic gray clip-ons he insisted on using over his Wayfarer rims. Tommy had managed to be well enough to make the move, and that was all that mattered at the moment, wasn't it?

She temporarily diverted her attention from endless overthinking and radio surfing to scanning the console's gauges. This U-Haul was a gas-guzzler; they'd need to fill up soon.

The sun, having tipped and ducked behind the clouds all morning, finally asserted itself. On instinct, June reached to lower both the driver and the passenger blinders. A cling shade she'd applied to the passenger door's window first thing this morning also continued holding the rays at bay.

"Better?" she asked.

Tommy nodded, eyes never leaving his tablet.

Falling Stars

Sun sensitivity had continued to be an issue for Tommy since his diagnosis. He couldn't play outdoors like other children, and naturally had his own ideas about that. Hence, a good portion of the contents inside their fifteen-footer—ones requiring a personal driveaway to their new destination—no ifs, ands, or buts. Stopgap lifelines never to be boxed, labeled, shipped, or otherwise. All for the little boy whose complexion had remained frost line white since June could remember.

The past two eculizumab infusions hadn't been easy for him, plus everything leading up to the move was beginning to tell on them both. Just that morning June had noticed the birth of a slight stoop in her bathroom mirror. She leveled her shoulders and pressed them back against the U-Haul's bench seat. June was thirty-five chasing fifty in the wake of receiving the awful news about Tommy—going on three years now.

In Arkansas, the game plan involved continuing Tommy's recent switch to ravulizumab, a less-frequent infusion option that packed an equal punch, something June weighed ever so carefully with his provider before releasing Tommy's medical records to Springdale.

Tommy had just turned six when the headaches started, those June expected to stop within the prognosed forty-eight hours following the final fitting for his first pair of glasses (the black Wayfarer rims he'd very carefully selected, ones like actor Jack Darrow wore as he'd rehearsed his upcoming role of Barnabas Collins in the television remake of *Dark Shadows*). Tommy's astigmatism hadn't been the whole ball of wax, though.

The headaches progressed, followed by bruising—at first only episodic petechial rashes, those tiny red pinpricks just under the skin— located mainly on his forearms and chest. They came and went as his little body pushed back for a few more weeks, until the verdict from flow cytometry testing returned: he had developed a rare blood disorder— paroxysmal nocturnal hemoglobinuria—a designated mouthful which meant cancer, that his bone marrow for some unknown reason had started producing defective blood cells.

Needle aspiration of bone marrow is no picnic. This, like many other macroscopic crucifixions (also known as diagnostic intervention) were little more than harbingers of things to come, June knew. She resented every last trace of it and began the process of slaying the dragon by retaining one of the best biopsy technicians in the Chicago area—for more tests would come. *Many* more. As a practicing oncologist (the hateful irony), June was tortuously in the know about what was in store for Tommy.

She'd treated paroxysmal nocturnal hemoglobinuria only a handful of times, a rare blood disorder so named after a preliminary and erroneous conclusion that destruction of red blood cells, or hemolysis, occurs only *paroxysmally*, during sleep. The classic symptom for 50 percent of patients was a toilet bowl full of bright red blood first thing in the morning, though subsequent clinical findings proved blood in urine isn't always visible *and* hemolysis continues around the clock.

Tommy wasn't spared the toilet bowl experience either, June recalled bitterly (although by then, diagnosis in hand, they both had grown increasingly indifferent and less surprised by the next shoe to drop). Damaged red blood cells being prematurely destroyed by his own immune system had given them yet one more of the telltale signs: a bloody mess.

The event was merely another click down the line. He hadn't screamed or cried. She'd almost wished he had.

Uh, Mom? he'd softly called. June herself had taken a knee. Next, she'd flushed the toilet, Tommy's huge blue eyes her whole world—begging for an answer she'd tried to give. Many PNH patients, she knew, never had to experience the toilet bowl shock—though hemolysis occurred constantly, and they, too, were in essence bleeding out. The anger had flinched inside her. In the normal course of things, she'd silently reasoned, this only lurked around the corner for prepubescent girls.

She'd also asked God why *that* particular symptom had to terrorize Tommy. Didn't they have enough on their plate already? The next on the tally for emasculating her son, June decided. Cancer was, after all, rarely *fair*.

Oh, how she knew it.

Which made Tommy's coping mechanisms for such terrors and embarrassments even more understandable. She held none of it against him, not one thing.

For June knew too much: Tommy had acquired a mutation of the PIGA gene shortly after conception, *not* inherited from his birth mother, a heroin addict buried in Odd Fellows Cemetery off County Road 205. The PIGA mutation, as it turns out, occurs randomly, and with no apparent reason. All the cutting-edge research remained deadlocked on this position. June also knew the median survival rate following diagnosis was ten years, though some patients—this was true—could survive for decades with only mild symptoms.

Other trickle-down data seeped between the lines, like Tommy's 83 percent chance of surviving an additional five years if he underwent bone marrow transplantation. And yet another roll of the dice: transplant too early, he would be exposed to undue toxicity, possibly resulting in an even earlier mortality from the procedure alone. Wait too long, he could develop other complications from the disease, rendering transplantation impossible.

Tommy's condition could escalate at any time. Short bouts with fatigue might become more pervasive and disabling. The longer he survived, the more likely the chances he'd develop blood clots around his liver, another life-threatening complication known as Budd-Chiari. At best, he would always tire more easily, particularly after treatments. At worst, he could lose his ability to swallow. For these and many other reasons June used her professional connections and had Tommy placed on a waiting list for a bone marrow donor within hours of his diagnosis, well in advance of his symptoms meeting medical criteria.

Tommy was intense. From the day June had brought him home from the adoption agency, he was the focal point of everything in her life. He commanded that kind of attention, as if the atmosphere imploded around him. Most people didn't like it. June didn't mind. He'd been a healthy baby. And he was hers. Very few people knew he wasn't her biological child, for their hair and eye color were identical. In the beginning, she'd felt a flicker of delight that his birth mother was dead, and his biological father, in the wind.

June's parents, Walt and Lilly Lucas, hadn't seemed overly concerned that their single, workaholic doctor-daughter was raising an adopted baby alone—that is, until his diagnosis.

Although June had never openly discouraged the idea of contacting Tommy's birth relatives, she now regretted her first, confidential glee that Tommy was all *hers*. The only possible cure for this kind of cancer was a successful bone marrow transplant from a compatible donor, preferably a parent, sibling, or half-sibling. For the past three years June had cast about for Tommy's relatives using an investigative agency in Chicago, a search that proved futile.

When additional testing six months ago placed Tommy in a subcategory for paroxysmal cold hemoglobinuria, June decided he would fare better living in a warmer climate, since destruction of healthy red blood cells can typically occur within minutes after exposure to cold. Chicago weather fell below fifty degrees Fahrenheit, the PNH delineation for *cold*, far too often. She'd gone to work immediately, submitting her application for a new state license, and orchestrating a new practice near her hometown in Arkansas.

In spite of it all, she knew they'd been lucky. Along the superhighway of many difficult things, Tommy had responded well to eculizumab, and his total reduction of red blood cells, white blood cells, and platelets had never tested as severe. They'd even managed to stay well during the COVID-19 pandemic while they hunkered down with the rest of the world.

Which didn't stop June from projecting the what-ifs. Aplastic anemia was another likely scenario in Tommy's future, she knew, and while this complication hadn't yet surfaced, she'd already outlined a pending schedule for androgen therapy. Not that she would ever consider treating Tommy herself, an occupational no-no. June already had the eyes and ears of the best oncologists in the business, plus their mutual respect. Most of her collegial suggestions for Tommy had been spot-on. Which made her even more wary of the chances that her emotional bond with her son might one day interfere with the best decisions, the right ones—hence, a single error she couldn't find her way out of.

When cancer hits home, there are some surprises—even for career oncologists. Intravenous dexamethasone, a mainstay for treating inflammation, made Tommy's skin burn. The filgrastim injections used to boost white cell production would sting if it came straight from the fridge.

On certain days, June waffled between shock and resignation. Others, she struggled to anticipate what Tommy really wanted versus the snarled knot of her own wishes. Was this enough for him? Would she become another caregiver guilty of perpetuating a situation where treatment would not lead to improvement? When was treatment no longer reasonable? Was she strong enough to make the difficult decisions? Could she live with herself afterward, that her opinions had not been completely egregious?

June was familiar enough with the new kid on the block, immunotherapy, to know that when it worked, it worked well. Tommy had the genetic markers for it, plus an adequate immune system response. He was strong enough to tolerate the treatment. The new frontier of using artificial intelligence as a precision medicine was already helping Tommy's oncologist plan more targeted treatments, using gene and genome sequencing to customize his therapy. The ability to measure—and therefore trust—the accuracy of blood biomarkers was much better than just ten years ago. She'd pored over every option—even immune system inhibitors like pegcetacoplan that had not yet been approved for pediatric use.

Offering immunotherapy to any cancer patient was, however, still a gamble. When the drugs worked, the disease seemed to melt away overnight. Yet little was known about which patients might benefit, and how much, from which drugs. Immunotherapy also came with potentially severe side effects that could lead to death—for once activated, a patient's immune system could attack healthy tissues alongside the diseased ones. For Tommy, this might lead to more eye problems, serious rashes, nerve damage, holes in his intestines, glandular and liver failure, or paralysis.

Nevertheless, June had heard enough end-of-treatment bells ringing over the years to know she longed for the same victory for Tommy, and nothing short of it. Risks accounted for, she agreed with his doctor to leverage everything. She also thanked their lucky stars and breathed again when their insurance company approved Soliris—*the most expensive cancer drug in the world.* As an oncologist, June couldn't help contrasting how many times she'd dashed off similar petitions to insurance companies without a second thought.

In June's workday world, the potentially exhausting avalanche of determinants and subsequent possibilities usually surrendered to raw and fearless medical training. Such protocol proved adequate for facing an endless stream of difficult daily decisions head-on—that is, ones about *all the other cancer patients* besides Tommy. Much more difficult, she found out, to lean on the grand scheme behind the training with those you dearly love.

Since her patients' lives hung on thinner threads than most, June's daily mindset always involved analyzing subsets within subsets, including how unique, how unpredictable each course of human treatment—and its outcome—could be. Try as she might, she'd never been able to successfully mask her own uncertainties about Tommy's future. That brutal evening in March after he was first diagnosed, she gave into his impulse to sleep in his Halloween costume.

Some patients had difficulty managing their pain, even with all the available therapies in place. Others arrived at the clinic gridlocked against pursuing any form of treatment. End-of-life discussions were always difficult, and June got very good at it. The error of overestimating patient survival and continuing chemotherapy beyond reasonable efficacy was always a concern.

Flawed choices to over- or undertreat were often driven by well-meaning family members anxious to spare their loved ones from pain, and decision-making frequently polarized. Families either begged her not to stop aggressive anticancer treatments or never to start them in the first place. From her own experiences with Tommy, she now understood why. Decisions that might seem good or right this week did not remain so. The disease always twisted and coiled its way to the next change, the next challenge, the next decision.

June didn't know many colleagues who wouldn't be tempted by a miracle cure—one coming down the pipe following months of double-blind, peer-reviewed trials in the form of a promising, well-tolerated chemical agent. When miracles didn't happen, though, Hippocrates bound her to revert to the *tried and true*—chemotherapy and radiation—to determine whether either of these could ultimately ameliorate difficult end-of-life events like collapsed lungs or broken bones. All the while believing that her patients should die of the disease and not the cure.

Tommy's deductive reasoning about his own dilemma at times outweighed June's best explanations. He'd already figured out, for example, why doctors were ultimately powerless to deliver the infallible prognosis—for himself, or anyone else.

"It's like a spaghetti plot," he'd told June the previous Christmas as

Falling Stars

he opened a Wikipedia page on his tablet.

In a separate op-ed article Tommy had also discovered how diagnostic projections could be compared to spaghetti diagrams used in meteorology, specifically cancer data—which is inevitably drawn from ensemble forecasts. When models from a meteorological ensemble are stepped forward in time, precision in comparing all the results becomes critical for accuracy and interpretation. If contours follow a recognizable pattern throughout the weather sequence, confidence in the forecast is high. If the pattern is chaotic and resembles a plate of spaghetti, confidence is low.

After June had skimmed the article and all but agreed with the analogy, Tommy bared his soul to her for the first time.

"Mine can't be *extrapolated* because it's part of a curse."

Tommy and his homeschool tutor, Molly Shriver, had just spent the week prior diving into pre-Algebra extrapolations, she recalled. "A curse?"

He nodded. "On my bloodline. The only way to undo it is to find the necromancer."

"You mean, like a magician?"

She'd pressed him for more, but Tommy shut down. Not too long afterward came the first of several bizarre rituals he loyally maintained to date. June watched from the wings, refusing to discourage any of it. She couldn't—wouldn't—put a lid on any of his outlandish ideas because she'd seen what invariably happens to patients who lose hope.

In days gone by, June had accepted that unto everything there was a season, including a time to surrender. She'd cringed in the face of therapeutic futility so many times, regretful that moratoriums weren't enlisted more frequently when continuing treatment proved useless, complex, and prohibitively expensive. Under the rules of desperation oncology, though, some doctors chose to do things differently, venturing into new and unproven territories. June simply couldn't do it. Patients deserved, she believed, to know when to quit.

She'd held hard and fast to such an opinion—until she found out about Tommy.

Chemotherapy, also a business (now the last thing on her mind), was nonetheless a damning bed partner. As a practice shareholder, how often she'd acquiesced to the bottom line: a reduction in treatment meant a reduction in income. Tommy's plight, however, initiated a whole slew of rethinking. Her own internal arguments snowballed; all the paradoxes magnified.

At any given time, a handful of her patients had potentially curable malignancies. Others would suffer unexpected, often fatal, treatment-related complications. Some had great responses, yet good responses didn't always equal health benefits. A sore reminder that oncology frequently walked into more unknowns than knowns.

June *wanted* to be able to provide Tommy with an answer for everything—especially now that he'd obviously begun seeking explanations outside the grid. For a latchkey kid schooled at home, this was a huge shift. Molly had recently texted June about his new "mainstay enjoyment of macabre fantasy," as she'd put it. One of the more difficult choices was leaving Molly; Tommy's brilliance and emotional intelligence came in part from her tutelage. At their new home, June had decided to step-up Tommy's intrapersonal experience by enrolling him in St. Elizabeth of Hungary Catholic School's first-ever primary class for children with special needs—and had second-guessed that decision every day since. He was starting midsemester too, so June had arranged for Molly to be available for Tommy on Zoom and still worried whether anything could adequately prepare him for the upcoming unknowns in his life. They needed a miracle.

It took only one miracle to convince most oncologists they were improving lives by continuing to treat their patients, and those moments shamed logic.

Yet extensive back-and-forth discussions about the pros and cons of frontline or even second-line chemotherapy required exam room time both unbillable and emotionally exhausting. Added to the mix, referring physicians often sent along their own emotional bias about how *their* patients were to be cared for. Far easier, June knew, to explain why someone *should* treat cancer than why they *shouldn't*.

As long as the FDA continued to approve anticancer drugs with minimal survival benefits, June maintained the stance that everything had to be considered within the context of her patients' wishes—even their resignation to die.

Several of the contents stowed inside their U-Haul were openly symbolic of such resignation. June chose to believe these items also represented Tommy's ability to cope. Their truck was one of U-Haul's *Venture Across America and Canada* Supergraphics Program rentals displaying the Manson Impact Crater in Iowa. Tommy had specifically chosen that truck after reading about the crater for several hours. He'd meticulously picked through the article several days ago and read (as he so often did) aloud to June:

The Manson structure is an invisible crater over 74 million years old, measuring more than 24 miles in diameter. It's also one of the largest known meteorite craters in the continental US. Experts think the original meteor was around 1.5 miles in diameter and weighed close to 10 billion tons. The crater is named after the small town of Manson, Iowa, near where the meteor crashed, to be discovered much later during water well drilling in 1912. Another 47 years passed before Robert Dietz proposed that the digs around Manson were of meteor-impact origin. Disappointingly, the crater's impact can't be seen; the inconspicuous hole lies underneath nearly 300 feet of bedrock and glacial till.

Prehistoric Iowa was low-lying, coastal land with mixed conifer and deciduous forest and ferns—a much warmer climate than today. Everything about the region's tropical environment shifted the moment the meteor became a meteorite. Anything within 130 miles was instantly engulfed in flames, and most life within 650 miles did not survive.

Scientists have identified approximately 150 visible impact craters around the world to date. Advancement in spacecraft orbital imagery confirms that meteorite impacts are a major earth-modifying process.

He'd stopped reading. "It makes sense, you know, why people used to think they were falling stars."

She nodded, deep in thought.

And Tommy had continued without further discussion.

The decision to cease chemotherapy—to resign to die—was both complex and intimate. Scientific data for guidance was quite frankly scarce and conflicting. Data that *could* be obtained was mostly in retrospect—on the autopsy table. In that context, it was much harder to provide a good death, let alone a cure. While treatment prolonged survival, it didn't necessarily guarantee a good end.

Most of June's colleagues followed the fundamental rule that any small possibility of benefit justified staying the course at all costs—even near death. Although the chances of a dramatic and prolonged remission were minute, they reasoned, how could they ethically deny medication to patients? They touted *hope* as an important defense mechanism against cancer, arguing that patients inevitably gave up with the discontinuation of chemotherapy. The same stuff, June acknowledged, that frequently exacerbated pain, fatigue, and dystrophy. She no longer hesitated on insisting the data went both ways, that announcing honest information—*even bad*—could carry some hope.

She was walking through that explicit valley of hope with Tommy. Even before his diagnosis, she'd rarely been ashamed to stand with one foot in and one foot out—first upholding her ultimate responsibility to counsel patients and their families *well*. She was also committed to determining when to stop anticancer treatments and focus on palliative, end-of-life care. Striking the balance was never easy or allegedly kind; she'd straddled that fence *oh-so many times*.

June's decision to specialize in oncology came after watching her grandmother succumb to pancreatic cancer. She was enrolled in premed courses at the time and disagreed with the cast-off approach toward her grandmother. She agonized over it. For some cancers, a paucity of tools was accessible to accurately assess prognosis in the elderly, to help with daily decision-making in their course from life to death. In the end, June had done little—except dare to enter the same arena and do things differently.

Only with certain cases did June advocate aggressive measures, usually for adolescent patients whose youth alone gave them more resiliency and greater chances for total recovery. And, while not neglecting to take inventory of the negative: the anorexia, the hair loss, the cotton mouth. She had to read between the lines when blood tests offered an oversimplified view of what her patients were otherwise experiencing.

Knowing even what *might* be in store for Tommy made it difficult to pull up the reins, to resist temptation to stay three leaps ahead. In her estimation, no amount of distance was far enough. Over the past twelve months, her parents' occasional doting over their only grandchild had shifted into hyperdrive; they were the force behind June and Tommy coming home. If not for their all-hands-on-board attitudes, June might've considered relocating Tommy much farther south.

Even her best projections these days often gave way to denatured directives and philosophies. While the average survival rate following chemotherapy administered near end of life was thirty-seven days, those same five weeks might allow a person to attend a special event, write a letter, or record a living legacy. None of this, however, could sidestep the value of dying with dignity. June saw the importance of respecting the enormity of many decisions, particularly the difficult ones faced by loved ones, those left behind. They lived on with the consequences.

June believed she was called first to comfort, next to relieve, and perhaps, if she was exceptionally lucky, to cure. And, failing to cure, the greater-than comfort could perhaps be simply offering more time—if that's what the patient wanted.

Particularly in terminal cancer scenarios, the medical community favored cessation of health care and provided directives *not* to resuscitate as the right decisions. But emotionally releasing something as large as a lifetime threw everything into slow motion, didn't it? And how could she expect grieving family members to believe they'd made the right decision, to arrive at any conclusion in a timely manner, all tidied up, boxed, and wrapped with a bow? For ending a life, *what* was timely?

Some days, her experiences seemed to alter her more than others. Tommy picked up on it too—whenever life's impossibilities had taken her down a notch.

Then, there were rules, standards, the classics—yes, three failed lines of chemotherapy only projected a small chance of success with a fourth, excepting HER2 tumors found in breast cancer. June understood very well why most oncologists stepped up the charge into treatment after the first diagnostic confirmations. The landscape at that time was —easier somehow. Relapses complicated things terribly. The only absolute predictability was how they would die: bedridden, constipated, dehydrated, in pain and, eventually comatose. Most brothers- and sisters-in-arms June knew were plagued with memories of patients they'd discharged home to die, particularly the younger ones. Those were the experiences they remembered, an education in humility.

Memories, especially in the weeks following Tommy's diagnosis, were an exquisitely unpleasant mix, echoes of all the stock phrases she'd used to date. She resolved once and for all she wouldn't be telling any more patients how brave they were, or how they could *win the fight*. For June had experienced an inevitable truth: when cancer happens to you or your own, it doesn't feel like a fight you can win.

Like other cancer patients, the beginning of Tommy's treatment was more predictable than anything else that followed. All of it was tough. She'd stepped through every second of it so far with Tommy, including the *red devil*—those repetitive phases of treatment that induced his overwhelming need to sleep from a tiredness that brought him to tears.

June's tendency to review her regrets in hindsight—the feedback from life's knee-jerks that inevitably found its way to the surface—hounded her. The question was always the same. Could she have done things differently? Her own mother was the master of rehashing bygones, always looking for a way to correct *some little something* in the past. She'd throw cognitive counterpunches at old choices until she became convinced she'd found a better solution. Were they doing this, June wondered, on the chances that future circumstances would repeat in the same manner as the bygones? After all, a direct replication was the only way a hindsight fix could be successfully applied, wasn't it?

And yet, June winced when people stuck out their chins and declared they *wouldn't have changed a thing*. So many life choices came in split-second delivery, without deep thought. Was this the ultimate arrogance, to suppose that one could not, would not, have done things differently?

And if so, just *how* differently? The paradigm of a reengineered past somehow impacting future events was still a far cry from predetermination, more akin to time travel. June didn't believe in predetermination, anyway. Not—really.

She maintained instead that at any given moment, she observed a world of probabilities and possibilities, a confluence guided by more variables than she cared to count.

Before she'd made the mistakes in her past, for instance—did she ignore the hints? The obvious? In the end, would she always and forever still be striving for, instead of the surety of what *had* happened, what she could've done? If life gave second chances, how would she then live? More nature walks in the park and less time at the office? Would *that* have been preferable to how things ended up? Would she have somehow worried less? Traded the urgency of the moment for something more important in the long-term? Set aside impossible choices for her dying patients and instead walked the dog? Chosen to own a dog in the first place?

Damn, I'm brooding again.

June shifted in the seat, forcing herself to sit taller. Her cell phone jiggled in the car cradle, its GPS clicking off miles and heralding another alternate route.

Three hundred sixty-two miles to Eureka.

She elected to remain on I-55 toward St. Louis and repositioned the phone in the cradle.

"Want me to read to you?" Tommy had propped open his clip-ons, eyes fixed on the way her right hand white-knuckled everything under its supervision, an unconscious praxis of June's while fretting. Of course, he'd picked up on her anxiety—he always did. Tommy suddenly grinned at her, a disarming and toothy one just wide enough to bare his uncommonly long cuspids.

A deep chuckle bubbled up within her. His smiles had a way of doing that, particularly ones which unexpectedly bloomed out of hours of wistfulness.

June had signed off on this U-Haul and its extra-wide bench seat for Tommy to stretch out and rest, a need she'd anticipated all morning since pulling out of Chicago before sunup. He surely must be tired by now, she imagined. The sparkle in his eyes seemed to say otherwise, though. *Still, maybe she ought to—*

"Sure," she said instead, and switched off the radio. "I'd like that."

Chapter Two

Part I

1 September 1939

On the second leg of our journey, while we are still some 1,575 nautical miles from Port of New York, the commander's daughter succumbed to her illness. Viscountess Agnetha Fallon is nary past nine or ten, and sickened from a bout of leukemia, the attending doctor tells me. Chief informed the ship's security crew at last port of call that the viscountess is bound for the States with her younger brother to a cure-for-cancer hospital in the Ozarks. Commander Fallon and the rest of his household elect to remain locked down near Cardiff and in the cross hairs of Germany's advancing front lines. Even at his rank, I hear that Fallon encountered a fair amount of difficulty securing safe passage for his children.

The girl's seven-year-old brother, Claudius, has an air of gumption I've not before witnessed in a boy so young. At Port of Southampton, the commander passed a note on the sly to our chief security officer, one instructing us he was satisfied leaving the dying girl in the lad's charge. The boy is exceedingly brave, it seems . . . though quite ill himself. I would find out a half hour or so hence that he too, is on passage to the Ozarks in hopes of remission.

The ship's naval surgeon got me on the horn at 16:43, to come to Female Isolation Ward on the double. From his clipped orders I knew he was belaying protocol as a favor, that he also had received instructions from Fallon. Instead of reporting his problem directly to the staff captain or chief of security he'd called me, one of four deputy security officers —and clearly a stroll down the chain of command in deference to nobility.

By that time, I'd had a chance to review the passenger manifest, catching on that Commander Jules Fallon was indeed one of the Welsh royals. He'd superseded his title of marquess as a military officer in Her Majesty's Armed Forces and retired his post some years past. Like several other commanding officers of the Crown, however, he'd most recently re-upped to active duty. Fallon and his wife had traveled abroad the spring prior on RMS Queen Mary, a trip likely for laying eyes on the medical facility where their children were destined for treatment. I didn't have the honor of meeting the commander then, for during those weeks I was furloughed in the States, helping Pops tan leather at our shoe factory in Hoboken.

As can happen with discovering a fly in the ointment, we already had several various and sundry issues brewing by the third day. Bridge received a telegram at sunrise that Hitler's troops had invaded Poland. The Germans had 57 stealth U-boats cruising these waters, and we'd already diverted course 100 miles south of our normal route, a tactical maneuver intended to navigate us out of torpedo range. The ship was running at capacity, transporting her largest number of passengers ever; what turned out to be *the* final peacetime voyage of the grand lady since she first set sail in 1936. With a full schedule in store plus the added weight of 2,552 fares, one stowaway, and several million in gold bullion, Cap'n had ordered the bridge crew to cruise at a cautious pace. While Our Lady had already set a Blue Riband record for crossing the Atlantic in four days at a top speed of 32 knots, Command was clearly driven by a different set of urgencies besides those of us now hunkered in sick ward.

I retired LCDR from U.S. Navy on 3 December 1937 and began my employ on the British ocean liner sixteen months after her maiden voyage, due in part to my parents' separation. Mum, London-born and U.S. naturalized in 1900, spent much of her life straddling two continents, lending more time lately in Nagy-Britannia per her own mother's failing health. Pops, tethered to the family enterprise in the

States, seemed willing to pony up for the whatnots and watch her come and go. My only sibling and older sister, Clara, expressed little interest in perpetuating the shoe business and married a wealthy attorney in California instead. I therefore divided my days off between both countries, and occasionally drove down to West Tennessee to visit a former shipmate. With war looming, however, Londoners were evacuating quicker than you can say Jack Robinson. By the skin of my teeth, I'd managed to book Mum and Nonna in Stateroom B450.

This was to be my last civilian stretch on the seventy-second voyage of RMS Queen Mary, having departed Southampton 30 August 1939 on schedule, set to dock in New York Harbor 4 September. I'd grown fond of the lady in the two years I'd sailed with her. England's ostentatious best, she dwarfed RMS Titanic by some 200 feet, with twice the tonnage. Her innards were bedecked with fifty-six varieties of highly polished veneer—*the real McCoy*—named for British protectorates who attended her coronation. Elaborate marquetry, carvings, and murals filled every ballroom, stateroom, and salon. Classic, but functional—with wood, glass, marble, metal, enamel, and linoleum in all the right places. She was earning her status as the world's ultimate ship, one of the most powerful ever built, just as the war in Europe escalated.

In the day, she set the bar for ocean liner luxury—frequently chartered by celebrities, dignitaries, and the very wealthy. We were hosting Mr. and Mrs. Bob Hope on this last peacetime trip, with Deputy Busby assigned to the ballroom in First Class to keep detail on the party. Deputy Stratton was rotated off-duty, and Deputy Meacham, in charge of the bullion. I, on the other hand, was making my way portside B toward Isolation Ward to collect a passenger.

As I rounded the ship's bulkhead, I immediately saw the doctor's predicament—his patient was no longer alive. They had yet to move the girl's body from bunk to cold storage because her little brother's arms were pinned across her waist, his face buried in the folds of her dress. I hadn't caught on yet why she was here instead of Infirmary amidships, but I would soon find out. Doc and I have a standing arrangement.

Dr. Dewey Langston, a lean and wiry Brit out of Norfolk, has premature greying ginger buzzed to the scalp and spends much of his downtime on the squash-racquets court. He volleys through his daily

Falling Stars

maritime routine in much the same manner, like a squirrel running a telephone wire. Thinking a stouter torso would give me an advantage, I once made the mistake of taking him on, and since, have had a more comfortable arrangement catching up with him over a weekly pitcher at Pig & Whistle.

Langston left the difficulty with the nurse and met me at the doorway in three quick strides. "Let's chat out here," he muttered.

I stepped to it after Langston, who headed portside, by rope storage.

Langston can be a nervous Nellie when it comes to job proficiency, and he undoubtedly believed he was in a pickle. My first assignment: to calm *him* down. He fished out a cigarette and leaned against the bulkhead.

"Smoke?" He tilted the pack toward me, its paperboard quivering.

I shook my head. "Obliged."

He lit his cig, took a long drag, and bridged his forehead with his toking hand. "Feck me, what a cockup," he muttered. Another drag.

"How's that?"

He shrugged with exasperation. "I bodged it." Glanced back at the ward. "Poor sod, in there blubbing his eyes out. I thought I could give him a little more privacy with her up here."

As opposed to the dispensary below on D Deck amidships, where she would certainly be, had she survived.

Langston checked his watch. "Dear God, it's been three hours already. We'll a fair bit of a pong in there shortly if I don't get cracking."

My take on the whole shebang up to this point was, Langston rarely *bodged* anything. Occupying Isolation Ward in such a manner (its quarters generally reserved for confining infectious diseases and stowaways) was quick thinking on his part. He'd managed to temporarily relocate our female stowaway too.

One sidelong glance at my vacant mug told him I'd been occupied elsewhere; I'd missed the main event. Security crew was spread thin over the imperial floating city on this trip, and tensions were high after receiving reports that Hitler had not just mobilized troops, but Luftwaffe and U-boats at Westerplatte. Nonna was waging her own war with dropsy, and Mum, a touch of housemaid's knee; I'd been to their stateroom twice today already.

I wondered if Langston knew anything yet. "Germany invaded the northern coast of Poland," I said.

Langston's eyes widened; he dropped his gasper. "You're fibbing me."

I looked down at the smoldering stub, suddenly the least of my worries. "Before dawn."

"Bloody Jerries," Langston muttered as he fetched his cigarette off the hull and put it out. "And where have I been? Well, here, I suppose." Langston lit up another and launched into an abridged version of the past twenty-four hours.

"Ah, well." He sighed. "We're in a wrench either way. So, here's it —we admitted her viscountess yesterday at fifteen hundred—fever, dyspnea, sick as a parrot." His shoulders sagged. "Said she'd been head down the loo since they boarded."

"I see."

"Gave her scopolamine, three hours' fluids, and pulled her off at twenty-twenty, temp normal, good skin turgor, no cyanosis."

My best guess, a reassuring medical summary. More importantly, Langston needed to talk this one out; I'd rarely seen him this tuckered. I knew better than to dodge in with questions. "All right," I said.

"She took a late dinner, and I discharged her to bed rest in her stateroom."

"Okay."

"Nurse Eddy, first shift—mentioned she saw the two of 'em taking a cuppa on the promenade at oh-nine-hundred. Not a parka or cap between 'em, mind you. Legging it around the sun deck."

I swallowed, catching on. "All's wet with the bed rest."

"Hells to yes, and then they alert one of the crew she's feeling a bit ropey, and she goes into cardiac arrest, right then and there."

"On deck?"

"Outer deck, in front of God and the rest." He shook his head. "How did he think they would manage all alone? No carer, no mum."

I could only counter that Fallon, for reasons lost on us, had arranged their passage this way, without the supervision of any traveling attendant. Strange, but true.

Langston wasn't appeased in the least. "I know, I know—he pigeoned a letter my way as well—but I'm telling you, mate, I'm buggered." He grimaced. "Now I have to ring him up, and say what, exactly?"

"You reviewed their medicals?" I recalled the boy clutching two thick folders, one under each arm, at checkpoint.

"That I did," Langston replied. "Somewise, I didn't sort her out completely, though. They've both got it, and it's rare. We've no setup to deal with such as that." He groaned. "Gor blimey, what if I lose the lad too? These are *nobs*, mate. Mark my word, I'll get my cards for this."

However true it may be that croakers aren't good advertisement—I wasn't convinced Langston was in the jam he thought he was in. This ocean liner would soon be commissioned for war and wouldn't be transporting any more civilians for a while. Langston and I were highly likely to re-up, so I seriously doubted anyone would sack him now.

Langston's *real* problem was getting last dibs on an irreversible complication. The two medical ledgers alone were proof in the pudding that a number of experts in Europe had already tried everything.

Better that I keep my trap shut, though. Langston needed to rehash a while more.

He continued reviewing his own shoddy performance and took another drag. The girl could've used a transfusion before sail, he surmised; she'd presented with at least four of the classic symptoms of deteriorating childhood leukemia. *Listless, underweight*, and *nodular* were among them. The only sign of irreversibility came too late, bruising that appeared postmortem. That, he concluded, was the riddle ex post facto: her skin was girlishly smooth and completely unblemished just hours before death—and it shouldn't have been.

"Should've presented with shiners from stem to stern," he muttered. Even her gums had been free of blisters, he told me.

No longer, though. My initial glance inside the medical suite hadn't just confirmed for me that the child was dead. When I returned to the doorway a second time, I realized I'd also inadvertently memorized the bruising patterns on her face and forearms, speculating at first sight how the girl might've fallen to her death.

The viscountess was an attractive child, skin milky and devoid of pigment, dark hair piled in braids on her head. Her Bonnie Jean Empire-waisted frock was selling like hotcakes in New York, its bright red and white polka dots and nautical collar all part of the latest style. I knew this because shoe factory trade follows fashion exchange between continents. I wasn't at all surprised she wore one; Fallon would want his children to blend into middle-class America as soon as possible. Claudius, too, was dressed in short tweed trousers and a sailor-style shirt straight out of *Montgomery Ward*.

Hearing Langston's recap of his shift, it was plain to me I'd been summoned for two reasons: to help him clear out sick bay, and to convince young Claudius Fallon to survive.

"You've a way with the ankle-biters, Gaye," Langston has said more than once over off-duty hooch. The lowdown shipwide about me was the same. I'd had my heart broken during boot camp and sworn off women, but not kids. Langston, on the other hand, was married to his work and satisfied with an occasional fling. I guess it's in the cards for me to meet Claudius Fallon. And if I can win the boy's trust, I just might be able to keep him alive.

This turned out to be my assignment, my mission—for the next three weeks. Within sixty days Langston and I would reenlist to active duty and later aboard the lady who earned her reputation as the Grey Ghost, the transport vehicle for U.S. Allied Forces in the next world war.

I hammered out a deal with Langston in the hallway that evening because he was my only true chum, and we trusted each other. If he didn't give my methods the high hat, I told him, I'd take care of the kid.

And Langston shook on it before I got the chance to beg off. "I need her in cold storage until we can sort all this out," he added. Which meant transporting her body to the ship's Ice Room two levels below— for our grand lady had no morgue. In the day, vaults were regarded as wasted space, and naval surgeons were usually far more opinionated about cause of death. A supply row of coffins stood permanently at the ready in H Deck Forward, near the cofferdam.

To date we'd only had one civilian death on record, and not on Langston's watch. Protocol in such an event was simple by standard, and determining a patient's demise without an autopsy, commonly accepted. Surgeons like Langston would simply fill out the necessary paperwork, embalm the body, and place it inside a coffin.

If a crew member died en route, we performed the customary burial at sea. A sailor would be sewn up in his own hammock, the last stitch made through the nose to ensure that he was indeed no longer with us.

The ship's linen service also provided three yards of canvas per crewman for these purposes.

Langston was still in a wrangle over this little girl's demise, however—so all of that had just flown out the window.

I hesitated at the doorway, reminding myself that the Spartan, but pristine isolation ward with three bunks dressed in white sheets tucked tight enough to bounce quarters and the two wall lavatories stationed in between was, albeit temporarily, Claudius Fallon's asylum.

As I entered the room, I could hear the boy whispering. I stopped and listened. It wasn't English.

In manus tuas, Domine...

Shit, I thought. That sounds like Latin.

In vita sive mors...

"You get what he's saying?" I whispered to Langston.

"Bits and bobs," Langston replied. "My first-year Latin's pretty dim —*super, subter, vomito*. Something about her hands, I think." He shrugged.

The boy raised his head, regarded his sister's gray face, and collapsed onto her belly again, sobbing. "Oh, Anya—"

I stopped a few paces behind him. *Heavens to Betsy, cat's got my tongue on just how to do this.* Seconds clicked by. I'd never thought about losing my own sister, a ne're-do-well for shoe mill toil or staying put in her own hometown, now the successful baby-factory wife of a five-figures Beverly Hills attorney. We saw them once a year at Christmas, and while I didn't concur with some of her choices, I missed her sorely in between.

"Viscount Fallon." My voice boomed off the walls despite my effort to address him gently. The attending nurse took a step back.

Claudius turned, snot and tears dribbling over his lips, pitch-black eyes on me. His red-rimmed eyelids and sunken, lusterless cheeks soundlessly screeched at all of us. A head of long black curls, wild ones, looked like they hadn't been combed in days.

I took a knee and removed my cap. "Lieutenant Commander Carleton Gaye at your service." I lowered my focus to the bright green linoleum floor in front of me.

When I looked up again, something in the boy's gaze caught me at eye level, like looking into the strength and resilience of a feral animal.

He never broke his spellbinding observation of me and, for an indeterminable amount of time, I noticed only oppressive silence save the drone of the starboard outer propeller six levels below. Neither did he turn back to his sister then, but slouched against the berth instead, expelling a long and shuddering gasp. I could've sworn his breath fogged the air between us; I felt its chill clap against my cheeks.

Then he raised his head slightly, and made what appeared to be a faint, involuntary chitter by clacking his molars together rapidly six or seven times. I have no children of my own, so this behavior was curious to me, plus a boy his age having cut a full set of adult teeth already, with extra-long canines.

Pops once had a big orange tom that lived at the factory to rout out leather-loving rats. I'd observed this cat doing something similar from time to time, when birds flew close enough to the windows. Whether he chittered from anticipation or frustration, I don't know. Deeply rooted behavior and primal hunting instinct made him practice the way to kill his prey quickly and efficiently. The old tom prepared himself for his dinner with a dress rehearsal of the same jaw movements required to sever birds' spinal columns. His chitters were no different, in fact, than the cries of his prey—audible twitters and peeps he used, perhaps, to lure them closer. The boy's by comparison were soundless.

Strange as it may be and all, I decided to let that be that. Claudius was no doubt in shock.

"We need to move her viscountess someplace more private," I began. Cold storage was located on D Deck, a straight shoot past the grocery store and food storage, next to the Ales and Stout. "You can come with her, by all means."

For a split second, Langston looked like he was about to shit a brick. I cut my eyes his way as a warning, and he managed to keep his nerve. I was working by my method on my time, however harebrained that might seem.

Without uttering a word, Claudius pulled a folded scrap of paper from the waistband of his britches and held it out to me.

"For me?" I asked the boy.

He nodded. I took it.

On closer examination, this was a letter addressed to me somehow —one sealed with red wax and the Fallon Family Crest—with orders

Falling Stars

specific and parlous enough to make my hair stand on end. *How the hell?*

It read:

Dear Officer Gaye,

By now you are likely midway to the States, and aware that Claudius cannot be allowed to return. I have taken the liberty of posting a sum of seventeen hundred U.S. dollars to your family's factory in Hoboken in exchange for your help. Your transport is stowed on F-Deck Forward, and in it you will find a Fisk Case for Agnetha's burial. The lad must report to Baker Hospital in Eureka Springs at once. I trust you will drive him there. He has further instructions for his sister's interment Stateside, as she also cannot return at this time to Cardiff.

It seems war is upon us once more. If we survive it, I will send for the lad in due time. Would you so kindly visit him whenever you are nearby? I fear that he will recover only to live alone in this world. I shall remain forever in your debt.

Cordially,
Commander Jules Fallon

I lost count of the times I reviewed the letter before I looked up at Claudius again—he, still staring a hole right through me. After tucking the note inside my uniform's breast pocket, I made a rough calculation about what I should say next. Perhaps simply the truth was best.

"Viscount, I have your father's orders to transport you and your sister to Baker Hospital after we dock. I understand he has made special arrangements for you on F Deck Forward." I took a breath. "It is my duty to take you both to F Deck immediately."

To be continued . . .

Chapter Three

Tommy finished reading the first installment of "Bad Blood" in *Philly's Argosy* just as they drove into northeastern St. Louis. Underneath his veiled disinterest, June knew he was totally revved about their hopscotch across the map to see his grandparents again. He would probably want to press on toward Eureka Springs, but June always checked in with him.

"Gas, snacks, and drive, or would you like to stop and eat in a restaurant?"

He raised his nose the same way he normally did when considering something important. "Gas and snacks," he said, and looked back down at his tablet. "There's two more episodes after this one."

"Gas and snacks it is." June smiled at him. "We'll cross the Mississippi soon, the Gateway Arch, on your right. Remember it?"

Tommy's face brightened. They'd passed through St. Louis twice before—when Tommy was three, then five.

"The world's tallest arch," he said.

"Would you like to ride up to the top sometime?" June asked. Tram tours took forty-five minutes to an hour, and June was naturally hesitant to place Tommy in any situation without recourse to wangle out. Sometimes it wore on her, rehearsing all the probabilities for future situations and scenarios.

"Did you know that it's earthquake proof?" Tommy asked. "It can also sway up to eighteen inches in either direction or withstand winds up to 150 miles per hour."

June chuckled. "And that makes me feel *so* much better somehow."

Tommy grinned. "I'm not scared of it." He bookmarked the page on his tablet and truly looked out the window for the first time that day, craning his neck to follow the glistening arch until it disappeared from view. Then he marveled out loud at the *way-coolness* of graffiti art here

Falling Stars

and there on the inner city's overpasses. June listened, thinking how much Tommy would enjoy seeing the arch at night, plus the city's Mural Mile, and when—if ever—she might bring him back. Her work schedule and his developing illness had already prevented them from leaving Chicago for the past four years. Aside from Zoom meetings, her parents hadn't seen June or Tommy since he turned five.

June knew it was only a matter of minutes before Tommy's attention would revert to what he'd just read, that he would have questions. The certain and awful fate of Claudius Fallon in the story haunted her—and she deliberated how she might best present her answers.

She totally *got* her son's immersion into strangeness, though, how *Philly's Argosy* and its fantasy fare—ever graphic and grim—helped Tommy as he stepped through his own dilemma *and* did keep him talking freely, always preferable to withdrawal.

He'd begun subscribing to the online pulp fiction magazine a couple of years ago. His main interest then was Elise Anderson's star column. His preferences lately, however, had altered—the subjects, more difficult. So she propped up her attention to answer some troubling questions.

"What do you think was wrong with Agnetha?" he asked.

June cleared her throat. "This was 1939, right?"

"Yuppers."

"We've come a long way with treating leukemia since then, you know."

Tommy pursed his lips. *Of course, he knew.*

In the thirties, June explained, relatively little was known about many childhood diseases, and leukemia was no exception. The first four primary types of leukemia had been identified by 1939, as well as the medical introduction of categories *acute* and *chronic*—but not until 1947 did a pathologist named Sidney Farber discover aminopterin, an amino derivative of folic acid that induced remission in children with acute lymphocytic leukemia.

June tried to summarize the history of leukemia into bits and parcels for Tommy's need-to-know hunger. There was no going around it.

Acute lymphocytic and acute myelocytic were two of the first four common forms of leukemia identified, she explained, while other subtypes like hairy cell were discovered decades later. The symptoms in many of the leukemias were similar, which included fatigue, weakness, weight loss, shortness of breath, fever, infections, and bruising.

The first bone marrow transplant was performed in 1957, and a slew of drugs designed to reduce or eliminate cancer growth were discovered and carefully honed for the next sixty years—6-mercaptopurine, methotrexate, cytarabine, vinblastine, vincristine, doxorubicin, chlorambucil, daunorubicin, fludarabine, tretinoin, imatinib, azacytidine, decitabine, dasatinib, rituximab—June knew them all by heart. While she suspected much of this *medicalese* went over Tommy's head, she dared not leave anything out, for she wanted him to understand the extent of medical science's advancements in treating cancer—*anything* to boost his confidence.

Researchers discovered a chromosomal abnormality linked to leukemias in 1960, she went on. Ten years later they identified the little bastards, chromosomes 9 and 22, which translocated and caused the disease process. By 1980, researchers had identified a human T-cell pathogen HTLV-1, the discovery of the first virus that causes cancer. Stem-cell donor programs emerged, and the first stem-cell transplantation for leukemia was performed in 1993. By 2008, genome sequencing was fully introduced for acute myeloid leukemia.

"That's why the doctors didn't know what to do for her in 1939," June concluded. "She might've had something called mixed lineage leukemia, which is the two most common forms of childhood leukemia combined. When they present together—and we don't see that as often, you know—"

"It's rare?"

June nodded. "With all kinds of weird stuff."

"Like the pissed mortem bruising?"

June held up a finger. "Postmortem. Occurring after death."

Tommy was onto his tablet again, following along in the story. "Oh, right." He nodded matter-of-factly. "The doctor was pissed."

June smiled. "He was in a tough spot, and in a highly unusual situation." The way Agnetha's disease progressed in the story was curiously *off* for any of the leukemias, she added.

Tommy suddenly broke into one of his cloak-and-dagger grins. "Like she really had something else all along?"

"Is this a spoiler alert?"

Tommy shrugged. "Maybe." He swiped the screen on his tablet. "*I think her illness came from a family curse.*"

June could see where this was going from a mile away. She nodded. "A curse, or—she might've had Li-Fraumeni syndrome. Claudius, as well. That would make total sense to me."

"What's Li-Fraumeni?"

June explained that the syndrome was named after the two doctors who discovered it, a genetic condition which is hereditary. Mutations in the gene TP53 caused it. Normally TP53, present in essentially every cell in the body, suppressed tumors while controlling growth and division of cells. The mutations, though, allowed cells to divide in an uncontrolled way and form cancerous tumors. Children with Li-Fraumeni mutations were more susceptible to a wide range of cancers.

"I assume we're going to find out more about their illness in the next two installments?" June asked.

Tommy stuck out his lower lip; he loved keeping her in suspense. June signaled the U-Haul to take the next access road off I-44, a convenience store in sight.

"I'm really at your mercy, aren't I?" She lightly goosed him.

Tommy giggled. "Now and forevermore."

Chelsea Dumont had worked after school at Archway Quick Mart for the past three years. As one of the proud *We're the Wolverines* at Vashon High, Chelsea called her dibs early about having two left feet and therefore passed up basketball. Her besties Aliyah and Taylor didn't, *good for it* with their athletic scholarships to attend UMSL next fall. Chelsea wasn't fellows material either, and this she knew—so on one signature Saturday after she turned fifteen, she made the decision to work her way toward college. Her Uncle Jerome owned Archway and was *dope* to pull strings for his favorite niece, whatever she wanted. When it came to his retail business, he was *fosho keepin' it in the family*. After his own sons announced they weren't jazzed about clerking petrol and coffee, and Chelsea told him she was, Jerome Dumont showed up at the principal's office the following day, ducked all 6'7" under the doorframe, and signed her vocational application form with his trademark JD.

Chelsea couldn't know for sure yet, but she'd kicked around the idea of majoring in history. Although several other *pushback* careers called out to her—political science, ethnic studies, social justice, and investigative journalism—she'd always been drawn to her past. The Dumonts weren't natives of Missouri; her family had relocated to St. Louis while she was in middle school. Self-identifying as Black Creole, Chelsea's ancestors were five generations deep from Plaquemines Parish in New Orleans.

Her extended relations (the ones she knew about) had thrown out the ethnic term *African American* several decades before other pockets in-country did—for identifying simply as *Creole* bore all the specificity any Dumont had ever wanted. The Dumonts were cafeteria Catholic too. While the label also included white Southerners in Louisiana proper, those Creoles were long since outnumbered by Creoles of African descent and people of color in and around the Acadian region, Cane River, and Natchitoches. Chelsea was one of them.

In quieter moments, Chelsea recalled her great-grandmother conversing in Creole, an autonomous language spruced up with wisps and swells of French patter. Some of Chelsea's finer memories came from her great-grandmother's yarn about biding time in the foyer of *her* grandmother's shotgun cottage, a tiny anteroom that doubled as a storefront for brightly hand-painted and 2-dimensional plantation souls printed on gift cards, hand-sewn prayer dolls crafted from swamp tree branches, piles of red mojo magic bags, and jars of pear preserves stacked to the ceiling. Curried inside every account was Chelsea's formative introduction to her own casual, easy-going manner for selling goods. As stories go, her great-great-grandmother had minded the store instead of the fields because she was lame—most likely from spina bifida. During low-traffic hours she'd played an accordion to entertain the work hands—short antebellum ditties, bluesy zydeco, Afro-Caribbean, or Congo-Square inspired folk songs common to southwestern Louisiana.

Fast forward to Missouri in 2019, where the Dumonts settled. Her dad was a cop at a time when it wasn't popular—anywhere—and transplanting to the Lou didn't make things any easier. Her little brother had adopted a sullen front after the move, quieter than he'd ever been. Chelsea, on the other hand, couldn't *not* be her usual bubbly, all teeth *grin to go*. She could chat up anybody. By the end of the first

Falling Stars

week, she had her two new friends A and T, a *lit* new circle of joy thick as her grandma's jambalaya. Chelsea was just that way, broadcasting *booyah* to the room wherever she went. Coming from a family of loud people (except now, her younger brother) who talked at one volume and engaged in boisterous discussions over just about anything, Chelsea understood her value as a social butterfly. Her uncle saw dollar signs and put her to use.

Chelsea quickly developed the ability to sell just about anything Archway Quick Mart inventoried—even those items shelved *way* outside their SKU designations. Try as she might to organize Archway, items stacked atop its hammertone Gondola were frequently left in a jumbled mess merely minutes after stocking up, because Uncle Jerome was bad to overbuy—particularly penny-ante imported crap and glittery gewgaw. Regular customers knew Chelsea could find anything in the chaos, that she couldn't care less if Uncle Jerome crammed his store with useless shit. *Make no difference,* Jerome always said; Chelsea could sell it. *She get some sucker to buy every time.* In an economic environment when many retailers struggled to fill their shelves or glutted them with stuff nobody wanted to buy, Jerome jammed through one of the worst supply chain disruptions in recent history without a hitch. He had Chelsea.

When businesses around St. Louis began to ramp up environmental sustainability efforts in the summer of 2020, Jerome had ordered three cases of recycled flip flops. Election year, Americana flip flops. They still had some of each mixed in with the meat-on-your-feet flip flops he'd just purchased for the 2023 Halloween season. Jerome loved—no, craved—making decisions on the fly. When he personally discovered the max styling power of Monkey Brains Hair Glue, he bought four cases of that. The second week in October, he'd walked into the store declaring that any of the remaining scorpion pops—all thirty-six assorted flavors, candied with real ones imported from Peru—were to be marked down for Archway's trick-or-treat "fire sale."

Overall, Chelsea managed to keep a lid on her amusement and hold down any forthcoming snickers. The self-perpetuating, comical workplace proved healthy for her, and Jerome's brouhaha over his niece's newfangled vocational success helped Chelsea emotionally sidestep a great chunk of international discord—the ongoing focus on police brutality and its *hits-home* price, the defunding of her own father. Some, but not all of it.

Certain days were tougher than others. After transplanting across *The Great Divide* (Jerome's personal insult for the state of Arkansas) Chelsea had no aspirations to move again any time soon. UMSL was looking rather good—especially in the fast company of A&T. Commuting to campus was the thing to do in the wake of COVID-19, anyway. *She fosho wasn't looking over the state line.*

When she started the online process, her undergraduate application to UMSL, she fretted through which of her four emails to use for creating an account, how to navigate the institution's mega drop-down menus, the call-to-action buttons, and *every last* contact field. For a Gen Z, things like this were normally *bada bing, bada boom* —but Chelsea's ACT score from last semester was teetering on the brink of oblivion at 19. She had one more shot before graduation, and if she couldn't improve it, she'd have to rely on class rank—a 3.35 overall GPA from those 17 attempted units throughout her high school career. She really didn't want to have to start her first semester at UMSL with any LEAP shit, either. It was *fosho nuff* to have to take the ALEKS placement assessment for math *after* she got enrolled. *If* she got enrolled.

That, too, did pass—and shortly after Chelsea received her acceptance letter to UMSL, she sat all but knock-kneed in the registrar's office. All she had to do now was turn in her completed high school transcript, but she couldn't rightly do that until spring. *Not* the same confident Chelsea everyone else thought she was. Though she'd sailed through several hard knocks, this *hurt*. Her little brother wasn't the only one who felt the disparity, either. Their father had assisted setting up the struts and frets upon the world's stage *and* in their home court by simply doing his job.

Which time and again turned her smile upside down. Chelsea had always loved her daddy, and *how she hated* being stuck in the middle.

Major Arwin Dumont III was stationed three miles away at Metro PD in the First District. He checked in on Chelsea regularly, the *only* way her mother would allow her to work at Archway. Most shifts—with few exceptions—were two to six and home for dinner. One of those irregularities occurred during her sophomore year, a night shift when

Falling Stars

Archway had a stickup. Chelsea made her dad swear on her grandma's grave not to tell her mother. And Arwin allowed Chelsea to continue at Archway under the agreement she would take only day shifts, although they both knew the likelihood of robbery at gunpoint was seven times greater in broad daylight—especially with the 2022 upsurge in crime. She therefore learned to quick-read people way beyond skin color, dress, or the height strip posted on the double door's inner steel frames at the entrance.

Chelsea loved nearly all the perks of being a daddy's girl, like Arwin's regular praise of her rapidly developing ability in profiling. He'd never openly pressured her, but inherently she knew he'd simply *go gaga* if she decided to major in criminal justice. She'd never told him that her investigative talents were birthed during multiple terse moments in the summer of 2020, watching the race riots play out across the country on TV. Her dad had sat slumped in his recliner under a cloud of anger. On one of those gloomy evenings, he told her he'd just discovered something new about his ancestral name, and the sheer irony of it.

Know what Arwin means? Take a fat guess. And no fair using your phone.

So she hadn't. *Sounds kingly to me.*

He'd sniggered. *I wish. It means* Friend of the People.

Woah. For real?

Woah, that's right. Ain't that a hummer.

They didn't get into any loud discussions that evening about beat bias or unchecked use of excessive force, departmental corruption or understaffing, the terror of being outmanned and outgunned, or any of the daily racket with those split-second decisions you can't walk back. Her dad was a master at reduction when he wanted to be.

That thin blue line just got thinner. He threw the remote across the room.

By the next morning she'd turned, however, from feeling bummed out with her daddy to the equally grueling task of pleasing her mother. Chelsea had always coddled a precise set of mom pleasers—some she kept stringing along, others to avoid maternal scorn. She always wore her hair braided straight back in long cornrows, for example, because Mom had more than once advised her (*no rug head in the face, please*) to show off her beautiful profile. At times, Chelsea felt the Fox News behind that item was, her face was her only asset. She was just big boned enough to carry added weight, particularly in her butt and thighs, and it bothered her. She hid this little niggle of insecurity nonetheless underneath a bright and booming voice, which bounced off the sneeze screen at Archway. She was good for this job—at least until she graduated from college. Sure, she'd briefly entertained the idea of applying for gig work after high school. But Uncle Jerome had promised to flex anything and everything around her college schedule, and the grand scheme to look elsewhere fell flat the next time she clocked in at Archway. This place was always home to her, never failing to give what she constantly craved: the chance to meet and schmooze new people every day.

Like those two coming at the door now.

Chelsea laid aside her cell phone, one piece of technology she'd never once been written up for at school or work—nor would she be. For Chelsea *loved* talking far more than texting. It'd always been that way with her, hadn't it? Arwin frequently bragged that his daughter was a true generational throwback.

"Welcome to Archway," she greeted them. The mom nodded; her eyes crinkled into a smile. The boy ran.

Chelsea grinned at the pair and set about doing busy work behind the counter in OWE mode—*observation without eyeballing*, she called it.

The mom, a year or so on the older side for having a six or sevenish boy. Chelsea calculated his age by his size, and the outfit—he wore a Chicago Bears hooded bomber jacket with a *some-big-bucks-at-Spirit-Halloween* Victorian vampire cape under that. Red satin-lined, not your average kid costume. A magnet for bullies.

Wouldn't last a day at Meramec in that get-up.

Chelsea looked away briefly and coughed. Children who ran around wearing costumes past their dates of service had always bothered her on several levels, anyway. Two weeks before, she could've sold them a case of trick-or-treat leftovers from Jerome's scorpion stash, but that train had left the station.

He had Mom's total attention, though. Not a doubt in Chelsea's mind he was her only. That's just the way things had played out between those two, she concluded—he, all big splash in this antiseptic little fishbowl and Mom, cleaning up after him. That, Chelsea decided at once, was the way they lived. The mom had waited longer, gotten older, to *fosho* start things out right—and yet something had gone very wrong.

Wrong enough to require they both continue wearing the CDC-approved N95 masks into the second season *after* the vaccines and the boosters, and boosters, *and boosters* when no one wore face coverings much anymore. Even Jerome was talking about *finally* taking down the sneeze screens. Like many of his decisions, that one came up in Snapchat as another ad hoc admission. First, he'd had concerns about the widespread Delta and Omicron variants, so they stayed up. Then he had the brainchild that screens might also serve as crime deterrents, *look after my favorite niece*, he said. They were a bitch to clean, though, and excepting these two, Chelsea hadn't seen a customer wearing a mask in—*well, that long.*

The kid, Chelsea decided. *Yuh-huh, immunocompromised.* His jacket's hood, his mask, and *those Polaroids* obscured all his face except a small section of skin under his cheeks. Chelsea had never seen anyone *that* white—not in person, at least. A level of white which made the poster child for St. Jude's look tan.

The boy moved quickly for someone who was ill, though, darting from one aisle to the next, as if he'd somehow already memorized the store . . . like an automaton, Chelsea noted. Mom, nondescript by comparison—solid gray sweatshirt over jeans—moved steady-ahead quick, not so much in a series of fits and starts, but in the directed way that people who work in large offices or institutions do.

While he shoveled items off the shelves, she went to get fountain drinks.

Their ride—a U-Haul truck with Iowa plates—was a sure tell those two probably weren't just moving across town, either. Mom speaking to him from one aisle over sounded . . . Great Lakes. Yuh-huh, if the jacket wasn't disclosure enough already, Chelsea would've guessed they were from Chicago.

When Mom pulled down her mask to sip the coffee she was dispensing, Chelsea immediately memorized what she saw. A pretty face, narrow nose, *dainty* even—and very expressive eyes. Hair slicked into a high ponytail long enough to just touch her shoulders, sort of an *un*tricked out, all casual for driving and such, except her hair and shoulders were also primed to work. Mom probably forced good posture and stood a lot at her job. The ticker on the front door pegged her at five-nine, but up close she appeared much taller—outright gangly, even. The kid piling on the groceries was also skinny but without the height.

Chelsea couldn't help herself. "There's shopping baskets over there, right behind you." She pointed toward the basket stand at the end of the aisle. The boy turned—only his head, though—*Holy Mother Mary Joseph and Jesus, he's got some range, like a goddamn owl* . . .

His gaze fixed on Chelsea. Mom casually glanced in his direction from the drink station.

Like that's a regular thing?

"Looks like you're going to need one," she agreed.

Chelsea couldn't really see his eyes, but could've sworn that for an instant they glowed red. Her spine went cold. The kid stared at her a click longer before he turned, crab walked his way over to the stand, and aimlessly dumped all the contents into the top basket. If not for that graceless action sequel, Chelsea would've been truly unnerved. She looked away just long enough to recover her cool.

A noise. *Here's Mom at the screen already,* fountain drinks lined on the counter, 8 oz. coffee for her—and a 32 oz. red cherry ICEE. *Geez, she's quicker than I gave her credit.*

Chelsea cleared her throat and stepped up to the register. *Something off about those two.* She couldn't put her finger on it, though. "What else can I get for you?"

"Is the pizza as good as it looks?" Mom had ducked to browse the giant slices displayed on the middle tray of the countertop food warming unit.

Chelsea grinned. "Why I subscribe to every dieting app there is, yes ma'am."

Mom chuckled, low and quick—then back to the boy, her real reason for the ask. "They've got pepperoni, Tommy." She pointed. "See here? It's red."

Which sounded—*well, not right.* Chelsea decided to ignore it for the moment and fetch a giant slice for Mom instead.

Falling Stars

"Will that be one, or two?"

"Two, please."

"Pepperoni?"

"Yes."

Chelsea ladled the slices into two takeout boxes, sealed the lids with Archway stickers, and grabbed a medium—*no, large*—plastic shopping bag from the dispenser before returning to the register. That last call came on the fly, seeing the kid wagging one very overstuffed shopping basket toward checkout.

Mom swooped in to assist, hoisting it onto the countertop.

Chelsea pulled the basket around the sneeze screen. "Let's see." Her usual quick assessment of the contents as she reached for the handheld barcode scanner:

Four Wacko-Wax Red Wax Lips
Two 9 oz. boxes of Red Hots
One 16 oz. bag of Cherry Twizzlers
One 8 oz. box of Boston Baked Beans
One 2 lb. bag of Cinnamon Jelly Belly jelly beans
Five sticks of strawberry flavored Rock Candy
One 1 lb. bag of blood orange Gummy Bears
One 1 lb. bag of red Swedish Fish
Ten cinnamon flavored Atomic Fireballs
One 20 oz. bottle of Big Red cream soda
One 9 oz. bag of Flamin' Hot Crunchy Cheetos

Her own mom would meet her at the door with a garbage can if she came home with all this jank, Chelsea considered. "You like your red stuff, don't you?" She glanced up at *whatshisname*—Tommy, staring a hole right through her.

"I eat only red things," Tommy said, nothing further.

Chelsea studied his expression a moment longer, lingering for a hint of a smile, another word or two, *something*. Nada, zip. The kid was dead serious.

Chelsea swallowed. "Maybe you'd like to top off all this with an apple?"

Tommy groaned loudly.

"That's a great idea," Mom interjected. "Where are those?"

"Just behind you on Aisle Two."

Mom set off for a Red Delicious while the kid glared Chelsea down. Yuh-huh, her only option now was to scan, bag, and ignore. She wasn't winning any awards with Tommy. *Man, what a dork.* She began ringing up the items quickly, hopscotching her way through *a pile of enough Red Food Dye #40 to rot out his tongue.*

"That's from *Dark Shadows.*"

Chelsea *quicklike* reviewed the last five seconds of her life and glanced over at Tommy, who had flipped open his clip-ons, huge blue eyes riveted on her. Yuh-huh, she'd quite unconsciously hummed the opening soundtrack for the show's 2022 remake.

Chelsea grinned at Tommy Blue-Eyes as she finished sacking up the reds.

A Shadows *fan, who would've guessed it?*

"I take it you'll be back here in January to see Jack Darrow, huh?"

Tommy's eyes widened. "He's coming to Fan Expo?"

Mom returned with two Red Delicious apples and placed them underneath the sneeze screen.

Chelsea nodded. "Just got the email this morning. How cool is that?"

No answer. Tommy was busy, thumbing on his smartphone. He stopped. "It's January twenty-sixth. That's a *Friday*, Mom."

Chelsea's best guess was *a Friday* was a good thing. Mom glanced down at his smartphone.

"Sure, Friday could work," was all she said. She opened her cell phone wallet and fished out a credit card.

Chelsea directed Mom to the card reader and continued chatting with Tommy. "If I can get the day off, I'm at the live Q&A and Rewatch Party for sure. Everybody's saying he looks a lot like Frid."

Tommy nodded. "He does."

Spoken like a kid in the know. A true throwback if he really *does* know, Chelsea thought.

He glanced down at his smartphone again. "Oh, *man*. He's doing a CGC Signature Series."

Chelsea rubbed her fingers together. "Spendy. I got a nine-point-eight Dr. WHO last year."

"Sweet. But a *D* or a *Blade* is better value. Even a low five on those brings a good collector's price."

Falling Stars

Chelsea blinked at Tommy in amazement. *Fosho kid's got to be older than seven, then.* She grinned at Mom and handed over the sack of goods. "Now I'm wishing he'd been around last year to keep me from wasting all my money—"

"I can help you out *this* year."

Chelsea was still taking in how *white* Tommy was as he stepped closer to the counter. He was being—*nice*. "You'd do that?" She glanced over at Mom. "He really seems to know his stuff."

"A walking microprocessor," she answered, eyes smiling.

"Well—if it's okay with your mom, you could friend me on Wiz's Facebook page." She looked at Mom. "I'm Chelsea Dumont, by the way." Chelsea couldn't help but notice that Tommy didn't look for permission—and Mom didn't seem to mind, either.

"It's fine," Mom replied. "June and Tommy Lucas."

Tommy's tiny thumbs were impatiently hovering over his cell phone screen.

"Oh, yes. I'm Martha underscore whoosis, all lowercase," Chelsea quickly added. Her middle school hero was Martha Jones in Dr. WHO, a medical student who became the doctor's traveling companion and girlfriend. Her dad *still* thought Martha was pretty cool.

"Got it," Tommy said, thumbing away on his smartphone.

Chelsea's cell phone pinged. And that was that. Her eccentric new friend turned ahead of his mom toward the door, the folds of his vampire cape shimmering and rippling under the store's LED tube lights.

"See you online, then," Chelsea called after them.

Chapter Four

BAD BLOOD
THE CASE OF CLAUDIUS FALLON
by Miles Cochran

Part II

3 September 1939

The viscount hadn't spoken to me directly, nor did he do so until after our arrival at the motorcar hold, F Deck Forward—nearly an hour later. Timing the body's transport was tricky, for we were approaching dinner, when the grand lady's passageways typically teem with passengers togged to the bricks. The eye is very smart, and no amount of mental arrangement can arrest a glance of what one *supposes* one sees, nor the split-second shock of determining it is *yes indeedy, right there in front of me*. We could only push ahead along the way I'd ordered and aim for swift passage.

Only one death had transpired on RMS Queen Mary previously, and that, before my service. I didn't find anything in the logs about body transport procedure then, and it had occurred off Langston's watch as well.

Courtesy some shop talk I'd overheard in mess, the engineer's lift by Forward Engine Room is a beeline from H Deck's Boiler Number One to the emergency generators located B Deck aft. Lead engineers had mapped out the detour for juniors, motormen, and wipers, to spare those workers the fuss of climbing ladders from H to B and potentially surprising first-class passengers with lengthy strolls to the ship's stern in mucked-up coveralls.

The emergency generators, it just so happened, were located adjacent portside rope storage and merely six paces from Isolation Ward. I mentally mapped the route, and in nothing flat Doc and I had consigned four stewards and a litter for Agnetha's transport, since this development should avoid the festivities and must needs navigate areas impassable by trolley, namely the stairwell to Number Two Hatch. Two stewards were required to carry, and two more to pilot and flank the body from sight. I was hard-pressed at the time to locate any of our heavier set stewards for the flank, and the one we called Gunner was only a mite bigger than any of our bellboys. He got that hatchet name from regularly gripping up for chump change at Pig & Whistle; everyone said he had big guns. Underneath his double-breasted steward's jacket, I could never tell.

Claudius walked directly behind the litter, and I took up the rear. Our trip to the engineer's lift would start with a short stretch past the ironing room, tourist accommodations, and quarters earmarked for twenty stewardesses. From there it made a sharp left past the ladies' lavatories, the aft stairwell, then straightway through tourist-class shops, barber side—with forty or so more paces to the lift located forward of the engine hatch. In my mind, this would be the most difficult leg of our trip, because I failed to account for what was set to happen afterward.

We reversed the engineers' detour, starting from Isolation Ward and making our way starboard, past the ironing station.

A couple of stewardesses at the pressing machines in there, winged white caps and backs to us.

So far, swell.

A short section of tourist-class staterooms flanked us, hull side. My every hope and intention was that their occupants were already seated for dinner on Main Deck. We'd almost reached the first inboard passage when I saw a stateroom door open four meters ahead. The stewards transporting the body had received strict orders to defer to no one and file forward, interrupted only upon my command—and that, they did. Claudius too, continued with his head down. I merely caught a whiff of a startled glance before the door slammed shut.

Inwardly I sighed, hoping for the boy's sake not all reactions would be as irreverent.

As we made a hard left at the first inboard corridor, the viscount began reciting in Latin again. With the stairwell at our right and the back of twenty stewardesses' quarters to our left, we were more likely to encounter a gaggle of tourist-class passengers and crew here, I knew.

In manus tuas, Domine . . . in vita sive mors . . .

Thankfully, he whispered.

Reditum eius anima . . . reditum eius anima ad me . . .

His emphasis—on the last two words, almost petulant. Mayhap the bald horror of his sister's demise alone was enough to throw him out of true, I don't know. I certainly hadn't prepared for this public display of bleating and soul-baring.

The stairwell, in use with tourist-class passengers going up, up to their dinner destinations.

A quick appraisal of its occupants told me none had yet stopped, hands gliding onward over the balustrades, entraining to the ship's yaw.

A gentle delay of one ivory Schiaparelli 20-button opera glove . . . there.

I dared look up into her crystalline eyes just as those garnet-red lips formed into a pristine and perfect "O".

"Clear the gangway, please!" *That* before I had the chance to reconsider, a total knee-jerk on my part. "Make way, ladies and gentlemen!" I bellowed when awareness about what I'd just done caught up with me.

They stepped to it, a steady stream of hands and bodies scurrying upward.

Two stragglers finishing up in the barber's had their chairs immediately rotated away to face the opposite walls.

Good on you. I nodded toward the shopkeepers.

Everyone in this section seemed to be catching on rather well.

We might even be able to log this one without incident.

Once past the staircase, we headed for a small section of the ship known as Fluff Alley, where the air is usually thick with a sour mash of counter testers' perfume and aerosol. The tourist-class patrons lingering here before their dinner call would most likely be too caught up in alleyway sales and services to notice us. Or so I'd planned.

What I hadn't counted on was Claudius gunning for attention, or whatever he was up to. His chanting had grown progressively louder,

Falling Stars

now glancing off the bulkheads like slugburger grease in a fryer—and with enough effort to leave his tiny chest heaving for air.

I didn't watch and wait this time, but countermanded the boy instead, again belting orders to clear the gangway. Shoppers who might've otherwise totally ignored us scrambled to vacate the ship's passage in a brief and shining moment of pandemonium.

Claudius stopped. I couldn't be sure, but he sounded winded.

"Belay there!" I roared. The four stewards snapped their legs into a precise halt. The flanks—Gunner and his associate, immediately executed right and left faces toward the body, their backs to the crowd —a simple, yet effective maneuver much like the way our old tom, by standing sideways, made himself look larger.

Claudius spun around, chest heaving, black eyes drilling me.

I didn't take a knee this time, really wanting to get a move on. I *did* make a mental note to lower my volume considerably and spoke directly to the boy. "Viscount, do you need to rest?"

A nib of that strange chittering again before he forcefully shook his head and turned away from me. I knew better than to tarry with that number of eyes on us.

I ordered all hands forward.

Claudius regrouped and continued somehow, his gaze trained downward. I would learn only later that this odd display I'd just observed for the second time was his own way of staving off a keen hunger for something bloody.

The engineers' lift was the finish line on this level, just large enough to accommodate our party—located aft of Forward Engine Room and merely a few more paces along the stretch. From there we would go down from B to D and surely bypass much of tourist class.

On D Deck we'd take what was known as Burma Road—a working alleyway portside. The entire alley was a two-tone shade of high-gloss polyurethane in gunmetal grey, none of the frills two decks above. Six exposed pipes thirteen inches in diameter snaked along the ceiling the entire length of the ship. The inboard walls were long and bare—for they encased boiler hatches five, four, three, and two. Skirting those boilers was a checkerboard of storage rooms and compartments for all things that sustained us—from the ales and stout to fruits in the ripening room, fresh and frozen fish, a butcher's shop that provided cut and frozen meats, eggs, bacon, and the wine room. Between the engine hatches, Burma Road tiered off into spaces for other necessary items like soiled linens, empty milk cans, potatoes, and boots. There again, we would also pass our ample dispensary hull side with its separate wards and operating theater, where Agnetha should've been in the first place.

The home stretch from amidships would take us yet past plenty elsewise, including a carpentry shop, printer's shop, plumber's supply room, an oil-filling station, a kosher kitchen—plus the firemen's, trimmers', and greasers' messrooms, the writers' office, and a swimming and bathhouse. At the very end was a bar, pantry, and lavatories.

Our chance encounters on Burma Road were more likely stewards and stewardesses bound for their assigned posts that evening, or so I'd anticipated. At the end was a portside stairwell aft of Number Two Hatch that would take us the rest of the way, two levels down to F Deck.

During the lift's descent (Claudius went silent), my mind twisted through a Lindy Hop between *coulda* and *woulda*. If the child had only died in the dispensary according to protocol, we'd have fared a much shorter trek, merely twenty-seven meters aft to the Ice Room on D Deck. As the die was cast, though—neither Langston nor Fallon threw a double.

Perhaps certain sections of Cunard's White Star Liner floor plans presumed too heavily upon the certainty of interminable life, spit, and cheer, for even transporting a body from the dispensary to coffin storage, H Deck forward required passage from midship to prow—not to mention stern to bow, which we were applying now.

I'd hoped Burma Road would be somehow less congested at that hour, but it was not. Upon disembarking the lift, I immediately saw the error of my ways, a passage brimming with far more occupants than I'd anticipated. I guess I'd placed the fear of God in our pallbearers, for they set out together in seamless stride, not a hint of a hiccup.

Burma Road's sea of humanity—stewards and guests alike—parted like high tide breaking over the alley's bulkheads. Word travels fast, and my inclination was, *these already knew*. We were headed into a procession regardless since most of our crew were British. A contagion of hats off, heads lowered, kneeling, and court curtsies had already begun—men, women, passengers, and crew alike—for the remaining fifty or so meters. As we passed them one by one, I faced the unnerving

Falling Stars

ordeal of holding back tears.

I guess a sailor could expect to mellow out after twenty-one months off active duty, but I never saw mine coming. Like many punks enlisting out of wartime, I'd done so wet behind the ears at age eighteen just after WWI, completed a long service record, retired, and was about to re-up for the very thing at thirty-seven. I hadn't pushed to make rank over some of my brothers-in-arms, more content to keep my nose clean and bide my time as a cog in the engine. My reputation for staying cool under pressure got around too. Sailors under my command knew exactly what I expected of them, and they always ate and slept before I did. My reaction time might be considered slack by some, yet this worked in the long haul. I didn't burn out. I was also willing to get my hands dirty, like we were doing now.

Perhaps *mellow fellow* was a misnomer for me, though, for I did develop a nervous condition in boot camp that I reckon had purely corporeal roots. During my first week's processing at Naval Station Great Lakes, my fiancé broke off our engagement. She was a longshore Jersey girl who, as it turns out, disliked large cities and Navy bases. By week three of basic training on the shores of Lake Michigan, I'd developed a rather odd syndrome. I quickly learned, however, to use it to my advantage.

Sailors cranking out the last of forty press-ups or running sandbags or adding ten live rounds at the firing range developed a kind of tunnel vision early on—I still heard about it over cheap whiskey years later. I, however, experienced another form of visual alteration under duress—the ability to observe the surrounding environment with my entire visual field simultaneously. I saw the room, so to speak.

I first noticed this heightened clarity of eyesight during timed trials climbing up ship scuttles. The recessed triangles marking the heads of every countersunk carbon steel rivet around those hatches gleamed at me as I scrambled through, rank few of them tightened due north, I also noticed.

Visual detail during those exercises always sharpened to the degree where fine edges of virtually any surrounding object became extremely clear and highly defined, like a camera or projector coming into focus. By Battle Stations 21, I'd refined my technique through fire and flooding simulation drills, abandon ship scenarios, and floating in near-freezing water. I've never experimented with psychedelics, though I've heard such states are commonly induced when dropping mescaline.

Enhanced peripheral vision gave me huge advantages. I'm not sure if it qualifies as a kind of cross-modal plasticity, because my visual field was never compromised—no blur or tubular darkening. I was wide open. Sometimes the gift still grazed me in a particularly swift performance of the Daily Dozen, my morning regimen at sunup, usually during the Grasp:

Pay special attention to keep the head up as the body goes forward. Keep the eyes fixed on a point directly in front when you are erect and do not let the eyes wander from that point as you go down and up. Exhale while the body bends forward, inhale while the body rises. When hyperextending backward the movement is slight, just enough to stretch abdominal muscles.

Repeat 10 times.

Even now, I trained my attention—that odd mix of perfect clarity—not only to the rhythmic advance of the rank and file in front of me (the boy's slouched shoulders, the way the fabric of his shirttail flapped as he scudded along), but also to gilded crowns and tops of women's fascinators and boaters as we passed, tops of hats not commonly pointed my direction. In suppressing the urge to weep, I memorized them all: various ways nylon tulle netting was sewn up into top seams, crown patterns of pearl-studded liners, tie-ins for lilting ostrich feathers and bows, staid slopes of down-tilted brims. And for the remainder of Burma Road, Claudius went along in silence.

A 1937 Packard Station Wagon waited for us exactly where Fallon said it would be. Also known as a Woodie, this beaut was an eight-cylinder Six Series, model 115-C by Baker-Raulang, one of the original sixty with a wheelbase just that long, and a tight fit between the other coaches. It gleamed army green from ox yoke to windshield, with exquisitely inlaid varnished birch running the length of the wagon. Inside it had contrasting leather, a wood-grain dash, and a built-in radio trimmed in chrome. The Light Eight carried the same three-speed selective gearbox as the Six with a single disk clutch and floor shift controls, hydraulic drum brakes at all four corners.

Oddly enough, I hadn't yet second-guessed Commander Fallon's choices, including his deployment of the Packard overseas. Assembled in Detroit, his was a left-hand driver. Until recently these station wagons were more likely to be seen in horse stables than in London proper or even Cardiff—for before the war, the station wagon was exactly that—a transport used to carry servants, luggage, and occasionally the owner between the palatial estate and the nearest train station. I suspected that Fallon had probably used the Woodie for these purposes regularly enough to familiarize the boy with some of its features.

I wasn't wrong. Young Claudius went immediately to the passenger side, popped open the door the ten inches' clearance it had, and wriggled his little body inside. He retrieved something from the glove compartment, squeezed his way back out, and handed a second sealed note to me. From there, he walked around to the rear and flipped down the tailgate like a pro.

I pocketed the note for the moment and peered inside with the rest of our assembly at the Fisk Burial Case. Up to then, I'd never actually seen one. Also known as a Fisk Mummy, these airtight, cast-iron coffins were invented and patented during the Victorian era of safety coffins by Almond D. Fisk, an undertaker more concerned about delayed burials and decomposition than the apparently dead or comatose being buried alive.

Fisk had believed his coffin would revolutionize the way the world handled death by preserving corpses for prolonged travel or other delayed interment. It also prevented the spread of diseases like yellow fever or cholera, then blamed upon overcrowding cemeteries. Fisk, a New Yorker, was familiar with churchyards spilling beyond their bounds and packed to the topsoil—sometimes several feet above the streets.

Production of these interment wonders, though, had stopped a half century ago. The business waned after Fisk's Long Island factory burned to the ground in 1849, when Fisk himself suffered injuries leading to his own death the following year. Sensational press in 1858, "Explosion of a Metallic Coffin," hexed any chances for new acquisitions, though W.M. Raymond and Company initially gave it a green light. A Fisk had, after all, successfully transported the remains of the Honorable Henry Clay from Washington, D.C. to Kentucky in the swelter of mid-July *to the entire satisfaction of the Senate Committee.* This wasn't, however, enough good press to straighten the record, and the coffin's production met its end in 1888.

Which made me speculate where Fallon had found this one, and a child's mold, at that. These were pricey—two to ten times the cost of wooden coffins. Shaped like a shrouded corpse, the Fisk carried the disgrace of looking more like an Egyptian sarcophagus than a stately mahogany, and the built-in face window sealed the deal for most Americans. The chance for mourners to behold again the features of their dearly departed was altogether too unsettling, it seemed. Still and all this Gothic curio commanded our full attention for a minute or more, its metal so artfully cast to replicate the delicate folds of cerecloth, the entire crest heavily adorned with angels, thistles, roses, oak leaves, acorns, and berries. Sealed with lampblack carbon, it glistened at us like some nine days' wonder.

If memory serves me, Fisk had included in his patent that . . . *surrounding air may be exhausted so completely as to entirely prevent decay of the contained body on principles well understood, or if preferred, the coffin may be filled with gas or fluid having the property of forestalling putrefaction.*

Which made me fetch the second note from my pocket at once. Surely Fallon didn't expect us to—?

I began giving instructions as I moved under the deck prism to read the note. First, the gurney had to be placed inside the wagon alongside the Fisk. To transfer the body in a respectful manner, we'd have to remove the Fisk from the cab and set it behind the wagon, on the bilge. A quick look-see told me everything I needed to know. I pocketed the note and moved in to take my share of the load in transferring the Fisk.

"Crikey! 'e bit me!"

I didn't catch at first who'd shouted out until Gunner backed away from the tailgate, his right hand unnaturally coiled, dark liquid dripping from his forearm. (In the incident log Gunner reported that he'd never actually touched the boy, that he merely tried to block the viscount from remaining underfoot during this risky operation.)

A soft thud near the right rear bumper was Claudius slumping against the wheelbase. I was there on the double.

"Viscount, are you all right?"

The boy's labored breathing and those strange machinations, his pale gums exposed, canines flecked and fully bared . . .

I needed to get him to the dispensary chop-chop and was about to put a hand on him regardless of his tendency to chaw—when he spoke.

"So—sorry," he whispered.

I took a knee. "I know you're hungry," I whispered back.

For I was also weighing in Fallon's second note, which had warned me to override any decisions to escort Claudius off the premises. It told me everything I needed to know for my next course of action.

When the boy grows faint, he must consume raw meat. Order him blue-rare steak.

I sent Gunner off to the dispensary for medical attention, assisted the stewards with transferring the body, and ordered the rest to fetch Claudius's dinner, bedding, towels, ceramic heaters, and rotary fans—for Fallon's instructions had already indicated the boy would refuse to return to his stateroom that night.

Claudius will likely insist that his sister is not dead, that he must remain with her. Give him immunity to do what he must.

In the bottom of the Fisk coffin, we found another note.

Do not autopsy, embalm, or attempt to preserve the body in any way. Do not enter her death into the ship's logs or try to inform me.

I excused myself momentarily and went to the nearest house phone just meters away inside the mail room, for I knew that however rattled he might seem, Langston would be quick to perform his duty, notifying next of kin.

"What's this with Gunner?" he wanted to know.

I promised to fill him in on the matter soon and informed him about Fallon's next request. At the other end of the horn, I heard him groan.

"What I'd give for an Anny right now."

"You and me both."

"It's all rather jolly unkind of him, wouldn't you say?"

"Yes, quite strange, I agree. We'll figure it out." I hung up.

The third note hounded me a bit, for it was about what I had yet to do Stateside.

You will drive the boy and the body to Baker Cure for Cancer Hospital in Eureka Springs. He will likely expect Dr. Baker to perform miracles for his sister.

The kitchen provided a flatiron cut cooked Pittsburgh blue, which the boy tore into with his bare hands and wolfed down like a hungry animal. He tipped the platter for the remaining liquid. After that, he was ready to talk.

"Viscount, I've ordered amenities to allow you to stay the evening, but the hold really isn't sufficient to accommodate you for more than one night." In addition to a small fleet of motorcars, most of F Deck housed recesses over all five boiler rooms with their overflow tanks, baggage and cargo, and the mail room. Noisy, isolated, and not temperature regulated, this was hardly any place for a sick boy.

I could tell by the way he looked at me already that he disagreed.

"I can't leave her," he replied. "She could wake up."

Which made me wonder if he fully understood the certitude of his sister's death, not to mention the airtight nature of her resting place. But there was no talking him out of it.

I nodded. "I'll prep the heaters for you. There's bedding and towels, a lavatory at the top of the stairs." I pointed toward the mail room. "You'll call me should you need anything else before morning?"

Though Claudius assured me that he would, I elected to stay with him for a while. He washed up satisfactorily in the gentlemen's lavatory on E Deck, and dutifully prepared his bedroll in the Woodie's wayback alongside the Fisk. I made sure the heaters were fully operational; nights mid-Atlantic have an unmistakable snap to them. As he settled in, I suggested we could post stewards to watch the body so that he might shower daily in his own stateroom and take in some fresh air in the evenings with me on the outer deck.

"Only those two," he replied after some serious thought. I obviously wanted to press for more, to reel him back into the luxurious accommodations Fallon had booked. I knew it well, "The Seven Stallions" stateroom, one of the ship's largest suites with a separate living room and breakfast nook, bookcase headboards over two queen beds, and operable portholes. Rich polished wood had massive carvings of Arabian horses, all commissioned artistry. By the end of that conversation, he'd only agreed to three catered meals and two stints away from his sister per diem.

The following morning, I was relieved to find him very much alive, alert, and ready to start his day. I took forenoon watch after his catered breakfast (another blue-rare upon request) while an assigned steward escorted him to his stateroom to shower and change his attire. He returned in just under thirty minutes dressed in a freshly starched shirt with slacks, his overgrown locks tethered into a tidy pigtail, sketch pad in hand. The steward escort (who'd also heard about Gunner) denied assisting him with any of it; Claudius had fully groomed himself, he reported. At which point I began to suspect I was entertaining an intelligence well beyond seven years old, and I made a mental note to find out why. With his hair dressed back, I also first noticed the boy's pronounced masseters, which gave me a much better idea about what they'd possibly done to Gunner's forearm.

"Lad was a wee bit *peckish?*" Seconds into that conversation, Langston's volume had gone up a couple of notches already. Turns out he'd been in the middle of pronouncing his second death that very same day, a Mr. Brandt from the United States, when Gunner had arrived. "He drags in looking like he pulled his arm out of a hasher and I'm thinking, *what's the stupid bloke gone and done now?* And that's it? *Peckish?* You're joking me."

I white-knuckled the receiver, still mentally sidestepping through the particulars for sanitizing my own log. "How bad?" I asked.

"Thirteen stitches."

Which surprised me; I'd hoped Gunner's triple-lined Cunard issue would've buffered the boy's bite somewhat. "How's he taking it?"

The line crackled; Langston was forever disconnecting the horn while he scuttled around the infirmary. "I put him on three weeks' light duty, and his grip-up's bodged for a couple more, how do you think?"

I swallowed. "I'll check on him, then."

"We really can't afford another row about any of this, right? You've a tight leash on the little nutter?" I suppressed a flinch at Langston's smear and did my best to convince him I did.

"Oy, I hope so," he mumbled. "I'm gobsmacked, I tell you."

I glanced over at the Packard, Claudius perched on the open tailgate with his sketch pad. *Could I manage him?* By then, I wasn't so sure. I signed off with Langston and went back to the wagon.

At the boy's request, the steward escort had also delivered a Kennedy tackle box from his room. A metal monstrosity half the lad's size, I was glad Claudius asked for help, and more than a little curious to see what he had in there. From where I stood, I could see it was packed with several sets of Grafos and Rapidograph styluses, pen nibs, graphite drawing pencils, charcoal, Faber-Castell kneaded erasers, and the like.

Claudius had popped open three cantilever trays and was busy at work, starting with a delicate outline of his sister lying in state. We'd replaced the Fisk into the wayback with the hinged face cover and window facing outward at his behest, and I could now see at least one reason he wanted us to do so, for only that vantage point provided adequate light to see her face. He'd pause from time to time, peer intently into the face window, then continue his masterpiece. I also noticed he was a southpaw.

I recalled finding a couple of photos tucked away in Nonna's family album when I was a kid, ones displaying some relatives I hadn't met. When I asked her about them, she explained to me that these were *memento mori,* that is, photographs commemorating the dearly departed. After a day or so I put two and two together and realized that some or all the people in those exquisitely contrived photographs were actually dead at the time they were taken.

The oldest in her stash was shot with a double-box camera around 1845—faster lens than a daguerreotype, but still requiring a typical three-minute exposure. As a result, my thrice-removed cousin, Nouvelle, propped alongside his brother and sister, was in pinpoint focus compared to the rest—simply because he wasn't breathing. In another one, two young girls with rapt and obedient attention toward the camera curled against their deceased mother on a chaise, all dressed in matching pinafores. The mother appeared to be resting quietly, eyes averted toward the floor.

The Victorian fixation on both sides of the Atlantic with photographically memorializing the dead incited a lot of creativity with props, gadgets, and staging—such as stands for holding bodies fully seated and standing, eye reconstruction using paint, even infants conscientiously posed and appearing to catch forty winks beside their favorite rattles. Death portraiture was popular for children in Nonna's generation because epidemics like diphtheria, measles, scarlet fever, rubella, typhus, and cholera plagued nurseries in England. Twentieth century improvements concurrent in health care and camera technology, however, had inevitably ended the demand for death photography. Life expectancy of children doubled, and with the development of roll film, Eastman Kodak, and 35 mm cameras, photography took its rightful station as a household pastime.

I expected that within the royal courts, though, old-school ways were still observed regarding *memento mori* and commissioned portraiture—that if the late viscountess had been in Wales, Claudius would be sitting with her for such an event. Since this obviously was not the case, he'd dutifully taken on the task himself.

After he roughed out a faint outline of his sister's face, he set to work employing several different tools, a range of pen nibs, and charcoal. A new and emboldened style with whorls and loops emerged, his stylus seeming to thrash about. Periodically he would pause, review his subject, and switch hands, drawing just as skillfully with his right. I could already tell by how it was coming together that he possessed some talent.

"You're quite good at that," I said as I walked past, my objective not to intrude.

"Much obliged," he replied. "I've swot at it a bit." He spoke a true South Wales lilt with its longer diphthongs and schwa, more emphasis on certain consonants and sibilants than Langston's Cockney, but not as harshly clipped. His cadence had a rounder rhythm.

As the day progressed heat would rise through the lower decks, I knew; I'd already set out replacing the space heaters with rotary fans while we talked. I would also need to order the boy's lunch, and couldn't help but wonder—was there nothing more we could offer him but blue meat? He certainly appeared anemic to me, and Nonna always swore by braised liver and lentil ragu. Perhaps it was none of my business, but I decided to ask, anyway.

The conversation following was one I filed away in my personal logs for a long time—partly because, God willing and the creek don't rise, I hoped the boy would surely find a way to outlive me. I could never bring myself to accept what he told me was true, no matter how forthright he seemed.

He would stick to the blue-rare cuts his father insisted on, he said, for this was the only form of sustenance keeping his illness at bay—and until more recently, his sister's. In the evening strolls which followed, his tale grew taller, and he confided in me rather candidly. Both children had suffered from a congenital disorder, he explained, crossing bloodlines against God's will.

I doubted God had much to do with it, but I held my tongue.

"A mutation, perhaps?" I suggested.

He considered this for a moment, eyes scanning the darkened horizon in front of us, hands dangling over the taffrail.

"Our blood is bad," he answered. "She and I, we are cursed."

At the tail end of the First World War, his mother, Baroness Claudella Scurlock, a descendant from a long line of druids out of Milford Haven, caught the eye of Marquess Jules Fallon. Fallon had roots in Ireland—and an ancestry of vampires. Extensively warned about potential consequences to their offspring by their forebears, Jules and Claudella, already quite in love, produced two children, both weakened hybrids some call dhampyres. The children were vampires—*and yet they were not.*

As I checked in on the boy over the next sixteen hours, he told me bits and pieces while he continued to sketch.

Fallon, he said, hunted for their food twice weekly in the mountains of Brecon Beacons, about fifty kilometers north of Cardiff. For a busy officer in the Queen's army, one round trip was easily a half day's journey by train or automobile, I knew. Which made me wonder how he found the time to travel there so often, and just how he *did* travel.

"He flew off," Claudius simply said. His face was covered in charcoal smudges by then; he'd whipped out another nib and set out blending in the backdrop of the portrait. At the time, I took it to mean his father had somehow deadheaded rides with the Royal Air Force.

Fallon then returned, he told me—not with boar, elk, deer, or other wild game—but flasks of blood drawn off wild Welsh ponies. As war in Europe loomed, he sent his bailiffs to capture some, and stocked his farm with them. He never killed them or drained them completely, the

Falling Stars

boy explained, nor did he require the children learn how to forage for themselves.

"Hold on," I interrupted. "How did you say he does this?"

"He mesmerizes them first, then nips them—usually on the hocks, and draws off some with a hose." Claudius also mentioned he didn't know where, what, or how his father ate.

I listened, flabbergasted. Fallon? A vampire? Generally lore regarding the undead had quietened after the First World War, resurging mostly for its entertainment value with the 1922 silent film *Nosferatu* and Bela Lugosi's memorable performance in the 1931 cinematic adaptation of Bram Stoker's *Dracula*. I had less difficulty believing Claudella was a druid, for Nonna had often spoken about coastal witches from Llanelli and Swansea.

Still, reports of revenants had incited panic from the shores of East Prussia to New England for nearly two centuries. The first case circulated in British news concerned Petar Blagojević, a Serbian peasant reported to have died and returned, asking his son for food. The son refused him and was found dead the following day. An outbreak of consumption in the village immediately followed.

Some stories—those involving government examinations and case reports—came better documented than others. Langston's grandfather, a vascular surgeon renowned for his innovation in arteriotomy and bloodletting, got commissioned from the civilian sector for some of those said investigations.

"Most ills tidy up on a dropper of arsenic and a pair off the turf," Langston had quoted his predecessor. *A pair*, that's right, turned out to be a couple of turf-harvested medicinal leeches. In an era when opening a vein or administering poison were the two best contenders against combat injuries, bacterium, and widespread disease, it is no wonder the bourgeois often blamed revenants for the calamities that engulfed them.

Even up to the turn of the century specter visitation was also popular in the States, reported particularly in parts of Rhode Island and Connecticut. Mum recalled neighbors in Westerly who, when their last living child came down with cholera, exhumed their dead and removed the hearts.

Vampire hysteria took a back burner during the Great Depression and (along with everything else) in the presence of Hitler's advance across Europe. The boy's insistence that he and his sister drank blood as part of their diet was troubling; I couldn't help but worry for him as he migrated to a new and strange country. What could possibly motivate him to maintain such claims? I'd never once suspected Fallon was anything more—or less—than human. And I could clearly see the young viscount was of the genius type. As it follows, I would come to accept Claudius was anything *but* human.

Gunner's arm healed completely over the following weeks, and while he continued blaming forearm weakness for his grip-up losses, any symptoms were relatively short-lived—a night or two of bed sweats without any long-term malady. If the boy had indeed been half vampire, I always suspected we'd have seen something more amiss with Gunner.

I was hard-pressed to protect the boy from the start, I knew. The task of guarding Claudius and his deceased sister in the New World had enough risks without him running his mouth. In the conversations which followed, I swore to keep what he'd unloaded on me in confidence, and strongly suggested he do the same.

On our last evening at sea I decided to introduce Claudius to Mum and Nonna, for they needed a distraction. Fear was palpable on board after receiving an urgent dispatch from the Admiralty to take every precaution. Britain had delivered its ultimatum to Germany the previous day, and within hours, any available deck hands were painting over portholes and rigging blackout curtains on doorways. Extra lookouts were posted, eyes peeled to sight periscopes or torpedo wake.

Both women were stir-crazy by then, and when they got wind of the viscount's upcoming visit, they forgot about any maritime danger or their ailments, and discarded wide-legged beach pajamas for Sunday best. For two church bells who'd rarely bumped gums outside their stateroom over the entire trip, they pretty much had the scoop on the war *and* the nobles, testament to *walls have ears*. Nonna had ordered a two-quart flan caramelized with eighty proof rum in keeping with her token afternoon tea spread for all her bridge opponents. The flan was a hit, I later found out. Claudius not only outplayed Mum and Nonna in three round games of Gin Rummy and Mau-Mau; he happily whiled away the evening in their stateroom.

I kept a steward posted with the body for the evening and very much recall standing in for a half hour myself. While I tended switching

Falling Stars

out fans for heaters and anything else I thought might make the viscount's space more habitable, I chewed over the bitter irony of Claudius passing hours alone in the hull with his entombed sibling. The amped-up schedule of everything going on all around him must've seemed nothing less than awful.

Part of my evening rounds included patrolling First Class Dining on C Deck, without a doubt the grandest room on the ship, and a tour de force in its own right—large enough to accommodate over eight hundred in one sitting. The table reserved for the viscount and his sister was located under the room's figurehead piece, a mural in oil staging the ship's summer-and-winter charted courses across the Atlantic. The map represented the journey between continents split into composite cityscapes from England and America, with a large Art Deco style clock top center. I stopped at the royals' table and collected their seating cards.

Mr. Bob Hope, it turns out, was manning the capacitor for an improviso performance upon Captain's request in an effort to calm frayed nerves. This was working. He'd just lapsed into a musical number and publicity plug for his starring role in the film *The Big Broadcast of 1938,* which had kicked up a wave of inebriated, off-key scat singing around the room.

. . . nothing in my purse, and chuckles when the preacher said, "for better or for worse" . . .

First Class Dining is one of the largest stations we cover, a room which stretches the full width of the deck and seventy-six meters longitudinally.

Walking the beat was generally a cinch, an analysis in latest intercontinental fashion while keeping an eye out for anything gone awry, whether persons or the decorum. I knew the room by heart. Floor-to-ceiling silver columns, which tiered off the deck above, called for several pints of polishing compound from engineering each week. Vestibules veneered in three shades of wood from Brazilian perobas equally hankered their share of oil. Portholes outfitted with peach colored ripple glass required weekly checks for cracks.

. . . and bills we never paid! How lovely it was, we who could laugh over big things were parted by only a slight thing . . .

The ceiling, a two-tone cream and peach with soffits veneered in

Mazur birch, had to be inspected for discoloration daily. A crystal inlaid dome six meters in diameter extended through two decks, the room's central canopy height, nine meters. Dining chairs carved from sycamore and upholstered carmine red were routinely rotated out of service and scrubbed. The floor, diagonally laid Korkoid, had integrated fabric runners to allocate traffic patterns. Checks for scuffs and frays—

. . . thanks for the memory of faults that you forgave, of rainbows on a wave, and stockings in the basin when a fellow needs a shave . . .

I turned away from the esprit—the tapestry paintings, bronzed doors, glass panels, illuminated friezes, metal foils, and pommeli—to go fetch Claudius. I'd seen it all once again, and yet I hadn't seen—not against the eyeful I'd just gotten in the hull when curiosity overcame me.

What I'd witnessed through the Fisk's plated window was yet another reminder that all was not as it seemed. I'm not sure what I'd expected to see, but I had ample mental recollection of posthumous blackening and streaking on the child's face. What I observed on my shift startled me: fair, white skin as flawless in death as in life, if not more beautiful. *Was that possible?* I'd need to run it by Langston.

Mr. Hope ended his stand-up with a parody for the times, a noisy one. His audience roared with laughter.

. . . thanks for the memory . . . some folks slept on the floor, some in the corridor, but mine was more exclusive. My room had Gents *above the door . . .*

When I entered the starboard passageway leading to Stateroom B450, I could hear Nonna's low-slung laughing, the way she usually sounds after she and Mum pour on too much giggle juice.

Mum met me at the door talking in whispers. She'd decided to sit out the last match and serve herself something stronger, she said, to speculate how long Nonna could keep an active hand of deadwood. While Nonna had retained her petite size and preferred drop-waisted or bias-cut gowns, Mum fought an ever-widening girth and stewed over belted day dresses in pale prints. She'd already discarded the matching belt tonight, I noticed.

Claudius had his sleeves rolled up, elbows on the table, cards tucked aside in one hand, his hair curly wild. Nonna, if truth be told, was under his spell—my Nonna, who kept her upper back stiff against the chair no matter what, a bluff which always brought to mind Whistlers Mother. The stakes were up and the play in the making, fierce.

"Such a darling little lamb," Mum said. "A bit stroppy at first, but nothing black pudding and flan couldn't fix."

I then noticed the remainders of blood sausage, crackers, and pastries on a brass serving cart they'd pulled up to the table. Mum touched her nose. "After he gobbled down that awful uncooked thing they brought up from the kitchen."

"Doctor's orders," I replied, and closed the door behind us.

Mum didn't move. "Ah, the lurgy. Well—if you're asking, I'd say he's a titchy thing all right, and I suppose he does need all the piss and vinegar he can get. We could use a few more days to fatten him up." She glanced toward the table. "I offered him a fizzy drink and all, thinking that's what the bairns like. But he just wanted regular tea."

"That figures," I muttered, and took Mum by the arm to steady her. Claudius evidently *had* discovered Nonna's flan; over half of it was gone.

"He said it was scrummy and had three helpings," Mum muttered. "Or was it four?"

"Four," replied Nonna. "I hope you haven't come to fetch him yet, dear boy. We're hot up in here." She cut her eyes at Claudius with a disdain she usually reserved for the old cronies she'd played a half century against. "Don't you give me anymore of your cheek, now, lovey."

A little too familiar, on second thought.

"Viscount," I greeted him.

"Hullo." Claudius grinned at me. It occurred then that I hadn't seen him smile—and for a child, his was an alluring one—with symmetrically excellent and perfectly formed pearl-white teeth, cuspids fully unleashed. It charmed us all, I think, with an innocent, evasive energy that disappeared into endless eyes. He was clearly tipsy, but happy—and at the time, I couldn't fault him for that. He pushed a stack of chips across the table and bought another card.

Nonna, for the life of her, had tried to get her usual advantage with the flan, but it was pretty open and shut that Claudius was about to best her again.

"We started up noughts and crosses, but he wanted to play cards like the big boy he is." Mum found her tulip glass of Cognac and plopped down in a chair beside him to kibitz. "Maybe you should go out whilst you still have something decent," she told Nonna.

"She doesn't," Claudius interjected.

I walked over behind Nonna. He was right; she didn't. She glared at him over her cards. "Maybe I do, maybe I don't." Discarded a four of clubs. "We'll suss this one out," she announced to Mum.

Mum ruffled the boy's hair and smiled at me. "He's a dishy, isn't he? Will make all the girls randy some years from now." She took his face in her hands and pinched his cheeks. He seemed to enjoy the attention, but I had to curtail a strong urge to step in, especially after observing what he'd done to Gunner's forearm.

After three more futile plays, Nonna let out an exasperated sigh and folded. For a seasoned card player, Claudius had indeed taken her by surprise, and totally under his charms. "Cheeky little monkey," she told me afterward. "He gave me those eyes and made me all fiddly, I tell you."

Both women wanted him to stay the night in their stateroom, and we had to turn down more flan several times. Until her death years later, Nonna would reminisce, "Poor lad, not a child-minder one amongst us. What was he to do?"

When Claudius stood up, he swayed just enough to put me on high alert, two quick strides to his side of the table.

"Steady as she goes, Carleton." Nonna sipped her brandy.

"Are you all right, Viscount?" I asked, ignoring her.

"He's just chuffed about his winnings," Mum added.

He's plastered, I thought, about the time Claudius righted himself and walked over to the coat rack to fetch his jacket.

"See," Nonna blurted. "The lad's not cucumbered, just a bit squiffy."

"Here, love," Mum said. "Give me a buss."

Claudius dutifully kissed her on both cheeks, a single peck for Nonna.

"Ta, love," Mum called after us.

"Toodle-pip and cheerio, twee one. We'll see how jammy you are when I raise you next time," Nonna added.

Falling Stars

The library aboard was a good one, and I found a Latin dictionary in a jiffy. I'd recorded the words from memory on the back of a kitchen order check. After I smoothed out the creases and began ciphering words to phrases, I was in for another surprise. The boy had repeated several times over his sister's body in Isolation Ward:

In manus tuas, Domine . . .

In vita sive mors . . .

Which translated, "Into Thy hands, oh Lord, in life or death." At that juncture, he seemed altogether more accepting of what fate had in store for him.

But as we transferred her body to F Deck, his prayer had changed.

Reditum eius anima . . . *reditum eius anima* ad me . . .

Return her spirit . . . return her spirit *to me.*

To be continued . . .

Chapter Five

The scenery changed at *Philly's Argosy* after we began running Cochran's material, which especially irked me because I knew the rightful heart and soul of the story was bound up in Gaye's devotion to Claudius Fallon and the journal we'd optioned. As the assigned ghostwriter for the series, I was endeared to Fallon already, drawn to underscore the cruelty of his extenuating childhood circumstances. *Gaye* had done that, not me—and certainly not Miles Cochran. Had Fallon been real, I would've enjoyed picking his brain for days. McWatters and I had, however, anticipated a racket—for Claudius Fallon was currently trending as one of the top one hundred urban legends on UL.

Sacks of snail mail started arriving daily, not just the typical piece or two. Online writing submissions tripled, and co-contributing aspirants were phoning every five minutes, it seemed. I was stunned when McWatters decided to give Cochran access to our interoffice fan email; I fiercely argued against it. Our followers were savvy, and we couldn't afford an autographed misstep while we crawled our way past a pandemic.

We hosted a video conference to walk Cochran through actions like signing in and answering some examples. The inbox maxed out anyway after a couple of days, forcing us to purchase more storage space—with me still questioning the validity of adding Cochran in the first place. Percy and I were friends above all the rest, though. When he noticed my carotid drumming "Yankee Doodle," he put an end to his secrecy and 'fessed up.

"He's my cousin."

"What's that?" My Eagles tumbler almost went flying; I caught it.

"Cockroach?"

"Yup."

"You're—related?"

"Sixth removed."

Hold the phone. From the water tower, I aimed my tumbler at him. "He's Gaye's—Clara's—"

"Grandson."

"*You're* related to Gaye?"

"As it happens."

Holy hell. That's why. The long view of McWatters's exceptional tolerance for Cochran's annoying antics in grad school and the rest was now mine. Cochran had chosen me to push the pencil, but surely McWatters—his own blood kin—had a far more implicit rapport with Gaye's story?

"Why me?" I asked McWatters.

"You're best."

"Not true," I countered.

"I'm too close."

Maybe, maybe not. I thought it warranted further discussion, but McWatters didn't—and I'd learned a long time ago when and where *not* to bump heads. We could save that one for another day. So I kept doing what I did and, when all of those emails remained unopened after another week, McWatters divided the list between the two of us and emphatically suggested we handle them. The snail mail he did insist we forward to Cochran. And for the next month McWatters phoned his distant cousin daily, supervising as much as he could over video chat. For an hour or more each day, McWatters and I would answer Cochran's emails, teaming up on some of the incoming questions.

"Name of stowaway?"

I checked my notes. While Gaye's journal mentioned a female stowaway in passing, the ship's manifest had no record of one on Voyage 72 West.

"None on seventy-two," I answered.

"Fictitious, then." *Clickety-clack.*

"Unaccounted for," I corrected.

"That's better," he said. *Silence of backspacing.*

RMS Queen Mary *did* smuggle an eighteen-year-old Evelyn Cooper on the voyage prior, I added.

"Relocation?"

"Huh?" I was busy staring down the next email. *Oh, right. First installment.* Gaye mentioned that Langston had moved a stowaway when he brought Agnetha and Claudius down to Female Isolation Ward. My notes indicated Langston had switched her to Male Isolation next door, I told him.

"With the fellas?"

I knew what McWatters was implying; gender segregation had its own stuffy guidelines in the day; somebody would call us on it. "Not *in* the ward . . ." I scanned my chicken scratch. "Nurses' Office."

Our blueprint of B Deck as built showed the nurse attendants' office adjacent to Male Isolation did have a hatchway separate from the ward itself. *Details, details.*

Clickety-clack-clickety.

McWatters could be so picky at times. *We were answering fan mail, for God's sake, like anyone would notice,* I inwardly fumed. At my left, Gram shook her head at me for getting all pissy. I took a breath. Percy compelled our excellence in everything, however misplaced or ultimately unnecessary—and normally that was okay by me. I just hoped Cochran didn't write something stupid that would come back and bite us in the ass.

The next question tiered off a similar idea; *they always had a way of arriving in pairs, didn't they?* This fan was asking if any record of Claudius or Agnetha Fallon existed on the ship's passenger manifest.

None, I typed.

How reliable were the logs, they also wanted to know?

They had their discrepancies, I'd noticed. I was still formulating what an intelligent answer to that question might look like when McWatters asked, "Why no morgue?"

And did someone really die on Voyage 72 West?

"A Mr.—" I scanned my notes, "F. Brandt," I read.

Gaye was correct about Brandt dying from heart failure on September 1, 1939. In terms of explaining to our painfully health-conscious culture how bodies could've been stored in the same compartments with food—it's hard to say, really.

Centers of Disease Control wasn't established yet. The FDA's first food standards issued in 1939 were about storing tomatoes, not dead bodies. And the Public Health Service Act, which covered a broader spectrum of health concerns including regulation of biological products

Falling Stars

and control of communicable diseases, wasn't law until 1944. Many years later, FDA Title 21, Sec. 864.9700 established procedures for refrigerating and freezing blood separately from food stored for consumption. Infection control and storage integrity practices simply weren't a part of the landscape, and D Deck's Ice Room was a centrally located, refrigerated option. After reviewing enough documents to break yet more ocular blood vessels, I was comfortable enough in saying that for the majority of the ship's service, cold storage was rarely needed for corpses, if at all. Those bodies were quickly pronounced, and they went elsewhere.

Generally naval surgeons were quick to authorize cause of demise and death, documenting these events in lingo that bounced from white coat expertise to layman's tinker. While researching "Bad Blood," I tried very hard to identify any death on record that could've possibly fit Agnetha's, hoping to raise the stakes in Gaye's ball of twine. I didn't find one, though. At the time this was so disappointing, I drafted several snarky one-liners from the ship's death archives for my editorial boneyard:

Skull fracture, laceration of brain. *Coroner overkill, anyone?*
Found dead. *Well, that tells us just about everything.*
Found dead in bunk. *That tells us a little bit more.*
Coronary thrombosis. *Now we're getting somewhere.*
Lost overboard. *Did they actually turn the ship around and look?*
Fatal fall from ship. *In a hurry to hit the docks, were you?*
Hypoglycemia. *Really? You can die from this?*
Collapsed on stairway. *Should've used the lift.*
Hepatic failure with coma. *You party animal, you.*
Crushed in a watertight door. *Er—where* were *you off to, anyway?*
Drinking tetrachloride by mistake. *Nope, not the vodka.*
Natural Causes. *My personal favorite.*

Total deaths logged during RMS Queen Mary's civilian service, such is true, were approximate and probably not accurate. Causes of death went unrecorded too. If our readers wanted to believe that Agnetha and Claudius were real, so be it. I chose instead to conclude that Gaye knew how to spin fool's gold into fact.

Through this process, Gram had been more present than ever. No doubt McWatters noticed I was testy but probably assumed it was stress as usual. Things were amping up, after all. I caught him glancing my way more often, trying to figure me out.

We were closing up shop for the day when McWatters got the call —actually a call waiting—for he was mid-sentence with his distant cousin in an escalating dispute over the correct usage of *that* and *which*. McWatters had covered the rules using three different examples of how the word *which* introduces nonrestrictive clauses. Which meant, he'd carefully explained, that the clause following *which* was unnecessary in contributing to the total comprehension of the sentence.

Which Cockroach evidently didn't comprehend.

Green eggs and ham, which are two of my favorites, always give me gas.

McWatters, stuck on *Play*, went over the example again.

"You *get it?*" he stressed.

Green eggs and ham always give me gas whether they're my favorite or not, right? he reiterated. It goes without saying.

"Which implies *whether?"* That question, directed toward me. Over time I'd also learned how to anticipate when any three-word *communicato* was mine, or for his Bluetooth earbuds.

"Right-o," I chimed in.

"See there?" *Clickety-clack.* In addition to fielding the incoming logjam on his Bluetooth, McWatters—*a human circuit board, as God is my witness*—was finishing up the last of his email pile. Although I couldn't hear Cockroach, I sensed by recesses and overtalk that McWatters was ready to flatten him.

"You want me to—?" I mouthed at McWatters. (Although the very last thing I wanted to do was continue that conversation.) He checked the ceiling with his eyes and shook his head.

"Nope, that's restrictive. Hold on. Philly's Argosy." McWatters's eyebrows shot up. "Speaking. Yup." A pregnant pause. "Really? One moment." He tapped his Bluetooth. "It's Fan Expo," he said to me, eyes gleeful.

I pointed at my cell. "Call Roach back?"

"Nope, I got it." He tapped his Bluetooth. "Later, dude." His jaw tightened. "The fan British?" Nanosecond. "Then don't." He cut his eyes my way. "No. *Hang up now.*" Tapped his Bluetooth. "Okay—let's see . . ."

Turns out Cockroach had saved the tail end of that cheerful scuffle to introduce his own personal dilemma concerning the British use of *which,* since Brits break the rules and use *which* restrictively and without commas. He felt it more appropriate to use that style of *which* when answering questions about content in the first two installments, he said.

Which nearly launched McWatters into orbit.

But—this wasn't one of the standard phone notifications about our booth rental at Wizard World, now Fan Expo. We were familiar with those, having managed to hawk our wares at the convention a handful of times before the pandemic shut everything down, then back at it again. Nope, *that* was us calling them; *this* was something more. I tuned out while Percy took the call, though—only because Gram had just dumped a cold shot down the back of my sweater. I glared at her, and she grinned—at the sack of snail mail. She was all about getting me home earlier these days, so I played along. I began sorting the mail (which Percy would hand deliver to Cochran later that evening) with Gram intently looking on, over my shoulder.

I'd come to enjoy stacking letters with Gram at the end of each day —a lesson in humanity, individuality, and personality. As envelopes go, they arrive in every shape, style, and size. A4's and 5's were popular, but so were #10's and C4's. We got bankers flaps sealed from end to end with custom stickers, die-hard collectibles like Power Rangers and Darth Maul. Euro flaps with the simple elegance of one monogrammed foil letter at the point. Art envelopes sporting Ginny Weasley Funko Pop and TWD.

Here and there we found some unusual ones manufactured from glassine or string & washer plastic, bubble or Rigi Bag mailers, Tyvek— even vintage airmail. I got familiar with custom designs from Fiverr and others recycled from invitations or classic wedding stationery. No end to the characters our fans admired, either, from Harry Potter, Marvel Legends, Mortal Kombat, and Mandalorian to throwbacks like Jimmy Neutron, Pee-Wee Herman, and Power Puff Girls.

Many of these letters were handwritten, penmanship from full-on Gothic to skinny Serif in every conceivable color to the nimble cursives in D'Nealian or even Palmer styles. More often they trotted out fonts modified by software engines to be generated by laser printers. A couple looked hot off a Brother Daisy Wheel while a lonely-only I found yesterday bore those random spacing carriage skips, uppercase alignment problems, and faded font tails characteristic of a manual typewriter like a Royal. Today's mail was equally entertaining. I was just about finished when I noticed the foil Euro flap in grey—and Gram placed her hand over mine. Deftly stamped at the flap's point was an authentic red wax seal, the letter F.

I turned over the envelope and stifled a gasp. The longhand (I examined it carefully) was not manufactured, and impeccably crafted. Spencerian script, the de facto writing style from 1850-1925, with flourishing like you'd see in Ed Bailey's letter concerning the looming skirmish at Gonzales in 1835—*come and take it*, that goldarn cannon that started the Texas Revolution in the first place—or in John Hancock's signature on steroids at the bottom of the Declaration of Independence. The return address simply read:

Tommy Lucas
22 Fairmount
Eureka Springs, AR 72632

Gram nudged me. Something in her eyes said *hang onto it*. Eureka Springs happened to be on my bucket list of places to see, a charming town on the National Register of Historic Places, perched in the Ozark Mountains. I pocketed the letter inside my briefcase and forgot about it.

Percy and I both knew the score by then, that the first two in the series were good—and the call from Fan Expo capped off the day. Cockroach had just received an invitation to chair a panel at the upcoming St. Louis convention in January.

Holy Shinola.

We had less than two months to prepare Cochran, who was way out of his depth. Unfortunately, with his newfangled publicity and meteoric rise to fame, Cochran was now convinced he was one tough hombre. *That* or *which*.

Wiz World.

Damn.

☆

Zero dark thirty came as early as June had anticipated, well before she turned their U-Haul west onto Missouri Route 86, the last hour of the final stretch toward Eureka Springs. For all the bluster and a parade of enough red candy to last for months, Tommy was fast asleep with none of it in his belly. And so it came and went with June and her son, a roleplay around keeping him alive, a fine-tuned system that often pushed the boundaries of rationality that only those two agreed upon. She'd take the stash to the clinic or donate it to a halfway house like she always did. She glanced over at Tommy and counted, *memorized* his respiration rate as she watched his chest go up and down in deepening shadows cast off by the setting sun. Such it was with Tommy these days; when fatigue overcame him, it hit hard—no matter how he fought it. He was deep in sleep, stretched along the full length of the U-Haul's bench seat under his Sherpa, his head resting near, but not touching, her thigh. At times like these, June wished she could prolong or avoid waking him altogether, but they had to stay on schedule with his evening dose of oral folate and prednisone.

June had managed once again to prevail upon Tommy to eat the pizza and an apple versus all the rest. After hearing him read the second installment of "Bad Blood," she also understood why Tommy had started asking last week for his hamburger cooked Pittsburgh blue-rare, which she overrode to medium, followed by a long discussion about salmonella, *E. coli*, shigella, and staphylococcus. At the time he seemed to understand, so his cross-reactivity came in asking for all things red with glucose today as anticipated. He hadn't countered her with his newfound indoctrination about blue-rare meat from *Philly's Argosy* last week, and June understood why—Tommy always reread his sources several times before approaching her with any new concept. He was, in the end, unremittingly introspective. All things considered, she was grateful for this feature of his personality whenever she was compelled to point out reality versus hogwash. If she leveled with Tommy on difficult topics, he usually listened.

While she mulled over what Tommy had just read to her, June couldn't help but wonder how Claudius Fallon would ever survive the odds stacked against him. Eureka homegrown, June came from old town blood—and she knew as well as anyone else around here that Norman Baker was one of the biggest curative shysters of all time, that his cancer hospital was bric-a-brac on the bones of terminally ill patients who died under his care. She couldn't fault Claudius's parents for their desperation, no—but sending a sick child abroad for an elixir from Arkansas' medicinal mountains was going on a lark, even then. In several ways, Claudius *did* remind her of Tommy. But the question remained: how much *Fallon* would Tommy ultimately need to emulate to maintain hope? Endorsing his staple diet was one thing...

As the headlights of their U-Haul illuminated the drive climbing up to her parents' hillside Queen Anne, what troubled June was an ever-growing niggle—her realization just how difficult Tommy's day-to-day eccentricities for her own mother might become. Some of these concessions, June knew, Lilly would never accept. Funny, after all the careful planning and choosing, plus the rigorous efforts in coming home, she hadn't fully considered how it might miscarry until now. Would they fit in? Had she made a dreadful mistake by bringing them here?

The home June grew up in was all that a Queen Anne architectural wonder tucked in Eureka's hillside vegetation could offer—a grand display of coral and ecru woodwork studded with gingerbread trim, fish scale shingles, and dentils. It had a commanding view of the town below, perched high on a bluff above Grand Avenue. A large polygonal tower grew out of the north side, three turrets facing each of the other cardinal directions. An asymmetrical façade and porch stoop opened to a wraparound from front to back, marked by classical columns and fine spindle work along the banisters, with cylindrical, weight-bearing balustrades at the corners.

June had spent a good chunk of her life on that porch. She wove dolls from dried sapphire salvia stems and tended her firefly collection there when she was four, studied into the witching hours wired on caffeine shots for high school finals there—and later, double shots for medical boards. She'd returned home the summer following her fiancé's death and smoked the more potent *salvia divinorum*, the diviner's sage that grew along the hillside, a twenty-five-year-old's funk on that porch —which she eventually put in her rearview mirror. She'd rocked her newly adopted baby on the same after bringing him home from Springdale the following year, and Tommy had seen his first snow at Christmas there when he was one.

The Lucas Queen Anne was elaborate, eclectic, flamboyant— replete with lead-glass windows, dormers, and a tiled terracotta roof. The old home had cantilevered, pitched rooflines, a dominant front-facing gable, and a second-story balcony with a pedimented gable. Lilly

Lucas was a master gardener, so the front yard tumbled into an ostentatious prairie garden enclosed behind Georgian wrought iron railing.

Walt and Lilly had systematically taken all the right steps in their lives—none of the howlers June seemed to run headlong into. Lilly's father was a wealthy oil baron, and Lilly, the sole inheritor. Walt had made a career as a chemical engineer for AstraZeneca that afforded him early retirement with a hefty pension, to spend more time fly fishing—and with Lilly.

Her parents kept the old home impeccably restored to its original charm and character. The rooms were spacious, if not a bit drafty. Because of that issue, this Queen Anne had two fireplaces with monumental hearths and chimneys. The floors were wide plank hardwood, each room finished out with elaborately carved crown moldings. The old house also boasted three showcase bay windows, one perched above the ground in front, a true oriel.

The rich corals and brass trimmings were ever as dazzling as they'd always been, June noticed. She cut the U-Haul's headlights and took a moment to force down a hollow feeling in her chest before waking Tommy. It *looked* like home, and yet she could not bring herself to say it. She announced to the sleepy pair of eyes looking up at her, "We're here."

It might be argued that in this outback of the Ozarks, Callan Masters also came from old blood—blood he would never reproduce—so that he, now thirty-six, remained forever its most eligible bachelor. Sole owner and proprietor of Fast Horses, a swank art gallery just off the fray on Cushing Street past Mountain, Callan didn't make a habit of reviewing days gone by while he worked—and work he did. His gallery was filled with evidence of toil over many years. Like much of historic Main Street's real estate, his studio was an eight hundred square foot cracker box, its main showroom a single L, the rest affording him a small office, storage, and a private half bath. Since his wasn't a large showcase space, it had a podium checkout and a rack of lithograph prints tucked inside an alcove by the front door that served him well—for customers who graced the space always found themselves somehow compelled to buy at least *one*.

The base wall color was traditional white, the floors, acid-washed concrete stained to a marbleized walnut hue. The gallery aptly functioned as a blank canvas, an open concept—nothing fancy like floating walls or stand-alone partitions bisecting the area to steer traffic flow. Fast Horses was always and simply wide open front to back, its only two pieces of furniture a couple of vintage skinny benches carved from elm to accommodate customers who needed to take a load off.

Oil paintings of famed racehorses lined the walls from top to bottom, each one illuminated under sleek LED track lighting in brushed nickel finish. The lighting remained the only feature of the gallery that Callan obsessed over, since he had inherited achromatopsia. Because of his light sensitivity he didn't paint in studio, and on any given day customers could find him on a step ladder adjusting the light heads just so or dimming certain tracks altogether.

Because he traveled frequently to study his subjects, Callan had arranged this lock-and-leave gallery for very little overhead and maintenance. Most of his serious investors met by appointment. The mortgage was paid, he didn't have any employees, and he didn't sublet. He'd finally installed a Ring security system only because city code required one, and he had a good HVAC unit that he topped off twice a year. Road noise and tourist traffic along Main outweighed any need for ambient music, but he did pull out an Ultimate Ears portable Bluetooth speaker from storage during the Christmas creep, these days walking back Eureka merchants' grand *Deck the Halls* and holiday sales well before Halloween. Next week he'd hang his four oversized Christmas ornaments under the awning outside. He cranked up the Yuletide Muzak before turning to make one last pass over the floor with a push broom.

He stopped; he needed to rotate in a couple of more festive pieces while he was at it—now that Thanksgiving was nearly upon him. Christmas *had* crept. *Again already,* he topped off the thought.

Fast Horses was always and inevitably about what hung on the walls, or the lithograph prints derived thereof. Only four portraits out of the fifty-some-odd others remained on permanent display. The centerpiece that drew eyes—and bodies—into the store hung prominently on the longest wall, east side of the gallery.

"Man o' War".

Callan had missed the superstar's racing years, something he'd always regretted. Widely regarded as one of the greatest racehorses of all time, he won all races but one during his career, equivalent to an excess of three million dollars in today's purses. A racehorse that typically won in front-running fashion with powerful starts, his stride measured 28 feet, still holding the all-time record.

When Callan finally met Man o' War in 1946, the famed thoroughbred was retired at Faraway Farm and near the end of his life. Though his swayback had grown more prominent with age, he was still huge, standing 16.2 ½ hands high, with flawless legs and solid bone. Even then as his handler, Will Harbut, had shown him, the stud held his head notably high, giving his audience a perfect profile of his Roman nose with its white star and stripe formation. Masters' oil captured the champion's signature stance as he stood quietly for them on that day. He'd also successfully managed to blend in the gold flecking throughout the stud's shimmering chestnut coat, which made this piece one of his most frequently commissioned copies.

Callan Masters had done well enough for himself, and he was no starving artist—but it hadn't always been that way.

The other pieces he never rotated out were "Adios Butler", "Secretariat", and "Zippy Chippy". Callan agreed to paint Adios Butler, a harness racing champion, as a personal challenge—and traveled to watch him win the Triple Crown for Harness Racing for Pacers at Yonkers Raceway in 1959. The job required studying stacks of photographs and publicity shots in an effort to accurately represent the horse's stride, tack, sully, and of course his driver, Clint Hodgins. An equally memorable commissioned trip was Secretariat's win at Belmont Stakes in 1973, another Triple Crown.

"Zippy Chippy", on the other hand, proved to be *the* icebreaker at the gallery. Customers who enjoyed trading stories about him always bought his lithograph prints. A New York bred gelding, his greatest accomplishment in the sport of kings was *not* winning. Zippy championed all the other Also Rans in the industry with a record number of 100 losses, a losing streak that nonetheless earned him a following. Aficionados like Callan attended several races in the '90s where he was entered to run, just out of curiosity.

Felix Monserrate, Zippy's owner and trainer, clearly had an emotional attachment to the horse, alleged to having traded a pickup for him. Monserrate colored outside the lines in the equestrian playbook—entering Zippy in high-stakes events and refusing to race him in claiming races. Zippy was also the consummate troublemaker on the track. He'd sometimes stop in the middle of a race or refuse to leave the gate, and he had a bad habit of biting. Ultimately, he was banned from every track in North America but Northampton Fair in Massachusetts. He earned $30,834.00 during his career and a track record of 0-8-12.

After rotating in oils of two other champions cantering across snowscapes, Callan checked his watch and stored away the push broom for another night. He'd locked the store's entrance with his cell phone a couple of hours ago but had forgotten to flip the shop sign. Pre-holiday sales and an influx of art collectors this time of year often kept him in the gallery after hours; the time simply got away. Such was *not* the case tonight.

He turned a small wooden sign that hung in the front window to show the town that Fast Horses was officially closed. Outside, shoppers had vacated the streets for a familiar dinner rush that included the locals' attempts to outrun tourists to Eureka's fine-dining establishments. Callan would soon head to one himself after tending a couple more items on the list. Once he'd determined no stragglers remained outside the store, then and then alone could he retrieve one of the oral syringes he kept in back and dose himself. Only he and his supplier knew about the blue juice that kept him, well—*who he was*.

Locked inside the supply closet was a medical grade refrigerator, a compact unit just large enough to store a year's worth. He could hear the faint hum of the unit from the doorway of his office, loud enough to know it was functional without drawing unwanted attention. A biometric reader mounted on the closet's doorframe recognized his face, his eyes. Callan rarely turned on any lights for this procedure. He walked across the pitch-black room to the supply closet, tilted the touchscreen upward, and looked into the capture camera.

A lever handle on the left side of the closet door buzzed open, and inside, a fridge spanned the second shelf. When he opened its door, luminous blue light flooded the hallway behind him. Callan was told the compound would glow until uncapped if it had maintained shelf life and was mixed properly—to destroy doses that didn't. Behind the refrigerator's second, glass-panel door, a white Monster rack

Falling Stars

manufactured from autoclavable polypropylene held hundreds of refillable glass syringes—216 at capacity, and enough to last an entire year while rotating off two days a week. He had thirty 1 mL Luer syringes remaining, a few rows to go before he met again with the cook behind its continuance.

At one time Callan thought the blue juice might contain a radioactive isotope used as a tracer, like gallium citrate. He wasn't sure what was being traced and he hoped they didn't find it. Later on, he learned that the liquid *did* contain an isotope derived from Actinium (not a tracer) that acted instead as an assisting agent in radiation therapy by emitting alpha particles that killed cancer cells. When paired with chelation, this isotope Ac proved effective in treating leukemia, lymphoma, breast, ovarian, neuroblastoma, and prostate cancers. He'd never had chelation or radiation therapy, and he didn't ask questions.

And so he went on living.

He closed the refrigerator door, leaned against the door jamb, and tipped the syringe using both hands to remix the liquid, a precise volumetric inversion ten times like he always did. Uncapped the tip, and the room went dark again.

After washing out the Luer syringe and returning it to the storage closet to dry, Callan set out to find some dinner, his first and only meal of the day. His metabolism had fallen rather naturally into this arrangement some time back, and he'd never felt a need to change what integrated so well with his lifestyle. Days were busy, nights were restless at times, and travel was frequent. He generally painted into the wee hours after spending the day minding the gallery, and when he was on a painting jag, his pants would begin to hang on him. Managers of all the local establishments he frequented would send him home with extra food. He'd started out small and grown tall—just over six feet, a solid stock of sinew and bone similar to the horses he painted.

For his daily groove therefore, Callan rarely changed his style, business casual—those slim-fit dress pants in black or navy, wool, or polyblends for warmer weather. He'd gone from straight and narrow to wide and pleated, cuffed to flared, back to the current ones that fit slim through the hips and thighs, belted just below his waist. He also wore neatly tucked, classic white button-down shirts with pointed collars in wrinkle-free twill or cotton blends, no tie. Leather cap-toe Oxfords were his standard footwear, although he occasionally dragged out a pair of running shoes.

The only vintage trappings he continued to wear during the crisp Ozark winters were two Herringbone Tweed Inverness overcoats, a Victorian-era style that fell past the knees and sported the trademark cowl. Fall weather this year had been unseasonably warm, an ambient 68-75 degrees on average. His watch said temperatures would drop to the mid-40s by midnight, though—so he pulled one of his overcoats off the hatstand on his way out the back door.

Not to forget his tablet, either—the reading he had yet to catch up on that had set him off in the first place. For now, he draped the coat over his arm as the back door locked behind him and stepped into the alley.

Since nightfall had come and gone hours ago, his eyes didn't have to adjust. Mesquite-fired meats roasting in kitchens downtown made him realize just how hungry he was. He decided upon the Grotto.

Callan hadn't checked his hair, face, or teeth—but hadn't painted today, either. With a slim chance of any stray marks, he went on. He was clean-shaven and wore his hair short and tight these days, all black and back in a low-maintenance, short pompadour over a flawless fade. As he set out, he sucked any remaining blue goo from his teeth. And that was that.

The Grotto was eight doors down, a wood-fired grill with wine on tap served from a historic rock building. It had a sub-street level cave setting that backed up to a natural spring and served a mean blue-rare any day of the week but Tuesday, plus bread pudding when his sweet tooth summoned.

He'd only gone a couple of steps before he picked up on something else—an odor northeast of town, out past Sheffield Dairy. It wasn't his sister, or anything that particularly stirred him ... except that it was *wrong*. He turned north, nostrils flaring.

A new arrival, a sick one.

His mum was the first one to identify his ability—*second sight*, she'd called it, which became equally olfactory and neurosensory as he grew. He could still recall her rocking him to sleep after one of the more frightening incidents when he, then three, saw through the skins of all those around him—the veins and arteries exposed in their necks, particularly the carotids. The disfigurement of how humans then appeared startled him, for without warning, everyone around him looked like cobras poised to strike.

The human carotid—paired with the jugular vein—takes on the distinctive contour of a question mark as it tracks down the side of the neck, twisting much like the symbol's own lobe and shoulder, and dropping behind the clavicle. Those blood-filled channels expand outward with every breath, he observed, and even more so if the individual was agitated.

When a cobra rears up and hoods, its neck flares laterally from the forces of bones, but at the time snakes to humans didn't appear all that different to him. Even after he became aware that, while ribs were responsible for the cobra's ability to hood, and normal lateral expansion of the nape when breathing made it so for humans—the anomaly still caught him by surprise. He eventually learned how to switch it off, though he couldn't help but see carotids when people were upset. He could also determine whether or not two people were related by the way those vessels circulated their blood.

Both senses, he now knew, were what remained of his own survival mutations for seeking out fresh blood—although he'd long since made other accommodations for obtaining the next meal. Now and then the blue juice didn't cap off things as nicely, and he had breakthrough sensory information that, quite frankly, he no longer needed.

Now grinds the quernstone in every tooth; thin fangs, tongues busy around the blue air—

He filed away the information about a new arrival with diseased blood northeast of town and went on.

When Tobias worked night shifts, he always saved Callan's favorite table in the corner, a two-seater tucked near the cave formations and an indoor aquifer. Tobias was half Caddo, one of the earliest tribal groups recorded to inhabit the foothills of the Ozarks—centuries before the arrival of Osage, Shawnee, Illiniwek, or Cherokee.

Tonight, he greeted Callan with a menu (although he knew his order by heart) like he had for the past thirteen years. He was closing out a large group in the main dining area, and astutely noticed the presence of Callan's tablet—which meant that once more, his friend had brought work to dinner. After a brief back-and-forth, Tobias whisked away as efficiently as he'd appeared, off to put in Callan's order.

At one point, he'd unashamedly hounded Callan to join him in cruising clubs and bars; now he regularly fished out his cell phone to show pictures of his kids. Not for lack of trying, Tobias had utterly failed to fix up Callan with anyone. In turn, Callan would chronicle the digital albums of his latest travels, and Tobias would end all those conversations with, *Báwsa'? Dude, you the man*, or something similar—plus a word or two about how nice those places would be to share with *a special someone*.

Grotto's subterranean magic, cool and dark, calmed Callan. Light gypsy jazz piped into the bar from wall speakers since the live entertainment had signed off for the evening. Tobias returned with a goblet of Lambrusco and a flask of water and scurried away again. Callan rolled up his shirtsleeves and logged in on his tablet to Wi-Fi, navigating to his own electronic subscription and the second installment of "Bad Blood" in *Philly's Argosy*. He'd been dreading this one for some time, and the day had finally arrived when one of Gaye's *shithead* connections got their hands on it—something Gaye would've never endorsed.

The last time Callan saw Gaye, the captain was on his deathbed in a hospital in Long Beach, California after taking a tumble in the bathroom. He was still fighting—*coherent, not coherent*...

The family—his sister Clara, and her various and sundry appendages—had trouble making out what he kept trying to say. Callan knew from the moment he arrived that Gaye was trying to tell *someone* about his logs. He'd been aware that Gaye kept war journals for some time as he watched him revise his thoughts in a series of Moleskine ledgers over the years. Gaye had always stored them inside a fire-resistant SentrySafe, but with age he grew careless, at times leaving one or two opened by his lounge chair.

Gaye had never married and, by 1967, sold all his shares in the Jersey Hoboken factory. He retired to Long Beach, California where he leased a guest suite behind his sister's mansion in Belmont Heights. Shortly before his arrival, *RMS Queen Mary* made her millenary-one transatlantic crossing, docking at 1126 Queens Highway on December 9. Callan—more of a jet-setter in those days—remembered all the dates, for that was an eventful year. He'd just finished visiting Jonathan Frid in

Manhattan before making the transcontinental flight with Gaye to help him unpack.

Frid was daytime TV's hot new sensation, having resurrected the flailing serial *Dark Shadows* starring as Barnabas Collins, something Callan had helped foster over a couple of weekend shoots as a technical adviser. He'd signed all manner of nondisclosure agreements with ABC, and at the time those had protected him. Callan still admired Frid for his integrity, knowledge, and practice of theatrical arts.

Gaye too, had worked as an adviser during the four-year reconstruction of *Queen Mary* into a hotel. By 1972, *Queen Mary's* original first-class staterooms were complete, and Callan could actually book the one he'd occupied during his first voyage to the United States. He continued to visit Gaye and the hotel every September, as he always had, for another fifteen years. After Gaye passed in 1988, Callan lost interest in the ship, having survived the only person in the world who fully understood him. *Queen Mary* experienced a series of ownerships—heydays to bankruptcies—largely due to maintenance and hull corrosion issues.

Following the COVID-19 pandemic, the property managers filed in 2021, officially closing access to the ship.

More than once during those last visits Callan was tempted to remove Gaye's ledgers but didn't. Instead, he helped his old friend remember to secure them away. Gaye had promised to give them all to Callan when he finished, but it seemed he was always finishing. At eighty-five he was no longer walking well and had to give up his volunteer post on the Queen. The ledgers were likely somewhere in his home, Callan knew—but unfortunately, Gaye was no longer conscious when he'd arrived.

Imminent exposure *was* therefore a very real and current threat *and* yes, an upset. Callan tucked his tablet inside his coat to finish his blue-rare mignon with the fixings.

Tobias checked in again and took the usual order for bread pudding and hot tea. "You off to the tracks anytime soon?" He replaced the empty Lambrusco with another one.

Callan shook his head, a grin more likened to an innocent baring of teeth in an effort to shake off his frustration about *Philly's*. "Painting season."

Tobias nodded. "Here again, isn't it?"

They dropped into their usual shoptalk and banter. "Are you heading out to the in-laws for the holidays?" Callan asked.

Tobias grimaced. "Erm—they *would* be coming here."

"That so?"

"Yah, wife's making me spaz with the whole white glove thing. Has me running the kids over to the mall in Springdale twice a week."

Callan chuckled. "Gee, what I am missing."

"Man—don't you even start."

The two continued jawing with their usual good-natured ribbing until Callan finished his dessert. In the course of all of this, Tobias never noticed Callan had rolled up his sleeves to eat, nor paid attention to the way he very intentionally exposed some uncommon artwork on his right forearm. Tobias always complimented him on the blackwork design as if seeing it for the very first time.

"Hey—nice tat, man." Given the holiday pressure he was taking on this week along with everything else, Tobias admitted he thought he deserved one just like it.

They discussed where it might go like they had many times before, since Tobias already had a Yakuza themed bodysuit colorfully inked on both arms and shoulders. Callan paid his tab and—like always—ran the next item up the flagpole.

Could Tobias ask the chef if he might prepare flan sometime?

Tobias never remembered to ask. Neither did he notice that his friend hadn't acquired a midlife paunch like he had. Nor did he age.

Callan felt better on a full stomach, and the wine calmed him. He was probably making too much of it, he decided. He'd lived in Eureka Springs this long without any trouble, and his tattoo was still working. Caution when traveling, that's all—and he didn't have any trips

Falling Stars

scheduled for a couple of months. He had time to decide on an appropriate course of action. And, if tabloid runs were like everything else these days, it was soon to be last week's news. He'd window shop for his customary half an hour or so and go paint for a bit.

An outdoor tavern across the way was closing down for the evening as he climbed the staircase to street level, the band on the balcony hitting up a remix encore of Eddy Grant's "Electric Avenue." The temperature hadn't dropped yet, either.

His father had taken him up to Electric Avenue in Brixton when he was four, London's first street lit by electricity.

Yes, he thought. *I'm relieved enough to shine this street.*

Coat draped over his left arm, Callan began—a series of full straddle, syncopated *ah-one two, ah-three four* catch steps and paso dobles into smooth drops and turns. From there he executed a couple of sharp spot Voltas, traveling diagonally along the pavement *ah-five-ah-six-ah-seven* in precise Latin cross steps, knees tightly connected as trained. After sixty-three years of practice, he had it all—smooth strides at one level with a solid, tight base; sharp, quick feet; full hip rotation and rib cage projection; fluid shoulder weave and drop; peak swivel of the hips and torso; precise syncopation on the quarter beats.

He'd started those naughty samba lessons in New York City while painting Adios Butler in 1959. An opportunity to perform on Broadway came up in 1973 that he turned down after some deliberation because he wasn't sure of his ability to effectively mesmerize an entire audience. To continue living in peace, everyone but Gaye had to forget who he was.

At the moment he was fine with showing out a bit, though, because he'd had the townspeople here under his control for years. It didn't matter who watched him when his sleeves were rolled up. He stretched out both arms and aimed the tattoo toward the barflies cheering him on from the balcony.

A jest drops from the collective . . .

The tattoo—his talisman—had required some painstaking study, creativity, and practice to become fully functional, and it hadn't happened overnight. He'd worked on it for his first forty years living in the States, after Gaye noticed he wasn't aging normally and had implored him to remain underground. Legally changing his birth name simply wasn't enough; he found out when ABC tracked him down to consult Frid.

Conjuring a spell to create confusion and selective memories in the public at large was no easy task, particularly since his art demanded that he interact daily with it. Fabricated memories, he soon discovered, could be particularly useful since they were practically indistinguishable from real ones. They could be forgotten, misremembered, or otherwise just as unhelpful. For a talisman to be truly effective, he had to combine one or more apotropaics—and some, the very defenses humans had long employed to ward off revenants. He studied two of his mother's spell books, a binding almanac and a Wiccan grimoire, to create his idea.

He had the first design fashioned from obsidian and wore it on a silver chain around his neck for a while. When bodywork came more in vogue in the late '90s, he got the tattoo. As time went on he had the talisman stamped into his business logo, over the front door of his house, and embedded in the underpainting around his signature on all his artwork.

His memory charm used parts of the Khanda, the strength of the Sikhs. While the original symbol had four weapons, for his purposes, he retained only three. He upended the left Kirpan—a single-edged sword known as the Piri—and pointed it downward to present on the Miri, or temporal side. Essentially, he'd just dropped spiritual supremacy into mortal space, which allowed him to complete his spell. The central chakkar was like a frisbee razor, representing eternal time. He infused that with Triskele spirals, the flow of existence—life, afterlife, and rebirth. The double-edged sword down the middle served to blend true with false.

The spell of obliviation, one that erased or deeply buried memories, was a part—whereas the false memory charm didn't allow a person's mind to fill in the gaps. Obliviation could be the more powerful option because people generally didn't question what they didn't remember. Sometimes that was necessary.

The false memory charm didn't eliminate memories altogether, but altered them, a much more complex process to complete. That spell could be used to change a person's recollection of a conversation or make them believe something occurred that actually didn't. After considering all his options, Callan chose something closer to a modify-memory enchantment at the eighth level. He found that in some cases

Falling Stars

he needed to use lower levels, those effective for as little as twenty-four hours up to thirty days. At the eighth level, the spell lasted a year. At the ninth, a lifetime. Casting always involved charming or mesmerizing the target, wherein he could either change the details of a memory, or permanently eliminate one. Memory spells could be modified using a remove curse spell, but he really had no need for those.

He held the eventide, and then some...

Callan continued swirling down the street—*how he loved these throwbacks.* He hummed along—*when was that again? 1982? The MTV deal that put reggae singer Eddy Grant on the charts.*

Out on the playground...

He turned, arms outstretched, walking backward the rest of the way, black eyes fixed on his audience. They could see his mouth moving, but no one could hear him.

It slips from the mind, heart, and soul.
All of this, hold loosely.
What you now see, you release.
So mote it be.

Chapter Six

Tuesday chalked up to be *bust a move* regardless of anyone's best inclinations or intentions. June could've just as easily slept in, but she knew as soon as Tommy opened his eyes he'd be entrenched in one idea, hell-bent on setting up his new room—*there*. Lilly thought everyone could use a day or so to chill and strategize how it all might go down in the most efficient and ordinary way, skip to the prettifying. Walt just wanted his little girl to be happy that she'd chosen to return to their neck of the woods, to truly *feel* at home.

In review, June was grateful for the small things—her parents' faces flushed with joy, although she and Tommy had rolled in well past dark, the tight hugs, the fawning over how much their only grandson had grown...

Tommy had gripped the martingale on his internal frustration (June could sense it from across the room) and delivered his level best during those first moments to ignore the fuss. He was now barely pushing out of 5T's and terribly mindful he wasn't growing at a normal rate, his awareness of this abnormality not so much from direct experience—yet. In Chicago, it came to his attention because they'd been ordering the same size for him for well over a year. June only hoped his introduction to St. Elizabeth of Hungary Catholic School wouldn't hand over any surprises.

Surely no one would bully him about his size in a classroom designated for children with special concerns.

June had chewed over that foolproof logic several times for months, and still felt dread for her son. With midnight upon them, she went along with her mother's usual pomp and circumstantial bedtime snack, relieved when Tommy missed the event entirely after rapidly falling back to sleep on a couch in the den after his evening dose. She stayed up with her parents for another hour over a cup of her mother's froufrou (organically sprouted, loose leaf) hot tea, just long enough for

Falling Stars

Lilly to lay out their urgent need to discuss the next day's plans.

"The moving van arrives at nine," June had countered.

Lilly glanced her way with muted consternation. "Oh. I didn't know that."

"Now you do," June said quietly, and checked Walt's reaction. He'd been methodically blowing on his tea for the past ten minutes to avoid drinking it; these weren't his favorite. *Of course, Lilly had planned a welcome home brunch like she always did.* She'd never dealt well with extenuating circumstances or situations on the fly, and June was well-versed in navigating her mother's need for surety. Walt didn't look up.

"And here I thought—" Lilly protested in her explicitly genteel way, the introductory *and here* implying anything afterward stood a good chance of being divinely ordained. Some of Lilly's mental tracks were banked steeper than others and required greater efforts to negotiate; June and Walt knew the drill. But Tommy was the equalizer.

June shook her head. "Tommy has first dibs on you, Mom." Sipped her tea. "Trust me, he won't eat anything tomorrow that he can't carry in one hand."

Which lent an idea. "Breakfast tacos?" Walt asked. He winked at June. What he meant was, he'd head down to one of the food trucks on Kingshighway first thing.

Lilly wrinkled her nose. Everyone knew how she felt about food trucks.

June nodded. "Loaded with tomatoes. He's really into red food lately."

"I could make strawberry pancakes." Lilly smiled at them sweetly, one last ladylike push for her original plan.

June hated these conversations, ones that left her with the unambiguous impression she'd let her mother down once again. Lately it seemed easier to cut her off at the pass, as Walt put it.

"Maybe tomorrow night?" June asked. "After we set some things up?"

"We haven't done breakfast at supper in a while." Walt looked at Lilly hopefully and choked down an ever so tiny slurp. He'd learned how to navigate the how-so-many difficult talkfests over the years, and in what manner to seal the deal.

The real message was, June and Tommy planned to sleep in their own house the next evening. Disappointment crawled into Lilly's eyes, an ever so tiny alteration of her polite smile that indicated *I'd rather make pancakes in the morning* and, *they're planning on staying here at least a few more days, aren't they?*

With breakfast reconfigured to Walt's taco takeout, June explained, they all could focus and conserve energy for other tasks—several of them, in fact. And while Lilly quietly conceded like she usually did, June never got full-fledged forgiveness, left to carry her own guilt for hours or even days until she finally mustered the fortitude to shirk it off. Sometimes logic fell in her favor and proved the point. They would spend most of Thanksgiving Day at her parents', after all. But the friction remained.

On her way upstairs, June pulled one of Lilly's blankets (with enough frays and naps for the rough-and-tumble little boy Lilly still believed Tommy was) out of the closet and laid it over him. In his usual magical way, Walt had gently persuaded his grandson to shed his vampire cape and bomber jacket soon after their arrival—*no, we won't put them in the closet, just here, across the back of this wicker Wakefield, the one nobody can sit in*—which was a good thing. This left only his sneakers, which June slipped off.

After his evening dose, Tommy had promptly taken his place on the claw-footed couch beside the Wakefield within arm's length of his signature attachments. When sleep overcame him, this couch—while just as superannuated as the rest—had ample breadth and three supportive cushions. June tucked in the quilt around Tommy and looked up in time to place an index finger to her own lips, signaling Lilly that, *while it might indeed be terribly improper to sleep in one's clothes*, the overriding concern at the moment was Tommy's sleeping through the night.

Everything else besides (and how she knew it) must leave the room, so June gathered Tommy's regalia and his shoes to go upstairs with her. *Out of sight, out of mind.* For Lilly's fixations about all the improper, not-so-right in the world at any given moment could be just as easily rectified if things were simply put away.

June's childhood room was at the top of the stairs, first door on the right. A classic U-shaped staircase just off the foyer wound its way along the walls toward the second story, its reconstructed wooden risers carved in the same style they were *circa* 1907. Getting around the creaks was always a twitchy ordeal, and June handled the staircase in her familiar falter-funk slither, the same old sneak-and-creep contrived around the second, sixth, and tenth steps she'd made since high school. Tommy didn't need any excuses to roll out before morning, to realize he hadn't slept in his own bed.

She made it to the top landing before the old house issued a gasp, something she was sure would awaken him. June froze. Listened. Twenty or so feet away she heard light snoring, the dull shift of the couch as Tommy repositioned.

When she'd moved away to college, June's room was plastered floor to ceiling with posters and photographs, one big collage of celebrities, friends, and family tacked on neon orange walls. Her old room had two twin beds with rainbow comforters and matching curtains. On Christmas break during med school, she'd returned home to walls repainted *canter peach* (according to the swatches), drapes replaced with plantation shutters, and the twins, with a Gettysburg queen poster bed on risers. Her comforters, too, had been superseded by an oversized and ruffled white-linen duvet. June never questioned her mother's exquisite and exacting period tastes, but she did miss her old room. Like the rest of the world declared outdated at one time or the next, Lilly didn't dispose of any of it, but had those items carefully removed to the attic. Walt had taken June up to see for herself how her beds, pictures, and rainbows had been devotedly stored away.

The Gettysburg (even at her height, with the help of its matching tiger maple chamber steps) had always been a *heave-ho* for June, especially tonight. She pulled a pair of pajamas from her suitcase and listened. Tommy hadn't stirred again, and for that she was grateful. *Nothing quite like dealing with the attitude about his bed*—she'd only had to botch that once.

Yet she'd somehow skirred over that item on her list, hadn't she—doomed already by the sheer unlikelihood of arriving with her own house in order, or the *how in the world* of ever explaining some of these bizarros to Walt and Lilly.

✯

June woke Tuesday morning to two wide blue eyes in her face, Tommy on point like the legendary cat that takes the baby's breath. Since June grew up without pets, she'd only had that unparagoned experience a couple of times in college with her roommate's Himalayan. Tommy was just as close.

"Where's my cape?"

June could've used an extra fifteen. She squinted at him sleepily.

"On the chiffonier," she mumbled.

"The *what?*"

June pointed. "The dresser, right over there."

He followed her finger. Satisfied, he straightened. "You smell like old flowers."

Yep, the tea. June groaned good-naturedly. She also noticed Tommy perched on tiptoe, top step of the chamber stool. "Careful stepping down, okay?" She reached for his hand.

"I got it, I got it." But he did allow her to help him, this time. He pushed off, darted over to the dresser, dropped to the floor, and began yanking on his sneakers.

June yawned and rolled to her side, raising a finger way too much like her own mother as she—

"I know, I know," he muttered. No time to untie last night's laces—he was going on leftovers today, cramming his feet into the collars.

"You do?" June asked.

"Teeth, face, hands, armpits. I got it, Mom." He mauled his way into the second sneaker, jumped up, and headed for the bathroom.

"I'll get you a clean T-shirt." June rolled out and opened his suitcase. Checked the weather on her phone. He wouldn't need a long-sleeve jersey like the one he had on now; seasonal temperatures were moderate here by comparison.

From the bathroom door she tossed a Chicago Bulls Space Jam T on the countertop, Tommy already a minute-fifty into "Drac's got Plaque" on his musical toothbrush.

"I'm going with Grandpa to get tacos," he said around the bristles, cut the power, and spat into the sink. Flashed an all-canines smile oozing blue toothpaste at her.

June, arms crossed, suppressed a chuckle and leaned against the doorjamb. "Better rinse that again."

He got the water going and stuck his face under the tap, eyes shining with excitement.

For a split second, June's heart relaxed. Here Tommy was, actually hyped about something outside his so-very-refined and narrow set of interests.

Free at last, free at last.

He was sponged down, dressed, and halfway out into the hallway before he slacked up.

"Mom?" He turned.

June had her hand on it already—*the cape, right?*

His eyes formed another question, though. "Will I need the ninety-five today?"

Yesterday was the last time June had checked the CDC COVID and Infectious Disease Data Tracker like she had for nearly four years now, particularly the community profile reports and vulnerability indices. *Did he need a mask?* Traveling, yes. Here, no. Carroll County was holding its own, with exceptionally low community spread of—well, anything, considering its recurring tourist traffic.

She smiled and shook her head. Tommy grinned back at her, then took off.

A good start for the day, June thought. No cape, no clip-ons. Just Tommy, excited about starting his day with his grandpa. She had time for a quick shower too. *Always grateful for the small favors, Dad.*

The U-Haul lurched and shimmied as Walt lead-footed the brakes backing toward the recessed entry of 22 Fairmount. June, standing in the driveway behind the ordeal, tried directing—before the sinkhole gnawing through her gut reminded her there was little use. She could only wonder how such a brilliant mind could drive so badly.

"Walt never did learn," Lilly had admitted once. June was only too glad Tommy was missing this part as he darted from room to room inside the house, choosing where his would be.

Their Queen Anne was solid white and curated as one of the first along several winding residential streets off Historic Loop 62B. The upper loop on the town's crest needed no four-way stops or stoplights because traffic calming came with the territory, the many curves and steep descents in those streets funneling down the rock face into the commercial historic district downtown. Streets like Spring twisted down the bluff in the direction of the original springs, meandering along rolling hills all the way into downtown. Five streetside pocket parks were scattered along this largely B&B neighborhood, accommodations grown out of the need to house travelers seeking curative effects of Eureka's naturally occurring mineral springs since its discovery in 1879. June and Tommy's new home was formerly a B&B and antique shop. The wraparound porch had made the sale for June, and now she prayed Walt wouldn't back the U-Haul into it.

Up to that point, Lilly had directed the movers with a measured amount of élan, enough to keep them tramping under the fret and strain of the larger pieces and where those might work. These men were husky enough, but June only hoped for their sakes Lilly let things stand where they stopped and didn't finagle them into any rearranging. They had a three-hour maximum, anyway—as June had carefully reminded her mother beforehand.

With a foot to spare, Walt cut the engine. June unlatched the roll-up door at the rear and hoisted it upward, *note to self* that from this moment forward, the day might as well continue on AutoPlay.

She'd correctly guessed that from Lilly's vantage point on the porch, she too could see all the contents in the van—*and there it was,* indeed.

Walt threw one leg out the driver's side as Lilly's scowl grew. Tommy bounded across the front porch with his own announcement, ignoring everyone else.

"My room's dope!"

"What's this?" Walt asked softly as he joined June at the back of the truck.

June swallowed; the answer came all at once. "That," she said, "is where Tommy has Zoomed—with you and Mom—for the past two years." It might've been simpler to say this was Tommy's very own special bed, yet oh-so much harder to explain. For carefully chocked between piles of packing blankets was a metal casket.

She'd had it personalized for Tommy, a relatively new concept, with one of his favorite images printed all over it in high-gloss enamel. The casket was standard adult size—78 inches long and 23 inches wide. June tried not to think on it much, the underlying psychological motive that he'd grow up to fit in it. The corners were sculpted, including all the classic working hardware, accessories, and full handlebars along the sides. They'd selected a half-couch design with a split lid for funeral viewing, and in order for it to function as intended, it was manufactured from tungsten steel. A huge mural covered the top and sides—an astrophotographer's composite image of the Andromeda and Milky Way galaxies merging 3.75 billion years from now.

Those photographs, originally downloaded from the Hubble Space Telescope as part of project AMIGA (Absorption Map of Ionized Gas in Andromeda) as seen from Earth, show the Andromeda disk filling the field of view as it hurtles toward the Milky Way, tugging and collapsing our own galaxy with gravitational forces powerful enough to set the night sky ablaze with new star formations. Tommy fully understood that the two galaxies were currently still 2.5 million light-years apart, and the merger a long time coming—although his quiet dissertation between sobs during his first bone marrow biopsy was all about how *way cool* that collision was going to be. While Tommy's decisions determined most of his bed's retrofitted features, June had chosen the star-studded print as a surprise. And it was a hit.

Other accessories that augmented Tommy's gaming and sleeping experiences also came at a price. At his request, the interior, matching pillow, and throw were black satin. June ordered extra padding, memory foam, and lining materials to make the base and sides amply cushioned. When the bruising had started, the last thing she wanted was Tommy injured by the way he slept. Directly beneath the split lid along the casket's right side was a drop-down door for easier access. Inside, a flat screen monitor was installed into the head section of the lid with an adjustable joystick clamped to a glide bar on the right, the command center of operations. June had the casket retrofitted with a balanced air ventilation system, since Tommy closed the lid to play video games and stream television. A house rule was soon to follow—that he always slept with the head section opened, joystick unpaired and stored.

The casket was coupled with a specialty scaffolding, engineered to act as a 4DX, movable platform and secured by adjustable, heavy-duty steel bier pins. The entire contraption was powered by electric actuators and set up to deliver 4DX, the kind of state-of-the-art film technology that creates an immersive, multi-sensory cinematic experience. On-screen visuals in Tommy's games synchronized with motion and environmental effects to enhance the action—especially flying, sailing, and driving.

His casket was wired to roll, sway, twist, pitch, and heave. The inner frame could incline his head and feet on demand, and the base had a back and bottom shaker as well as a back and bottom tickler. Modified vents provided face air, air shots, warm air, and wind. LEDs embedded along the sides produced strobed lightning.

June had drawn the line when it came to water, scents, and bubbles. With improvements in technology, though, even these features had become environmentally safe and functional for Tommy's Rube Goldberg device. An individually targeted email June received from the retrofitter several months ago announced its new water-repellent fabric, liner, and drainage assets now available. After a brief back-and-forth, June arranged for an on-site reconstruction that would allow Tommy to experience fog and snow in his casket for this year's Christmas present.

Tommy's project—even for a leading interactive technology company—was a first, an odds-against concept from the word *go*. Tommy had conceived of the idea after spending a day at Universal Studios, the last family trip he and June made before he got sick. Some design decisions were discoverable and had to be painstakingly greenlighted, like the degree of head incline necessary to avoid motion sickness. Others were economical ones, like deciding whether to use industry standard biodegradable and fire-resistant hydraulics and pneumatics, or the more flexible and precise electric actuators.

June had therefore long since cast aside all morbid overtones about the casket, for Tommy had spent some of his happiest moments in there. As the years passed, she came to regard it as a pricey bed and flight simulator. The four heavies, having just parked the last of the appliances in the kitchen, returned one by one, lining up on the porch alongside Lilly.

"I need all of you over here," June called.

"Tell them it's fragile," Tommy warned.

"This piece has some sensitive technology," June explained. "No hand trucks. You'll need to carry this one inside the conventional way." She turned to Walt. "Let's lower the ramps, okay Dad?"

Tommy had selected one of the home's front rooms for his own—a round tower capped off with a cupola at sixteen feet. The room was probably a drawing room or smoking room originally, set just off the main foyer. It had three large windows, but Tommy wasn't concerned about exposure to light at the moment, June noticed. She thumbed a note on her cell phone to measure the windows for installing blackout roller shades. The entrance to the tower room had huge, solid double doors. June tested one of them; it clicked firmly into the sill.

Walt eyed Tommy and whistled. "Are we going for the Capitol Rotunda here, little man?"

Tommy straightened and pointed. "Right there in the center, yes."

When Lilly vigorously shook her head at June, June focused instead on directing the movers.

"We can run the power source—" Walt scanned the walls for electrical outlets.

"Nope, look here," Tommy said with a grin. "See, Grandpa?" He tapped a floor outlet in the center of the room with his toe. "I don't know about the amps, though."

Walt squatted by the outlet. "How much you need?"

"Thirty, I think."

Walt braced himself to stand—a slower process than four years ago, June noted, and walked around the casket, checking the labeled specifications. "Yeppers, we're going to need a new floor box."

Lilly tapped June on the shoulder as the movers began setting up the bier. "This is *not* the place for this—or his room, dear," she whispered.

June shrugged. "All we need to do is close these beautiful French doors when we have company."

Taking everything into account, June had allowed for even this unexpected turn—in fact grateful that Tommy was psyched about having a bedroom on the first floor, a level they both could comfortably occupy while he adjusted to his new lifestyle. Most kids his age would pine for a bedroom upstairs. A lot of empty space at 22 Fairmount, such was true—but given Tommy's circumstances, limiting his activity at times was advisable. Of course, Lilly would undoubtedly continue giving pointers from here on out and try to fill the old house to the brim if June budged one inch.

"There, there, Lilly." Walt had overheard. "Maybe it's time we take a break and get into those breakfast tacos, eh, Junebug?"

Her special pet name, reserved as an affectionate warning to cease and desist, June well knew.

He turned to the movers. "How about it, boys? I got extras, plenty for everybody."

⭐

Eleven-year-old Casey Wenner had watched off and on for two weeks from the salon window for the arrival of their new neighbors—jazzed when they finally showed today, *of all days*, as her mom, Dawn, had complained. Casey had *like, a way long time ago* discovered her own strategy for turning a blind eye to those moods, for Dawn had a way of reinterpreting what people did far and wide according to her own chaos. Today was turning out to be *salon heavy*, as she'd ranked it, especially when the hot water heater feeding that section of the house crapped out again.

Casey sometimes listened when she wasn't busy forming opinions of her own. Dawn had collected some scoop on their new neighbors over a month ago from an ancient realtor lady she all-too regularly bleached caramel blonde—full cap, whatever remaining hair picked through the holes—while they gossiped through the entire process. From that client Dawn had learned that a single, out-of-state doctor bought the house for use as a primary residence and wouldn't be continuing the B&B or the antique shop. Dawn had a classic *smize* reserved for certain kinds of news, and Casey understood what that meant: more bookings for them.

The realtor was semi-retired, so she didn't have *all* the information, whether this doctor was male, female—or how they self-identified, or if a family came with, and such. Casey naturally hoped any boys over there were cute and girls, into virtual reality. When Casey wasn't hustling to submit classroom modules on time or baking for their own B&B, she lived on VR.

And eavesdropping.

Casey's avatar was always and only herself—mid-back length brown hair, brown eyes, the kind of girl no one notices. The only difference was height. Casey was going through her *Great Dane* stage, yep, taller than most boys in her class, and would be oh-so glad when that was done. Dawn frequently mentioned that Casey got her hair and eyes maternally, the height from her AWOL dad—and reminded her to be grateful for all of it, as Dawn had only grown to five-five and stopped, a freak of nature she'd always regretted.

One day, my curves just marbleized, she'd repeated a gazillion times. *All the nicotine on God's green Earth* (Dawn vaped outside) *won't scare off this extra twenty, will it?*

Lately, Casey had noticed her mother only kvetched about her body every other Thursday, when the supply truck ran. Perhaps she had a thing for the driver, who knew. Casey didn't care. They were the proud owners of Purple Passion B&B and Dawn's Hair Glam, the only refurbished Victorian on the row painted electric lavender. Her mom didn't have time for a man, anyway.

Casey was fairly sure about that, for she knew the raw dirt of her own history; Dawn hadn't shielded her from any of it. Her mother had staked her claim on this house after *affair with married man number two* left her penniless and pregnant when he flew the coop. She'd hung by her thumbnails to make a go of it, raised Casey all on her own, and tried hard to forget about men. Whenever she remembered, Dawn had a whole section of seedy paperback romances (*amenities* for the B&B) she borrowed from.

Casey for the most part was a good kid who stayed out of trouble, with an unmistakable inclination toward hearsay and snooping like her mother. About the only common interest they didn't share was VR—*don't make me play anything with the word* reality *in it, sweetie.* Casey didn't push for that anymore, satisfied instead to have her very own thing. She and her mother were otherwise pretty much in each other's faces much of the time, VR Casey's only opportunity to cut and run from Dawn's Jenga of unresolved issues and personal enslavements.

Purple Passion B&B had ample room for two guest suites, their own living quarters, and a hair salon large enough for Dawn to lease out two extra stations. Between those enterprises Dawn had managed to make a decent living because child support checks didn't come. Casey worked hard as well—baking her all-star muffins and cupcakes for all the breakfasts, her after school chore. Blueberry, pumpkin, chocolate chip, and cinnamon roll were their standards, for Dawn had a solid belief in jinxes and wouldn't let Casey color too far outside the lines. In the spare (when that *did* happen) Casey had created a growing list of unrated classifieds, however—muffins made with barbeque potato chips, sour gummy worms, brussels sprouts rolled in ranch dressing, fried drumsticks over peanut butter, and cotton candy under licorice wheels.

At that moment Dawn's cell phone stood in the windowsill on speaker and on hold with the plumber while she swept between customers. The other two hairdressers, Katie, and Jeremiah—*praise God Almighty, she'd muttered*—didn't have anyone on the books this morning. Casey, out of school for Thanksgiving holiday, had parked herself at the same window, watching.

"Er—Mom? What kind of doctor did you say it was?"

The cell phone crackled, but no one picked up. Dawn frowned at it. Back to Casey. "I'm sorry. What?"

"The people moving in next door."

"Oh. Pearl didn't say." She began looking around for the dustpan.

"It's over by the nail station," Casey said, eyes never leaving the activity across the street.

Dawn made a colorful remark about her own disorganization, which was really more about mentally taking too many different directions at once, Casey had learned.

"She didn't really know much at all," Dawn grumbled. Which was all kinds of disappointing because it went without saying Dawn was fiercely aware that a chance with a doctor, whether by true love or even misinformed conjugation—might mean they both didn't have to work so hard.

"I think it's an undertaker."

Dawn snickered. "Get outta here."

"I'm *serious*, Mom. I just saw them take a coffin inside."

Dawn stopped sweeping and walked over to the window. "For real?"

"Uh-huh."

"I *do* wish Pearl had known more." She snatched up her cell phone. "I'll text Katie; she'll find out." She hesitated, glaring at her cell phone screen and *the damned plumber on hold*.

"I'll do it," Casey said, and took the phone away from her.

Dawn looked out the window dreamily. "While you're at it, maybe you can Google how much morticians make?"

Casey, thumbing away on her mom's cell, rolled her eyes—but Dawn, stalled at one of her more self-important junctures, totally missed it. "Maybe we should take the good doctor some muffins later, you think?"

Walt's midafternoon errand to a hardware store off Interstate 62 for a 30-amp floor outlet morphed into a burger stand lunch and quest for fudge in Eureka's historic downtown, its mishmash vibrance one of the reasons June was drawn back to her native home. Not many things in the Lucas household were completed without good chow somewhere in the fine print, and June was happy to see the town again, charming as always, a truly unforgettable step back in time.

These Ozarks grew into crossroads for many activities not long after the first Osage Chief dug out a holy basin near Main Street, the future site of Basin Park Hotel. For the latter part of the twentieth century Eureka was either boom or bust, a place to lay low or live high on the hog. Railroad magnates, bank robbers, bootleggers, gangsters, and whorehouse madams all made fortunes here. When the local economy swooned again in the '70s, a maverick counterculture migrated in and saved the town with breakout craftsmanship.

Eureka Spring's loop—a combination of Late and Folk Victorian, Gothic and Revival, Gable Front and Ozark rock cottages, rustic log cabins, tree houses, bungalows, and hippie craftsman—all tumbled into a mishmash of twisting two-lane streets that coil around a shopper's and artisan lovers' paradise. The springs brought it all into a *city of staircases*: quirky one-off shops, quaint boutiques, world-class dining, lively taverns, recherché art and jewelry galleries, celebrated spas, bathhouses, and just the right amount of local audacity.

Here entire stores were dedicated to items like kites and kaleidoscopes, Amish quilts, tinctures, beading, salsa, cooking oils, vinyl, aura photography, tobacco, handcrafted furniture, or fashion-forward yard art. *Stranger things* were always the norm, sought after by those who chose to play here or stay here. Merchants poured their arts, wares, and souls into these streets, shops featuring oddities like extinct toys or trained rabbits that handed customers their change, receipts, and merchandise at checkout.

In some ways, walking Main Street was still like entering an old west boomtown, its steep boardwalks and limestone tunnels tiering along several street levels, all shrouded under a canopy of Ozark white cedar, yellow pine, or juniper garnished with kudzu vines, bloodroot poppies, and Dutchman's Breeches. Only in Eureka could this many unique shops, artisans, and miscellany thrive. Patrons could dine underground or on a mountaintop, take carriage rides or ghost tours, hang out with the locals for coffee, commission street art and music, receive services from alternative and native healers, or tour protected public springs lionized with decorative rock originally carved and inlaid by skilled stonemasons. If that wasn't enough, during the winter months when the dense underbrush dwindled, visitors could look east of town and see a white, cross-shaped outline of the seven-story statue of Christ created in 1966 by Emmett Sullivan, one of the sculptors of Mount Rushmore.

Even Tommy's school, St. Elizabeth of Hungary Catholic Church, was included on the National Register of Historic Buildings. Originally constructed as a small chapel in 1882, it was built from locally quarried dolomite with a unique bell tower separated from the church proper.

Holidays had always carried a hyperactive scramble of creativity—all manner of artfully placed gewgaw strung along the historic tumble, with colorful lights cranking 24/7 and every imaginable piece of unconventional Santa's schlock one could wish for.

In June's best-laid plans, she wanted to gradually introduce her son to all of it, but today, Tommy was apparently set on taking everything in one gulp. After devouring half a bag of old-fashioned cherry sours at Two Dumb Dames Fudge Factory, he led the charge on short notice, pressing through the bright red double doors into the greater outside. The red stuff was a total hit, and he was flying pretty high for three in the afternoon, June noticed, following his own altimeter as he discovered more and more.

"Hold up, Tommy." She caught up with him several doors down. "Let's wait for Mom and Dad, okay?"

Tommy popped another cherry sour in his mouth, impatiently hopping from one foot to the next. "They're talking too much." Which was true—Walt and Lilly had run into a couple of old friends from Holiday Island they hadn't seen in months. He pointed toward the Basin Park Hotel. "I want to go that way."

When he got to the limestone archways at the hotel's entrance, he wanted to cross Spring toward Flatiron Flats, Eureka's own iconic four-story recreation of New York City's Beaux-Arts style tripartite skyscraper on Fifth Street. Thankfully he stopped and held out his hand. When June took it, he pointed at the flats' brick-and-limestone encased bow windows.

"That one's *lit*," he said.

"Sure is," June agreed, no time to elaborate the details. As soon as the coast was clear, Tommy was ready to cross the street.

Tommy and June were halfway down the south side of Spring Street before Walt and Lilly caught up with them. Walt's forefathers had originated along the Croatian coast of giants, and he really had no issues keeping up using one lanky leg or the other. He had to mete out his progress at a slower pace for Lilly, though—whose running gear, as he called it, came plagued with the standard amount of shortage from her Dutch ancestry.

"Where we headed, Junebug?" Walt asked just as Tommy broke off from them again.

June really had no idea. "Just one more stop, I think," she offered. Her top strategy for getting Tommy back on track was the need to connect his bed to a newly installed floor outlet, which they had yet to complete. She'd learned over the years, though, not to play any card until she absolutely needed it.

Several shops later, Tommy turned and headed down an alley staircase, two flights of weathered deck cedar toward Center. The end of that street was not generally as congested, so he looked both ways and crossed, June right behind him. He hotfooted it across Mountain toward long-defunct sawmills bordering German Alley. June glanced up at the shop sign, the destination that had lured him somehow.

Fast Horses.

She shrugged at Walt and Lilly. "What's this?"

"That's Callan Masters' art gallery," Lilly called.

June spun around. "Tommy, stop right there."

Amazingly, he did just that. June walked over to him. "Give me the candy."

He groaned loudly but did so.

"Hands out, palms up." She sprayed his hands with hand sanitizer. "Two minutes, no touchy." Her eyes snapped.

Tommy nodded, his gaze downcast. That's when June knew he'd

worn himself out just getting here. "We'll come back again soon and stay longer next time," she promised. She was all-too familiar with Tommy's implosions, the moth before the flame.

"Okay," he answered quietly, and hurried away.

"How long has this been here?" June asked.

"Well—ah—" Walt began.

"Five or six years, I think," Lilly declared, although she didn't look her usual certain.

New shops did pop up frequently around this vacation magnet, but June knew the mainstays endured for decades. She shook her head, trying to sort it out; June thought she knew Eureka like the back of her hand.

"Lilly wants a 'Knicks Go'," Walt said, rubbing his thumb over his fingers. *Spenny.*

Lilly nodded. "He won the Pegasus World Cup."

June laughed. *Her mom? A horse?* "The print, or the real deal?"

"Why—" Lilly thought about it. "I have the perfect place for either one."

And Walt muttered something June didn't catch.

Several art investors gathered around Callan Masters at the east end of his gallery in a lively and ongoing discussion about the expanding digital art arena using non-fungible tokens. For Callan, the viability of NFT's was old news; he'd spotted that trend early and bought into digital platforms years ago. Nonphysical forms of traceable and verifiable works of art sold in fractional shares was the wave of the future, and he'd hopped on it without a second thought. No one questioned that he had a long-term vision for his artwork, though no one recalled just how long he'd been at it, either. He'd had a continuous demand for his pieces however they were sold or auctioned since the midforties, art that continued to appreciate in value. Digital art was yet another opportunity to sell his work directly to consumers, a way to give art investors access in open marketplaces. This discussion had ended several minutes ago for him, but he continued to listen politely, especially when he saw the boy wearing horn-rimmed glasses and a Bulls T-shirt enter the gallery.

He leaned out from the investors' huddle ever so briefly for a better view of the boy's mother—*well-cut shoulders accentuated by a racer back tank, legs that went on forever in skinny jeans*—and ducked quickly back inside the circle. The kid hadn't interested him so much, except for the smell. He was the sickly one who'd arrived yesterday, Callan knew it.

The greater irony, that this boy's smell had originally turned up north of Sheffield Dairy, he remembered—*the* homestead where Eureka Spring's mother aquifer originated, called *Grotto* by early townspeople. Tent dwellers in the area discovered that spring and several more like it with the help of indigenous peoples. All the springs were considered sacred by the tribes, so settlers created an enclosure of limestone and ornamental stonework to encase the grotto. Stone masons carved *Esto Perpetua* above its stone entrance, translated *may she endure forever*, a summons for the water to prevail and continue healing all those under its power.

The boy had insisted on coming inside Fast Horses, and she, standing nearby as he scrutinized each painting, didn't touch him or yank him around like other parents usually did with their curtain climbers. Instead, she mothered him with—*captivating tender mercies*, Callan observed as she leaned in and spoke gently to him. She was a perfect match for the little guy, with the same sleek black hair pulled into a high ponytail and blue, blue eyes. Just how his own sister might've looked about now, had she lived. She wasn't wearing a wedding ring, either. He quietly cleared his throat. Then he saw their carotids.

Humph. How about that.

So Callan forced himself to stay hidden inside a discussion he no longer cared about because he had one cardinal rule: he couldn't let himself grow fond of anyone he'd outlive. Far easier to love vicariously through the lives of others, he'd learned. He'd lent a couch to Tobias more than once, and that was how it had to stay.

And so it was, she entered his broken world...

After a couple of minutes she took the boy's hand, and he followed her out the door.

Tommy was no worse for wear when they finally arrived home, to June's relief—which made her begin to question her own accuracy at reading things lately. No doubt her own personal exhaustion from an unflagging sweat equity to make *rights* out of *wrongs* over the past three years played a role in this. *She'd really forgotten how to turn it off, hadn't she?* No one who rode in Walt's Series II Land Rover today had long to mentally stew between the yaws, however. He wheeled the antiquated SUV into the drive and alighted with one last, bounding stop.

"Looks like your hoss made it just fine," he announced.

The driveaway delivery—June's teal Audi e-tron—had indeed arrived in one piece.

"Sure does." June smiled. *She really needed to teach her dad how to drive.*

Even Lilly, one hand parked on the dash as insurance, chased her own thoughts about the rough ride with what a successful day they'd had. The furniture was placed, and all the boxes distributed to their appropriate rooms. They'd returned the U-Haul at lunch, and only had to try out the new floor outlet in Tommy's room for his—*contraption*—before heading over for her strawberry pancake supper. *Neat and tidy.*

June had to admit—some neat and tidy felt good.

"What's with the purple house?" Tommy asked Lilly.

"That's the Purple Passion," Walt cut in, pointing.

June looked; he was right. The sign in the front yard plainly said so.

"It belongs to the Wenners." Lilly lightly touched Tommy's shoulder and glanced over at June. "You remember Dawn, don't you, dear? I think you two were in the same class."

June listened halfway, preoccupied with Tommy—how he hadn't dodged Lilly's affection like he usually did, and how he seemed genuinely interested in what she had to say. The better part of five seconds clicked by before some remote high school memories came wandering back. *Oh, yeah.* They hadn't exactly run in the same circles. While June was studying protein synthesis of *Arabidopsis thaliana* in a plant genomics lab, Dawn was discovering how to make money by taking her clothes off in front of her laptop's webcam.

Lilly chattered on about Dawn's enterprising streak with her B&B, plus a hair salon, pointing out the three hooded hair drying stations spaced six feet apart on the porch. At which point Tommy and Walt ducked inside to install the new floor outlet.

"Clever, isn't it? She left them that way after the pandemic because

some of her customers like sitting outside," Lilly went on.
"That is—effective," June offered.
"I think she has a daughter about Tommy's age. She's a single mom too," Lilly added.

Mutually beneficial common ground for—? June had some prolonged practice with anticipating Lilly's underlying agendas. She listened for a minute or so before turning to go inside.

The hums and thumps of a casket systems check carried into the foyer, Tommy going full-on tilt, bank, and whirl when June and Lilly entered the room. For all intents and purposes, his casket was fully functional.

Lilly gasped. "It does all that?"

"Some *thingy*, huh?" Walt stood a few feet away, watching.

It's the best—maybe the only—*way he can play, Mom,* June wanted to say. Then again, perhaps over time Lilly would come to realize this for herself.

Walt rapped on the side of the casket with his knuckles. "My turn, buddy."

Lilly frowned. "Oh, Walt."

"Huh?" He grinned at Lilly. "I can fit in there, and he'll show me how."

June chuckled. "Good luck." Who knows, she thought, it might improve his driving.

The casket settled at geometric horizon. Tommy popped open the lid and sat upright, his blue eyes beaming.

The doorbell rang. *So that's how it sounds.* June listened.

Lilly leapt into action. "I'll get that." She grabbed one of the double doors and expeditiously motioned for June to close the other.

Walt shrugged and grinned at June. "Go on, see what they're selling. I'm all over this; we're hotter than a TSA checkpoint in here."

June chuckled, walked out, and shut the second door behind her.

Lilly, waiting at the entrance, wasn't about to do anything until she saw the coast was clear. She peered around the casing and through the decorative frosted glass panel, exclaimed, and rapidly opened the front door.

"Dawn, hello! What a nice surprise!" Lilly gushed.

Even in a salon apron Dawn Wenner oozed cleavage and curves.

With a somewhat higher fat index than before, June noticed; age hadn't been kind to Dawn. The senior class had voted her most likely to succeed modeling lingerie for Wonderbra in Indonesia, a smear Dawn had proudly set her sights on regardless. *How could I forget.*

Her daughter Casey was a lesser endowed version of the young Dawn Wenner, and very definitely hers, with a cute face much like a little mouse, June observed. She was embracing the unseasonal weather in shorts and a T, holding a small wicker basket draped with a red gingham bowl cover.

"Lilly?" Dawn threw her arms around June's mother with the zeal of a church parlor meet-and-greet. "Well, of course it's you!" She looked down at Lilly's hands. "We haven't seen these in a while."

"Yes—my nails are a mess. Fall gardening, you know. I'll be in soon, I promise."

"You better, Hon. We can't have you going around town looking like that."

La-di-da laughter, June noticed. Even Casey looked bored.

"Do you remember my daughter June?"

A faint spark of recognition with somewhat less warmth. "Oh, *sure!* You went off to—"

"Chicago," June answered.

"Medical school," Lilly echoed.

"*You're* the doctor?" Casey asked.

"She is," Lilly preempted June. "An oncologist."

Casey pulled out her cell phone. "Could you say that again?"

"Sweetheart," Dawn chuffed. "Wherever did those manners of yours go?"

Casey stuck out her lip. "But I thought you wanted me—"

"Casey," Dawn cut her off. *That* was a warning, June noted.

"It means she helps people who have cancer, honey." Lilly smiled sweetly at Casey. Which gave Dawn time to recover.

"Well, you're just as slim and gorgeous as ever!" Dawn smiled daggers. *Some things, just so unfair,* that said.

Behind them, Tommy opened one of the huge double doors and stuck out his head.

Casey was on it quicker than a cat's sneeze, craning to see around Lilly and where *the coffin she knew was in there* might be.

Falling Stars

Lilly's eyes flashed an all-points bulletin June's way. "We're still in a bit of a mess in here, I'm afraid, or we'd invite you inside." She turned toward June. "I don't suppose Walt needs any help in there?"

"Nope," Tommy replied from across the foyer.

"I'll check," June said. "Nice to see you again, Dawn, and to meet you, Casey."

"Who's that?" Tommy asked as June shut the double doors behind her.

"The neighbors," June replied. "Maybe go out there in a minute and say 'hi'?"

"Not today," Tommy said, watching the casket. "I need to monitor him."

June stifled a giggle; Tommy did have a point. "No kidding," she said. "What's he playing?"

"*TrackMania Turbo*," Tommy said.

The casket's lid opened a crack. "Man, this is awesome," Walt called, and shut it again.

June, standing by the door, could hear the ongoing conversation outside.

"Tommy's about your age, I think."

"I'm eleven," Casey answered.

"Oh! You're in middle school, right?"

"Yes ma'am."

"Well, Tommy just turned nine. June adopted him as a baby, and he unfortunately has cancer."

June white-knuckled the door handle. *Too far, Mom.*

"Oh, my stars, Lilly, that's awful! We're so sorry," Dawn exclaimed.

"Yes, yes. We take it one day at a time."

June turned to Tommy. "Will you keep these doors shut a couple more minutes, please?"

Tommy cut his eyes at her, then back to the casket. "Is that your idea, or Grandma's?"

June gave him a *don't-mess-with-me* look and shut the doors behind her.

"Does Tommy attend school?" Dawn was asking.

"St. Elizabeth's, when he feels up to it," Lilly replied as June rejoined them.

Dawn grinned at June. "Why, that's just around the corner. Casey catches the school bus downtown. She'd be happy to walk with him, wouldn't you, sugar?"

Casey glowered at her mother.

"Oh, I imagine Walt will probably take Tommy most of the time," Lilly said, "since June will be commuting to her clinic in Rogers."

June mentally filed the correction for another day, that she would actually rotate as a staff oncologist out of clinics in Rogers and Springdale three days a week and do the rest remotely from home.

"You know, weather permitting—" June interrupted, "I think Tommy would enjoy walking to school with Casey now and then."

"Honey, are you sure about that?" An *all things considered* inquest from Lilly.

"I don't see why not," June said dryly.

"Well, then. It's a date!" Dawn nudged Casey, definitely looking two seconds from meltdown. "Give them the muffins, dear," Dawn said through her teeth, and nodded toward the sign in her front yard. "Feel free to text me at that number anytime, June."

⭐

"*Mom*," Casey growled when they were out of earshot.

"Oh, don't you *mom* me," Dawn snapped. "Sometimes, Casey— you just really don't know when to shut it."

"But you said—"

"*No.*" Dawn stopped at the Passion's porch stoop. "*No, ma'am.* I said . . . well, *good night*, we even made a pinky swear on it. The stuff that goes on between these walls stays between these walls."

Casey fished her cell phone out of her back pocket. "*Well,* just in case you still wanted to know, the stuff that goes on between *those* walls comes with three-hundred-eighty-five grand a year."

Dawn swallowed. "You're serious?"

Casey nodded. "You could change your sexual orientation and give it a go if you want. I don't mind."

"Casey Denise!"

Hands on the hips and the *middle name that curled her toes*, a hard count toward things heading sideways for sure.

"How can you even think that way?" Dawn's most disapproving look.

"Just sayin'," Casey mumbled. Maybe she really should dial it back, though; she didn't want a little stepbrother, anyway. "News flash, young lady." Hands still on hips. "Your mother is *eternally* straight, even if the majority of men are assholes." Dawn turned to go inside. "And you didn't hear me say that last word, either." Nothing much made Casey lose her cool except when her mother volunteered her willy-nilly for stuff. Part of what brought on that ugly was, there was no way of getting out of *those*. Casey didn't want to walk the weirdo kid next door to school on the first day or on any day, for that matter. And Dawn always had to end those conversations by texting Casey some misspelled, sanctimonious shit like *you shall reap what you sow*, or *the good Lord won't give you more than you can bare*. Casey glanced down at her chest with a matter-of-fact *nope, not yet*, and *Good Lord, you'd better not ever*.

Tommy's new online friend martha_whoosis a.k.a. Chelsea Dumont had friended him yesterday shortly after they left the convenience store. He'd hopped on a brief thread to confirm Chelsea's screen name for *Eve Online*, a massively multiplayer space game she played on Thursday nights—particularly *Invasion Expansion,* third chapter, *when she could get on*, she'd mentioned. Tommy had encountered *the cluster* with the video game's overcrowding and usually opted to play *Star Conflict* instead, sometimes with Molly, which happened to be tonight. The game could've been handpicked for his casket's unique 4DX setup since it offered some one hundred ships to pilot, unlock, and upgrade. The ships were what made the game, of course, and tonight he had the challenge of flying a big-ass frigate for some pretty intense dogfighting inside the asteroid belt Kuiper, the rim of Neptune's orbit. Half an hour into repeated failed attempts to level up, he had an incoming Zoom call from Molly.

"Talk to me, Undead Lucas," she said, still using his screen name.

"I've got more time in here than you think," he announced, opening a thumbnail of Molly's Zoom in the sidebar to continue his hassle with his *smaller than a destroyer but still a big piece of...*

He knew Molly was watching the clock on Chicago time, but he'd been granted an extra hour before lights-out, kudos for keeping a lid on today—more or less.

Molly sniggered. "How'd you manage that one, Lucas?"
Incoming volley, pitch and ro-o-oll
"Damn," Tommy muttered as shrapnel filled his field of vision.
"Better cut out and try another sector tomorrow," Molly advised.
Tommy didn't like it, but he knew Molly was right. He signed off, and Molly in her Penrose gaming headset filled the screen. He grimaced.
"What's that on your face?"
"Colloidal oatmeal," Molly replied. Whatever it was, she'd smeared the same shit into her eyebrows and loaded up her earlobes.
Tommy squinted. "Not your best look."
"Yep, you get the true *moi* tonight." Molly chuckled. "How's the new digs?"
"Killer," Tommy said. "I'll send you a video of my room."
"Moved in already, huh?" *Clearly Molly knew how fast he was crackalackin', didn't she?* She knew all kinds of stuff.
"Here's some info," Tommy said.
Molly read the bottom of her screen, eyebrows raising in surprise. "OMG, really? You're going?"
His mom had greenlighted Fan Expo, Tommy told her, after a new online friend he'd met at a convenience store in St. Louis had invited him to go. Martha_whoosis had just messaged him about another new addition posted on Fan Expo's Past Events Page for the upcoming convention: a CGI holographic collation of recorded interviews with Frid and live chat with Darrow.
Molly promised she'd get tickets ASAP and reminded Tommy to send the video of his room before they signed off because he'd gone on and on about how *way cooler* this one was than their home in Chicago, that it was all old and creepy just like the one in Collinsport. It even had a forest behind their back yard, with a big ol' wrought iron fence.
Tommy powered down the monitor and opened the lid. He still had to go to school, and he missed Molly already, but how hard could it be, anyway? For now, the only light in the room came from an old Tiffany floor lamp, and his mom had hung dark sheets over the windows, which worked just fine for him. The shower running in his mom's bathroom had stopped, so he only had, maybe ten-point-five more minutes—*and he had so freakin' much to do.*
He wanted to go back to Fast Horses and ask the *curator* (new

word of the week) if there were any paintings of wild Welsh ponies and visit the Crescent Hotel—formerly the Baker Cure-for-Cancer Hospital—to find out if Claudius Fallon had indeed been cured. He needed to catch up on new episodes of *Dark Shadows*, and he was so close to unlocking the next autophagy level on *Vampyr*, an action role-playing game set in 1918 interwar London about a doctor who awakes in a mass grave as a vampire. He also wanted to message martha_whoosis to see if she'd be online Thursday, if she thought they could play *Eve Online*.

He wondered if she might consider *Vampyr* and raised his nose in thought. *Hmm, likely not.* He'd leveled up past III on most skills like coagulation, body condition, prowess, and fast regeneration. For tactical maneuvers and quests using claws, spring, and hard biting, he knew it would take martha_whoosis several months to catch up. And she might choose combat over harvesting, who knew.

June decided to give Tommy an extra few beyond the hour before calling lights-out because she wanted to unpack three more boxes and review the day—particularly the two minutes that bothered her more than all the rest. What she'd seen in Fast Horses had knocked her for a loop, requiring every ounce of vim she possessed to hide it from Tommy. Thankfully, he was too distracted to notice, and after mulling it over, June decided to drop the matter altogether. Every last shred of emotional intelligence she possessed fired off like a Klaxon, and while curiosity had her by the throat, further inquiry wasn't an option. Not now.

Master's artwork was stunning. From the moment June had entered the gallery, his imagination captured her complete respect, how someone could bring this much beauty into the world—and at a time when it was so needed. His painting style was renaissance realism, a roomful of magnificent beasts poised to charge off the walls. Many he'd captured in chiaroscuro, a technique that incorporated pitch-black backgrounds and striking contrasts between light and dark. Others he'd crafted equally well in *sfumato*, a technique perfected by Da Vinci where paint blends and molds imperceptible transitions between light and shade.

She'd only needed a split second and a sidelong glance to neurologically embed the memory when he momentarily leaned out of the group; that was long enough. Out of the corner of her eye June saw Callan Masters, the man she assumed was the artist, and he wasn't some back-of-the-hillsides yayhoo. Near her age. Tall and slim in hip-casual business attire, white sleeves rolled up. Dark eyes and hair, an arched nose with a hint of a hook at the tip, curved firmly from the nasal bone. A diamond-shaped and highly angular face somewhat due to pronounced masseters, making his jawline widest at the temples. A slightly protruding chin. No wedding band.

Her Capricornian table manners told her it was only practical that a man *that* good-looking at that age in Eureka Springs either had someone in his life or wasn't scoping for a reason. The chemistry had surprised her; she hadn't felt that way in a very long time. And Tommy wasn't likely to forget her promise to return to Fast Horses, either. She shook her head, annoyed with herself for promising anything. Maybe Walt would take him? *There's an idea,* but it didn't make her feel any less troubled somehow.

Chapter Seven

BAD BLOOD
THE CASE OF CLAUDIUS FALLON
by Miles Cochran
Part III

4 September 1939

Our last day at sea, an encrypted telegraph came in from Pops about an influx of cash into the factory account from the British Consulate. I got him on the horn to explain the money, plus our contingent procedure for disembarking, but I don't think he fully followed until he saw me motor the Woodie down the ramp onto Pier 90's passenger terminal at the Hudson. In the thick of an embrace with Mum and supplied with a second wheelchair for Nonna, he seemed as shocked to see me as I him, or that we would ever find one another among the Stateside *Welcome Home* ticker tape and hoopla surging all around the docks that Monday evening. In the light of recent events, we were grateful to reach the mainland at all. World War II had begun.

    Claudius sat quietly on the passenger side, his dark eyes taking in the shoreside frenzy and New York traffic. I felt for the lad even more then, with no one to greet him, and I ruminated over what kind of reassurance to offer about arriving in this strange land. I'd felt that way on foreign soil myself—captivated, yet isolated. But for now, we were doing things the American way.

    Pops came bearing a large bag of potato and kasha knishes from Yonah Schimmel's on East Houston Street. Draped over his other arm was a Guards coat packing a U.S. atlas, a roll of greenbacks, and a convincer. I took all of it, since we had a thirty-five-hour drive ahead of us, a trip that would probably entail roadside stops only. After weeks of summer heat and a long drought, heavy thunderstorms along the northeastern seaboard had cooled the air to its usual nose-clearing smack.

Although I'd been running on fumes the past four days, I'd primed myself to make the excursion on a few catnaps here and there. Mum and Nonna really wanted to invite the viscount for a layover at our Jersey farm, but they also understood the nature of the mission. We couldn't delay, on the chance that he or his sister might be helped; we were soon to be off.

"Unless we get gummed up, I should be back late Sunday," I promised Pops. I knew he would need my help at the factory after I completed the captain's list for placing RMS Queen Mary in dry dock. We'd just gotten our first large order for M-42 service boots that would push the standard twelve-hour days to fifteen, conditions that led to CIO pickets and riots like the one in May at a coffin factory in Erie. The end of the decade had been marked by a moderate number of sit-downs —the tool and die strike in Detroit—and, closer to home, McNeely and Price's Leather Tannery walkout in Philadelphia. Pops was always preparing for the next shit to hit the fan, especially following news like the International Fur and Leather Workers Union's demands to boycott Japanese goods in 1938, or their more recent denouncement of Hitler in January as *a monster, hatching plans to conquer the world.* Hoboken factory employees had remained simpatico, but we both knew how quickly things could turn.

On the passenger side, Mum and Nonna were smothering Claudius with glum goodbyes, for sending off the boy in any fashion went entirely against the grain.

"The little dearie, now—we won't see him again for yonks, will we?" Nonna, buttoned-down in her own wheelchair, shot the last part across the bow at me.

"Latter October, perchance," Claudius interjected. His generally dispirited gaze had a flicker of hope this evening and took me by surprise. Then again, Mum and Nonna seemed to have that effect on him.

"We can treat him to the fair!" Mum exclaimed. She'd convinced

Pops to take a Saturday off last May to attend the World's Fair with me while I was on leave. I nodded in agreement; the fifth World's Fair had opened in Queens to a construction cost of 160 million dollars and FDR's commencement address touting America having *hitched her wagon to a star of good will*, all its parks themed "The World of Tomorrow." New York World's Fair Corporation had truly outdone themselves this time.

"There's an idea, nowt the lad can find his way back," Nonna muttered.

Which set Mum sideways. "Tosh if he will, Carleton will go and fetch him. This plan of yours really takes the biscuit, you know," she snapped at me.

"It's not his," Pops countered.

Nonna leaned forward, hands clamped on the door shell. "Oh, give me a peck, sweet one."

Claudius kissed her cheek as affably as he had the previous night, and that was that.

"Just make sure the boy gets what he needs," Pops added. I always thought it odd, since at that time he barely knew what we were up against. But his grip on my forearm was firm, his smile compounded with unmistakable dread.

I covered his hand with mine. "Abyssinia, Pops."

"Off you go," Mum murmured.

"Cheerio, fellows!" Nonna called as we drove away.

We took Canal Street out of the city toward Newark, Claudius silently eyeballing everything. He even turned around in his seat as we started through Holland Tunnel; I'm not sure he'd ever seen anything like it. Going twelve years strong, its gleaming cream-colored tiles clipped past as we made our passage under the Hudson River toward Jersey City's Twelfth Street. One of the more significant challenges, I explained, was how to draw out carbon monoxide fumes from the 1.6-mile tunnel in the first place. Part of the solution was its circular design and automatic ventilation system. Four buildings, two on each side of the Hudson, housed eighty-four immense fans that provided an exchange of air every ninety seconds.

I tuned the radio at a low volume, Hoboken's own Knickerbocker Broadcasting, WMCA 570 AM, as we drove our way out of the city. It occurred to me this might be a good way to introduce the viscount to the States and the way things were—from breaking news to common vernacular to entertainment, like the back-to-school advertisement now airing for the new film adaptation of L. Frank Baum's children's fantasy, *The Wizard of Oz*.

I'd read somewhere that Metro Goldwyn Mayer's budget topped three million dollars to make this *wonder show of shows* in glorious Technicolor, one very likely to be held over in theaters across the country. Starring child prodigy Judy Garland as Dorothy, Jack Haley as Tin Woodsman, Burt Lahr as Cowardly Lion, and Ray Bolger as Scarecrow, it trailed NBC's *The Wizard of Oz* radio show that ran six, seven years ago. Sponsored by Jell-O, that one aired three days a week in fifteen-minute segments around quitting time, a diversion on the yellow brick road for the ride home. The announcement went something like this:

Now playing, The Wizard of Oz comes to the screen in a magnificent presentation of Technicolor, songs and dances, camera wizardry, and spectacle. When Dorothy the Kansas kid finds herself whisked away by a cyclone to a never-never land of gorgeous color and incredible happenings called Oz, you'll miss a lot of fun if you don't whole-heartedly go along. A whiz of a wiz he is and yet, with all his magic, even old Oz himself couldn't work the wonders of this season's rainbow lollipop of entertainment—a super-super that's worth every penny. You'd have to be pretty old and crotchety not to like it, and if you're feeling that way it might, just might, make you feel ten years younger.

Claudius listened intently, absorbing every word. My throat relaxed a bit, and for an instant, fascination appeared to override the urgency of his sister's status. As for me—no matter how far we drove—I couldn't, in truth, forget that we carried a body in back.

"I hear it's a good picture show," I said.

He nodded. "Fancy I'll see it, yes." It dawned on me then, the life he must've led until now, a boy born into the privilege and hardship of choices, accustomed to carefully weighing in what he brought into his own circle of affairs, so to speak. Because of this terrible authority, he was now driving his sister across the continental U.S. to be buried. And unless he was somehow allowed to return home sooner than I expected, the closest box office was in Little Rock. How terribly messy this was, I regretted.

Seven miles later U.S. Route 1 crosses the Hackensack and Passaic rivers by means of the Pulaski Skyway, a causeway over three miles long. Arching steel deck trusses clear the water by 135 feet to make this bridge one of the country's first four-lane superhighways. Over some sections the trusses carry the roadbed on top, *a drive into the sky*, Pops calls it, who rather enjoys the jaunt himself. At the rivers, a series of cantilever trusses sandwich the structure to stabilize the bridge top to bottom. Spanning those waterways are iron behemoths with massive diagonal braces, lateral struts, chord rails, and connection joints arching thirty-five feet above any motor coaches passing underneath.

Claudius rolled down his window to look above and below, paying particular attention to the one-hundred-foot concrete piers holding up the deck.

Oh, lean from the window, if the world slows down . . .

A single white stripe in the middle of the highway separated four lanes of traffic, which I suppose he wasn't familiar with, either. I explained to him that over the water, cantilevers balanced road compression with upward truss tension. He seemed to understand, nodding at me. I could see it in his eyes, an odd mix of relief and weary resignation.

I talked to him a bit to calm him down, detailing some of the exhibits at the World's Fair I'd enjoyed, ones I thought might draw his interest. Like many public directives dreamed up in the armpit of hard times, the park was a full-blown extravaganza from one end to the other, all 1,200 acres of it, formerly an industrial ash dump. It drew government agencies, corporations, and civic groups from around the world in large numbers to build exhibits and pavilions with national pride—namely Britain, France, Greece, Italy, Japan, Jewish Palestine, the Netherlands, Poland, USSR, and the countries of the Pan American Union.

The park's focal point, I explained (the pair of knock-your-socks-off contemporary buildings with long lines staged to enter) was the Trylon-Perisphere set. Folks filed into a sleekly simple boxed entrance at the bottom of a huge white spire 610 feet tall, the Trylon. Displays inside the entrance hall immediately introduced the brainchild—*interdependent farm and factory, trade and craft, city and country.*

Falling Stars

From there, spectators were ushered toward the world's two longest escalators, each bound for different levels inside a huge, also-white globe 180 feet in diameter, the Perisphere. Once inside, visitors stepped onto circular ramps advertised as magic carpets, which in reality amounted to very slow-moving conveyor belts. The exhibit radically demonstrated a new way to approach life, nonetheless—a visionary appeal to manufacture a better world within the next twenty years.

The show started with *Dawn of a New Day* above dark shapes in the bottom of the sphere and a gradual fade-in on Democracity, a giant model of a planned, symbiotic region. A commentary by newscaster H.V. Kaltenborn dished up a better life in this world of tomorrow by employing interdependence and design. Forward thinkers were concerned about creating better living environments with adequate sunshine, air, greenery, and mobility, all to replace the congested canyons of American cities. Looking down into the center of the sphere, we could survey a utopian model city surrounded by seamless projections of living murals above it on the dome's gypsum tiles. When dusk set in, Democracity lit up with a beautiful star-spangled sky on the dome's walls. The mural featured ten groups of people from various walks of life marching slowly out of the darkness, side by side and singing in unison. The show ended with a fireworks display.

People loved the cinematic experience, I added, courtesy Eastman Kodak projectors and RCA amphitheater sound. When finished, crowds left using a 950-foot spiral ramp called the Helicline that encircled the exhibit and exited the Perisphere three stories up.

While I had the viscount's full attention, I also shared a mishmash of glorious words from a program I got at the show, namely *this isn't just a city of the future, but a symbol for a way of life. Yet you can start building this city tomorrow morning with no trick materials, no imaginary machines. Here is a city with built-in greenery, a perfect traffic system, industrial and residential towns that together constitute Democracity.*

That future city was a hard idea to fancy, I admitted, because most Americans were only familiar with cities and towns that stopped abruptly where the boondocks begin.

Claudius knit his brow together, trying to understand. "The outlands?"

I nodded. "Backcountry. We'll see our fair share of it as we drive west."

I think the boy was having trouble apprehending the sheer size of eight million acres, but I told him about it, anyway. The central concept of the show was, if we parcel that many acres at a time into 70 different towns, we *could* have farms, residential areas, industrial complexes, and sociopolitical centers coexisting in the mix.

"Will they do it?" Claudius suddenly asked. It took a moment before I realized he meant *us*—whether or not our American ingenuity would roll up its sleeves and ever create such a world in the future.

"It's a bit of a stretch, I think."

"It sounds lovely," he said.

I kept in mind the boy's own artistic streak as I framed my next response. The river of industrial capitalism and progress, I explained, could be ever as resistant to change as fiscal strategy in the Queen's Court. In severing ties with our mother country, Americans had in some ways erected institutions and attitudes equally as formidable, cities with factories and lives that never left those cities for anything better. Modernism and its rebellious attempts to revitalize the way we saw art, politics, and socioeconomics would certainly be cataclysmic on whatever soil it was employed, but it was doomed to remain a pipe dream for now. Riding in on the heels of the Great Depression seemed a good time to introduce change—and we had—but it remained doubtful this utopian dream would be met with enthusiasm by the workaday masses. As a member of the armed services, I couldn't seriously consider such a future with war looming, and Claudius understood this. America was still hanging onto neutrality, and the fair would continue for another season, but that kind of pricey restructuring was a dead duck in the face of financing the war machine needed to defeat Hitler.

If America joined The Allies, I wasn't so sure we'd ever get back around to it, I admitted. With an economy largely recuperating on orders for war materiel—many Americans remained loath to get mixed up in Europe's War. I didn't tell this to the boy (should he choose to come back to New York for a visit) or that some countries already under the Axis regime had pulled their pavilions early, or that while Mussolini's Italy was present with a 200-foot waterfall, Germany had refused to participate. Without a unified front in a world of parks, all bets were off

Falling Stars

about what might happen in ours.

Seventy miles west of New York City, Route 22 progressively winds and climbs along the Appalachian Trail into Easton, Pennsylvania. This stretch of William Penn Highway is known as ridge and valley—variegated terrain with rolling hills that surprisingly won't reach elevations much over 1,200 feet until Pittsburgh—but steep enough to fool you otherwise. For miles are nothing but wooded hillsides, largely swamp maple and sycamore, with dirt roads scatting off the two-lane sidewinder here and there. Even in September, the wildflower carpet is something to see. Purple cornflowers, masses of ribbed stalks and vines belonging to common fireweed, creeping spurge, pokeweed, mountain mint, and yarrow thickly populate the valleys. Popping up here and there along the hillsides are bright red rays of New England Asters and white crocus clover. Tossed in between the foliage are sedimentary folds of hikers' heaven where the Blue Ridge Mountains originally piled up into rocky faults of sandstone, clay, and shale.

We would continue on this backcountry two-laner well into the night, passing through Allentown, Harrisburg, Lewistown, and Mount Union before we connected up with Route 40 southwest of Pittsburgh. The sun was low in the sky as we approached Easton, and Claudius admitted he was just as hungry as I was. I suggested we find a fill-er-up and a café in town, eyes out for one that looked like it served steak.

Some say Easton lies strategically behind the Delaware River. On the east side of town is Bushkill bridge, a petit through-truss causeway far less the expanse of Pulaski—merely 1,020 feet—but equally necessary. This bridge was new, open a little over a year—four lanes braced and bracketed, pedestrian sidewalks on either side. Reinforced for heavy equipment, it was the only bridge over the Delaware that could transport such, in case New York was evacuated during the war. Pennsylvania has the largest German population per capita in the States —and I would find out later Nazi sympathizers had sized up Bushkill the following year around the same time two NYPD officers were killed investigating a time bomb planted at the World's Fair's British pavilion.

I was near the viscount's age when Pops and I made a couple of road trips to Pittsburgh for a pair of lasting machines wholesaling at cents on the dollar. Pops always had his ear to the ground for deals on used line equipment, and this was one of those trips. We'd stopped at the Seip Café in Easton on our way back to Jersey, a restaurant with an interesting history. From the 1890s it held a reputation for outstanding food and service, *the* place to top off an evening after theater at Abel Opera House. Through the years we went back several more times, until I enlisted in the Navy.

Seip Café had evolved from a popular oyster bar called Garren's, where lunch patrons stood at the counter with saltshakers and ate oysters *half on the shell* as quickly as they were opened or took out *twelve in a box*. Through a string of business mergers, marriages, and seventeen-hour days, Seip became the uptown Manhattan-style dining experience in a three-story limestone building decked to the nines with carved wainscoting, designer wallpaper, and white-linen tablecloths.

By the time electricity lit Easton, it boasted six dining rooms, two of them exclusively for ladies or gents—and had expanded its menu from oysters on the half-shell to include shad roe and dandelion salad, deviled crab, steaks, prime chops, clam chowder, hickory-smoked hams, and gourmet coffee. Locals probably still argue about what exactly happened, but I suspect Seip faltered like many among us during the financial upheavals leading into the Depression years and had closed.

Recently the restaurant had reopened with a gala that made Easton's front-page news. First and foremost, it still served steak—and fit for a noble, of which I was ad infinitum aware. When I recalled the menu, that was my choice. I pulled off the highway up to a pump at an Esso station we frequented whenever we came through these parts.

Today, a gas attendant much younger than the familiar old fellow who'd serviced us for years came out to greet us, reminding me once again how time flies. He was too young to be drafted, a perky little fellow who bobbed when he walked and wore a heavy starched station uniform a snatch too big for him. He was quite taken with the Packard and a mite curious about our cargo in back too—rustling around to the driver's side and stiffening to attention when he saw my uniform.

"Mighty fine evening," he said to us with a smile. "She's a real looker you got there, sir. Fill 'er up?"

"Yes, son." To keep things rolling, I thought it best not to clarify ownership at the moment—and I *did* need to change into my civvies. "Can the boy wait inside while I use the facilities?" I asked.

My guess was locals hadn't seen many Woodies like this one, and

Falling Stars

the attendant dragged his feet a bit, distracted by its novelty. Inside the terminal, he pulled out a metal stool for Claudius, where he was to wait for me. My heart did a flip-flop when I returned in four minutes on the dot and saw through the pane glass windows that he was no longer sitting there. I looked again. He was squatting in the corner, picking through the motor oils, coattail dusting the floor.

"She uses this one," he said, holding out a quart. I added two quarts to the tab, once again mystified by the boy's intelligence. Back at the car, the attendant had topped off the gas, checked the fluids under the hood, and aired up the tires. I put our purchase on the floorboard behind my seat and got in just about the time the attendant threw open the passenger door, Genuine Joe whisk broom and a little dustpan in his hand. Claudius glanced at me, uncertain.

"Swing your feet over this way, Viscount," I said, "Up here, on the driveshaft."

The attendant stiffened again, knowing *something* about the title, but not enough. He meticulously swept the floorboard a few minutes longer than necessary and bowed his way out. "At your service, Your Eminence."

Claudius shot a sideways grin at me. I had to purse my lips to keep from hooting.

Within minutes we were pulling up to Seip Café, located just off Route 22 on the town square and Third. Claudius was okay with parking the Woodie by the window near one of the front dining rooms where we could keep an eye on it.

We got a table on the first floor near it and settled in to order dinner. Our waitress, convinced I was in error when ordering the boy's cut blue-rare, politely corrected me to medium-rare. Seip had her uniformed in black formal attire along with the fellows, and she was exceptionally good at what she did.

No, he really wants bloody, I wanted to say. But of course, I didn't.

"Just barely seared," I offered, and leaned toward Claudius. "If they overcook it a smidgen, Viscount, you'll be okay with that?"

Soon afterward I decided I was pulling a brodie every time I called the boy by his title in public. Sure, I let it slip now and then, but as situations emerged, I quickly began to realize the longer he remained in this country and the less people knew about him, the better.

Either the waitress made it her business to figure it out, or someone in back cleared her up. She fawned over the viscount for the rest of our dinner and put our tab on the house. He dove into his steak with the same gusto he always had, earning whispers and stares from the upper crust patrons around the dining room.

"Let me cut that for you," I quickly suggested, sliding his plate over. He challenged me with an angry glance, and I made quick work of it, should he decide to make a spectacle and go for my arm in the process. From there on out, no matter how hungry he was, he made sure to cut up his dinner first.

For dessert he tried the mincemeat pie and talked between bites about the course of his treatment—scheduled to be completed within six weeks, he said. I caught on then why he believed he could return to Jersey by October. Considering what ailed him, it seemed a rather quick fix to me, but I assured him he'd always be very welcome, that Nonna intended to best him at cards even yet. Since my current beltline and upcoming military physical required me skip dessert, he confided that the pie was tasty, but not as good as Nonna's flan.

The silver interurban Liberty Bell line rumbled out of the square as we walked out of the restaurant, Claudius watching until it disappeared from view. He commented it was noisier than the ones in Cardiff, and I explained to him that some of the grades between Easton and Allentown put strain on their traction motors. This gave the ridership a diverse travel experience that included bursts of high speeds, numerous stops, and yes, the noise.

What he said next took the cake. "I can drive if you like," he said, explaining that his father had taught him *years ago* on their farm, that he had been driving back and forth to Cardiff on a near-daily basis since. I warned him that driving on the right side of the road could be a tad hinky although he was obviously accustomed to a left-sided driver. He didn't seem fazed at all, insisting he could see better at night, anyway. Route 22 to Harrisburg was a straight enough shot, so I consented. I'd have a couple of hours to evaluate him before taking back the wheel for the steep switchbacks from Harrisburg to Lewistown, I reasoned.

He had a special cushion he kept in the wayback to bolster him just high enough to see over the steering column, and with the bench seat pulled all the way forward, his feet barely reached the clutch and brake.

Falling Stars

In all fairness, he drove just fine. After a hiccup or two understanding the rotary and traffic signals in town, we were back on Route 22.

As of yet I wasn't totally comfortable with our arrangement, so I told him some more about the World's Fair to calm *me* down. In the Westinghouse Hall of Power was an example of something called an electric stairway or *escalator*, I explained, the same device used to transport us from the Trylon to the Perisphere. What packed the house more than anything was the robot, though—Electro the Westinghouse Moto-Man—a seven-foot automaton weighing over 265 pounds. He could speak about 700 words using a 78-rpm record player, smoke cigarettes, count on his fingers, and sweep his cubicle clean. He had a steel gear body and a motor skeleton covered in gold aluminum skin and photoelectric eyes that could distinguish red from green.

Claudius wanted to know exactly how the robot worked and I told him what I could. His walk, I admitted, was more like a shuffle on roller skates that produced a loud electronic hum. The Broadway-commissioned MC who introduced him stuck to an orchestrated script using commands into a telephone handset that followed three-one-two syllable patterns with stiff pauses between phrases.

"Will you come . . . down . . . front please?" I reenacted, demonstrating how the operator held the handset as a light flashed at Electro's midriff.

Claudius listened intently, never taking his eyes from the road.

I repeated what I could remember from the show. *I'll be very glad to tell my story. I am a smart fellow as I have a very fine brain of forty-eight electrical relays. It works like a telephone switchboard. If I get a wrong number, I can always blame the operator, thank you.*

Claudius giggled uncontrollably, the first I'd ever heard the boy laugh. I went on, telling more of Electro's bad jokes like *my brain is bigger than yours* until he was howling with laughter.

Somewhere between drawing castles in the clouds for the viscount about exhibits and shows I'd seen at the fair—GM's 36,000-foot model city of the '60s with double-decked streets, Billy Rose's aquacade swimming girls, a time capsule to remain buried and unopened until 6939 —I began sawing logs.

✯

I shuddered from sleep when I realized the Woodie was no longer moving, accessing all at once that we were idling on the grass shoulder, roadside. The viscount was studying the atlas, squinting against the sun's first rays. I sat up suddenly, and he yawned.

"I must—" I began, stopping short. We were on the west side of Cambridge, Ohio—where Route 22 feeds into 40. We'd blown past Harrisburg and the switchbacks up to Lewistown, Mt. Union, and Ebensburg. God, I thought, he'd somehow driven through Pittsburgh and over the state line into Ohio while I slept. I checked my watch, my flesh crawling.

That was—physically impossible.

"I suppose I might kip a bit now," he said. He did look sleepy to me.

"How the hell did you do that?" I demanded, unable to censor my fright.

"She's a good set of wheels," was all I could get out of him.

Under a shroud of turbine and steam they brooded past Ohio...

While Claudius curled up to sleep, I pulled into Frisbee's Gulf Station for more gas. The route from 22 to 40 was plainly marked and a whole lot less complicated than navigating Pittsburgh, so my guess was, the viscount had truly given up his place behind the wheel from exhaustion. We agreed to forgo the first of three squares in interest of making time, and I strongly suggested he use the facilities. My legs were stove-up from tight quarters while he'd driven, so I walked around the station yard while the attendant serviced the Woodie.

Cambridge was a small, yet affluent city located along the Factory Belt that had boomed out of humble beginnings as a railroad outpost. Since the late 1800s it had hustled retail and manufacturing establishments fueled by profits from mining coal, what Indians here had once called "rocks that burn." Four major railroad lines converge at a double track and loop at Union Station—*Central Ohio Railroad Company*, the *B&O Railroad, Cleveland and Marietta Railroad*, and *the Pennsylvania Railroad*. Teddy Roosevelt had stumped through on his presidential campaign trail here a couple of times. Known for its glass and baseball, Cambridge also happened to be one of the targets of Confederate General John Hunt Morgan's months-long *ride and raid 'em* through Guernsey County. After the Civil War when everybody got into baseball, Cambridge was home field to Casey's Colts, an aggregate of baseball players whose fame earned some of their team invitations to

Falling Stars

join the big leagues.

The leg from Cambridge to Indianapolis was a little under five hours, putting us on the outskirts of its Washington Street straight-shot after lunch rush. My stomach's steady rumble woke up the viscount, and he sat straight up, rubbing his eyes like any normal seven-year-old. In those moments I questioned the inconsistencies I'd already documented—no matter how strange.

Though not New York, Indy had its own Midwest traffic on a main commercial corridor that cut directly through the middle of the city. The most expedient use of our time, I knew, was lunch on Monument Circle. This would also give the viscount a chance to soak up some of the local flavor. I was almost sorry I hadn't been eyes-open for the trip through Pittsburgh. The boy had a way of observing the world around him that had convinced me already; he needed to live to see more of it.

Monument Circle is just that, a rotary in the center of Indiana's capital city that showcases the Soldiers and Sailors monument, a tribute to those who served in the Revolutionary War, the War of 1812, the Mexican War, the Civil War, the Frontier Wars, and the Spanish-American War. Although our country is young by comparison, I admitted to the inquisitive viscount that it *was* a lot of fighting for 250 years.

The tribute requires 330 steps to reach its base and is just fifteen feet shy of the Statue of Liberty. Primarily gray oolite limestone Indiana is known for, it includes sculptures of pre- and Civil War era governors Morton, Clark, Harrison, and Whitcomb. All around the monument are statuary groups and astragals, *War and Peace, The Dying Soldier, The Homefront*, with four corners dedicated to Infantry, Cavalry, Artillery, and Navy. On top is a female statue named Victory holding a sword in her right hand and a torch in her left.

"She's a lofty one, isn't she?" Claudius grinned at me.

"Yes siree," I summarized, "that just about says it all."

From Monument Circle, Claudius could see what makes up Hoosier extravaganza and why Indiana recently adopted the state motto *Crossroads of America*. If we went west on Market, we'd drive up to the front lawn of the Statehouse itself. On the north side of Market is the nine-story Traction Terminal that handles hundreds of trains per day. Directly across the street from the terminal is William H. Block's eight-story department store. The city had a fairly new fleet of buses, pulling up to stops at the circle's ten and four.

Spanning the entire northwest quadrant—which captured the viscount's attention—was the old English Hotel, all twelve stories magnificently Gothic Revival and Victorian inspired, 200 rooms built in one continuous curve around an opera house. Its large and distinctive balcony has been used as a bandstand, a popular location for political addresses and a good place for live updates on World Series games. Here some 50,000 Hoosiers packed shoulder-to-shoulder to hear FDR in October 1932, then on his campaign trail to the presidency. The hotel also has thirty-one stone medallions, each weighing around 250 pounds, a ribbon of portraits affixed above all the second-story windows. English, the owner and proprietor, displayed (and within his own right to do so) roughly half with his own family, the rest either governors or early settlers. The original transfer car location was located at the hotel's south end, but celebratory Hoosiers made quick work with an iconic snapshot—bunting and flag decorations included —of removing the entire platform in 1893 for the Grand Army of the Republic encampment parade.

Retail here was huge. From Meridian we could see Hook's Drugs, Russet Cafeteria, Florsheim Shoes, and Goldstein's. From Market I recognized Harry Levinson's Hattery and others, plus the rooftop of Joseph's Jewelry & Loan Co.—Indy's version of a flatiron wonder— thick and robust, bricked and mortared with neoclassical dentil patterns along the roofline, studded with floppy awnings, metal fire escapes, and multiple chimneys. The building was plastered with huge signs advertising everything from diamonds to sporting goods, overcoats for three dollars, and check cashing services. One sign even said Joe had money to *loan on anything under the sun*.

We circled the monument again and detoured two blocks north on Meridian to park. As we backtracked our way on foot, Claudius was drawn to a newsstand near Ohio Street. I bought a copy of today's *Indianapolis Star* straight from the bundle while he picked out some things for himself, postcards of the Knights of Pythias building, the Benjamin Harrison Home, Christian Schrader's turn-of-century art, plus a copy of Victor Green's *The Negro Motorist Green Book*.

We talked about his purchases while we walked back to Monument

Circle because he wanted to know everything I could muster on those subjects. The Knights of Pythias fraternal order, I explained, was one of a handful that didn't rebound over the Atlantic, founded instead in Washington, D.C. by a music composer. The viscount was familiar with secret fraternal organizations, he said, several in his own royal order having served as Freemasons.

The Knights of Pythias building shown on the postcard was another of the city's beefy flatirons, an ornate, eleven-story stone and terra-cotta sensation erected in 1907 at Pennsylvania and Massachusetts. At the time it was the second-largest flatiron in the nation next to yours truly in New York.

Indianapolis artist Christian Schrader began exhibiting his black-and-white sketches around 1912, a nimble stipple engraved style portraying everyday goings-on in the nineteenth century original mile square.

The Benjamin Harrison Home, a former residence of our twenty-third president, had sixteen rooms, a primarily Italianate architecture trimmed in red brick. Harrison built it on Delaware Street, starting a migration of wealthy landholders northward. It had bracketed cornices, a three-story bay window, oak-trimmed staircases, and parquet floors. The front porch with Greek ionic scrolled columns was added in 1896.

Not all U.S. presidents had such fancy homes, I mentioned. Millard Fillmore, Warren G. Harding, Abraham Lincoln, William Howard Taft, Herbert Hoover, and even our current president lived in simple homes. After FDR was treated in Warm Springs, Georgia for polio, he built a house there.

"That homestead is pine," I said. "One-story, six rooms."

As for Victor Green's *The Negro Motorist Green Book,* Claudius was familiar with the blight of segregation in his own country. Colonial imperialism had impacted seaports in Cardiff just as much as any other part of Nagy-Britannia, especially after people of color were brought over from Jamaica to fight in the First World War. Many settled in London when the fighting was over, only to enter into a different kind of skirmish when white soldiers returned and agreed the job market was glutted. Job shortages had initiated violence, and during 1919 (a few years before Claudius was born, he claimed), race riots in Glasgow, Liverpool, and Cardiff, injured hundreds and killed others.

I explained that Green's back-pocket liners were all about helping colored people navigate lunch counters, bus stations, schools, public restrooms—wherever *regulated and segregated* reigned supreme. It even helped them know where to drive, I said. This was one of the first copies that included locations in Indianapolis, details of consumer venues in the Hoosier capital. There were entries about restaurants, hotels, bars, and more—many of them located just north of us along Indiana Avenue. Indianapolis also had a large Black Republican voter constituent. Four-time Olympic gold medalist Jesse Owens and his wife Ruth had visited Indianapolis three years ago for one of their meetings, I mentioned.

Claudius then said—quite matter-of-factly, he did—that he wanted to study Green's guidebook and send home some suggestions. As I was equally curious about what drew his heart, we conversed rather freely concerning his own country's state of affairs and those worldwide. Despite the strangeness that came with his illness, I grew to admire his thoughts very much.

Wheeler's Lunch falls into a pattern of new super diners and is advantageously located on 8 West Market just off Monument Circle, a popular place for shoppers and politicians, since it's only a couple of blocks from the Statehouse. Starting with the bulb-lighted marquee over the entrance, the restaurant is built to impress—Streamline Deco Jazz and Moderne, what some call machine aesthetics—architecture focused on mass production, functional efficiency, and abstract design straight out of Bauhaus Art School in Germany. None of us wanted to admit the influence at the time, but we lived in a world that had just floundered out of the well-heeled Roaring Twenties into the grips of recessional austerity only to be rescued by industrialism fueled by war against the Germans.

Contemporary, clean and shiny, Wheeler's had many of the new architectural features I'd recently seen at the World's Fair, including chromed ribbing, smooth wall surfaces, ziggurat motifs, and intense colors composited into resin, alloy, and glass. The diner still had the vertical emphasis of Art Deco—twenty-foot ceilings supported by huge tubular columns.

Booths lined both sides of the building, and a long soda fountain bar ran front to back, the diner's centerpiece, offering the efficiency of showcasing mouth-watering temptations and providing a central kitchen in one. After taking our places at the bar and staring down two long menus, we both ordered rib-eyes, the usual specifications applied to the boy's. This wasn't as big of an ordeal here.

Someone had left a backdated copy of *The Indy Star* on the counter, front-page headlines "Germany's Airplanes Bomb Warsaw; Poland Charges Reich as Aggressor." I asked, and the waitress told me I could keep it. This was an important write-up for me, news I needed to study.

While I read the Hoosiers' take on the German aggression, Claudius drew on the back of our check with a pencil he'd borrowed from our waitress. This was the first time he'd sketched since we left the ship. Since he worked with such fierce concentration, I suspect even our best roads made drawing in the car impossible.

When I finished the article, I glanced over to see what he'd drawn, and my hair stood on end. He'd lickety-split replicated the Soldier's and Sailor's monument true to form—without once referring to it. I asked him if I could see the sketch for a moment and held it up toward the front window to compare, my skin crawling.

Every angle, light, and shadow, right on the money.

How did he do that?

He gave his little masterpiece to our waitress, who—just as doggoned about it as I was—made him sign it before she taped it up high on the glass display case.

Minutes later we were on the road again, navigating our way out of greater Indianapolis. We chatted about more notables in these parts, though I must confess the extent of my knowledge ends just south of St. Louis—making me in every respect a damn Yankee. In the Deep South, I admitted, Claudius was pretty much out there on his own. I didn't say this to frighten him, but to introduce the idea that he was always free to contact me with any questions or concerns—even if I couldn't answer them. He thanked me and pulled out his stack of postcards, shuffling them until he found the one he wanted to show me.

"I ken it'll be all right," he said quietly. "She's a glorious place, don't you think?" He held up a postcard for me to see the massive stone and red-topped Baker Hospital perched high on Eureka Springs' West Mountain (*nearly 2,000 feet above the sea, atop the Ozarks,* it read). Spilling down the bluff were equally Romanesque structures within the city, the hospital itself magnified and encircled with a graphic loupe, as if to say *yep, here she be.*

Once a fireproof luxury hotel called the Crescent, this grand villa sits at Eureka Spring's highest point, towering over the city, the Ozark's *castle in the sky.* Masonry, concentric Roman arches, and dormers contribute to her glory, features that have held fast since her grand opening in 1886. Its original construction cost was $294,000, part of that to outsource stonemasons from Ireland for fitting eighteen-inch stones from a quarry near Beaver without mortar.

Commissioned by Eureka Springs Improvement Company and The Frisco Railroad, the grand lady at one time was written up as America's most luxurious and opulently furnished hotel—one that features large, well-ventilated rooms and unmatched service. Midwest businessmen in the railroad industry saw the opportunities to cater to high-end clientèle and fill railroad seats, of course. In the day, Eureka Springs was hopeful, the *Eureka Springs Times Echo* hearkening the investment as *entering a new and exciting era.* City fathers expected the Crescent to attract notables, and it did—because everyone knew the reason the town existed in the first place was H_2O.

Water analyses performed in 1894 and 1925 in Carroll County summarized water samples from these springs as notably *pure, odorless, and low in solids.* The only remarkable levels at the time might've been the calcium carbonate concentration at 128 ppm in Magnetic Springs, but otherwise she was declared as *a table water of excellent quality for general use.* The U.S. Surgeon-General's report that the waters contained a certain amount of radio-activity was well-received as well. With more than fifty springs like her spuming healing water, the area and this hotel were visited by thousands of tourists in the late nineteenth century.

The old hotel fell out of favor with tourism in about ten years, though—with less traffic during the winters. It coasted for a while as a women's conservatory in the winter and what it was originally built for in the summer. During The Great Depression, it went belly-up.

An enterprising fellow from Muscatine, Iowa named Norman G. Baker had bought it for a song in 1937, his second run at a cure-for-cancer institution. City fathers were delighted when he made plans to turn it into a radio station, pharmacy, and sanatorium. He ran a national ad campaign that exceeded a million dollars, a piece of which the boy now held in his hand.

I couldn't help but notice that the postcard's ballyhoo seemed overcrowded with perks and draw—what I would later begin to call *Bakerisms*.

Where sick folks get well.
Cancer-tumor-curable without knife-radium-X-ray-serum.
Operated by Norman Baker Inc.
The Switzerland of America.

If this was somehow supposed to be confidence-inspiring about dropping off a sick boy in those Dixie hills, it wasn't.

Claudius put the postcard away, and I resumed my litany about Indianapolis—anything to ease my growing suspicions.

Washington Street was known as the National Road in those days, and on the west side of the city it ran alongside Military Park—the site of Indiana's first state fair in 1852, and later a Civil War encampment, Camp Sullivan. Today this piece of real estate was a long stretch of grass with a smattering of aptly placed historical markers. A little farther down, George Washington Park had been developed in 1929 for gentler days with baseball fields, croquet courts, and brick ovens. Local Boy Scout troops used that park for day hikes.

The Washington Street Bridge, a city attraction since 1916, features seven spans of closed-spandrel arches from white limestone pavers locally hewn. It crosses the White River and the Central Canal just south of the city's historic pumping station. Though Christian Schrader never sketched the National Road high bridge in its modern form, I always thought it a graceful and magnificent subject, and Claudius agreed.

I shared a bit about John Dillinger, who staged his largest ever bank robbery six years ago in Greencastle after his gang had terrorized the state following his escape from prison in Michigan City.

Here too, was the world-famous Indianapolis 500 that claimed Floyd Roberts's life during a spectacular pileup during lap 107 last year. Wilbur Shaw, still reeling from that loss one year later, had remarked when he won the Indy last May, "This is a screwy business, but I'll be back again next year."

The west side of Indianapolis is a mise-en-scène mixed bag, one that reminds me how far progress is from perfect. The way we tend our waterways is yet another thing, I believe, we'll be forced to rethink. As you cross over White River, you can see industrial shale piled along its banks. Also on the west side are abandoned factories like the Duesenberg, where Fred and his brothers developed some of the best racing engines in the world, ones that won three Indy 500 races, and once home to the Duesenberg Model J luxury car.

A more recent development here are the slums, commonly known as Curtisville Bottom, a slur after Vice President Charles Curtis, Hoover era. Like many cities during the Great Depression, Indianapolis has its own sprawl of shacks and huts covered with tar paper roofs—Hoovervilles, they're called—where the unemployed live along the southwest banks of the White River. The settlement runs three-quarters of a mile from Oliver Avenue up to Washington Street, not the best parting shot, and you want to make it a point to stay in your car. The viscount, if he was stirred by it, said nothing.

Go back, go back to Indiana . . .

We'd only gone fifty or so miles when Claudius offered to drive again, although it was still several hours before dark. I didn't need any shuteye just yet, but I thought it might give me a chance to get a better look at the newspapers, so I agreed to make the switch until we reached St. Louis.

I went back to the 1 September issue, curious about what else happened on this fateful day. From my own perspective we'd lost two lives on board. I'd met Viscount Claudius Fallon and received a year's wages from the British Consulate. Germany had invaded Poland. *What else?* I read about the new Indiana State Fairgrounds Coliseum, officially finished on the same date. Rifled through several pages toward the middle.

What was I scouting for?

There.

Buried in the neighborhood section I found a two-inch filler, a smear of yellow journalism whipped up by an enterprising reporter who'd ferreted out some news concerning the goings-on of Norman G. Baker, proprietor of a cancer hospital in the Ozarks. It seems Baker had once stamped through rural southern towns in Indiana working in machine shops, tool and die companies, later forming a vaudeville troupe for staging his own mental shows and a psychic named Madame Tangley. He'd founded K-TNT radio for his own personal diatribes and proxy summaries about the ills of aluminum cookware, radium, and X-ray. His anti-vax ranting during the bovine tuberculosis epidemic in these regions had garnered some attention, as well as his slurs against *belly-and-throat cutting medicos* in the fields of doctordom in general.

K-TNT was his advertising enterprise and the assigned acronym for *Know the Naked Truth*, of which he was convinced he knew it, the story said. He declared he could diagnose cancer from handwriting, made anti-Semitic remarks, and praised Hitler, all on K-TNT—a now defunct station after FCC charges for illegally boosting its signal to reach scores of Iowans from that high-wattage pulpit. The story went on to say that he had money on hand, and quite a lot of it, having spent some $50,000 renovating the Crescent Hotel. He'd moved all of his staff along with 140 patients from another hospital in Muscatine to Eureka Springs.

At the time, the news was merely sitting on a cusp of indecencies to be found, stories eventually reported in papers from Davenport to St. Louis and Huntsville to Austin. Baker would be written up in *The Daily Times, Mid-West Progressive, Iowa City Press Citizen, The Madison County Record, Fort Worth Star-Telegram,* and *Austin American-Statesman*—to name a few.

This was a developing story, one that newsrooms were sure to pick up and run—and toward the end of the month, they all did just that. Baker had received a federal court summons on 1 September 1939 for mail fraud. I spread the paper across my lap, doing my best to hide my alarm.

Good Lord.

Chapter Eight

Tommy, index finger suspended over his tablet, was about to launch out loud into the next section when June interrupted.

"Not a great place to stop, I know—but it's time to head over to Mom and Dad's," June said quietly. She'd just pulled the final batch of her super-easy cherry turnovers out of the oven (two packages of frozen puff pastry dough, two cans of cherry pie filling, four egg whites to seal the edges, twenty minutes at 375°). One well-tenderized round cut (marinated, salted, and pounded) for grilling to medium was already packed on ice on the contingency Tommy *would* turn up his nose at Lilly's deep-fried turducken, which wouldn't pass as red—no way, nohow.

Gaye's story was beginning to work on June. Until recently she'd held onto a version of history that Baker Hospital had treated very few, if any, children. What was surely in store for a young boy in the *Switzerland of America* left her feeling nauseated.

"Those smell good." Tommy digitally bookmarked his place.

June smiled, knowing how important cherry turnovers might weigh in when it came to managing a successful Thanksgiving lunch at her folks'. She'd hoped Tommy would continue on yesterday's normal streak, but this morning he'd come into the kitchen once again wearing his cape and clip-ons.

"Would you like some red icing?" She'd prepared for that as well.

Tommy nodded eagerly, back on his tablet, opening the Super Mario Run app, a couple of short courses he could double jump through while June finished up in the kitchen. She'd decorated the first half-dozen turnovers using a piping bag (zags not too unlike QRS complexes on an EKG) when Tommy suddenly looked up.

"How old do you think Claudius Fallon would be today?" he asked.

June had just popped a dollop of icing in her mouth for a try; it was

Falling Stars

surprisingly good. Factoring in the chronological age Gaye had attributed to Fallon, seven in 1939, June already had a number in her head—but she also saw Tommy working it out on his tablet's calculator. She washed the icing off her fingers and waited.

"Whoa. He'd be ninety-one," Tommy said.

June nodded. "Correct."

"Could he still be alive?"

"Yes, some people live past one hundred."

"Do you think he got well?"

A more difficult question to answer. June wanted to say *how very highly unlikely in the clutches of a monster like Baker*, but she didn't. She knew Walt would be happy to share his extensive library on the history of Eureka Springs and the Crescent Hotel, including its discreditable years as Baker Hospital. Tommy would inevitably discover all those things, wouldn't he? For the time being, however, she didn't want to rain on his parade—unless the story took a real dive. *I need to be reading ahead in* Philly's, *ahead of him.*

"Put that away for now and help me finish up," June said.

Thanksgiving at Lilly's in some ways always evolved into a competition to outdo the last one. Walt had all the fires going because the *snap* had arrived, as he called it, his weather vane *whipping in a nor'easter*. Tommy surrendered his bomber jacket but took a rapid step backward when Walt offered to take his cape.

"And just where's those peeps this morning, kiddo?" Walt teased, bending down to peer behind the clip-ons. June checked her dad's gaze with a look that said it all, *it's one of those days, Dad*, and Walt got it. He usually did. Lilly, on the other hand, might not be as easy.

A pumpkin collection pushing the borders of unmanageable dominated the house again this year. The familiar and oversized plaid one that reminded June of a giant pincushion was the dining table centerpiece. For the moment, Tommy seemed completely distracted by the decorations, even raising his clip-ons for a better look while he scooted through the house. In the living room, Lilly had a large selection of pearlized and ceramic lighted harvest pumpkins as well as delicate art glass ones in translucent oranges with pale green stems.

"Look, don't touch," June warned. Until yesterday, a connection to any environment apart from his tablet, casket, or revenant regalia hadn't interested Tommy. Stepping outside his wheelhouse, while an opportunity for personal expansion, could also become an opening for fallout, she knew. Try as she might to anticipate any missteps, June realized she ultimately could not dial into them all.

Tommy pointed at the pumpkin express train on top of Lilly's Shaker hutch. "That one's way cool."

June nodded, grateful Walt had put it up high.

And those were just for starters. An equally dowdy pumpkin scarecrow sat a little too close for comfort beside one of the hearths, and June made her first task to move it over a couple of feet. Thankfully, Tommy had returned to the front anteroom and plopped down in the center of the floor, trying to count the ones displayed there, mostly pumpkins made from galvanized metal and velvet. Those tumbled into the next room, a mixture of large Casper pumpkins and diminutive Jack-Be-Littles and Baby Boos. Then came Cinderella pumpkins with those rambling curlicue vines. Festive tiger-striped and sugar pumpkins (the latter, better suited for eating) were in apt proximity to the kitchen. And the grand pooh-bahs—those huge, twenty-plus-pound fairytale pumpkins traditional to the South of France with their heavily ribbed brown skins bejeweled any remaining free space. Tommy finished his tally in the anteroom, moving into the drawing room. Warty goblin pumpkins had caught his eye, and the urge to resist touching was palpable. June watched him linger for a moment before he sat down once more to count in this room. At Christmas, they'd do it all over again with Lilly's Teddy Bear collection.

Lilly had Walt haul out all these decorations yesterday, June was sure of it, while she'd spent the last twenty-four hours preparing way more food than any four humans could eat, a tradition handed down by her own family. June walked around the dining table and, after thirty-six years, she still admired it—though very little of it was red.

The only space left was a twenty-four-inch oval for the platter of deep-fried turducken, which Lilly refused to call by *that classless name*, she said. Food covered the ten-server table—candied *crème de la crumb* sweet potato casserole requiring five pounds of sweet potatoes, air fryer bacon-wrapped asparagus, frozen ambrosia with heavy cream and extra maraschinos, butter flake rolls, hot water cornbread, Cajun black-eyes, and Walt's pumpkin soup, always a little heavy on the pepper. Lilly had also baked a pecan pie with a sour cream crust, Amarillo carrot cake with insanely rich frosting, and cranberry orange cookies. Compared to everything else, June's tray of turnovers seemed paltry. No place for squeezing them in on the dining table, either. She offloaded a couple of turnovers onto Tommy's plate and put the tray on a sideboard nearby.

The spread was perfectly timed with their arrival—dishes precisely placed on the table while Walt carved the turducken straight from the oven. When he started pulling out his favorite countertop grill for the steak, Lilly jumped in.

"What's that for?"

"A little something for Tommy," Walt answered.

"It won't take long," June added, and reminded her dad under her breath that Tommy liked it medium.

"But I need you to finish carving the turkey and say grace," Lilly countered.

"Dad can go ahead and do that while it cooks," June interjected. "I'll watch the grill."

Without ever looking up, Walt waved off them both. "I got it, I got it. Turkey's as ready as it'll ever be. Why don't you take it to the table, Junebug?"

Ever the switchback and skate around Lilly, who didn't have an ounce of room for spontaneity, June fumed. Life was scripted, and anything else by her mother's playbook was rude.

Walt, who could be lightning efficient during such troubled times, had the grill going at a low sizzle and was seated for grace even before Tommy found his plate with the turnovers.

"Why don't you sit across from me instead, Tommy?" Lilly pointed to the empty plate across from her, the one normally reserved for June. Tommy, distracted by the pumpkin tally on his tablet, plopped down with oblivious compliance in the seat opposite Lilly. June quickly switched the plates, earning a scowl from her mom.

"You'll need to put that away while we say grace, Tommy," Lilly insisted.

Tommy stopped his calculations and glanced up at her. "Do you know you have two hundred seventy-three pumpkins in this house?"

"That sounds about right," Walt quipped.

Lilly pretended to act interested. "*My lands.* That many, really?"

Tommy nodded. "Thirty-one in the foyer. Sixty-six in the drawing room. Eighty-nine in the living room. Forty-two in the dining room. Twenty-seven in the kitchen, and eighteen on the stairwell."

Lilly blinked at Tommy, clearly not knowing what to say.

"From thirty-nine boxes in the attic." Walt added, stirring his tea.

"It comes with my condition." Tommy shrugged, showing Lilly his tablet. "Arithmomania. You see, I *must* count everything first and then categorize—"

"You need to remove all that, young man," Lilly interrupted.

Directives in lieu of trying to understand. June sighed.

Tommy shook his head. "No can do. I got a bad sunburn yesterday."

"The first I've heard about this, Tommy," June said. At the moment, she was more concerned about getting at the truth than casting off her mother's ire. He knew better than to feign illness or injury; that was an old rule.

"Even my eyeballs hurt."

"Nothing grace and a good meal won't fix," Walt offered.

"I thought he overdid it yesterday, myself—but nobody's asking me," Lilly added.

"No, we're not," Walt muttered.

"Just hang your cape over the back of your chair like we do in the restaurants," June instructed, an old trick that allowed Tommy to imagine he was still wearing it. He'd learned the bonus behind keeping his cape clean; a trip to the dry cleaners meant three days without. Tommy got the message, and that was all he needed to do as far as June was concerned—to neutralize an ailment that didn't exist. He took off his cape and clip-ons immediately.

"You mean—you let him wear that out in public?" Lilly scowled at Tommy, then June.

"It keeps him from getting sunburned," June shot back.

"And there's that," Walt said quietly. "Shall we pray?"

Walt's grace was short and expedient, and he was off to tend the steak. Lilly was up, too, whisking away Tommy's plate and shoveling a serving from each dish onto it. June could only watch in exasperation as her mother returned with a plate covered with all things *not red* and picked up Tommy's fork. Tommy had just conceded his two favorite possessions, but a single gesture of mitigated compliance was ultimately never enough for Lilly, was it?

"You need to try a bite of each thing," Lilly ordered. June held her breath as Tommy silently scowled at the plate she set in front of him. Dissatisfied with his response, Lilly made the mistake of squeezing his shoulder, and *oh-how to not see it coming,* June observed. She internally flinched as Tommy winced, bared his teeth, and growled at Lilly. For a split second against a backdrop of stunted November sunlight, his canines seemed even longer than usual. Lilly froze mid-air, fork in hand.

"That's quite enough, Tommy," June said quickly. "Go sit down, Mother."

Tommy bolted, his chair teetering after him.

Walt, steak in hand, caught the back of Tommy's chair in free-fall. Lilly hadn't budged an inch, her face screwed into a flabbergasted pout.

"I think that might be a good idea, Lilly," Walt said quietly. He slid the all things not red plate aside and replaced it with a single, medium-cooked steak.

And Lilly made sure to punctuate how deeply hurt she was by ever so gradually and meticulously placing Tommy's fork on that plate just so.

Damn it all to hell. Anger threatened to gush into recklessness before June caught herself with an internal fair warning to choose her words carefully. *Just take away this focus and give him something else instead.* Tommy had always responded better to casual suggestions when he was upset. June took a bite of turkey, making sure he could hear her utensils tap the plate, and called out to him. "Steak's ready."

After an eternal fifteen seconds and another bite of food that didn't claim any of her attention, Tommy wandered back into the dining room. He took his place at the table, carved up his meat into large hunks, and devoured it in gulps. Lilly held her tongue, but June caught every avoirdupois of her struggle. Walt introduced a new idea, the upcoming Christmas parade next Friday, *weather looks mighty fine for it and all,* the only topic that got a unanimous vote.

When Tommy was finished with the steak, he specifically requested two of June's turnovers on a fresh plate that hadn't received any cross-contamination by other food items, in those very words. June had to chock her lip to keep from laughing; she didn't dare check Lilly's reaction. Tommy finished *those* turnovers just as quickly, topping off his string of indiscretions by licking his fingers before asking to be excused from the table. He took his tablet and left the rest.

Once Lilly had determined Tommy was out of earshot, she dove into the deep end of that dilemma.

"You shouldn't coddle him so much," she began.

Walt gave June an uncomfortable glance. He wasn't going to step in, not yet.

June took a breath. "It's important that we don't derail his confidence at this time, Mother."

"While he runs ramshackle over everyone and everything around him?" Lilly shot back.

June paused to consider whether or not Tommy's behavior currently met the definition of *running ramshackle*—and just long enough to give Lilly a driving edge.

"That kind of behavior won't fly five minutes at St. Elizabeth's, and you know it," she persisted. "He has no manners to speak of, and he needs to learn what's acceptable—or he's in for a world of hurt."

His world is already lined with hurt, June wanted to say.

Lilly's face softened. "I realize he has special problems, honey."

"Yes, he does," June said.

"And none of this has anything to do with helping him get better." She made a sweeping gesture toward the regalia still at his chair—the cape, the clip-ons.

June leaned forward, eyes leveled on her mother, words hissing. "Don't you *ever* let him hear you say that."

"*Well, then*—I think I'll drive Tommy around town for a little bit, would that be all right?" Walt pushed back from the table. He swallowed, eyes on June. "Nothing strenuous."

June smiled at him. "He'd also enjoy looking at your library."

Walt glanced down the adjoining hallway. "I think he's already back there."

★

Mom wasn't kidding, Tommy observed. *Grandma can be a real diva hard-ass on some days, and Grandpa has one helluva library.* Some castaway pumpkins had found their way into that room—but all these were *really-really beaters*, either threadbare or chipped. Tommy cautiously picked them up one by one and examined them. *Nope*, Grandpa hadn't tried to fix them that he could see. It appeared he'd saved all the broken ones for himself, probably after Grandma asked him to store them away permanently or even trash them.

Walt seemed to have a way of doing that, stockpiling the unsalvageable. Tommy made sure he put the pumpkins back *tie-dee— exactly* the way he found them and signed in on his tablet. Since these broken pumpkins were once every bit as much a part of Lilly's collection, they needed to be recorded too. That brought the official house total to 278.

Tommy laid aside his tablet on an immense rolltop desk and began scanning the titles on Grandpa's bookshelves, dozens of books, all sizes, about Eureka Springs—pictorial histories, a book of postcards, *other days* and *hidden history* memoirs, pioneer tales, and books on area legends and lore that included ghost stories from the Crescent Hotel. A couple, *dead-up stanky*—and Tommy suspected they'd been locked away in a dark and creepy library somewhere before Grandpa bailed them out. Walt had a small section on Norman Baker too, and a paperback even subtitled *His Life Story*.

Moments later they were headed up Ellis Grade in Walt's Series II, yo-yoing along a winding two-lane highway that eventually connected up with Prospect Avenue where, as Grandpa explained, they'd drive by Crescent Park and down to St. Elizabeth of Hungary's rectory. They wouldn't tour the Crescent Hotel today, only a quick road trip to escape Lilly's *ring of fire*, as Walt put it.

Ellis Grade eventually ended exactly where he said it would (rear parking and the grand entrance to the Crescent Hotel merely a hundred or so feet down Prospect), but they yawed right instead and around the next corner at Crescent Drive, a steep slope downward toward the church. If it snowed again this year, Walt explained, the hotel's surrounding gardens (exactly like photos Tommy had of Tuileries Garden at the Louvre—*with more shade, he corrected himself*) was quite something to see, Walt went on, and then they were already halfway down the bottom of the hill. Even at Walt's irregular twenty miles an hour, it was all going by *way* too fast.

"Can we pull over?" Tommy asked.

"I think we might do even better than that," Walt said, and detoured into a parking space behind the church. From that vantage point, a five-foot limestone wall separated them from the historic Catholic rectory located some fifteen feet below the parking lot. The dome, *way cool,* wasn't transparent like the Tiffany one at Chicago Cultural Center, but it was special, Walt said, because St. Elizabeth's was the only church where parishioners entered *through* the freestanding bell tower outside. They talked for several minutes, comparing notes. Chicago's might be older, Walt agreed, and designed originally by Tiffany's mosaicist J. A. Holzer., but St. Elizabeth's was truly inspired by the Hagia Sophia in Istanbul, Turkey. Which made Tommy even happier, because this was old-world stuff straight from Europe and what once was Constantinople—the domain of druids and vampires—right in his own neighborhood.

Chicago Cultural Center was a happier memory, one before he got sick. Mom took him to see the Tiffany dome when he was five—with its 30,000 pieces of transparent glass shaped like fish scales, bound by ornate iron framing. The dome was huge—some thirty-eight feet in diameter—like looking up into a giant flying saucer, he remembered. His mom had explained that during a restoration in 2008, artisans discovered multiple red stained-glass panels that had been installed backward during a previous repair in the midthirties, not allowing the light to come through the way it now did. With the red-tipped ones cleaned, reversed, and restored by hand, he remembered the blinding light, even near sunset, and squinting so hard his head hurt. He was more interested in the twelve signs of the Zodiac top and center, anyway, and locating his, a June 7 Gemini, and his mom's, a January 7 Capricorn. June had pointed them out to him, but the dome was so huge, it was hard to follow her finger.

He'd always found it *way cool* how they shared the same day, and that both birth months started with the letter J, and his, his mom's very own name. Synchronicities he discovered like these, the way they often shared like-minded thoughts, made it harder to consider at times he was adopted. He didn't care much about it, anyhow—except when it recently became *yes-how-critical* for him to prove his lineage from vampires for medical reasons. They had yet to locate his biological father, though. Maybe that was the way it was supposed to be, mystery before truth. Mystery diverging toward truth, truth diverging toward the mysterious. *Gnarly.*

After they'd visited the Tiffany dome, Mom spun him around in a rolling laundry basket on the roof of her clinic, *the most kick-ass thing,* he remembered. Manufactured from commercial grade canvas and tubular steel frames, he'd imagine he was crawling into an escape pod instead of a laundry basket. She'd sneak it out of the supply room, line it with a fresh sheet, and in he'd go. As his pod launched with Coriolis force, Tommy watched the night sky's star canopy turn into one humongous gyroscopic spin high above him. June would check in with him and reverse directions frequently, but he never once asked her to stop, no matter how dizzy he got. Then she would lock the wheels, lie down on the roof beside his pod, and talk to him through the canvas about the stars she could identify.

"There's a magic here you won't find many other places," Walt suddenly said.

Tommy, deep in his own thoughts about the *super coolness* of viewing stars in a flat spin, wasn't prepared to respond. "It-it's very old around here for sure," he stammered, ashamed when he couldn't cough up something more intelligent off the cusp.

Walt didn't seem to notice. *Yeppers,* he went on, *the kinds of magic in these parts didn't come out of LA in cheap washed oak or the Costa Nova cottagecore nonsense you see these days.* He pointed toward the Crescent Hotel sprawling across the bluff some two hundred feet above the church. "There used to be a statue of St. Elizabeth of Hungary right up there somewhere too." He seemed a little unsure where exactly that was, but he explained she was the patron saint the church was named for.

Tommy didn't say anything about what he knew already, but he had the full goods on St. Elizabeth's, ever since Mom had shown him the school's new website. He'd also Googled Elizabeth's canonization to discover that, among the litany of stations, people, and plights she was sainted for—hospitals, homelessness, bakers, beggars, and widows— was the death of children. He'd never shared it with his mother and wondered if Walt knew.

Walt certainly seemed to know everything else. He pointed out the Stations of the Cross leading down from the freestanding bell tower, *not a bell in there anymore, it's gone digital.* All the statues around here were carved from Italian marble, he said. Then they were back onto specifics once again. Since Mom said his school started *erryday* at 7:30 a.m., Walt was fairly sure they'd assemble inside the dome at least once a week for children's mass in the church proper.

"Behind those big wooden doors in front," he said, "is a very special place. Do you understand?"

"I think so," Tommy murmured. "It has pink ceilings, marble floors, a ginormous chandelier . . . and *red* candles." He'd already decided the candles might make the rest more tolerable.

Walt chuckled. "That's the upshot of it." His smile slipped away as he studied Tommy's face. "If you respect each of those things, Tommy, the church will be a peaceful place for you."

A simple nod was the best Tommy could come up with there and then, for he wasn't about to touch on his little problems with crosses, mirrors, or holy water. Or the mosaic inlays that would challenge his arithmomania even on a good day.

Walt glanced out the window again. The sun was breaking through the clouds, just as bright or brighter than the day before. "Maybe we'll tour the grounds later this weekend?" He touched the skin on his own forearm. "Don't want to add insult to injury. Besides, I promised your momma we'd just cruise around a bit, you know?"

Tommy nodded. "Okay by me."

Walt made a fist. "Knuckle bump?"

Tommy grinned. He leaned across the console and gave his grandpa a solid one, and just far enough to see—around Walt's shoulder, past a couple of cars parked alongside—a chrome-plated Goddess of Speed hood ornament belonging to a 1937 army green Packard Six.

The hair stiffened on Tommy's neck. "Um—" he pointed. "How long has that been here?" He'd left his tablet back at the house, or he could've looked it up. Tommy was out of the car and several yards away before Walt managed to unhinge himself from his own seat.

"Hold up there, Tommy," he called after him, waggling his door shut. Tommy heard the car door half-click behind them. And there it

Falling Stars

was. Tommy quickly reexamined every word in *Philly's Argosy*, a story Walt didn't know about yet.

A 1937 Packard Station Wagon waited for us exactly where Fallon said it would be. Also known as a Woodie, this beaut was an eight-cylinder Six Series, model 115-C by Baker-Raulang, one of the original sixty with a wheelbase just that long, and a tight fit between the other coaches. It gleamed army green from ox yoke to windshield, with exquisitely inlaid varnished birch running the length of the wagon. Inside it had contrasting leather, a wood-grain dash, and a built-in radio trimmed in chrome.

Damn, he had the shakes. Tommy crossed his arms. *Be cool, be cool.*

Could it be?

"That's a thirty-seven, isn't it?" Tommy asked.

Walt nodded. "Correctomundo you are. One-fifteen C." He walked around the car with Tommy, studying the wagon intently.

The Woodie, waxed to the max, was in impeccable condition—as if it had rolled off the assembly line yesterday. Which left Tommy second-guessing how *that* could be.

"It's not a kit, is it?" he asked.

Walt stopped, both hands shoved into his pockets the way he did when he gave something a good looking over, like the first time he'd inspected Tommy's casket. "Nope," he answered. "This is the real done-deal."

"Have you seen it around here before?"

"I—have," Walt faltered, clearly struggling to call up the details. He shook his head. "And as best I can, I don't recall who owns it at the moment."

"But—somebody does," Tommy pressed. "Somebody who lives around here, right?"

"Yes, yes. I believe so," Walt mumbled, suddenly seeming impatient. "You know, we probably ought to be heading back now."

Tommy dawdled a bit, wishing he could look inside the Woodie. When it was clear Walt wasn't waiting around, he tagged after him toward their car.

The radio! He'd totally forgotten about it.

A built-in, trimmed in chrome.

Tommy broke away, ran back, and peered through the passenger window for anything he thought looked like an old AM radio—

No way—but there it . . . just like Gaye had described. One more tick down the list in vouching that this *was* Fallon's car. Which got Tommy thinking.

What was Fallon doing at the church? Could he even go inside? If he came back later this evening, was there a chance they'd meet?

Tommy turned away from the vintage car and scanned the grounds. Yes, there was shade all around, but he still had his doubts Fallon could tolerate sun for very long, even if Gaye hadn't really mentioned it in his story. Yes, he most likely drove after dark. Tommy also knew in his heart that if Fallon had survived, he was probably older than ninety-one. Which brought him to the inevitable question.

Just how far was the rectory from his house, anyway?

Mom had mentioned it was within walking distance, but he hadn't paid much attention at the time. He turned away and ran toward the Series II, where Walt was waiting quietly. "Hey, Grandpa, can I borrow your cell phone?"

Walt had stopped, several feet back from his SUV. "Didn't I shut that door?"

"Uh—yeah, I heard the click." Tommy followed Walt's gaze. The driver's door was wide open.

"Like I said." Walt squinted up into the trees, as if something had dropped down and done this. "Here, many things are possible."

Tommy walked around the Series II to check his own door, open a crack, just the way he'd left it. He raised his nose to the sky, no wind to speak of—and said nothing, not wanting to hoodoo any possibility of the mysterious among them but determined to get what he now needed. He could see Walt's cell phone on the dash.

"Borrow your cell phone a minute?" he asked again.

Walt had braced himself to scrutinize the overhead branches one more time by parking his right foot on the running board and his arm along the roof rail. "Yeah, sure," he finally said. "Let's head out."

Maps was pretty straightforward, one way to school from home—and the most direct way, a four-minute walk. Mom was right, this was going to be a cinch. Right on Fairmount, right on Prospect Avenue, right on Crescent Drive, down the hill. He could probably shave it down to a minute if he cut through the big-ass gully behind their house, but he'd have to climb the fence. He hadn't checked it out until now, but that ravine also ran behind the Purple Passion and the rest of the homes on that side of the street. Casey had probably hiked through it on her way to the bus stop a time or two, he decided. He could ask her.

Grandpa of course made a pitch-and-swing by their house for Tommy to get *a feel for the course of things,* he said. What Walt didn't know was, Tommy had already decided he *for sure* could sneak out to the rectory later this evening after the sun went down.

June's systematic way to de-stress after taxing clinical encounters and troubling family moments was *the brutal 60* on her Tonal home gym. While Tommy headed off to play video games in his casket, June powered on the AI-monitored flat-screen hanging on the north wall of her bedroom, a digital platform that would allow her to heave up to 200 pounds of dynamic weight in virtually every direction. Anybody who thought she got those guns naturally had a rethink coming. With quick cues on the touchscreen, she was soon sweating with an interactive monitor and mirror, but no live coaches, on-screen socialization, or HIIT classes today. She needed time to think, to hear only the metric hum of her own blood boil.

This Thanksgiving had unfortunately delivered an irritating string of incidentals that nevertheless required agonizing analysis through every curl and press, a slow burn in the belly of the muscle that coiled on command until it ached. Form and technique were more important on days when June felt required to question her life, and her gym allowed her to do so with a real-time guidance—an exacting range of motion on every lift, calculated pacing for concentric and eccentric, a digital spotter giving her a nice *final* edge-off when her arms or legs threatened to give way. Today's workout was a curated program, preset to one of her favorites, and particularly grueling for equally grueling thoughts.

Her mother, sans elocutionary intelligence at times, did have a point. June really needed to help Tommy reframe several of his ideas, starting soon. That kind of reset, she knew, wouldn't happen overnight. An even bigger part of all of the above was what Tommy currently accepted into his thought stream. At the risk of unhinging his imagination, June knew she must first prevail upon him to reconsider his fascination with Claudius Fallon. With progressing hemolysis and more aggressive treatment cycles, Tommy would soon have to come to terms with what was going on inside his body regardless of all the mental madstones he held onto.

And June's hour was up. Her on-screen stats announced she'd just set a new benchmark.

She grabbed a towel, flicked off corrosive and sweaty thoughts, and walked across the room toward her desk. She hadn't corrected Lilly a couple of days ago about her commuting schedule because it was a conflation beyond her mother's understanding, that a big part of her clinical experience and direction also happened right here in her own home.

June's transition into a collective clinic practice with higher e-visit demands called for an extra-large work surface with all the bells and whistles—a triple-bay black desktop outfitted with multiple USB ports, an ergonomic and virtual Bluetooth keyboard that projected onto each bay using a rotating laser camera and smartphone station, a holographic mouse, and three 32-inch touchscreen monitors daisy chained to each other. The center section had a stand-up desk option with an electric undercarriage. Although Tommy had mentioned she ought to buy a gaming chair, June preferred to shuttle between the three stations using a height-adjustable lab stool.

She listened a minute before signing in, the hum and drone of Tommy's casket at full tilt. Yes, she needed to handle this first. June opened up the search bar and purchased her own online subscription to *Philly's Argosy*, logged in, and began reading where they'd left off.

Per my usual when anything got my goat, I dialed into the Golden Age of ether, *the radio that roars in every home . . .*

The viscount, with his strange ways and means of sitting in silence for long periods of time, didn't seem to mind at all. After rolling through several stops of radio static, I found a station spewing classical gitbox, and quite good—for I was all nerves with nowhere to put it. An apex station straight out of Nashville, W4XA was one in a bundle experimenting with hi-fidelity shortwave AM independent from WSM Nashville. It didn't showcase *Grand Ole Opry*, but did its own thing instead, *solid hours of the world's greatest music* as advertised, purely classical. We were in luck, because, as it turns out, tuning into its frequency was a major limitation for many radio transceivers—though Gambill's Moto-Home had come out with *a small radio converter to pick up WX4A for $12.95*. What no one knew at the time was, midday solar radiation was extending W4XA's already experimental modulation, and it could be heard as far away as Australia. Although we were already experiencing superior sound quality, advancements in frequency modulation eventually determined *that* was the way to go, and all these shortwave stations transitioned to FM within two years.

Next came a piano classic, a waltz—which induced Claudius to reach over and turn up the volume. He nodded and smiled at me, his eyes lucent.

"Opus thirty-nine, number fifteen," he said.

My knowledge of classical composers had its limits. "Haydn?"

"Brahms."

We listened, the music's charm enabling me to gradually kiss off the hoo-ha I'd just read in the daily yap. Even years later I wondered if somehow the viscount was behind this too—especially given what happened soon afterward. *Could he—?*

We were well into the second refrain when Claudius added, "Anya and I, we danced to this."

I nodded, not wanting to interrupt the sweet, but very short waltz. The viscount explained that his sister had also known the piece on piano by heart. Shortly before Germans occupied Czechoslovakia, she'd requested their royal string quintet perform it while they attended an investiture of a knight commander.

"I think I should like it played at her exequy," he said.

So . . . I thought (following out the term more commonly used overseas), he's conceded. *He's accepted that she is indeed gone and there is no hope for her revival.* I also realized I had no further instructions regarding Agnetha's burial, that at the very least I'd need to arrange for a priest on short notice. Beyond a simple service graveside, I wasn't sure what I could guarantee the boy in this neck of the woods.

"It's a nice arrangement," I answered.

On the other side of St. Louis, we'd soon be heading into territory where the bottom dropped out, the Deep South. Merely one hundred fifty or so miles below the *show me* capital in the dead of last January's winter, more than fifteen hundred sharecroppers—men, women, children, young and old—all evicted from their homes, had organized one of the largest roadside sit-downs ever. Spanning miles of highway that converged in the bootheel of Missouri, blankets and sheets flapped around stick frames.

Protesters had unloaded corn shuck mattresses from their jalopies —cook stoves, wash tubs—the lot of what they needed to survive and made camp in the ditches. I'd seen the photographs. Into the horizon either direction stretched all manner of household items, articles normally found inside four walls: iron headboards, wood-burning stoves, quilts, sheets, rocking chairs, makeshift tables, pots and pans— whatever they could pile onto pickups and haulers. If their cars and trucks were running at the time, they'd parked them around the encampment to shield their loved ones from road debris and prevailing winds, but it was messy by design.

Their plight was a product of foul weather, falling crop prices, mechanization of cotton production, and New Deal agricultural policies. As the Great Depression had yawned on, landowners tried to save their own shirts by evicting tenant farmers and hiring day laborers instead. The protest in New Madrid County made an uproar in Washington and gained the immediate attention of First Lady Eleanor Roosevelt in her newspaper column, while FDR had declared the Great South a general disaster zone and put the secretary of agriculture to work on it.

All said, I was pretty sure we'd see remainders as we drove farther southwest, and Claudius would want to know about it. While he'd slept I'd switched Pop's sidearm from the overcoat to a paddle holster under my waistcoat. I didn't want to set the boy on edge, but I did point out the first vagrant sharecroppers we approached and instructed him to reduce his speed.

The viscount, as it turns out, was familiar with the dusters and black blizzards that decimated parts of Nebraska, Oklahoma, Texas, Kansas, New Mexico, and Colorado. For the young fellow he was, he saw the scope of things with amazing acuity—such as the contributory five-year drought and failing *everything* forcing tens of thousands of already poverty-stricken families to foreclose on their homes and migrate from the Dust Bowl—in the middle of a worldwide economic depression. By that time nearly sixteen million acres of land in the Texas and Oklahoma panhandles were dirt piles, *enough acreage for two Democracities, was that fair,* Claudius asked, and I had to admit, potentially one hundred forty cities and farms was aplenty, yes. What a better place the world could've been.

I saw many times how Claudius possessed a larger view; he'd already seen U.S. economic lechery on his own soil, witnessing now how impactful situations like black rollers in the Great Plains could dismantle farming communities—an entire nation—the world—in one way or another.

I made a point when we finished discussing the roadside demonstrations to draw his attention toward our efforts in putting the economy back together again.

The Works Progress Administration, I explained, was a federal program focusing on infrastructural improvements across the country and creating jobs—for example, those displaced farmers if they signed up. The Public Works Administration was a select group of private firms that received government funds for contracted projects.

In Missouri both relief organizations got busy with *All Things Twain*. The renowned author's name was assigned to a memorial bridge, a lighthouse, and a museum in Hannibal—an elementary school in Brentwood, and a handful of park improvements.

Many of the new bridges and road construction we'd already seen, including retaining walls and sandbagging, were also part of putting people back to work. When it came to ideas, the worker-bee ingenuity of the American way was seemingly inexhaustive. WPA and the numerous federal divisions that spawned from it, *alphabet soup agencies*, I explained, tackled a list of constructing or refurbishing virtually anything: courthouses and other municipal buildings, museums, state and national parks, schools and auditoriums, fairgrounds, cemeteries, armories, and public housing. Many of the murals and frescoes gracing the innards of almost any bureaucratic building were funded by PWA. Post offices across the country had gotten those by the hundreds, I explained, and Deco dabbers were still cranking them out. New post offices sprang up everywhere. We'd even developed programs to construct and maintain fish hatcheries, tree seeding, public swimming pools and bath houses, high school bleachers, opera houses, golf courses, fire lookout towers, and resettlement farms like the Osage in Pettis County.

Something in Brahms' compositional magic started it, I think. We were barely into our first hour of midafternoon conversation when, hell's bells, I was nodding off again.

⭒

Tommy took a graceless nosedive to the floor, *not* part of the plan or his original idea to bail out of his casket with it running *Rockin' A Thrilltown Donkey Rodeo,* a really *cool-o* video game simulation where players rode revenant donkeys side-saddle, the general strategy to stay strapped in and dodge sanguineous bites. He didn't want to use the door, because that would switch the unit into sleep mode, and he thought he had time to shimmy out during a reset—but the casket bucked into the next sequence already, the main housing's flange caught him by the ribs, and tossed him across the room.

... bussin' donkey balls, damn, that hurt ...

Tommy placed one hand over the spot on his chest and held it for a minute, not daring to move. He'd made a mess of a racket hitting the floor—and *shit-to-Shinola he was going to miss this chance to dip out, wasn't he?* He listened for footsteps. Two doors down he could hear his mom's Tonal blasting Brit Pop, *sounds like Spice Girls.*

He'd filled a pillowcase with all the candy they'd picked up in St. Louis and three pair of shoes, probably not quite sixty-one pounds, but heavy enough to keep the program running.

Flippin' yeah, it worked.

He watched the casket on autopilot and grinned through the pain, knowing this one would leave bruises for sure.

But it was working. Mom would never know he wasn't in there unless she heard him leave—and she wouldn't be finished with Tonal for another hour or more. He crawled to his feet, grabbed his cell phone, and carefully cracked open one of those great French doors. Snaked his way along the wall toward her room, listening.

... donkey balls, it hurts ...

... Tonal, Spice Girls, still cranking ...

Tommy forgot about his jacket as he shot out the front door and bounded down the porch steps just as the sun slipped behind the trees. He dodged a pothole in the road and didn't stop running until he turned

Falling Stars

onto Crescent Drive and had to bend over at last, wheezing a lot more than he should, he knew.

. . . donkey balls, it's cold . . .

He was nonstop shivering already, fully aware he needed to press on before darkness set in. He really didn't want to call attention using his cell phone's flashlight if his eyes could adjust to the dark like they usually did, and he didn't have that far to go.

Damn. From here he could see already that the Woodie was no longer there. Tommy went along several more yards and crossed the road to the fence line to make sure. He stopped, staring at the empty parking space.

I'll find you, revenant.

He'd see that old car again, *he had to.*

He took stock of his current condition, *only a dull womp now.* Tommy crossed his arms tightly over his chest to keep out the cold.

. . . donkey balls . . .

He turned to go home.

June had been reading for about five minutes when she noticed Tommy's casket sounded louder than usual. When she stepped out of her room, she immediately saw why. One of the double doors was open, so she went to the door, watched the casket pitch-and-whirl a few times, and decided on second thought not to interrupt. She still had a story to finish.

Dawn preferred eating out for Thanksgiving, and the Wenner tradition was the all-you-can-eat buffet at Myrtie Mae's. Casey was flat on her face in bed afterward, however—still wondering *how*, and maybe someday, *why*—she had stuffed her face with little remorse at the time. It was too close to that time of the month and now she was paying for it.

Casey was hands down on the brink of sinking into a full-blown pity fest when she looked out her room's one-and-only casement window and saw the weirdo, sicko kid who now lived next door galloping down the street, *yeah, he's definitely on the run*, a full-on ghosting. *Hmm.* She watched him ape walk around a pothole in front of their house. What a dork, she thought. But he's got some balls, sneaking out at night. *Maybe he isn't totally uncool, after all.*

Chapter Nine

I jerked upright from my catnap as the Woodie banked hard left. A quick scope of our situation assured me the boy had complete control of the vehicle—he'd just underestimated the degree of shoulder pitch steering off the highway catawampus in the dark. We'd shored up the Fisk with some equally elaborate staves Fallon had supplied in the hold, but a dull thud from something shifting in the wayback alerted me. The Woodie's headlamps dipped and bobbed over a gravel lot that spilled into a roadside duo, a full-service gas station and diner, cars and trucks parked around—always a good sign. Claudius deftly pulled the Woodie up to the pump and stopped.

Cripes, I'd slept for hours. By my watch it was near eight.

"Where are we?" I croaked.

Claudius found the location with his finger on the atlas lying between us. "Morrellton, it seems."

"Still in Missouri?"

"Aye, yes."

I opened the passenger door and saw by the dome light that we were already well past St. Louis, though—and once again ahead of schedule somehow by a couple of hours. I decided to give it a rest. Considering we'd driven past (for laying our hands on a blue-rare and dodging backwater hooligans) where I'd planned to be our last stop before Eureka, Claudius had done all right.

For the Morrellton pit stop was not without its consumer guarantees—among them *finest high premium gasoline or double-your-money back*. Also emblazoned across the front of the accompanying diner in uppercase letters was *STEAK DINNERS*.

"Well, look at that," I muttered.

Claudius flashed those canines my way, a grin hinting that he'd managed to see this one a mile away even after dark.

Falling Stars

The prices weren't too shabby, either—hyped-up barn ads on the front three of the diner selling rooms (somewhere) for fifteen cents, hamburgers for ten, hot dogs for five. Gasoline, nine cents a gallon.

Stick your brand names all over a signboard, Ma—

The service attendant here too, made eyes over the wagon—lickspittle and the rest, and suggested we park it near a light pole, back side of the station and visible from the diner *if we was stoppin' over, yowza*. I checked the Fisk in back, and minutes later we were seated in a booth by a window where I could keep an eye on things. This clapboard mess run was a cracker box build chocked up on cinder blocks with plank floors, plyboard booths, half-a-dozen stick tables and chairs, its north wall lined with newspapers—poor man's insulation.

We only had about nine or ten hours' driving time ahead, a task I was good for while the boy claimed some rest. While he finished off a steak that could pass as medium-rare, I tanked up on joe, enough to guarantee a trip to the pisser and eyes-open until we reached Eureka. I went ahead of Claudius to the pit latrine behind the diner and paid the check while he took his turn.

When the boy didn't return directly, I forced myself to give him a minute and accepted another refill on jamoke. I'd just walked back from the checkout counter to lay down a tip when I noticed the situation out front.

Firmly as coffee grips—and away!

What was this? Two, three rugged nogoodniks shooting the breeze on the other side of the Woodie, plenty soused and looking for trouble. Pointing, howling at the moon. One dangling a bottle of giggle water.

Claudius, halfway across the lot, headed straight toward them.

I hit the front door reaching for the piece under my coat. Those hoodlums were every bit my junior, but I knew they couldn't outrun a first-drawn bullet. Or at least, in the thick of things, that was my strategy. As it turns out, I didn't even make it to a full draw. They stumbled *goggle-eyed* backward in the general direction of an old pickup parked on the far side of the lot, piled in, and lead-footed it out of there.

They'd scoped out I was packing iron—or so I thought.

From the handful of trips visiting my old shipmate in Tennessee I'd picked up more tidbits besides his momma's sweet Southern patter. *No-*

goods in these backwoods parts, he'd warned, *they don't cop and run like the big boys in the city, no sirree—they'll stand their ground punch-drunk.*

I didn't question their quick retreat beyond being grateful, though —for just ahead of me Claudius had stopped, and I thought I saw a curious little adjustment of his shoulders. I was so jacked up by that point, I decided my eyes had fooled me once again.

"Viscount!" I caught up with him, and he turned.

Arc lamps have a funny way of buzzing on and off in general, a persistent hiss when rods need replacing—and this one did. By the weakened beam casting off into the shadows, it appeared to me the boy was not at himself, likely the ordeal had worn him through somehow. His forehead seemed larger, and as I helped him into the car, I thought I could see knotted veins just under the surface of the skin around his jawline and neck.

Beyond the lamp's dim flame . . .

I knew better than to dally on the chance those gadabouts wouldn't come back—and didn't take time then to examine him more closely, not until I was seated behind the steering column. By the dome light I could see my imaginings had once again gotten the better of me —the boy was simply winded from his exertion, and very pale. Once I'd put enough miles between us and Franklin County, I did what I could to set him straight.

"Viscount Fallon," I began, "you're aware it is my duty to deliver you safely?"

A pause. "I am."

"And you've seen I carry a firearm?"

"I have."

I didn't want to spook him, but he needed to be informed. I swallowed. "You must realize, son, that people may try to kill you in their ignorance."

He said something then that would've chilled my Christmas dinner for six to come, if it hadn't been so ridiculous. I never countered him about it, and I often wondered—since I had none of my own—if he was cracking wise in a flight of fancy the way children sometimes do.

"They can try," he said, "seeing I'm half gone so far."

The boy fell into a sound sleep after that, and I made good time going west on Route 66 to Springfield. From there our high-gear road reverted to dirt, the surfaces more level in sections here and there, where WPA remains in active status. We crossed the southern state line into Arkansas around 0300 hours and turned onto a progressively windy and steep-sided mule trail of a road that, while ever casting west, bends sure enough south, east, and north again toward the Missouri border several times—slowing our headway now and again to a crawl. We pulled into Eureka Springs at daybreak.

The town seat has some noteworthy Romanesque and colorful buildings—native limestone structures as well—but Main Street is dirt, and with hard times, several merchants are boarded up. The community, enclosed by craggy woodlands, has stick shacks built into the sides of the bluffs and sections along the outskirts where panners still pitch tents.

Baker Hospital, located on the north crest of West Mountain, is categorically on the lofty side of town, as Claudius had mentioned, the road here a steady climb and true test of one's carburetor. Constructed from massive stone masonry more common to European castles, the five-story structure literally crowns the town from all directions and provides an expansive overlook of green valleys below. I later learned that Isaac S. Taylor, the architect of the Union Station Hotel in St. Louis, had designed her. She was honestly as pretty as her picture, everything the boy's postcard had promised—complete with Roman arches and a red mansard roof.

For her grand opening in 1886, the hotel came furnished with the latest Edison lamps, electric bells, sewage system, and steam-generated heat. Contractors used native marble for the entry fireplace and local wood for her newels and balustrades. At one time, she had billiard rooms, a bowling alley, and tennis courts. As I understood it, Baker had taken her as she was, sidestepped the need for any recreation, and refurbished the interior in an Art Nouveau-Deco blend with the same colors you'd find in a Tijuana brothel.

Claudius and I got out of the Woodie, stretched a minute, and walked toward the lobby.

First impressions can be encouraging, like the carpeted entrance and the large, covered porch lined with chipper-looking patients in loungers—ones who apparently chose to spend the first hours of morning outside of their rooms. Some greeted us *howdy-do* and *g'mornin'* as we walked past.

Lavenders and salamander oranges aside, the grand lobby was just that—with all her velveteen, tapestry, elegantly carved woods, and delicate décor preserved from the previous century. The only hint of institutionalism was a nurse in a white-aproned uniform who came up to greet us.

"You must be Claudius," she said warmly, stooping to the boy's level. "Welcome to the Ozarks, Viscount." It sounded a smidge coached but helped me momentarily worry far less. She explained to us that his room was still being prepared, and in the meantime she would try to catch his assigned doctor before he started making morning rounds. I pulled her aside and told her about the viscountess.

She looked down, then back at me with a set smile reserved for these kinds of unfortunate circumstances. "I'll let the doctor know," she said. "He'll probably want to take a look at her too."

Earl J. Tassemon, I later found out, is an osteopathic physician, as are several on Baker's medical staff—doctors who more readily incorporate home remedies and pay particular attention to posture and the dynamics of movement. Just as the nurse had promised, she managed to find Dr. Tassemon on his way to the infirmary, and he soon came down the hall to greet us.

Tassemon walks with a cane—an old sawmill injury from his teens (he admits rather openly), one that doesn't slow him down much—*he's several steps ahead of us already in fact*, as we head out to the Woodie. He's about my age and a bit portly, a cue ball dressed in pomade, his Oxfords scritching as he goes. For here was Tassemon's first task, to officially pronounce the viscountess and declare nothing more could be done. When he saw her body had been stored in a Fisk, he stiffened a bit before fishing out a pair of cheaters to peer through the plated window. He opened the hinged outer face plate—and looked.

After the better of fifteen seconds, he straightened. "Viscount Fallon," he addressed the boy directly, "if I open this, her viscountess will no longer remain as unblemished and beauteous as she now is." He took the boy by the arm. "Come, look at her now."

I was a bit stumped by his informal bedside manner with the viscount, but Claudius seemed to have taken a shine to him. He stood quietly beside Tassemon and looked through the little face window with the same intensity I'd seen him do so many times already.

"It's a nicer way to recall her, don't you think?" Tassemon asked.

A single tear rolled down Claudius's face.

It occurred to me then that he'd expected his sister laid in some form of dormancy.

Commander Fallon had arranged for the boy to have private quarters on the second level. The rooms take on a more institutional feel, of course, everything tidy white—from the two hospital beds to a chest of drawers to the dressing screen in the corner. The only space he will share is an adjoining balcony with the room next door.

Claudius was scheduled to receive his first treatment after breakfast. Under Tassemon's purview (and a flourish of his pen on a note to the kitchen), we were permitted to have room service and a private dining experience on the balcony. I would soon come to realize why Tassemon had set us up this way, but at the time, Claudius was enjoying a blue round steak overlooking the Elysium of the Ozarks just outside his window. He'd even kicked off his shoes and socks for the affair, temps here averaging warmer and humid. As he dangled his feet off the balcony, I was reminded once again he was merely a boy.

"Anya fancies gardens like this one," he suddenly said.

As farewell's demeanor beckons well or ill . . .

I was unsure how to respond, because with each passing day he'd appeared more resolved to accept that his sister was gone. I decided to treat it as a slip of the tongue and agreed the grounds were landscaped well, or something innocuous like that. I saw no value in vexing the boy as he tried to settle in. His apprehension was growing by the minute, and he'd already asked if I'd remain in the room during his treatment. I said I would. He suggested I might stretch out for a spell, that I looked like I could use some sleep. I told him I first needed to arrange for a priest for his sister's service. He nodded, his gaze drifting downward.

"Is that a conch of thunder I hear?" he suddenly asked. I listened, unable to supply him with a ready answer to the question, for there wasn't a cloud in the sky.

Treatment for the various and sundry types of ailments that checked into Baker's ward were primarily injectables, and a lot of them. In those days we called them *hypos*, short for hypodermic, or a rapid delivery of liquids through a hollow, carbon steel needle into the skin. My own experience with the rapid delivery of a typhoid booster under the skin of my buttocks wasn't a pleasant one.

Although I later became familiar with other types of injections besides the old IM in the keister, I never liked the premise at all. I lived through intravenous ones for blood draws or *to go under* and afterward, drag around the old IV pole—the intra-arterial, a hateful alternative for some forms of chemotherapy, and the intrathecal, directly into the spine. The one with which I was about to become very familiar was something Tassemon discussed with me afterward, the possibility of administering an intradermal, or *just-under-the-dermis* injectable on the underside of the boy's forearm, where both skin and hair are sparse. A much smaller needle, he said, but nonetheless, a needle. And those hollow points were being used to rapidly force Baker's Formulas 4 and 5 into patients several hundred times a day.

Since the first injection used on an Irish lady in 1844, the *hypo* for the most part remains unchanged. Therefore, the dreaded *nurse will give you a hypo* and here she comes.

The doctors primarily gave the injections here, rotating sites as needed—in the upper back just under the shoulder blades, the fronts or backs of the shoulders, the abdomen, the lower thigh, and sometimes just outside the kneecap on smaller patients—not to forget the dobie favorite. Tassemon later confided that some of his peers referred to themselves as Baker's "Tommy Guns," considering the number of injections they administered on average.

Tassemon arrived shortly after 11:00 a.m. with two nurses, one pushing a medical cart, the second laying out the boy's mess kit—which amounted to a little stack of toiletries, towels, and a hospital gown.

The doctor, I think, was tuned into the need for efficiency over everything else, requesting his nurse attendant to pull the cart beside the dressing screen. The cart had a low rattle when she rolled it across the hardwood—spilling into a deeper rumble, the first audible peal of thunder since the boy had mentioned it over an hour ago. Outside, the sky had all of a sudden grown black.

"Pop-up thundershowers," Tassemon said to me. "We get them regular around here in autumn."

I'd just returned from arranging for a priest at the rectory down the hill and, unsure of what to do with myself, stood at ease by the door. Tassemon didn't ask me to step outside, and for that I was momentarily glad.

"No need to gown him for the first one," he instructed the nurses. And to Claudius, "Step behind the dressing screen here with me if you will, Viscount."

He talked quietly to Claudius during a cursory examination (I would find out later, for determining the best injection sites) and ordered a twenty-gauge needle.

"We'll start with two cc's subscapularis," I heard him say to the nurse. At that point, all four were behind the screen, the boy's shirt draped over the top. "I need more light," he added.

No dilly, I thought. *This room's grown dark as a mug of murk.*

The supply nurse stepped out briefly to switch on a bedside lamp, which didn't do a lot.

Formula 4, we all later found out, contained .18 of 1 percent hydrochloric acid, .03 percent salt, a trace of potassium phosphate, and the rest, water—all guaranteed to burn on entry in a very nasty way.

The boy, as was his constant, seemed to take it quietly—without a peep or even so much a whimper, and I feared they'd killed him already, or that he'd swooned. I'd just about decided the latter was more likely when Tassemon—*he's bailing out*—stumbled backward, fighting for a foothold—and the entire screen crashed to the floor not fifteen feet away from me. The screen pitched the medical cart as well, hurling an entire supply of formulas 4 and 5, ampoules rolling every direction. The stool they'd sat him on was splintered. The supply nurse was passed out on the floor, the attendant flattened in terror against the back wall. About that time, something very large flushed down from the ceiling.

And the viscount, now he comes out for a landing . . . here he comes, and what a great sight it is, a thrilling one, just marvelous, coming down out of the sky, pointed directly at me, the mooring mast—

I instinctively reached for my sidearm before I remembered I'd locked it inside the Woodie, *oh—*

He rides majestically toward me like some great, mighty bird . . .

The creature that dropped in front of me, however, was no longer nobility, the boy I'd transported halfway across the continent, the world

—for *oh, something far more terrible* . . . the thing coming at me *is it Claudius?* I gauged standing six feet upright in the boy's breeches, cuffs coiled up to its hocks, and through the dim I could just make out the face, indeed the boy's—hair still neatly pinned back in his favorite pigtail, but the masseters—far more pronounced, sharp cranial ridges running ears-to-mouth, skull bossing, and distended veins boring their way out of his skin . . .

The nurse attendant vomited.

The eyes made me at first question the rest, for they appeared quite ordinary, irises his usual black—until I realized that while the left focused dead ahead on me, the right rotated independently to monitor the doctor now crouched in the corner at his four o'clock. Perhaps the boy's cockeye could've somehow humored us all had he not blinked. When he did, I saw a second lid recoil across the sclera.

I'm gonna step aside where I cannot see . . . it's terrible, I'm gonna have to stop for a minute because I'm losing my voice . . .

I shrank back, the small of my spine ramming the doorknob, nowhere to go but the ground . . .

I took a knee, and while every last ounce of horse sense shouted at me not to do it, I extended my hand. My vision shifted and I saw the room.

Sweat beading on my forearms.

Tendrils of the nurse attendant's last meal pouring out of her nose.

Tassemon gripping the edge of the hospital bed.

I've dropped out the rope close enough to take hold of him, and it's starting to rain . . .

The storm was upon us, rain slamming the windows like wadcutters, water sluicing down the roofline in buckets, air charged with the next electric explosion. The affairs around the room weren't necessarily warm, safe, and dry, either: Tassemon, at the ready with his cane, for what good that will do—the nurses, useless—no one arriving to save us.

Then I notice a proboscis on each shoulder (*yet not proboscises*) for the boy no longer had any arms, his hands attached by the wrists somehow at the tops of his acromion processes, fingertips dangling— those same slender artificer's fingers *trilling, trilling* as he grew yet taller. He chittered then, the same peculiarity I first observed on ship—

canines flared, sawbill fangs now—*oh* . . .

Something dark cohered to the boy, and while I argued within my right mind he wore no shirt, he released—tightly cockled membranes of wet skin, *wings* . . .

And I—I've seen this overseas, yes—*where, though?*

Nycteris thebaica, the Egyptian slit-faced bat, unfurling. The beast before me, its hideous cousin.

That I could tell, he stood aright on his own legs, somewhat—

But the feet. *Oh.*

Rearward toes, smooth shapes of each calcaneus *facing me*, gnarled tarsometatarsals hooking the floorboards *behind him*. He bore his weight primarily on the left because the right one flopped abnormally outward, palsied.

And I would review his struggle in every adrenaline-fed and sickening attempt I witnessed in the next world war—creature or infantryman—to crawl, absent hindquarters, *oh, run, Jesus*—s*cramble falter scrabble falter run*—away from harm . . .

He limps in my direction.

I hear—panting.

It's me, I can't breathe.

And though the viscount's not generally right either way—I assume because of his condition, the bad blood that determines what's left in or out—he's changing still, mutating somehow around even these . . . disfigurements—

When his talons come in, he stops, face twisted in pain, and issues an ear-splitting shrill, misery that slices through my nasal passages. Tassemon grabs his well-oiled head in a pitiful attempt to arrest his own agony.

With the addition of talons, the boy's maimed foot abruptly stands aright, and he springs forward, sailing overhead onto the wall behind me. The downdraft knocks me over, on the floor.

Its mighty roaring, wings biting the air and throwing it back like a gale . . .

I simply don't have any strength left to move. A sulfurous and sickly-sweet odor, something battle-stations rank—

Going up, up, with him as he scales the ceiling, fifty or more glass ampoules rising off the floor. But not for long. Somewhere up there he

screeches again, and they fall . . .
That smell, it's coming from—
The ceiling's on fire.
Oh, get out of the way! It's burning and crashing! It's crashing terrible! Oh, get out of the way, please . . .
And the beast is crawling through it.
It's burning, bursting into flames, and it's falling on the mooring mast and all the folks agree that this is terrible . . . oh, the humanity and all the people screaming . . .

When June heard Tommy's casket switch to sleep mode, she stopped reading. *Unusual for him to go lights-out before curfew, but apparently, he is.* She digitally bookmarked her place and walked softly to his darkened room, where she could just make out the outline of a mound of blankets above the main flange, ambient autumn moonlight shimmering over the open lid. Tommy was fast asleep.

She backed out and gently closed the huge double door, for Gaye's story had her full attention at the moment, every page of its awfulness. She had to get back to it and ultimately make some tough decisions about how appropriate the material was for Tommy. For at some point, she might have to censor his reading, however dollars-to-cobwebs difficult. This wouldn't be the first time she'd had to store his tablet away—but June knew how resourceful Tommy could be. He'd discover a way around it, she knew. Her son was hooked on "Bad Blood," and what she really needed to do was find a way to convince him it was just a story.

I came to, in the hospital bed Claudius had offered me earlier that day, evening sunlight spilling into the room and Dr. Tassemon standing over me.

"There, now," he said, stalling me as I tried to sit. "Take it slow, sailor. You took quite a blow to the noddle."

Langston called them plonk migraines, and that's what it felt like.

Claudius was sitting outside on the veranda looking no worse for wear. I blinked at him in disbelief.

The doctor caught my dismay. He nodded and talked to me under his breath. "The boy's at himself again, or whatever he verily wasn't when that squall came through."

"Y-y—you saw it, as well?" was all I could manage.

"Let's just say I'll recommend we suspend his treatment for today and review. He doesn't like needles."

A visual sweep of the room told me everything was back as before, all tidied up, only the lingering odor of pine cleaner reminding me that anything untoward had ever happened here.

And—the ceiling, spotless.

"The fire—" I faltered.

Tassemon gave the boy a cursory glance and muttered, "I saw snakes up there, myself—and the attending nurse, faces of all the patients who ever wept in front of her, enough to tip anyone's teakettle."

He handed me a note with an address on it. "Meet me there after seven. I think we need to run this one up the flagpole."

☆

The address Tassemon had slipped me was downtown, so I decided to stretch my legs and head out on foot. Claudius took dinner in his room, and I did my best to reassure him we'd hatch a treatment solution. He was more anemic-looking than ever; this worried me. He also seemed saddened by the adequate distance I maintained following the morning's events.

The address took me to an old building with a speakeasy grill on the door, no surprise, since several businesses in this section—even once first-class hotels and stores—stood neglected or closed. I fished out the note to check the address.

I didn't have long to wonder, though—for here gimped Tassemon *chop-chop* around the corner. He'd traded his white lab coat for a full length "breakwater" raincoat.

"Officer Gaye." He shook my hand. "How fare you this evening?"

I assured him I'd recovered for the most part, and he rapped the door a couple of times with his cane. I overheard the husky Joe who admitted us, then the barkeep call the doctor Jax, *three unsanctified letters in the alphabet his momma had smeared him with*, he told me, therefore the middle name abridgment to J.

Somewhere in the telling I later found out he bore at least one name from his father and the other, from an old flame and prizefighter. Truth be it, I don't think he really liked either one. I ordered my usual hooch at the bar and noticed Tassemon stuck to ginger ale. He directed me toward a booth in the back of the establishment away from the billiards and nickel-in-the-slot, *a corner with my name on it*, he said.

He propped his cane on the end of the table before setting down his mocktail and easing into the bench with a stiffness not too unlike Nonna. I followed suit.

"About the boy," he said after we were seated. "He won't survive a week in the lopsided lap of this *power of mind over body* nonsense, you know."

His expression took in my shock. *Is that what this was? If true—why in God's thunder had Fallon agreed to send him here?* Tassemon was ready with an answer for that too. "I met the commander and his wife at the hospital briefly last spring. I think the endeavor is more about getting the viscount out of the country than curing him. Europe's going up in smoke, wouldn't you agree?"

As sure as I was headed back over there, yes, *yes it was.*

He looked down at his drink. "The formulas—they don't work."

Somebody's—nickel—stopped . . .

"You mean, for the viscount's exceptional condition—"

"For anyone." The doctor sipped his sugar ale. "We'll get back to that. Let's go over what happened in the room."

"Let's." I knocked back my own drink, feeling sickened by it all.

"I think the boy has a form of leukemia, but that obviously doesn't explain everything."

"No, it doesn't."

"My evaluation is he and his sister are dhampyres. Has he told you about this?"

"Some, yes."

"He's never turned on you?"

Those episodes . . . a quarter-dozen times on ship, and Morrellton. That's why they ran.

"Not entirely," I said. "Not like this morning."

"It harms him when he changes. If anything, that's what will kill him."

In my ire, I inadvertently lowered my mug with a vise grip, sloshing my ale a bit. *So noted.*

Tassemon did and stepped up the pace. "If I were flying solo, you see, I'd have referred the boy somewhere else from the beginning."

"But you're not."

"There's the bald horror and unbounded gall of it all," he said quietly. He stared into his ginger water a moment before proceeding to tell me how he got here. In better days, he said, he'd completed a certificate in biochemistry and toxicology in Minnesota, his osteopathic training in Missouri. Married a federal judge's daughter and Georgia débutante, started a *highfalutin* practice in Alpharetta until drinking became a problem. Divorcing his wife required half his earnings at a time when things became financially hard in general. He'd joined Baker's staff eight months ago, managed to stay sober for seven, and actually saved a little money.

"What's in the formula?" I asked. For we were back around to that.

He shrugged. "We all signed confidentiality agreements. Nobody knows. And I don't have the equipment to test it."

It seemed best, considering, not to hold any punches. "If you had said equipment, would you?"

Tassemon leaned forward and lowered his voice. "Oh, I can, and I will. Snaking it out, that's the trouble."

I think Tassemon knew things were off with the job from the start and had regarded himself as a plant inside a quack institution from day one. He saw right up front that he couldn't *air out anything* to the medical staff Baker had relocated from his first clinic in Muscatine. He'd been planning on leaving the hospital for a couple of months, the timing of his exit and procuring interim employment for bankrolling the ex-wife the larger issues. He had to play his cards right, *and not during a full moon*. Granted he wouldn't advise giving any of Baker's Formulas to Claudius—keeping up a ruse for six weeks while giving the boy something else wouldn't be a doddle, even as his assigned doctor.

The only other acceptable methods of administering Baker's Formulas were orally (Baker himself had downed an ampoule of Formula 5 during one of his mental shows) or intradermally, in smaller amounts delivered into the underside of the forearm. Tassemon believed his peers would report him for changing the viscount's treatment plan if they found out about it. And he'd tried the location best suited for hypersensitivity on Claudius already: his back.

"I can switch them out with sugar water administered orally and decline nurse assistance for two, three weeks—maybe longer," he said. "After this morning, I seriously doubt any of the staff will want to rotate in there with me, anyway."

Which set me on edge, knowing how quickly the rumor mill could destroy the boy's chances for a life here. "There's no way to keep a lid on this, is there?"

Tassemon sniggered. "Not to worry. We've all seen enough to shake the *aplomb* out of our tree already. I'll remind fellow staff that his viscount is a client of privilege, his affairs, confidential."

I breathed again. "Much obliged."

"It goes both ways." He shrugged. "The boy's survival could be a real feather in Baker's cap about right now."

All things considered, we'd arrived at a *most fortunate time*, he went on, because Baker was *snatched up in the hurly-burly* of preparing for his court date later this month. I told Tassemon a bit about the op-ed I'd seen in the *Indianapolis Star*. He wasn't taken aback in the least.

"That, and a whole lot more no-account from the same place." He sipped his sugar ale. "I don't even know where to start. If they arrest him, they'll go after the hospital."

"What will you do?"

"I'll agree to testify and pray to the high heavens I don't land in the big house with him."

"There's nothing here to cure the boy, then?"

Tassemon held up a finger. "Baker doesn't have it. But I might."

He was the only doctor on staff with a chemistry degree, the reason Baker assigned him Claudius in the first place, he said. And for the next fifteen minutes he watered down the boy's medical notes as much as he could, for he believed the viscount's illness had started with recessive genetic traits that, in his case, triggered spontaneous and unchecked genetic mutations, among them leukemia.

Tassemon's digression into the boy's sympathetic and parasympathetic response was lost on me, but he rounded out his explanation with a proposal to immediately start moonlighting trials incorporating Eureka's healing water and the blood of select animals (rabbits, wild pig), at which point I mentioned Claudius's stories about

Falling Stars

the Welsh ponies. He smiled at the claim, not from skepticism—but out of genuine admiration for Fallon's resourcefulness, I think, hand-over-maw as he considered where he might go about procuring such ponies in Arkansas.

I told Tassemon about the amount of reliance the boy placed on horses' blood keeping them alive, and the possibility that his sister might revive on the journey. At one point I asked Claudius how he'd know if she'd resurrected.

"I will smell her," he'd said.

My own experiences with necrotic flesh weren't pleasant. I was curious.

"Like the blood she at first consumed," the boy had answered.

Tassemon listened with interest. "I think you're onto something there."

Without getting too far ahead of my cummerbund, he explained, he expected *the most efficacious curative blood was*, as he put it, likely to be extracted from local marine life like primitive brine shrimp, a species unchanged since the Ordovician period. And while he shared some of the radio doctor's disdain for knives and radiation, he also mentioned the possibility of adding in an isotope that could be instrumental during radium therapy.

"You'll need funds for that," I said.

"And the commander's blessing," he added. "He'll need to approve the change."

"Maybe not," I countered.

Tassemon groaned. For *though I be one of Baker's dozen*, he'd quipped, he hung onto his own code of honor—which, I was about to learn, was all-important to him.

"Buddy, I'm six ways to Sunday behind the eight ball here already," he grumbled. "You've seen the crawl."

"Hear me out," I said.

And at the risk of showing my hand too early, I launched my idea, for I trusted Tassemon, and he was going to need a job. He was all Claudius had at the moment—besides returning to Jersey with me to die. I explained that Fallon had released funds to me for the boy's continued care, enough to get started. We'd keep the commander updated about his progress and petition for more money when necessary.

By the end of that conversation, we both were sweating and Tassemon signaled the barkeep to tick up the overhead fan.

"Another one?" He pointed at my dimple pint.

"I think I may," I said, and he ordered another round for me, temperance for himself. He fell quiet for a moment and studied his cane. "This—this isn't an old sawmill injury, you know," he mumbled.

Said the doctor I'd decided to trust. "That so?"

He shook his head. "Sawmill's a story I can go about my day with."

He went on to explain he'd been bitten while hunting pheasant by a swamp rattler as a young adult. Quick use of a venom suction cup had saved his life, but the muscle was gone. *It still gets to me,* and he readily admitted that the viscount had managed to tap into one of his greatest fears. While he saw a ceiling infested with massasauga pit vipers, I saw mine.

"Battle Stations twenty-one," I said. "Ship fires." Our drinks had arrived. "How does he do that?" I asked.

He slid his glass from one hand to the next, studying the suds. "The amygdala," he said.

I wasn't familiar. "Pardon?"

He leaned forward and spoke very quietly to me. "Primal responses. On the level, here—while we're all worried sick about the little baboon, I'm telling you, what he does is exceedingly primal and therein lies his power, power enough to claim us all."

I swallowed. "I never doubted it for a minute."

He sipped his mocktail. "I can write you an order for that if you want. Druggist is one block over."

And, after years of covering for the sinker, a part of me was relieved to have it out in the open. He took a pen out of his coat and with the same cursive flourish provided me with a prescription for henbane, *to help with your paroxysmal nervous and asthmatic condition.* I took it and thanked him.

"You probably should keep some secobarbital on hand for these kinds of things—but I'll let you work that out with your ship surgeon."

The previous spring, Commander Jules Fallon commissioned an above-ground companion crypt for his two children in a cemetery east of town, a local burial ground founded by the International Order of Odd Fellows. Much like the rest of the terrain surrounding Eureka Springs, the cemetery comes with a series of crests and dips, all shrouded by thick foliage.

Land originally owned by homesteaders, recorded burials here began after 1880. I was glad of it when the priest decided to ride along, for the acreage is ample for getting turned around—and he, also contacted by the commander, knew where their plots lay. I would've failed to find them easily also because they are a full plot and inscribed with the single identifier *Scurlock*—the boy's maternal maiden name, nothing else.

I polished my Cunard issue and boots to spit shine and donned the uniform once again for the service. Out of his travel chest, Claudius chose something equally formal—probably one of the suits he used for court dress, a black single-breasted coat with silk revers, waistcoat, black knee-breeches, silk stockings, and black shoes. Customary after 1908, he explained, he was allowed to wear an ordinary dress shirt with lace cuffs. For this occasion, the top hat and sword were omitted.

The priest had notified the grave digger for an extra set of hands to unload the Fisk and place it inside the crypt. Upon our arrival I noticed a couple of 1930 Ford Model AA work trucks parked around. I assumed rightly so at least one belonged to the digger. The other was a petrol peddler, a tank truck—except in place of the tank, something like a hurdy-gurdy with a maroon-colored veneer and fifteen or more glimmering pipes crowded into its casing.

I hadn't expected to meet Norman Baker; Tassemon didn't anticipate his return before the end of the week, and his daily driver I'm told was a white Cord. But here he was, the quintessential entrepreneur from the corn belt who'd discovered a natural ability at showmanship in his younger years and how to become the sole profiteer from it. He wore a respectfully dark pin-striped suit for the part albeit giving into a Tijuana lavender necktie. Still eye-candy for his audiences at a half century, Baker was white-haired, slim, and sharp-featured, eyes glistening for the next opportunity. He'd sniffed out this one and now greeted us with infectious enthusiasm, ready to offer his services. From what Tassemon had already told me, I put two and two together that the truck belonged to him—from a former gas station enterprise in

Muscatine, Iowa.

After paying his condolences, Baker volunteered to perform the Brahms' opus Claudius had wished for on the contraption aboard the tank truck. I found out later he'd invented the instrument himself, patented as a Calliaphone (an air-powered pipe organ) *its beautiful thunderous volume pleasing for attracting adorable atmospheric conditions,* the ads read, *tones that can be heard for a mile.* Baker had primed many of his Calliaphones to mechanically play a handful of vaudeville tunes from paper rolls that automatically rewound. These organs also could be played manually, as he was doing now, and to his credit, with some degree of skill.

Stop-look-listen.
Once heard, never forgotten.

And so the music man of Muscatine was heard for miles around Eureka Springs that day, although I'm not sure Brahms aficionados would've agreed upon the method of delivery, the acclaimed composer's classical waltz insulted by ear-splitting carny wheeze.

We met back at the hospital to complete the boy's paperwork a couple of hours later.

Baker's office is one that also blends the yesteryear of plush tapestry and veneer with a Deco six-sided desk, another Baker invention. From there he additionally operates an art correspondence school, a local radio spot, Tangley Calliaphone sales, a populist magazine, and a supply company.

The majority of the paperwork had already been completed by Fallon. My part was simply signing in good faith that the boy had been delivered to be treated. Tassemon said he didn't think Baker would try to bilk Fallon for more time like other patients, because the hospital could really use some timely favorable publicity. A six-week miracle cure of a royal figure would do just that. My orders were to store the Woodie in our factory until such time I would come back to retrieve the boy.

I couldn't shake the pit in my innards as I farewelled the viscount, particularly when he sidestepped my handshake and threw his arms around me. I took a knee and hugged him with all my heart.

Mind slugged to spittle, muttering in hell . . .

"Promise me, Claudius," I said, "that you will draw a little every day."

He did and agreed to post a letter or send a wire weekly. After this and a handful of other inculcations, I pointed the Woodie east toward four hundred orders of combat boots.

To be continued . . .

Chapter Ten

When Tommy heard June coming down the hallway, he put his tablet on standby and lay quietly in the dark until she left. He'd just about finished the November 20 issue of "Bad Blood," second pass. Mom really didn't like the scary stuff, he knew, so he lay wondering how he might skip those parts when he read out loud to her again. He really didn't want to have to wait until midnight Sunday for the next installment, either. And of course, with their discovery of *the* Woodie, he also wondered if it was asking too much to imagine Fallon alive and well somewhere nearby, even if Grandpa couldn't remember the owner. *Unless he'd sold the Packard to someone else.* He needed to find out. Tommy sighed.

With that came a *donkey balls* owie again because dark violet welts had raised within minutes. He'd inspected them in the bathroom mirror after the fact, *hell yay-uh* he'd hit the side of his casket *way* too hard. Tommy threw off the top covers and squirmed around, trying to find a comfortable position. He'd just missed hooking up with martha_whoosis—she'd been *on* during his trip to the rectory—she messaged, *try again next week?* And he answered *for sure, no biggie, something came up.*

He closed his eyes.

Sister of Mercy Madeline Nygard, the parish's new teacher, came with credentials and accolades a mile long. This, among other benefits implicit to St. Elizabeth of Hungary Catholic School, had settled matters for June when selecting a classroom environment that might work for her son.

Sister Madeline had made her first vows at the Benedictine Sisters of Scholastica Monastery in Chicago ten years ago. Degreed in archaeology and anthropology, she worked as a paleoethnobotanist in Armenia before returning the States to complete her M. Div. with an

Falling Stars

emphasis in special populations. She'd also served as an assistant campus minister for a parish school in Missouri before accepting the teaching position at Eureka Springs. When Tommy commented he thought someone who dug up bones for a living was *wicked*, June corrected him that Sister Madeline had chosen a subfield of anthropology, the study of behavioral and ecological interactions between protohistoric peoples and plants—that she'd probably spent much of her time analyzing pollen, charred seeds, and residues. More importantly, she was a new resident in this community—something they shared in common.

Since the 2023 fall semester had just introduced St. Elizabeth's elementary level for children with special needs, the principal arranged parent-teacher conferences for all incoming students before their first day of class. Tommy's was 9:00 a.m. Friday, so June settled on strawberry Pop-Tarts, something she knew Tommy would wolf down without a fuss. They'd just popped up in the toaster when he walked into the kitchen shade-less and cape-less, she noticed. He'd picked out a solid long-sleeve T and his favorite jeans—even better. *He did have his tablet—*

"You'll need a jacket," June said, the plate of toaster pastries in hand.

Tommy groaned and headed back to his room.

June munched on her own Pop-Tart, grateful for the once-in-a-blue moon *that's all I gave him to gripe about so far today.* They didn't have time to get into "Bad Blood" this morning, or the installment that left her lying awake last night. Later, she reminded herself. Always—*later,* cued up the old tapes to broadcast. For while she scolded herself for procrastinating anything, June instinctively grasped that the prerogative to set aside anything for *later*—even bones to pick—meant Tommy was still with her.

Mom was too busy adjusting the e-tron's seat heaters to notice he wasn't wearing a jacket, *chill by me*, Tommy thought. Shrugging on a shirt earlier was hard enough—*donkey balls, it hurt*, and he'd decided right then an extra layer would simply make things *way* more uncomfortable. They were already at the rectory before the heat got going and he wasn't really *that* cold, anyway. He tried leaving his bomber jacket in the footwell when they got out.

"Don't forget your jacket," June said. She was *way* busy fooling with her phone and didn't seem to notice how he dragged it along the sidewalk behind him, either. So he made it down past the twelve Stations of the Cross to the big front doors *no problemo*.

Sister Madeline was waiting for them at the entrance, ergo Mom now busy saying hello to her. He studied the situation from where he stood. She had more wrinkles around her eyes than Mom, and she wore something that looked like a habit, he was pretty sure—gray instead of black, a long navy-blue veil attached to a coif, white stockings, and running shoes. She had a rosary attached to her belt and a large silver cross hanging around her neck.

Tommy tried not to look at the cross, but it was super shiny, so he had to cock his head to one side and squint at the top of Sister Madeline's coif to take it out of his field of vision.

"What *are* you doing?" June said through her teeth. And a little louder, "Sister Madeline, this is Tommy." Mom pulled him along by the shoulder, which didn't feel too super-duper, either.

He shook Sister Madeline's hand and mumbled *hullo*, his gaze on the tips of her fuchsia athletic shoes.

"How about those kicks, Tommy?" she asked. Her giggle sounded like little bells.

"One tradition I disregard," she said to June. "Too many ankle injuries in the digs."

"I can imagine," June replied.

Before Tommy had a chance to ask Sister Madeline about her injuries, though, she ushered them inside the dome, *a very special place* Grandpa had called it—up to then seen only online, and it was ... *pink*. Or to be accurate, the arches and their intrados were pink. The ceiling was a nice dark blue with gold pointy stars all over it. And the big, gobby chandelier right in the middle, just like in the video. Super-slick marble you could sock skate on.

Yes-way too many crosses, the fancy budding kind just like the ones in the Vatican, he figured—everywhere. Life-size statues of holy people much bigger than he was in the vestibule and red candles, actually *gosh-more* things painted red than he'd planned on. A zillion doves monogrammed into yet another ginormous arch over an altar in the sanctuary with a jumbo-jet portrait of Jesus praying or maybe stargazing, he wasn't sure which. Too many pieces of stained glass to count. And angels *genuflecting* toward the podium, his new word of the week. This was going to take some work.

Sister Madeline walked them into the sanctuary and stopped, explaining that the students assembled in the *rotunda*, she called it— *every blasted day of the week* before heading to the classroom. Mass on Fridays.

"Classroom's this way," she said, and he noticed her running shoes squeaked *Middle C* like his when she walked back outside. They'd converted the priest's carport into a *study hall* just for this class last summer, she went on. In one of the six tablet armchair desks set out in two rows Tommy saw a rather thick orientation packet. The classroom didn't have any windows, *good thing for a vampire, newsflash*, and it looked like a long list of rules and regs Mom needed to hear about. He tried to very politely and not-so-weirdly ask if he might go outside.

"Put on your jacket," June said. He put one arm in and backed away, stepwise, really surprised by Mom being all fine with it—and then Sister Madeline suggested he pick out a favorite saint on the grounds to tell her about when he came back, and he was *outta there*, headed for the church parking lot, on the lookout for the Woodie. He tossed his jacket on top of the e-tron and looked up and down the parking lot.

Not here, not yet.

Tommy decided the best way to surely jinx ever seeing the Woodie again was scoping *yes-way* too much. He'd have a look around, maybe find a statue along the way for Sister Madeline. He stood inside the rectory's freestanding bell tower with no bell, the one that straddled the main sidewalk—for maybe a minute. Of course the statue in there was Saint Elizabeth of Hungary herself, *no-duh,* and then he noticed the great pile-on of moolah shining up at him from the church gift shop's wishing roof (*he'd get to that later*) because he *then* spied *another* garden down the hill a ways, farther out from the hotel's park and church proper.

He hadn't gone *that* far—scaling a *way-high* embankment along the road *up three, down two*, when he decided to check out how difficult the *way up there* was for hiking (in the event he'd ever need to take a shortcut to anywhere), and up he went. Crawling under the bushes was probably a better option, looked like, which meant he'd need to clean up some before he went back down to the church, *for sure,* he was thinking—when he saw it—*over there*—a little cave whatsit in the hillside, *cool beans, yuppers*—*a grotto?* Except as he squeezed his way through the creepers, he saw this was much bigger and barred up with a deadbolt, *not a tourist thingy,* no historical marker or any special name for it like the rest of the stuff on the church grounds, just an old, *bunged-up* POSTED sign nailed on a tree.

And Tommy wondered *why that was,* especially if this was a natural spring or *maybe even a parish catacomb*—could be, right? He knew he needed to get back to the church, though. *Check it out later, not that far from my house, no prob.*

When he returned, Sister Madeline and Mom were standing in the parking lot—*ruh-roh*—*not as many rules and regs as he'd originally thought,* and there was no hiding he'd been *MIA,* Mom giving him *the look*—so he decided to run with it.

"Does the church have a catacomb nearby?" he asked Sister Madeline, a question he thought might score with her since he suspected she really once dug up bones for a living. And she was smiling, he noticed, when she shaded her eyes and looked down the road.

"Excellent question, Tommy," she replied. "Did you find a cemetery?"

He figured as much, Sister Madeline checking to see if he knew the difference. Tommy shook his head. "No, a catacomb."

"You mean a tunnel?"

"A burial vault."

Sister Madeline wasn't smiling anymore. "For real?"

"Yep. Right over there." He pointed.

She followed his finger with her line of sight. "Eureka does have a number of grottos—"

"That's private property, Tommy," Mom interrupted.

But while he had Sister Madeline *woke,* he didn't want to lose the opportunity. "It's not part of the church?" he asked innocently.

Sister Madeline shook her head. "I think your mom's right." The only *burial vault* she knew about was the *rotunda* itself, she said, *without a body of course,* erected by Richard Kerens in memory of his deceased mother Elizabeth in 1908, a columbarium added on the grounds later. Kerens had left on business and farewelled his mother right on the very spot where the bell tower stood, she said—then a stairway leading down the steep hillside into town—and Elizabeth Kerens had passed away while he was absent. She went on with her little history lesson *blah-blah* about the bell tower being constructed a year later and dedicated along with the memorial chapel to St. Elizabeth of Hungary.

"Which is my *fav*," Tommy said, trying to *keep it righteous with the teach, no slackin'*. "Saint Elizabeth's in there."

"That's right, Tommy," Sister Madeline said, her laughter sounding like little bells again. He glanced over at his mom, knowing she couldn't be *that* upset with him, not really.

★

Callan Masters formally put down roots in Eureka Springs four months after World War II ended, in December, with two purchases—a storefront space on Cushing from the city and then-land parcel number 915 from the county.

In 1945, parcel 915 was little more than a wooded ridge overlooking Crescent Drive, a half-acre tract with a once-active, seasonal seepage spring. That one had dried up from overuse with increased municipal and industrial demands during early settlement days, years before Callan arrived. Any ground water once weeping from the rock basin on parcel 915 officially stopped in 1905 when county authorities decided to blow the cavity using dynamite. The resulting fifteen-by-twenty-foot cave was incorporated into the county's jail system the following year and held a record as unbreachable—since the bedrock, as is much of Arkansas, is cherty limestone, dolomite, and quartz.

From the turn of the century until sometime before Callan bought it, the sheriff's department used the cave as a quarantine jail for sick prisoners during outbreaks of encephalitis, influenza, and polio.

The entrance had a single jail gate with a deadbolt, just large enough for one person to pass through without difficulty. Inside, the area was excavated like a coal mine, natural partitions dividing the space into two cells. The interior was left unfinished, riprap and exposed jags from the discharges functioning as the primary wall and floor structure within each hold. An ample amount of drain holes were blasted along the hillside for air, several of them plugged with turf over time.

The interior could be expressly damp during rainy seasons, not so much a concern about prisoners past, those dismissed to live and die where they lay on straw mattresses—but for Callan's art, a problem. He remedied that using a similar construct he'd observed in the Fisk—two racks of custom-built metal storage cases much like museum archive boxes, and an equally solid one for his paints.

While his studio in town *could* burn, this space was naturally fireproof, temperature-tolerant nine out of twelve months, and secure—*the* location where Callan went off-grid to paint for many, many years. The jail cells provided an extra level of security for the artwork he kept padlocked inside them when absent.

He did have a Wi-Fi hotspot he brought along with his tablet, though—for ease of communication, sales, and networking. Callan painted in the rear block, the one with the least available natural light, and found over time it kept his art on point. On overcast nights he often set out a kerosene camping lamp a few feet away from the three-legged stool where he sat to paint. He'd purchased a tall one from a local shop in '46 with custom-turned cherry stretchers and a hand-carved tractor seat for long hours. He kept a metal Bishop easel set up most of the time, an elegant nouveau piece with filigree and florals.

Everything Callan owned fell within a two-mile radius, for he walked much of the time, even after Gaye finally delivered the Woodie in the autumn of 1945. By then he'd lodged on Spring Street for five years, a shack he'd originally let upon being discharged from Tassemon's care, when squatting in Basin Park Hotel was no longer an option. Those were tenuous times.

He didn't think about it much anymore, at least not until he came upon the "Bad Blood" series. Even in summary, it brought back too much. The next installment went live at midnight tonight, and he dreaded what Gaye—Cochran, *damn him, the dickhead nephew, that's who*—would write next. But he didn't have long to worry about that, for he'd just picked up a smell some thirty feet down the trailhead as he stumped along in the dark toward his cave after dinner.

The kid—

He won't remember it, not in a month of Sundays, Callan reassured himself. For he had long since sealed the area with his talisman, his memory charm—over the years having relatively little problems with trespassers. He supposed the sickly one and his fetching adoptive mother could be visiting family for the holiday—*where was it on the first?* Yes, *Sheffield Dairy*...

They might be staying at a nearby B&B, he supposed, a bit of sightseeing before heading back to their lives elsewhere. Which suited him just fine.

Something about the odor unnerved him, though, more than he cared to admit. He closed the jail gate behind him and tried to remember. *What was it?*

As he sat with his 3/8" flat brush primed to overpaint, he realized.

Phenol.

His windpipe closed suddenly. Callan leaned forward and coughed to clear his throat. *The kid smelled like them all, he did*—those unfortunate souls subjected to Formula 5 so many years ago. At Baker's appellate hearing, prosecutors presented evidence that the standard injection contained 28.4 percent carbolic acid. When Baker couldn't mentalize or shame the malignant tumors out of his patients, he shot them up with poison, took their life savings, and looked the other direction. Even after ninety-four years Callan still ground his molars in anger.

But more importantly—how could a kid be smelling that way *today?*

His nostrils flared for another whiff, the odor scattering, almost gone.

That's what it was, all the same.

He frowned at this thing he had little recourse to deal with. The fated prisoners left in the cave to die were a far easier matter to settle, for with that difficulty, he knew exactly what he must do. He'd swept out any remaining straw, pressure-washed the walls, performed clearing rituals from his mother's gramarye, and burned sage for a week before he began exorcising any remaining wraiths from the property. One in particular he'd hated to part with was a fellow who went by *Alonzo*, a real cut-up who'd hung around to meet his *bambini* due sometime that spring. When he'd figured out he could pass through the bars, he'd mess around by distending his belly and pretending to get stuck. On the longer nights, Callan didn't mind the entertainment.

And they had laughter to spare sudden tears . . .

Yes, he thought, I could use a good joke about now, and preferably one that's not on me. For a holiday, Friday store traffic had remained steady until midafternoon, when he agreed with a neighboring merchant that closing up shop early in the face of a pending Saturday rush was the right thing to do. He'd eaten leftovers at home, pulled out his Harding University sweats and runners, and broken with all manner of custom this evening. In some ways that set him sideways just as much as the kid's smell, his attractive mother, or his own secret life smeared all over social media. *Damn*, it'd been a long time since anyone or anything had pushed his buttons. He tugged his sweatshirt sleeves past his forearms and went to work. *Slacks and saddle Oxfords tomorrow morning,* he reminded himself. He needed to put this behind him.

Some things were easier to unsee than others. One of—if not *the* reason he remained cautious about any social entanglements, especially now.

Callan had owned the gallery twelve years before he allowed himself to fall in love, the first and only. She was sixteen, a twelfth-generation Angolan-American with flawless sacatra skin, a housekeeper for one of the hotels. Biologically he didn't appear a day older than she, even if his naturalization papers said differently.

Her name was Milja, and their first pillow talk brought with it her tearful admission she couldn't bear children. Piggybacking on an emergency appendectomy was Arkansas' sterilization policy, and her stepfather had signed away her rights to conceive when she was ten without knowing what he was doing. Milja therefore became one of the last targets of the declining eugenics program, one of twenty-seven state projects that legalized sterilization of inferior peoples—immigrants, Blacks, indigenous, poor Whites, and disabled—those a society soaring into a postwar economic boom thought it couldn't afford.

He loathed her fate. Yet he never could bring himself to express how inwardly relieved he was not to propagate his own illness.

And so he once traced the visionary company of love . . .

She was brilliant, and he taught her Cornish, which she read and spoke with ease. During their short decade together, he helped her obtain her secondary diploma and apply for senior college programs.

They could not marry. Arkansas was one of sixteen states that wouldn't repeal its anti-miscegenation laws until the bitter end, in 1967. She maintained a separate residence. Her siblings scattered, residing mostly in Louisiana, not much to do with her after they found out she was *consorting with a whitey,* no.

After Milja received an acceptance letter to Harding University in Searcy, she didn't come back to Eureka Springs anymore. She refused money whenever Callan offered, insisting on working off her room and board near campus. When he was on the road with painting assignments, he'd visit her every chance he could.

Harding University had only just integrated three semesters before Milja arrived, she and a handful of other Negro undergraduates. The campus climate, as he recalled, didn't splash any headlines, or echo the country's current themes of segregationist pushback or social unrest. The calm among the common folk at times, he remembered, was equally if not more insidious—unmistakable airs of hostile public indifference. He could feel it hanging around them especially when they were in the city.

Milja's entrance into a recently desegregated, small-town college during the high-water mark of the civil rights movement wasn't Callan's first choice. He worried about her constantly during the demonstrations, the sit-downs, the escalating efforts to kill Jim Crow.

Promise me, Milja, he begged her one evening. *Don't march, don't protest. Study hard, finish your degree, and that will make all the difference.* He knew then she didn't believe him even as he implored her.

We will wear you down by our capacity to suffer.

The arduous fight to establish solidarity in schools, theaters, restaurants, hotels, streetcars, buses, cemeteries, parks—virtually every kind of public facility—was *a too-long time* and *a too-long a-coming.* Even the Southern Christian Leadership Conference's systematically planned, peaceful marches initiated from pulpits across America had incited more radical race riots in the urban ghettos and a much larger so-called Negro revolution than anticipated.

Regardless, Callan planned to surprise Milja with dinner and *the* question a semester before she graduated. She was running late, still on campus, so he sketched on a small pocket pad he reserved for such times while waiting in the foyer of her boarding house. When she'd finally arrived, he saw immediately something was dreadfully wrong.

They killed him, Callan—oh, they shot him in Memphis! And Milja never got past it. Then twenty-four, she'd become increasingly aware the boy she'd fallen for remained not a day past eighteen and, that difficulty alone separated them more than any caste, race, or station in life—more than all the violence or death of Blacks and Whites combined, or the assassination of the civil rights leader himself.

He would never grow old with her, and she clearly knew they would never travel time in the same way. So she persuaded him to use the talisman he'd recently minted that hung about his neck to make her forget.

Milja graduated the following year with a Bachelor of Arts in English and married a fellow Black ministerial student. Callan heard they'd settled in Little Rock and had adopted two boys. He found her once, lugging a sack of groceries into the quaint parsonage where they lived, and she was the first indisputable proof his talisman had worked.

She thought he was a door-to-door Kirby vacuum salesman and told him they already owned one.

He didn't seek her out anymore until he saw her obituary in the Arkansas Democrat-Gazette many years later.

That—that is in the past, Callan reminded himself, *as is the rest I have somehow survived.* He took a moment to talk himself down, embracing the grim reassurance he was merely stewing over *potential* future problems, not real ones—not yet. While he painted, his worries escaped him as usual, and before long, it was midnight already.

Chapter Eleven

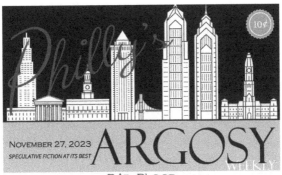

Part IV

18 September 1939

As he is true to his word, Claudius dispatched a post to me the day after I left the Ozarks. It is one of several items overstuffing our letter box at the post office on Grand Street this Monday, one I am keen to read while I wait for the bus to the factory.

He pens a rather elegant cursive for a boy his age, I think, and in clipped telegram style much like the cablese I've reviewed overseas in submarine control rooms. Also enclosed is a four-by-five delicately etched drawing of the gardens outside the hospital.

Since mail-order is a vital part of Baker's various and sundry enterprises, there's a postage meter in his office of operations as well as a combination letter and package box on the grounds. While this makes mail runs easier for the boy, the possibility that all outgoing posts can be intercepted and inspected from that six-sided desk does not escape me. Because of matters confidential to us, it appears the viscount has decided to err on the side of caution.

ALL WELL, AGRESTIC AT TIMES. REFLECTING ON ALLEMAND, SEE ENCLOSURE.

NALIME,
CLAUDIUS

I read through it twice, determining for the skinny I'll soon be tossing out Pop's desk drawers at the factory for a telegraphic code book we keep there. I suppose if Baker did intercept the letter, he may very well have pulled out his own cipher. While Tassemon and I discussed the possibility of using code, I wasn't sure Claudius would hop to it. But he did. *Baker will likely suppose it's argot Welsh*, Tassemon had surmised, since the viscount doesn't appear old enough for formal schooling and English is his second language. *I don't know about that*—I'd opposed, not totally sold on the idea. Tassemon was counting on Baker's distraction in preparing for his court appearance to load the bases in our favor—maybe a little too much.

All in all, his hunch thus far proved correct, for the enclosed letter and drawing seem to hold their original creases, and when decoded, Claudius isn't revealing any house secrets. Translated, it reads:

All is well, affairs at present unsettled at times. Please refer to the agreement that was made to see what we would entertain. I will only do what is absolutely necessary, Claudius.

For the life of me, I've missed his point—and must crack the decode, as it were. I sat at my desk with the coder wondering why Claudius hadn't simply used Latin. I didn't have time for it right then; Pops was waiting. Perhaps something would come at me later.

Our first order for combat boots, then known as service shoes, was spittle in the bucket, one of those early half-gestures America lobbed toward her own economy under the guise of supporting the war effort. We wouldn't ramp up munitions production for another year, hardly a little more than jack-shit willing to stick our toe in Europe's "war of nerves." At that point it looked like the States would pull up the covers of stubborn isolationism for a coon's age, Pops and I agreed.

News covering the Stateside scene that autumn was cagey and boilerplate, Americans being Americans. First-rate wheat crops reported in the Dakotas and Kansas cattle fattening faster than their usual farm standard. Attempts to return the bustle and laced corset to the fashion market after Paris openings said we could, railed by fashion critics as medieval and protested by the Lane sisters in Hollywood (the hourglass figure, it seems, won't be back). Catholic Nuns learning the Lindy Hop in a Chicago parish while communists celebrated their twentieth anniversary at Madhouse stadium. A mass Negro baptism in Newport News. The World Cotton Conference, The Davis Cup tennis competition. Ann Miller staging new and scandalous dance moves to the *Mexiconga* and Bimelech, the Hopeful Stakes.

Underlying all that audacious verve came those hourly bulletins airing over an excess of forty million radios, Europe's War is the chief commentary, trailed by speculations whether FDR will run for a third term.

And Nonna announced she agreed with the old Greek theory that war commences every thirty years out of generic curiosity while Pops argued wars wage far more frequently. After all, he said, *we're all vainglorious and greedy when it suits us, every last one. Except for Carleton,* Mum shot back. To which I must admit there's a difficult state of mind, to recalibrate one's basic urge for self-preservation, even in the smallest of ways. Most of us don't come hardwired to do that, or to examine any misplaced drive to survive even if it ultimately underpins the insanity of killing others. And Nonna's Greek philosophy does hold a point, just how many everyday decisions we make using our generic, lopsided history, and likely very short ones—of thirty years or less.

Pops briefed me about these service shoes, a test batch using new Quartermaster Department guidelines for rookies in training. The specifications laid out beside the lasting machines had altered the fleshout, hobnailed boot used in WWI into a new look indeed—polished grain-out uppers, toe caps with brogue holes, and leather outsoles. As we followed those orders over the next year, the M-42 would give way to a second one designated as a garrison shoe with an outside counter pocket, lighter laces, smaller eyelets, and a stacked leather heel. When our army would actually put feet on the ground in the European theater of war in 1941, both were replaced with a heavier, unlined boot with a full rubber heel. And finally, boots in the trenches had options to employ those bothersome canvas leggings in other ways with the evolution of the double-buckle cuffed issue.

Until such time we actually went to war, we remained busy manufacturing doubles—the mandatory army allowance for every new blister foot—two, not just one pair of those first service shoe generations for drills and maneuvers on our own soil.

I've considered in years since that Claudius arrived at the best and the worst of times. In several ways his calling card was impeccable. There are days I simply cannot conjecture how our world arrived at such a fix, although long exchanges over bottled sunshine usually parse out that the Second World War was simply unfinished business from the first. Any soldier or sailor worth his salt knew we were headed back across the pond. Only a matter of when, yes.

Hapless years can generate political machines and gestapo muscle for empowering tyrants, and we had created both. Some historians peg the rise of the Third Reich as far back as the roaring '20s—starting with an attitude. For the first time ever, a saturation of Americans were moderately affluent. We began to spend, and we liked it. Conspicuous consumption emerged as an American entitlement, but underneath that fat dollar craze financial classes splintered. By 1929, the richest 5 percent had one-third of all personal income in the country.

Enter Herbert Hoover, *a good man gone belly-up in bad times*. Universally admired when elected president, he'd barely gotten a running start before Black Tuesday. The US stock market crash at the end of October 1929 was truly a shock wave heard worldwide, and hard times fell on our own turf like never before. By 1933, thirteen million American workers were unemployed. But it didn't stop there. Soon more than thirty million people were out of work across the globe.

Hoover's blunder of frequently and publicly predicting imminent upturns in the economy made him a laughingstock. In retrospect he was probably too cautious with financial aid, putting money toward business but not directly into the hands of jobless workers. Because of those choices he appeared uncaring and became the dour symbol of all that went wrong. Mum saved some newspaper clippings, front-page photos of crowds jamming the nation's capital in 1932 demanding direct action while Congress pounded out the Reconstruction Finance Corporation.

That solution was an attempt to bail out failing banks, state governments, and railroad companies. Hoover used the Federal Reserve to encourage business loans and bolster industrial growth. His incentives stepped up a public works system to provide jobs. He *did* cut taxes to encourage consumer purchasing and enlisted federally funded buyouts of crop surpluses for export sales. This was a start, but it didn't move fast enough to stop the global repercussions that concocted the Second World War. Japan lost its lucrative American market for silk. International trades began to collapse, and pervasive national self-interest replaced any international cooperation. Midwest farmers packed what belongings they could fit in their cars and headed to California. Once-successful businessmen took to the streets wearing sandwich boards—*WANTED, a decent job by a decent man, age 39, paying on home, college trained, native, purchasing, accounting, traffic, 18 yrs. Union Steel, best reference*—some hawking apples, cigarettes, or other wares people might purchase.

The insidious reality of the *I'm so low, I'm looking up at down* Great Depression made old virtues of thrift, tenacity, and willingness to work no longer enough to make any difference. Thousands of jobless men and boys roamed the countryside, stowing away on freight trains and essentially becoming hobos themselves.

Also mooning the year 1929 was the bull's butt of what some had once called farmer's delight, those grander agricultural yields and surplus crops delivered by improved farming methods and machinery. We simply couldn't eat all we grew, resulting in a steady, but significant decline—22 percent—in farm prices over ten years. Corporate profits, however, still soared at 62 percent with an unleashed commercial giantism and scarcely any regulations. But the average worker's income only rose 11 percent. Since those wages didn't go up proportionate to industrial production and profits, the household law of averages couldn't afford an ever-increasing quantity of goods. Without consumers, prices dropped. Many products fell into disuse and disrepair or rotted in the fields because harvesting and farm-to-market sales were no longer profitable. Then came the face-plant of the moneychangers, some 6,000 banks to fold after Wall Street's collapse. In Germany, half the men between sixteen and thirty were out of work.

Adolf Hitler snaked like crabgrass through concrete, not too unlike several other self-made discontents in his day. This was a pivotal point in the Cold War polemics that Pops and I continued to pound out years later—whether or not the Führer, the most reviled dictator of all time,

Falling Stars

had started out as a free-floating proselyte or a yellow-bellied jackboot. We agreed that the political and socio-economic climate gave him a toehold he didn't dare lose. For the first five years Hitler managed to gain his objectives without any war at all (in point of fact we prefer to leave out of the argument) and used, quite simply, his well-rehearsed theatric rhetoric and wide-eyed oratory to prey on his enemies. With clenched fists and sweeping gestures he exploited centuries-old divergent interests of Britain and France, their mutual suspicions of each other, and their fear of war.

Germans were as weary of poverty and economic disorder as the rest of us and looked back with nostalgia on better economic times during WWI. They needed another war to boost their national reserves, and Hitler was ready to seize the gambit. His political platform promised more jobs and the golden egg of reinstating Germany to her former glory. Part of that national greatness also involved territorial expansion —*lebensraum*—which amounted to claiming Central Europe as his own.

In the middle of the night on 27 February 1933, Hitler stepped up his game. The budding proletariat-born chancellor was granted special emergency powers for *the protection of the people and the state* after a single government building in Berlin caught on fire. From that smoke of opportunity, he garnered a propagandist tilt that would slingshot him to the top. We could *Heil Schicklgrüber* and throw mud at him until the cows came home but he was way ahead of us as we toasted "Auld Lang Syne" into 1940—and just how much we were about to find out.

While we washed down our sack lunches with cream sodas, I studied the viscount's correspondence more closely. Pops was fretting over a matter with invoices, one I'd rather avoid until he absolutely calls me in on it. I'd parked my backside on a stool a few feet away, by one of the windows overlooking the Hudson River—one with less industrial soot and grime deposits—*ghosting* it's sometimes called. Coincidentally, because I chose to review the letter beside a reasonably unsoiled pane instead of at my desk, an occasional flash-blinder from water lapping in high noon sunlight exposed something I've up to now completely missed.

I saw words, a lot of them.
He's hidden words in this picture, by golly.

The first ones I discovered were neatly printed along those willowy narrow stems of forsythia in the left foreground, and so precisely integrated into the shading I almost missed them.

Only in darkness do shadows come clear...

The news in the forsythia alone was dreadful enough to make my blood run cold—and Claudius was on a roll. Tucked inside the folds of flowering monster chrysanths, even in those diminutive, tightly budded peonies, across lotus blooms of giant magnolia trees, under the darker sides of philodendron ivy—along the crosshatched decaying stems of half-a-dozen palmate leaves felled to the ground from surrounding sweet gums—was evidence of the boy's day-to-day mission, his cautious inspection of what lurked inside the walls of the cure-for-cancer ward where he resided.

It seems Baker turns manic in the evenings, and on a couple of occasions over the past week has roamed the halls and engaged with insomniac patients in the most curious of ways, Claudius reports. Many of the newer admissions like the viscount are riding on old propaganda that once attracted worldwide attention about cancer treatments and cures at Baker's former hospital in Muscatine. We are a few years in advance of reel-to-reel taped radio, and Baker's unrecorded programming in Iowa went away with his license to broadcast years ago, so his nightly appearances in the hallways of the Eureka Springs hospital are admittedly his own stage reenactments for those souls so unfortunate to have missed the original events.

In the clinical case of Mandus Johnson, Baker had announced over the airwaves on one fortuitous Monday in May 1930 that he was inviting medical doctors far and wide to attend a publicly broadcasted healing demonstration on the grounds of his K-TNT radio station, call letters for "Know the Naked Truth." Johnson had started out—according to Baker—*with a sore the size of a bean on his head* that spread to cover his entire scalp *while those incompetents associated with the AMA also known as Amateur Meatcutter's Association treated him*, Baker was sure to mention. According to the radio doctor, that well-attended rally in 1930 (some 32,000 people) would prove once and for all that cancer was indeed being cured by the treatments at his hospital.

During the demonstration one of his staff physicians removed the cancerous top of Johnson's skull without anesthetics, pain, or blood loss—the remainder purportedly on the mend from merely three treatments at Baker Institute. The top of Johnson's head was held up for inspection, exposing his brains. Some onlookers fell out or lost their lunches. To balance the act, scores of cancer patients from the institute took the platform in tandem to give testimonials about the remarkable results of their treatments. A skin cancer was lifted out with tweezers from the face of another patient before the crowd.

And of course, preparations used to kill external and internal cancers were on exhibition. Baker held up a small glass vial containing a quarter teaspoon of yellow powder he said was neither poisonous nor potash—and sufficient to cure five hundred cases of external cancer. He drew a four-ounce bottle of black liquid out of his handkerchief pocket (for eradicating internal malignancies, he said) and drank the contents. Claudius wrote that Baker also claimed Johnson was still alive and well nearly ten years later.

I think Claudius was more disappointed about one of several false advertisements promising moving picture shows at Baker Hospital, of which there were none. I'd talked up *Oz,* and he wanted to see it.

Details along the underbelly of the philodendron were even harder for me to stomach, how Baker continued flimflamming dying patients with his *whack magnifique* while one woman rooming down the hall from Claudius screamed with every injection. One day he couldn't hear her anymore, he wrote, and Tassemon informed him she'd been moved to the hospital's Psych Ward. Claudius knew something was up because of his hyperacusis; he should've been able to hear her regardless. When the boy asked if he could go visit the woman, well— *fine by me,* Tassemon had answered, *but this dog and pony show has no licensed psychiatrist in the rink, and I can't get in there myself.* Tassemon had already told me he could only surmise what happened behind those sealed doors; he suspected it wasn't good. Psych Ward took up an entire wing.

Before his first week was up Claudius had also learned about a pair of submachine guns Baker stored behind his desk. The viscount simply thought it an odd place to keep firearms, but he said Tassemon had informed him Baker was convinced one of several enemies he'd made along the way would try to assassinate him sooner or later if *those pill-pushing and soulless commercializers of man's suffering don't take me down first.* His high-octane paranoia determined many of the hospital rules and regs too. The nurses—*I've attested to it at half past midnight thrice already this week*—Claudius wrote, were only allowed to remove deceased patients from their rooms to the morgue at night. *He doesn't like a body count upward of two a week*, Tassemon clarified.

Two trials for my immedicable condition purposing swine numbles—Claudius also mentioned, had apparently met with some success. Tassemon logged that the boy's turgor was improving rapidly, *most efficaciously my colour,* the viscount added.

I remain uncertain about the lengths to which Baker will go in maintaining an operating hospital in the Ozarks. With the long arm of the law after him it doesn't look good, and desperate men do desperate things.

"How's our little nipper settling in?" Pops interrupted my reading. Strangely enough, he had no idea how accurate he was. When I looked up, he was grinning, a self-satisfied mug I've learned to read down the years. The invoice issue was obviously resolved, and—for all the times I carry a stiff upper lip, we'd both agreed to a ten-hour workaday transparency a long time ago.

"I'm worried about him, Pops."

Tommy wasn't ready to go lights-out with the viscount jammed up like he was, and it wasn't a school night, really—*and* Mom had treated him to ice cream after they drove out to the parish office on Passion Play Road to be fitted for his school jacket (*not really a uniform*, they said, *you'll wear this in cold weather, and you're expected to arrive with it in good order*). He guessed he hadn't bombed the meetup with Sister M., Mom didn't act *that* upset, even if he was t-rexin'. Ergo he might be able to take this out to two a.m., he hadn't heard her moving around in a while, but he could see her desk light was still on, a barely-there streak under his door.

From the parish looking west was, *no fibula*, the ginormous Christ of the Ozarks, *yes-way* tall even a mile off, and he'd speculated whether Fallon had ever climbed that statue, because anyone knew he could, right? He'd have to ask Gramps about the World War II stuff, most of it above his play grade, but he wasn't going to let that stop him from looking for Fallon.

Falling Stars

He hadn't added a wish to the secret slot in his casket in a while, especially the yen he was after now. A special pad of narrow parchment for doing just that was in his backpack, so he released the ramp and rolled out, bracing his ribs—*donkey balls*—and shuffled across the room. If this wasn't better by next week, he'd have to tell Mom, and she'd *yurp-yurp* ground him for life.

He sat on the floor beside his backpack and after a minute or two of braining it wrote under a nice full moon in his best Spencerian script:

Find Claudius

He'd thought about begging the snot out of it but had discovered a while ago—*not*. Wishful thinking didn't save him from the needles. Ordering it up like a console command seemed to work better.

Since his casket came loaded anyhow, Mom had no problem springing for a memorial record tube as long as he used the special paper only. A secret chamber was pretty *cool-o*, especially considering the nosy neighbors, *if* Casey should ever come over to see his real digs. The little cavity fabricated into the corner by his left foot on the outside of the casket was just large enough to hold three wishes, covered with a metal knob and chromed with the same stuff as the handlebars—*abut* (today's new word) to them, in fact, *super-duper* incognito—and *sealed to prevent water seepage*, the sales brochure had said, no-duh.

He'd studied it, though, and learned something else about memorial tubes like his, *really* for funeral directors to include a little tag inside so a body could be identified without opening the casket, helpful in locations like New Orleans where cemeteries often flooded and washed out old graves.

Eureka Springs didn't have to deal with their dearly departed inside drifters, Tommy was pretty sure—and his casket was rather unique. He used the memorial tube his own way; he took out last week's wish and added the new one with the other two. He really needed to get going and finish the next section in *Philly's* before Mom came looking for him. And by Monday he'd work out how to glue his cape to his school jacket, *yuppers*.

⭐

The third week the boy went radio silent, and I fretted until I received a post a few days later from Basin Park Hotel. He'd moved into a room with Tassemon, he wrote. Up to then I knew little about what had transpired at the hospital or how dicey their situation got. From our previous conversation at the local blind pig, I knew Tassemon was set to draw the shades on his employ at the cure-for-cancer establishment —he just hadn't determined how soon the dominoes would tumble. His plan to give his resignation notice was confounded by the arrival of the viscount and how he might legitimately secure the boy's medical discharge into his own care on the sly before six weeks were up.

Tassemon didn't think he could convince Baker—or any of his colleagues, for that matter, that Claudius was cured after only two weeks of treatment at the hospital *although the boy is responding favorably to my home brew*, he wrote.

During the second week, it turns out, they were busy cooking up a ruse—*not the most brilliant one in my playbook*, Tassemon later admitted, but a plan, nonetheless. The consensus was his boss was likely going to jail, so when Baker headed out for his court appearance on the afternoon of 21 September, Tassemon and the boy put their operation in action. This very well might be their only chance, and they took it.

Tassemon was familiar with interventional use of barbiturates (he had, after all, prescribed me henbane and suggested a prescription for secobarbital). The Mickey Finns he had access to were tetrodotoxin, the Haitian zombie drug, and pentobarbital—used for anesthesia and euthanasia.

After some discussion, the viscount said he thought he could induce his own tonic immobility, or at the bare minimum mesmerize those who tended him into accepting he'd succumbed. In the event of his failure to do so, the viscount agreed for Tassemon to have pharmacologia accessible. We were years away from reversal agents, but Tassemon had prepared his own *revival compound for raising the boy's acetylcholine levels if we should need to do it*, he wrote.

The evening Baker departed for Little Rock, Claudius grew ill and vomited up his dinner. Tassemon remained after hours at his bedside while the viscount's condition worsened into the night. *A right good show of it by half past eleven*, Tassemon wrote, *the viscount is, for all intents and purposes, dead as a doornail*. The boy had quite effectively drained the color from his face, lips, even his nail beds, he said, such that *all left for me to do was to pronounce him*.

Tassemon, I'd observed, could work an angle when necessary, and in his obvious distress, he accompanied the body to the morgue to document the viscount's death. Since every patient admitted to Baker Hospital signed a county permit waiving autopsy, none were performed —either there, or at the medical examiner's office.

Staff doctors simply had to tick off the boxes on a short-form postmortem report, *a fill 'er in and circle,* Tassemon wrote, with a simple narrative examination and pertinent findings to cause of death. Like the rest of Baker's operation, postmortem examination was cursory and external, *although those forms have yea-big anatomy charts with body sections and organs as if we were set up to saw open the pitiful bastards,* Tassemon wrote.

Just outside the hospital, a hauling truck belonging to a sexton Tassemon had generously paid idled with a casket in back—*after I purchased said casket for myself from the local undertaker and arranged for the sexton to accept delivery,* he wrote. This is where things went sideways.

Normally the morgue was unattended at such an hour, but Claudius wasn't the first body to arrive. One of Tassemon's colleagues had also stopped in, *wearing his dinner jacket, mind you,* to pronounce—also not the norm—and Tassemon *had a hankering he was onto us.* When he produced a carefully manufactured letter Claudius had crafted—the commander's order for his son's immediate burial—the colleague, *a one W.D. Dull, a nasty chump and every bit as bull-headed as his name suggests,* Tassemon said, insisted they put the boy's body in a drawer and wait for Baker to sign off on the transfer. At that point Tassemon could see beads of perspiration starting to soak the sheet covering the viscount—and slipped half a tablet of Nembutal under his tongue when Dull turned away *to listen for breath sounds in his own cadaver, all coattails for show, I'm certain of it,* Tassemon said.

By that point Tassemon was worked up and on the clock for giving the boy his reversal agent. He pounded his cane on the floor and loudly announced that under no uncertain terms would he defy the wishes of the Queen's Commander at Arms, that Baker might very well be gone for weeks, and he would go get the radio doctor on the horn immediately. He stormed out of the morgue and slipped into an alcove off the hallway, impatiently watching the secondhand on his watch click just past three minutes, *a fitting amount of time it would take me to gimp to the nearest house horn and back,* he fumed. Then he walked back into the morgue.

Thankfully Dull didn't call his bluff and had apparently left all in a rush, Tassemon wrote, *bottoms-up in the smack middle of his report. I flew open the back door, the sexton thankfully on point to assist me getting the boy into the cab, and off we went.* Around the truck's jolts and jounces, Tassemon produced a syringe of his revival serum and uncapped it with his teeth, for *the viscount lay lifeless across my lap, I'm telling you—and I feared we'd killed him yet.*

He was about to inject the boy in the thigh when Claudius stuttered upward, *all teeth and cuspids in my face, the sexton hollering out and nearly steering us into the ditch,* he said, *and if I hadn't bellowed the boy's name loudly, I'd surely be missing an ear.* Tassemon assured me Claudius had piped down immediately when he realized—*as I have mentioned aforehand, he really doesn't care for needles.*

With the casket placed in the crypt and the boy safely stowed away at the hotel, Tassemon's troubles weren't over. Baker posted bail after his arrest in Little Rock on 22 September and was out the next day, informed and enraged about what had developed in his absence. Baker called Tassemon into his office after the morning rounds and demanded to know the details of the viscount's demise. Tassemon, of course, insisted the boy was too far gone from the beginning and left it at that. And although certain levels of indiscretion weren't beyond Baker, exhuming a body wasn't one of them. *That silver-tongued grifter is in enough hot water as is,* Tassemon wrote. The only remaining power Baker had was to fire Tassemon on the spot, which he did.

And in the following weeks while Tassemon pounded the pavement from one *locum tenens* to the next, he encouraged Claudius to remain in the hotel room until the hospital officially closed its doors. Even so, much of the boy's ability to confound the memories of those around him was well underway. When Claudius began to hawk his artwork on Main, even patrons who wanted more of his art never could seem to find him again. I suppose even if the boy had met Baker in the streets, his escalating power to spellbind his subjects left him little to be afraid of. The viscount continued posting weekly to me, and I continued wiring Tassemon money. Treatment switched from swine to cattle to prawns and stepped up to a chemical complexity beyond me. The boy reassures me he grows stronger, that he no longer has tired blood. He'd hoped to visit Nonna by Christmas, he said, but a hiccup in locating a food laboratory in good stead for researching and preparing Tassemon's biological product—the one it turns out he'd consume for life—was going to keep him in the Ozarks a while longer.

June read the paragraph a second time, now feeling compelled to take a different direction before she discussed *Fallon anything* with Tommy. She needed to ask her dad about some local history. How to introduce those questions was another matter. Walt loved to read but she was fairly certain pulp fiction wasn't a fit.

And explaining why Tommy was gobbling up a fantasy series called "Bad Blood"—*well?* If Walt breathed a word to Lilly, they'd never hear the end of it. June grabbed a pencil and jotted down some questions. *Maybe start with these—no need to preface madness, right?*

Everyone knew some strange things had happened in these hills. Life was messy, no matter how much June tried to make it right.

Five minutes before Tommy's school orientation she'd gotten a text that her first day for clinic onboarding in Rogers had been moved up from Wednesday to Monday. She'd planned to be home on Tommy's first day of school—*the one day that was fucking necessary,* she stewed. But she couldn't rightly say no, could she? *It won't improve our situation if I have a meltdown over what might happen,* she kept reminding herself.

Callan stared at his tablet in disbelief. Many accounts Gaye had recorded in his logs were personal, and never intended for public consumption. He was a sailor honoring his duty to the Viscount of Wales as if he were his own son, and like many military men of his era, Gaye was hardly loose-lipped. Up to now many of these sentiments Callan had never known about.

After breaking out of Baker Hospital, he and Tassemon continued exchanging letters with Gaye until he deployed for war. In wartime, correspondence fell off somewhat, brief reports from Gaye through V-Mail—those all-in-one, featherweight aerogrammes with bright red templates—*give me the hair and hide on single-sided, standard letter paper—fold, lick, and seal.* Victory Mail used a nifty technology that reduced letters to microfilm with Kodak's Recordak machines and reproduced them on sixteen-pound paper overseas. But Callan could no longer include his sketches. He drew small panoramas in the corners that Gaye enjoyed deciphering, he wrote—*particularly when the line sorters are on the blink and fail to adequately flatten your posts before filming.*

Gaye had also recorded in his journals before he left—*through the 1940 mud season,* he called it—a stepwise account of weekly tweaks Tassemon ordered into the winter months until the viscount's medical formula was complete and his symptoms all but eradicated. The story in *Philly's* included the doctor's Miranda to Claudius: *should you ever feel the need to turn, boy—don't do it.* For with every turning, Tassemon had explained, *your chances of staying your disease grow less.*

Gaye spent the winter of 1940 dividing time between the shoe factory and RMS Queen Mary, securing her in dry dock. Tassemon retained the services of a laboratory for the viscount's *medical food,* he christened it, and cleared him for travel in March.

The trip to New Jersey Callan recalled with fondness. By racking up hours and sales at a local butcher shop where he worked, he'd managed to come into a train ticket and two weeks off. The butcher treated him fair enough for a boy his age and even offered him a low-rent option, a shack he owned on Spring Street. Tassemon came to the end of his agreement with the hotel and hung out his shingle in Springdale.

The first winter wasn't kind; the Spring Street lodging was poorly insulated and damp. The butcher periodically gave him older, uncured cuts to carry home that made him sick, but Callan ate them anyway, for he was always hungry. When temperatures dipped under zero Celsius, he bunked in the Basin Park Hotel lobby with other down-and-outers who would otherwise freeze overnight.

With warmer weather in March, he fared somewhat better, so Gaye didn't know about the inadequacies of his rooming house until he returned to the States years later, at the end of the war. Most of the viscount's monetary allowance coming through the Bank of England went toward the development of his medical food.

On the Jersey visit, Gaye questioned him a couple of times about the *ease of his living arrangements*—he was suspicious, Callan could tell. And he'd given him extra money when it came time to leave. The alternative to stay in New Jersey wasn't possible yet, although Callan had wished for it, and Mum and Nonna tried once again to solicit it. He needed to continue medicine trials until Tassemon saw fit to stop them, and at the time he thought his treatment was temporary. He'd also discovered that Eureka Springs was a good place to lay low.

Callan tried *not* to best Nonna at cards and he ate flan until he thought he would burst. Even with calling his hands early he bested her every game. She didn't seem to mind her losses as much as she had on the ship, *fiddle me, lovey—them's the breaks*. He also noticed the blood didn't move as freely through her carotids as it once did, and her eyesight was failing.

He was going back to Eureka, and Gaye was going off to a war the States could no longer avoid. Callan recalled even now every exacting deliberation in policy meetings he'd attended with his father the fall of 1937, after Hitler annexed Austria and occupied Czechoslovakia. The commander saw war coming down the pipe two years before the Führer's blitzkrieg through Poland or the Ukraine, and he'd tried to stir some action from the deaf ears in those boardrooms. Fallon knew the Reich was training six-year-old boys to fight in open-air camps in Germany; he saw where Europe was headed.

Most of the talking heads in that assembly assumed Fallon's five-year-old son, the one sketching faces on a pad in his lap, had little interest in the political diorama going on around him. No one present knew his real age, a secret Commander Fallon had very carefully guarded. He'd charged Callan with three sealed letters for Gaye's eyes only and one for himself. In his own were requisitions to make no further contact with Wales until the war was over. How Callan had longed to send a post, especially to his mum. But letters could be intercepted, and he had a duty to keep them safe.

Three years after the assembly in Wales and an ocean apart, Gaye shipped out to Australia the third week in March, where he recorded the excruciating details of destroying the ship he so loved. *We stripped her hull of the signature red, black, and white and made her gray,* he wrote. His was the detail that removed two-thousand stateroom doors and refitted all the sleeping quarters with rows of bunks and hammocks. *The lovely carpeting, veneer, and Art Deco is thankfully secured safely in storage along the Hudson,* he continued, *for we gutted her and made boutique shops into senior military offices; the Promenade Deck, standing room bunks; the first-class swimming pool, toilets.*

Gaye summarized, *any remains of her previous splendor is gone. She is now a killing machine fortified with cannons, angle guns, and rocket launchers. The lady has eyes on the ocean floor and wears a degaussing girdle that can neutralize underwater mines—no kiss-off for this ship, by golly.*

The sailor who, until his own death meticulously followed Commander Fallon's directives and remained loyal to his son's development wouldn't return to the States until the end of the war. He'd already transported Callan halfway across the continent, introduced him to a new world, and ensured he would never suffer his sister's fate. If Gaye had never done anything more, Callan thought, that would've been enough.

Perhaps Gaye found some satisfaction in helping him; at the time, Callan couldn't tell. Gaye continued his meticulous documentation of Hitler's movements into the fall of Paris in June. *And so the Stahlhelms marched rank and file through the* Arc De Triomphe *while civilians wept openly in the streets—and we'd only just delivered 5,500 troops to Scotland ...*

Callan reread the final paragraph in Part IV.

10 July 1940

I dispatched a wire to the viscount at 2100 hours following a five-hour enemy air raid on Cardiff shipyards that unfortunately involved the town, over two hundred homesteads. We have confirmed that the farm estate belonging to Commander Jules Fallon was destroyed as well, and I am now in custody of executorship documents from royal probate attorneys. I must speak with the boy at once.

Thankfully, *Philly's* didn't go into all the grisly details. Callan read to the end of Part IV and that worrisome *to be continued . . .* and stopped. He clearly remembered the conversation with Gaye, the grimness and exhaustion in the old sailor's voice and his surprise at the boy's true age—that chronologically the viscount was eighteen.

Tassemon was of course more informed about biological

immortality in vampires and had openly explained that the viscount's rate of aging would *follow out its own tendencies*, he'd put it, considering *your revenant genes first disorganized by a congenital disease process and current changes in cellular cytokinesis from the daily consumption of your medical food*. While Gaye was left guessing the viscount's true age until he started assisting the boy with inheritance receivership and naturalization, Tassemon had him pegged from the beginning.

In 1940, Tassemon believed the viscount might never grow to biological maturity. The only explanation he had for the boy's apparent immortality was *an arrested process of cellular division and the telomere shortening that should accompany that, you see*. Tassemon also mentioned he thought the viscount had inherited his father's telomere length, which could account for his own biological resistance to aging.

As years went by, however, Tassemon tweaked his original prognoses when Callan matured and albeit very slowly aged. He continued to mail Callan newspaper clippings about any new study in negligible senescence, a phenomena also found in a number of wild animals and organisms that appeared to have no biologic mortality after reaching puberty.

Observations from other species grew in number—from the Galapagos tortoise and the Greenland shark to starlings, sparrow hawks, naked mole rats, and collared flycatchers. When cancer research first termed *cell immortalization*, Tassemon had contacted Callan immediately, for these findings offered yet another possibility: the viscount's childhood cancer had contributed to a telomeric sequence unique to his own body, since cancer cells themselves express an enzyme responsible for lengthening telomeres. Tassemon remained convinced that both the viscount's cancer and remission had contributed to the unique and ongoing changes in his rate of aging.

The two continued comparing notes until Tassemon's death in 1978, for with every consecutive calendar year, the viscount seemed to age less. The question was, however, in the end a rhetorical one: Callan couldn't chance what might happen if he discontinued medical intervention. And yet, there were lonely days when he wanted to. When the war was done, he'd gone back to Cardiff once to visit his parents' graves. And while sorrow had threatened to reduce him to a blubbering nitwit, he instinctively knew what his father expected of him, that it was no longer in Wales.

Chapter Twelve

Mondays were nasty sum bitches, Casey didn't care how much Dawn evangelized *being ever grateful for her schoolyard days*, or some other dumbwise shit like that, Casey hated every single one coming and was pretty sure her mom hadn't hit the books like she claimed, *not even.*

Also bearing down on this Monday following an a'ight, chill holiday with low expectations (she *did* have to brush her teeth on day three) came the totally inconvenient horseshit with *being a reproductive woman* (according to Dawn), something Casey hardly cared about *if ever,* she grumped, an event requiring three extra tampons in her backpack this morning.

She'd discovered online how she could nix such dumb luck by crash dieting on diet soda and sugar-free bubblegum—but Casey really liked food too much. Another possibility was sneaking some of her mom's blood pressure medicine and contraceptives—but *you betcha* Dawn would notice. *So totally unfair*, her mom caught onto any little whoop-de-do when she felt like it.

Casey had copped to the futility she was stuck with Bloody Mary for the long haul, especially after her mom laid down the law about *what happens when you go against the good Lord's wishes for the feminine parts He gave you.* She shrugged on her backpack and heavy-stepped it down the stairs.

And this wasn't about trans or gender-bending, even.

Casey was set to continue mentally ranting against female troubles if not for *the oddest thing stumbling across our yard in the dark under a golf umbrella*—OMG. It's that kid—*whatshis?*

Tommy.

Yeah, he was all hers, this freakin' shitshow.

Casey quickly stepped back from the window and peered around the casing in the event she wanted to call it and skip the walk down the hill. She could hear herself whining already, uh-huh, *not being good for it today, cramps and such,* and Dawn would put her on toilet duty forever, Casey just knew it.

She got Mondays off and was sleeping in.

But what the effin' thunder is he wearing?

A motion-sensor floodlight on the side of the Purple Passion snapped on, and Tommy jumped back. Casey saw it though, looked like a cape. *A vampire cape.*

Humph. Give him two—no, one day of my kind of tampons and see if he still has a blood fetish. She opened the door and stepped outside.

"What's with the cape?" she wanted to know. Tommy kept walking, head down, obviously not any more thrilled about the *walk-to* than she was. Casey slammed the door and caught up with him.

"Part of my uniform," he answered. *If safety pins in his school jacket counted,* she guessed that made it so. *Except—*

"Halloween's over," she remembered. But that was stating the obvious. The next part was really important, and it wasn't easy, getting a word in around his monster brolly. "Your teacher will make you take it off, you know."

Tommy didn't answer.

"And send you home with a bill for destruction of school property," she added, tugging one of the safety pins.

He stopped and glared at her. Casey couldn't see his eyes, but she could feel them.

"Don't touch those," he growled, and took off again, turning right on Prospect.

"Okay, okay. I'm just sayin'." She caught up with him. "What's with the granny shades?" She'd never seen clip-ons before, but she was pretty sure only old farts wore them.

"I have sun sensitivity," Tommy answered.

"You mean, like a vampire?"

"I am." He bared his teeth.

Casey gave him a dirty look. "That's creepy, you know. Maybe you should keep those inside on your first day."

"Maybe you should stop telling me what to do." He went on, hopping over the grooves in the sidewalk.

Oy, that figures. Casey watched him repeat the process every four or five steps, then a right on Crescent. *What a freak.* And *well duh*, it looked like he knew his way plenty around here, anyhow. But she wasn't allowed to diss him or leave him, not after his granny said he had the Big C. They'd already bought a coffin for him, *Jesus H. Christ.* Which she also needed to ask him about. When the time was right.

Casey assumed he had the umbrella for the same reason as the granny shades because her Apple watch said no rain today or tomorrow, either. Some of the jerkbags who hung around the neighborhood called her *The Weather Channel,* but she was the one who had to walk in it coming and going to Mill Hollow bus stop—the other side of downtown. Umbrellas were overkill, though. No one carried them much anymore when wearing a hoodie worked just fine. She did wonder about the Samsonite briefcase, *yea verily.*

"Don't you have a backpack?" she called.

"This has a combination lock," he said over his shoulder.

Casey caught up with him again, slipped off her backpack, and showed him. "Zipper clips."

He stopped, set down the Samsonite. "Let me see that." He popped up his clip-ons and inspected her backpack locks, *TSA on steroids,* this was.

"Hey, watch the Mary Poppins." Casey stepped back.

"My bad." He tilted the hilt away from them, his big blue eyes looking genuinely sorry, *gotcha.* Then the clip-ons went back down, Samsonite up, and he was off again, flea-hopping the sidewalk grooves.

"Who's going to steal from you at a church school, anyway?" *There's a thought, Dracul.*

"I'm not worried about that," he answered. "It's for keeping things *out.*"

Casey didn't get it. Then—*oh, yeah.* "You mean like silver or garlic or—hang on a minute—a mirror or a crucifix, maybe?"

"All that. Or a communion wafer."

"Well excuse me, but it *is* a Catholic church. What's wrong with a communion wafer?"

"It's not red. I eat red things."

"Oh, right." *Jeez, there's OCD for ya.* "I saw you sneaking out Thursday night, by the way."

Not the *oh crap* she'd bet on. He looked like he didn't give a rip.

Falling Stars

"What's it to you?" he said flatly.

"Where'd you go?"

"Just looking for a shortcut."

Casey giggled. "Believe me, you don't *ever* want to do that." She knew every hobbit trail and shotgun alley from here and the bus stop, one for every freakin' day of the week, and a pair of other details the new douche didn't really need to know about.

"Why not?" he asked.

"Ticks. They're all around here." She did her best Nosferatu impersonation. "And they drink your blood."

He actually grinned for once, a nice smile, *if he wasn't a third grader and the rest, so god-awful trippy.*

"Would they be red?" he asked.

"*Ew*—now you're just being gross." They'd reached the rectory's parking lot where a nun was waiting.

"Careful what you ask for," he countered.

"Oh—touché, Tommy Lucas. See if I walk you to school again." Casey grinned at *the teach* and waved.

"Not tomorrow," he said in all seriousness. "Wednesday, maybe?"

And if I wasn't so busy shooting myself in the butt already, Casey thought, I'd have a better comeback like, *how we'll skip every Wednesday from now to eternity. Mondays, Tuesdays, Thursdays, and Fridays too.* But he'd caught her off guard.

"Sure," she said, and continued down Crescent Drive.

Sister Madeline had *yup-yup* figured out how to *roll tide* in her classroom *anyhoo*, and before he'd totally caught on, Tommy was benched in his own armchair desk, *every last freakin' piece of his stuff* locked in the sanctuary's central coat closet, tablet and cell phone included. *Insane.*

Tommy *brained* the first fifteen minutes of the school day in dismay. *Makes no diff,* even if he'd decided on Day Zero to try and keep things under wraps, or that he could break out on all the other one hundred nineteen days (he'd counted) that remained in the calendar school year. Or whenever Mom left at dark-thirty like she did this morning.

Sister M. had his number.

Yezzir, she gave the rest of the chumps right along with him an efficient, two-minute intro to *everything Tommy Lucas*, allowed him to demonstrate his goods and what's more, how easily they came off and stowed away in his Samsonite. She even managed to give him a snappy, *perfecto fold-it* lesson with his cape and made him trade that out for his sack lunch, label it, and stick the bag into the classroom's mini fridge.

The morning *meet-ya* in the *rotunda* was just that—a *smokin' hup-two at 7:30 A on the dot, she wasn't kidding*—five students moving along single-file toward the classroom, all walking but one.

Trent Busby, code name Bumblebee, was the only student who couldn't. He was the oldest in class, fifth grade, and new to a wheelchair after last year's run-in with spinal meningitis. Trent got his handle from his power chair, the one tricked out with smart technology that stood him up, sat him down, spun on a dime, and constantly collected information on driver behavior and the environment, he'd mentioned.

Trent was a cool dude, *yuppers*—maybe the only student there who knew what it meant when things got really, really hingy—like two weeks in ICU. His wheelchair was his desk, and he really enjoyed taking a victory *spin-on-a-dime thingy* whenever he *got* the answer. A little tiresome at times depending on how many questions Trent aced, but Tommy was also now *zonked* about gracing the classroom with maybe some new cape tricks, who knew? Since Trent looked like an older, bigger version of himself, Tommy tried real hard not to let his classmate's *heyo* get under his skin on the first day. Besides, here were three others with their own mojo.

Stacee (*spelled with two e's, she was most anal retentive about it*) Rains reminded Tommy of Gollum, a bony little girl with bulging eyes in second grade who wore a beanie, never took it off, *no indeedy*. She constantly rearranged her desk and reordered her words which, *duhvcourse* changed her answers, and she had some sort of anxiety disorder, he didn't catch the name, but he was pretty sure she had no hair, and in spite of being medicated she twitched. He tried to tune that out too.

Gerard Miraval's family had immigrated from Peru, and he couldn't sunburn because of *equatorial pigmentation*, he said that. He *did* have the best tan there, and his birth name was Gerard-*o* but he went by Gerard in class, fourth grade, and really preferred answering to his gamertag, Unit Fiver-Niner. Gerard was considered high functioning and on the spectrum, and he *defo* played *Eve Online*. He said he'd show Tommy *how to cheese through Invasion Expansion sometime* if he wanted, although it didn't sound easy at all.

Delia Cook was a third grader like Tommy, hearing impaired since birth, with bright red hair, big freckles, and a cochlear implant over her right ear—*and* a real bookworm who mostly kept to herself except when Sister M. called upon her. She had an odd voice that *came with*, he noticed, and she also knew how to sign. Every now and then Sister M. would sign back, but M. had a firm rule about that as well and didn't allow Delia to use her other language to talk smack.

Then the day (*shazam*) was over already, and Sister M. assigned everyone homework modules. He'd gotten *way* past the morning funk by then and squared it with Sister M., he was good for walking home all by himself, *no big deal*. Since he was pretty tired he decided clip-ons were plenty, the extra stuff like books made his Samsonite pretty *durn* heavy. Sister M. sanctioned his walk home alone, then decided on second thought to *go-with* to the top of the hill.

"I checked out the property you found," Sister M. said. *Funny*, what happened last Friday was *somezheimer's* until she mentioned it. He'd been way too busy the past couple of days with his cape and his ribs and he'd totally forgotten about it.

"You went down there?" he asked.

"Nope, title records. It's a cave—once a quarantine jail for the county and now posted as private property. No public access."

So that's what the sign means. "Really? I couldn't tell," Tommy fibbed.

"It doesn't belong to the parish either," Sister M. went on.

Hmm. "We can't go in and see it?"

Sister M. sighed. "I'm afraid not." She grinned at him. "And you're talking to someone who *digs* caves." She chuckled, *the little bells again.* "Corny, I know."

"What about a class project?"

"There's an idea," Sister M. said. "But not on site."

"Bummer," Tommy muttered.

"Yes, it is," she admitted. "Trent couldn't go, among a couple other reasons, like the legal requirements for obtaining a working geostructural analysis *if* they could locate the current owner for permission. It all meant time and money. They could, however, still do a class project reviewing old county records and historic documents, Sister M. went on—but she no longer had Tommy's interest, for *yowza* he saw the Woodie pulling into the parking lot behind the rectory.

Sister M. was on her way to the Crescent Hotel on an errand and said goodbye at the top of the hill. When Tommy was pretty sure she could no longer see him, he ran *hubba-hubba* back down the hill to the rectory. He thought about stashing his goods (they did *slow his roll*) under the park's hedges but that idea didn't really come up until he'd already reached the rectory.

And there she be, the model 115-C Baker-Raulang.

He set down his Samsonite and circled it, admiring the *sublime* that she was. *Damn, was he sucking wind.* And he'd been so *straight-up* sure his ribs were better today.

For six weeks between Thanksgiving and Christmas, Callan always took a break from the downs. And while store hours frequently overlapped with his working schedule during the holidays, he'd always considered those first weeks of winter his painting season. Tourism and sales could be unpredictable even during the so-called Christmas rush, one that came and went according to global economy and events clearly beyond his control. Coming out of the COVID-19 pandemic, painting season had exponentially lengthened into the new normal of 2023.

Usually, his wealthy clients would place orders for one of his newest this time of year, or occasionally an older original with no provenance history and never before displayed in his studio. Here was the second trip by appointment this week, which meant flipping his shop sign to lunch break during a midafternoon lull and going to his cave to retrieve said artwork. Often he drove those acquisitions directly to his clients' homes using the Woodie as a hauler since some paintings were quite large, and their metal storage cases, heavy.

He'd just pulled into the parking lot behind the rectory, locked up, and started down the trailhead when he picked up the scent. Checked his watch. He had an extra few, and by the odor he knew the sickly one was very close by. So he backtracked several yards toward the edge of the parking lot out of curiosity and stood behind a tree, watching the activity around the Woodie.

The sickly kid never heard them coming, unfortunately—three hoods that rode the streets downtown on stripped-out mountain bikes looking for trouble. Callan had seen them loitering around the shops before, middle-schoolers who'd grown up in trailer parks, cut classes, and didn't belong on this side of town. All three ran around in thrift shop Gangsta, mostly black and neon green hoodies and low-hung shorts with skater stripes. Because they knew their turf, they usually just wheeled by and yelled insults, which he hoped for the boy's sake they'd be doing now.

"Hey, bloodsucker!" The biggest one yelled. *There's an interesting turn of words*, Callan thought, *haven't heard that one in a while*, but those creeps had eyes and ears on the street and had probably heard something about the kid Callan hadn't. The bigger one skidded to a stop and snatched up what looked like an umbrella off the pavement.

"What's this?" He broke it over his knee.

That's pretty brassy. Callan hesitated. When the sickly one went after him, feisty as he seemed, the hood shoved him down. And Callan was on it. He hurdled the hedge and ran straight toward the fight, the sickly boy now doubled up on the pavement.

Callan wasn't sure anymore about what *could* happen, it had been so long—since he'd consulted Frid, in fact—but he did feel his shoulders repositioning and his jaws extending as he ran. This was a chance he'd have to take. He was turning, he just wasn't sure how much.

By the collective reaction, plenty. One of the smaller hoods pointed and the other two spun around to look, eyes widening in disbelief. They bailed and ran for their bikes, all but the biggest, somehow thickheaded enough to try to stand his ground. Callan leapt onto the roof of the Woodie and growled. That's all it took.

The cast was a quick one, more like spitting the confabulation in their general direction, tailing them with it.

This memory, what haunts your sleep,
Bind it here, this be its keep. And so it is.

The sickly one had passed out the moment he hit the pavement, so Callan had a second or two to reset. He yanked off his Inverness overcoat and draped it over the boy, his first concern the kid might go into shock. He wore a school jacket, one of the hoods having ripped his shirt underneath, and Callan could see bruises already coming up, *not a good thing*. He should retrieve his cell from the car, he decided—when the kid came to.

"Did they take my—" The boy straightened his glasses and tried to raise up.

"Easy does it. Go slow." The only item besides what once was an umbrella was a briefcase lying several feet away. "No. No, they didn't. It's still over there."

The kid sat, grimacing as he did. "I'm good," he said, holding his side. Flipped up his clip-ons. "Who are you?"

"I'm Callan."

"*You're* Callan Masters?"

The boy's ice-blue eyes followed every move Callan made, and while he knew he'd have to hedge on some things—*damn Philly's*—his legal name was still secure.

"That's right."

"My grandma thinks you're hot. She wants one of your paintings."

Callan couldn't suppress a grin and prayed his teeth were back in due order. "She should come by the studio sometime."

"We all were in there last week, but we couldn't stay very long, and I need to ask you, are there any paintings of Welsh ponies in your gallery?"

The part about Welsh ponies was more than just a coincidence, and certainly concerning. Would a kid this young read *Philly's?* Callan shook his head. "Just racehorses."

The boy's shoulders sagged. "Oh, well. I guess I better go home now."

"Is home close by?"

He pointed. "Just over there, four-point-two minutes if you Google."

Callan helped him to his feet, and by the weight of the Samsonite, he wondered how the boy would manage. He draped his overcoat across his arm and picked up the briefcase.

"Shall I carry this? It's pretty heavy. I'll walk with you, okay?"

"Uh, okay." The boy brushed off his jeans.

Callan scooped up the mangled umbrella. "Toss this?"

The boy sighed. "Guess so."

Callan tucked it under his arm.

"Do you know who owns that car?"

Callan shook his head. "She's a beauty, isn't she?"

The kid's eyes flashed with frustration. "I really need to find the owner," he said dully.

"Perhaps someone who goes to the church?" They started walking.

"Maybe." He folded down his clip-ons. "Don't you need to get back to your studio?"

"Lunch break."

"Really? It's sorta late for that."

"Busy day."

They walked for a minute or so in silence, Callan speculating whether the boy would come clean about his injury when he got home. Given he was sick already, he might try to hide it. Callan recalled doing something similar himself.

"What's your name?"

"Tommy Lucas. Me and my mom just moved here from Chicago last week, she's an oncologist, and I go to school at the church."

"Really? I didn't know they had a school there."

"It's new, for kids in special situations like me. I have a blood disorder they say is cancer but it's really an anomaly, a curse on my bloodline."

"That so?"

"Yes, I come from a line of vampires."

"You don't say?"

"Nobody believes me, but it's true." He bared his teeth.

"Those are some biters, all right."

"I have a cape and a casket in my room too."

Were kids nowadays always this chatty?

"It's a 4-D player when I'm not using it for a bed or streaming TV. Standard adult model, serial number zero-nine-seven-B-two-M-six-D. It's way cool."

Callan narrowed his eyes. "You're really not joshing me, are you?"

"Nope." Tommy hopped over a groove in the sidewalk.

"What grade are you in, Tommy?"

"Third, supposed to be in fourth, but Mom and Sister Madeline didn't want me to stress out this year because it makes my red blood cells explode."

"Really? That sounds painful."

"Not so much. I just have to aim straight when I take a leak at Grandma's."

Okay then. Callan wasn't sure how to respond to that one.

"Well, this is me."

"The old Brighton place," Callan murmured. He'd seen the first restoration *circa* 1947, and some since.

"I'd invite you in for a rare steak or something, but Mom's not home yet and I don't know how to cook."

"That's very generous of you," Callan said. "Much obliged."

"What's obliged?"

"Mm-m—another way of saying thank you." Callan handed over the two-ton Samsonite to Tommy and caught how he did his level best not to flinch.

"Do you think those *creepoids* live around here?" Tommy asked.

Callan shook his head. "They won't be bothering you again." He waited until Tommy looked him in the eye before continuing. "Promise me something? Let your mom know you got hurt after school."

And that went over like a lead balloon.

"Whatevs," Tommy muttered, turned away, and stumped toward the house.

★

"*Mom,*" Casey groaned. She hadn't been home five minutes, *for real*—before Dawn was sending her on another garbage run, the meanest of mean. *She* had to take muffins next door *again. So unfair.*

All because her mother seized the spare today to vape and snoop, and thought she saw the *drop-dead* art guy she called eye-candy walking Tommy home after school. Dawn wanted to know *way hella more* about that, she said, and she expected Casey to find out pronto. And of course, Dawn had grilled her about this morning for all the *bushwa* she needed to satisfy her that Casey had *indeezy* walked the fruit loop to school. At five sharp his mom still wasn't home, and Casey rang and rang the doorbell like a bazillion times, but no one ever came. She left a plate of leftover cinnamon roll muffins with a crapload of maraschino cherries (red for the undead) at their front door and walked

Falling Stars

ever so slowly back home.

Dawn wasn't pleased with *no show info*, no wowzer for Casey. Her mom already had trigger thumb from searching for text messages she forgot to save as contacts, and now she was ice fishing for June's.

"Here." Dawn handed the phone to Casey. "Find her number for me and I'll call her when she gets home."

Donkey balls, it hurt. It took all the *how now brown cow* Tommy could muster to *squeegee* out of his long-sleeve T, and he had to lose it *yesway* down in the bottom of the garbage bin (the big-ass one in the garage), so June would never find it. *Not* a good idea that she ever hear about what really happened after school, he figured. He had to come up with something better. *Super drat* yeah Tommy wanted to tell her about meeting that horse painter guy, but he couldn't and stick with his *yes fibula* story, could he?

When he finally found another T just like the *rip-torn* he'd worn to school and changed—*nope*, he wasn't good for much—no *Rockin' A Thrilltown Donkey Rodeo* or homework modules for sure. He was sweating bullets, hot and cold at the same time.

Tommy lay very undead still in his casket for a long time before he settled for restreaming the new 2022 *Dark Shadows,* the episode that officially introduced actor Jack Darrow as Barnabas Collins—although the app also listed two *just out* episodes in the cue, *cool beans.* He'd gotten to the part where Willie Loomis discovers a dusty old coffin chained up in the Collins mausoleum when his own casket lid swung open—and all it took for his mom to spaz out was one look.

On his way out of town, Callan stopped at an ironmonger's store for hardware to hang the piece he was driving out to Pea Ridge. A stand of umbrellas caught his eye, and after carefully examining a couple of them he drew out a black one, a far more appropriate size than the golfer the boy dragged along to school today. It had a reconstructed brass parasol handle just heavy enough to knock out bullies and a vintage design fit for any old-world vampire. He smiled, a bit surprised this store carried these, and the owner confided he was trying them out. Callan bought two.

Pea Ridge was an hour's drive around the Ozark Highlands' Beaver

Lake with brightly colored fall leaves that always drew in pre-holiday travelers. The road trip calmed Callan and allowed him to temporarily set aside his dread about what Cochran would write about him next. He had to remind himself that he'd managed to blend into the world by his own wits and outsmart the American general public so far. Yet he also knew that the open-book, hardline investigative, *click-on-social-media-and-hurl* society he now lived in made it more and more difficult to stay underground.

He'd decided not to cast forgetfulness or even false memories on Tommy today, for he wanted the boy to remember all the details about the incident that harmed him. And while Callan could've selectively confused Tommy's awareness about his own part in it—for some ungodly reason yet unclear to him, he chose not to.

Callan knew he was taking chances, yes. All bets were off until he found out for sure, but he had a hunch that the boy was also reading the smear about him in *Philly's*. The pulp histrionics were probably above Tommy's grade level, but the vampire stuff was right up the kid's alley and he had it bad.

No question about it, he'd mail the umbrella, for Callan knew not to gamble on meeting Tommy's mother. From what little he'd observed already she was too precious, and he couldn't allow himself to risk falling in love.

⁕

June internally kicked herself all the way to Eureka Spring's emergency room, everything she could muster not to come unhinged (*she should've been home today, she knew it*), not a doubt in her mind what was shaking and baking with Tommy when she found him febrile and saw the bruising under his ribcage. Her day had been productive but long at the clinic in Rogers, and traffic wasn't kind at rush hour. She hadn't made it home until after six.

Tommy admitted he'd injured himself—*really-really*—way back on Thanksgiving Day when he tried bailing out of his casket on a lark, thinking he *for sure* could make it over the side without disengaging the drop-down panel. He knew better, June inwardly fumed. How many times had they reviewed the risks of opportunistic infections in cancer patients? Pain, redness, and swelling anywhere—not good. Fever, really not good. And lung infections—well.

June's strategy to formally introduce herself to Eureka Springs Hospital under less extenuating circumstances was no more—and while the ER team did workups on Tommy, she wasn't spared the joy of missing the incoming call from their next-door neighbor. Not a good idea to ignore Dawn, she knew, but June didn't feel up to wading into feckless drama at the moment, either. She stepped outside where crickets provided white noise.

Dawn's main objective seemed to be informing June that she'd seen Callan Masters, *you know, the gay guy with the art studio downtown, we need to have coffee sometime and discuss him,* walking Tommy home. She wasn't sure what Masters was up to, she said, but of course she wanted to make sure Tommy got home okay, and Casey had left more muffins at their front door (*did she get?*) and had also mentioned she and Tommy had agreed to walk to school together again on Wednesday. June archived the pathological oversharing for later, on the outer rim, beyond the blur of her more critical concerns—thanked Dawn and ended the call. She also made a mental note to text Sister Madeline that Tommy would probably miss school tomorrow.

The remarkable news was he had no broken bones. His urine sample showed a low white cell count consistent with infection and fever. Tommy wasn't thrilled when they started a line for IV antibiotics, *and that's just too bad,* June dismissed, he knew what he was in for when he broke the rules.

The doctor in charge agreed to run ahead of the curve and treat Tommy's as bacterial illness. He would go home with ten days of erythromycin, and his next ravulizumab infusion schedule would have to be altered. Since clotting was a very big deal (June reminded Tommy once more) they'd repeat a protime if he experienced increased bruising or pain. If he didn't improve in a couple of days, June also had orders for filgrastim injections to stimulate his bone marrow to produce more white blood cells.

The only thing Tommy enjoyed, he said, was collecting the sputum culture because he felt like spitting after *the whole enchilada.* With any luck, June hoped, the culture would come back gram-positive, an infection less resistant to antibodies his body could make. When Tommy tearfully told the doctor he really didn't want to miss school, June was surprised—and touched. She repeated the importance of catching things early if he *really-really* didn't want to miss out, and he seemed willing to listen to her—at least for the moment.

June texted Sister Madeline about Tommy's upcoming absence at 10:00 p.m., and at 10:01 p.m., her phone pinged with a reply. Sister Madeline was shocked, she texted, because Tommy had seemed fine the entire day, and she'd walked him to their street corner after school herself. June laid aside her phone, an introspective sift and sort for the truth. Dawn was always and fundamentally full of it, wasn't she? Nothing would change if June gave Tommy the third degree, so she didn't. June also decided then and there *if* Callan Masters was in their neighborhood and she wanted to know why, she'd go ask him herself.

Chapter Thirteen

Partly in protest of holiday-hyped commercialism, Callan didn't hang the four oversized spangles under his studio's awning until after the parade, the first week in December, on Thursday, end of the day. Happier memories of yuletide holidays as distinct and separately occurring events stoked his culpability to keep things that way, even if neighboring shopkeepers pegged him a minimalist or worse. His ornaments had always struck him as gauche, anyhow—although they apparently did the job and kept traffic coming. Only after he'd gotten them up again did he notice the weathering—and that wasn't smart, not for holding the operational age of his business in question. Callan was meticulous about maintaining the gallery to keep his cover, and here he was, slipping.

"Better line up your ducks, old man," he lectured himself. He'd change those out next year.

If Callan was willing to accept a modicum of personal immunity, he got it—from the fifth and final installment in Philly's (just out Monday), where for all intents and purposes the editorial department had slapped the cuffs on Cochran. Gaye continued spinning some details too close to home, but "Bad Blood" concluded with an open-ended stance concerning the continued, if ever whereabouts of Claudius Fallon. Which suited him just fine, he was happy to remain an urban legend.

He was still on edge though, probably a good thing.

He'd changed his work schedule after last week to avoid driving to the rectory during school hours and started making most deliveries after dark. The Woodie otherwise spent much of the time in an enclosed garage behind his house. Callan had considered doing an electric conversion on it, but if at any point his car became a sole identifier, he knew he'd have to part with it.

He tried not to dwell on the possibility too much, for unlike his forebears, Callan's sacrifices were modest thus far—he was sure of it.

He was, in truth, the end of the line—no longer sanguivorous, never needing to hunt his next meal from blood as long as he drank the blue juice. Last year's supply chain shortages did unnerve him at times, this was true—because he had insufficient proof of how long he could exist without it, or what he would revert to. And he hoped he never had to find out.

The generations before him were feudal warriors who outlasted their human counterparts by hundreds of years, vampire knights swearing allegiance to King Caradog ap Meirion and fighting for the crown in exchange for land and rulership. They migrated away from lynch mobs and executioners when necessary, but his own father had secured (and not without trepidation) a certain level of amnesty in Wales fighting the Queen's wars. The political landscape turned into a mudslide following the First World War, however. Fallon cued his children to remain vigilant, for discovery was ever on the cusp even then and there. Fallon's own ancestral ascent into nobility protected them up to a point, but policymaking could be damning, one of the reasons he farmed their own food. And Commander Fallon had no recourse for advising the son he sent overseas to die how to navigate his own individual freedoms. When Callan departed New York's harbor with Gaye all those years ago, he feared being studied, and he still did. To that end he no longer second-guessed any effort, however great or small, to remain underground.

Another cold snap had arrived, and Callan hadn't bothered with a jacket, so after fifteen minutes of northerly wind whipping through his dress shirt, he decided he'd decked the halls long enough and lugged his step ladder back inside. On his way in he flipped the shop sign to CLOSED, and, on his life, those center track lights are off again. So he set up the ladder and went to work, his stomach reminding him he really needed to take his medicine and eat.

He didn't appreciate the lights going pissy on him, and he was hungry—and when he heard the front door's motion sensor chime, he remembered his cell phone was in back, that he hadn't locked up. The sensor didn't chime shut, and on second thought he suspected the wind had done it, but he could also tell someone was standing behind him. The door sensor chimed closed. Inwardly he groaned and didn't concern himself to look around, but outwardly, he put on his shop voice. A customer was a customer, after all.

"Welcome in," he said, still haggling with the lights. "Feel free to look around. I'll be done here in a minute."

A cell phone ringing, not his ringtone. He kept going with what he was doing, half hoping the shopper behind him would take it outside like people often did these days, and leave.

"Hi there, Dr. Lucas," she answered the call.

Callan turned a tick too suddenly and the step ladder twitched. He righted it on cue using a flamenco stomp, but the boy's mother, cell phone pressed to one ear, was on it in two quick strides, a firm grip on the ladder's rear side rail.

"I got you," she said, big blues looking up at him. Then back on her call. "He has a PICC line? Okay. Let's stay with IV Raltitrexed, take it down to two-point-four ML on this cycle."

Nurse chatter escaped the cell's earpiece, and Callan listened in curiously—perky banter about a reduction in treatment time too. And he wondered how well all those measures ultimately worked.

Wounds they wrap in axioms hard as hail . . .

"Yes, fifteen minutes," she continued, "Thank you." When she looked back up, he was pretty sure he was still ridiculously admiring her, forget the lights.

"Hi, I'm June," she said. A pensive smile. "I know it's late, um—I didn't see the sign posted that you were closed until after I came in. I'd like to see 'Knicks Go', I'm thinking a Christmas gift for my mother?"

Callan swallowed. *Make the sale and get her out of here.* "Surely. 'Knicks' is right over there." He pointed and watched her walk across the studio. "Yes, there. Third from the end." He stepped off the ladder. "I'll put this up, back in a minute."

He propped up the ladder against a wall in the back office, the hum of his medical grade refrigerator sounding unusually loud. Callan chalked it up to a dreadful gift of Spidey sense in hazardous times and began rolling up his sleeves. Took a breath, grabbed his cell, and walked back out into the gallery.

She stood at standard viewing distance from "Knicks", her gaze taking in everything. Since Callan had seen "Knicks" plenty, he studied June instead in her black duffle coat over turquoise scrubs, sneakers, high ponytail—probably straight in from work.

Falling Stars

"This is lovely," she said. An inquisitive smile. "You're a lefty." Not a question. She could see he pushed the paint, no fooling her.

"Yes, I am."

"How much?"

"'Knicks' is twelve-five," he said.

A flicker of disappointment in those blues, he caught that. Callan crossed his arms over his chest. "I—have a new 'Knicks' off site, slightly smaller but equally nice, for ten."

She smiled again. "I'd like to see it."

And there's how to arrange something, but not now, surely. His stomach growled. "You hungry?" he asked her instead.

She chuckled. "Starved. But I can't tonight. My parents have had my son since three, and I need to go rescue them."

He grinned. And how he knew that—the kid was a handful. He had his doubts Tommy told her about the scrape after school, and Callan hadn't mailed the new umbrella yet, either—*because he was afraid of this very thing, damn it.*

She fished out a business card. "I'm on call Saturday. Free tomorrow night, though."

He took the card. "Tomorrow night it is, then."

"Meet here and walk? Just text me when you're ready," she said.

Exquisitely casual and a little pushy, but he guessed that's how she got things done. "Fair enough," he said. "I'll have the painting here for you." He tucked the card inside his shirt pocket.

"One moment," she said, gazing at his right arm. "May I look at that?"

His tattoo, *hell yeah.* He'd like to make the sale, but he also wouldn't mind if she forgot about him and dinner altogether.

She popped out a pair of red cheaters and took his forearm in both hands, gently rotating it from side to side as she studied the pattern. "Did you design this?"

"I did." And he wished she'd never let go.

"I'm normally not a fan and I usually advise patients to remove them, but this one's really nice," she said. Cheaters off, smiling up at him. "Tomorrow night, then?"

Eyes sharp with pain, burning blue—

He nodded. "Until then."

Callan locked the door behind June Lucas and watched her walk to her electric vehicle parked a few cars down. *Damn, is she gorgeous.* He switched off the lights and stood for a minute or two in the dark trying to decide how fated this might be, *on Pearl Harbor Day it was,* eighty-two years later. Given her megadose exposure to his talisman, he doubted she'd remember—so he didn't go out of his way to cast a spell.

✯

June aimed a string of unsavory terms at herself and made a U on Cushing. Fast Horses had already gone dark, *she'd blown that one way over the top, yessir,* a kick-ass tendency she and her late fiancé argued about fiercely even before she started medical school. He'd called her a tight-assed studyholic, and now she struggled to turn off the doctor.

She drove for a mile or so along Highway 23 before settling on a more comfortable point of view. Lowered her chin, squared her shoulders, and willed even this to be okay. Nothing but a casual business dinner to fork over a metric shit-ton of money for a Christmas gift that might buy her mother's patience with Tommy for about a week, that's what this was. Masters just happened to be the fulcrum. Not her best analogy, but that's all she could find at the moment. He certainly didn't seem overeager about doing the dinner thing or maybe again, he was gay—but she hadn't given him a chance for a word in, had she? June came full circle to raw nerves and a scolding, she needed to hit the Tonal tonight for sure.

How grateful she was for an option less than twelve-five because—*coming home with a framed print for Lilly?* No can do. June had, enough already, waded through the muck too many times lately, and the cost of Tommy's Christmas present alone would set her backassward. Not to mention his tuition, old medical debts (professional discounts included), and as of last week, those added emergency room charges. She could do ten, but *shit*—did she step in it back there. No surprise if Masters decided to ghost her for dinner, yet another reason she refused to date.

June found Walt and Tommy huddled over a pile of books at his rolltop desk in the study, a delicate operation setting up tiers of possibility among the threadbare Teddy bears Walt had chosen to rescue this year. June knew her dad had spent the past week in the attic trading thirty-nine boxes of pumpkins for fifty-seven boxes of Teddys—

not counting the ten-foot tree or the indoor and outdoor lights, a combination of retro bubble and globe, Lilly was very specific. Every single room was a spillover much like the pumpkins, and, with any luck, Tommy had occupied himself counting every last one of them this afternoon, a built-in reprieve. Since Tommy's most recent ER visit, Walt insisted on driving him home each day, including June was free to pick him up.

Walt had both fireplaces going full tilt, a warmth that was welcome. The old house whispered the signature rosemary-tomato broth in Lilly's Caroler Beef Stew, reminding June why yes, she would gladly continue to buy reassurance her mother would love them this way. Evenings like this one also called to mind why she'd chosen to move back home in the first place. The old prognosticator, however, was difficult to disengage, for June had managed Tommy by herself for a long time—and her thoughts were already charging ahead toward tomorrow's weather. If temperatures cooled much more overnight she knew she'd better plan on driving Tommy to school regardless of how much he protested. June checked the weather forecast on her cell phone.

He'd grown almost—sweet on Casey, it could be—walking with her every day since he got clearance to return to school last Thursday. The maraschino muffins were a hit, even if raccoons plundered the first ones before June found the plate after Monday night's ordeal. Like a good neighbor, Casey brought more, a big enough wowee to prompt Tommy to ask June's permission for her to come over and play video games with him sometime. Gee, June mused, if only alliances came that easy when we got around to adulting. She didn't want to hurt Casey's or (sigh) Dawn's feelings about tomorrow, either. Maybe Casey could ride with? Or if the front shifted and allowed them to walk tomorrow, she still needed to put a weather-contingent plan in place. *And here I go again.* June filed that one away until after dinner, removed her coat, and pulled up a chair alongside Tommy.

"Looks like Congress is in session," she said.

"Hard at it." Walt blinked at June over his bifocals. Tommy, nose inches away from his book, was intently giving neon-yellow highlighting a new meaning.

"Is all of it important?" she asked him.

"Yuppers." Tommy didn't look up.

"Seems like I remember somebody else who was handy with a highlighter." Walt grinned at June, already doing her level best to stifle a giggle. She picked up an old Steiff Teddy bear leaning against the end of the desk, one of the larger ones with those trademark elongated toe pads and scruffy red mohair. He'd graced the foyer for years with his flattened fur and patches where the material was completely worn away. *Prince Hairy.* June smiled; he was one of her favorites. Lilly had found this guy in an auction, originally a display toy in FAO Swartz department store.

"His growler went out," Walt said, then back to his own book. June could feel the built-in sound box in the bear's back where a short red pull string was attached.

"I'm going to fix him," Tommy suddenly announced.

June glanced over at Walt. "Really?"

"He might be a take-home if you know what I mean," Walt said.

Tommy capped his highlighter. "Grandpa said I could try."

Walt closed the book he was reviewing. "Big school project next week, we're looking for what's what about—" he read a sticky note posted on the desk's tambour groove, "Earl J. Tassemon, D.O."

"June! You're here, finally," Lilly interrupted. She stood at the door with an oven mitt on each hand. "Can someone help me set the table?"

"I need to start the steak," Walt announced. He knew the drill by now.

"I've got the table," June said, motioning Walt toward the hallway. In a lowered voice she told him about Tommy's original source for Tassemon, the five-part story in a pulp fiction magazine called *Philly's Argosy.*

Walt frowned. "Now it makes sense. I thought it was mainly about the Second World War, he had questions about all the goings-on. It sounded authentic enough to me—and I found a list of sawbones who testified against Baker. But Tassemon isn't on it."

"Delia Cook is profiling an anonymous benefactor who contributes ten thousand dollars a year to the food pantry. Sister M. said I could do the same thing with Dr. Tassemon, but I'm profiling him on the premise he really was on staff at Baker Hospital," Tommy declared, still hunkered over his book.

June crossed her eyes at Walt.

"Sounds like he's got it all figured out." Walt winked at June and turned toward the kitchen.

She really hoped so, since Sister M. had e-mailed her two write-ups on Tommy already, one for refusing to open his Bible in class, and another for pocketing a communion wafer in last week's mass, which happened to be Holy Communion. The second time she sat Tommy down and carefully explained the critical nature of his conduct, June had an epiphany. She suggested (risks considered) Tommy create his own apotropaic inversion to protect him from all things commonly vexing to vampires so he could get on with the business of school and life without these added distractions. He didn't like her idea very much at all and told her in that many words—but a day or two later, he apologized and said he'd figured it out. On the plus side, his protector-deflector didn't involve his cape, umbrella, or red food. Tommy had, in fact, carefully hung the cape inside his closet last Tuesday. She wasn't sure where the golf umbrella went (she kept forgetting to ask) and neither appeared to be coming out again anytime soon.

June half-expected Tommy to put in an order for a Stefan Salvatore daylight ring, or some other ad hoc tween rage commonly believed to protect vampires, but he surprised her yet once again.

"Grandma gave it to me," he'd told her earlier this week as he pulled the lucky charm out of his backpack. "I think it'll do, donkey."

Lilly had gone into her jewelry case and presented Tommy with a dime-size pendant in white gold. This curio, a vintage starburst with a tiny, beveled glass center, came from one of the downtown jewelry shops when June was about Tommy's age. Because it was a star, Tommy handpicked the charm from an array Lilly offered, and it came on a white gold chain. He explained according to his own arbitrary rules how the starburst magically protected him three ways. The white gold only looks like silver, he said. The beveled glass centerpiece wasn't large enough to reflect anything *or show that my own reflection is missing.* And with all its tiny pinpoints, the exploding star was still his favorite symbol of all time, *no-duh.*

June held no illusions; she still skated on thin ice every day with Tommy's conduct. Yet she couldn't fault his fascination—no, not really, with Gaye's story in Philly's—for she, too, no longer saw her hometown the same way. She'd read most of her dad's books on Eureka Springs history, and the pulp fiction story added some new elements. That's what it was, though—pulp. Once again June planned to talk with Tommy when she finished the final installment. She needed to get back to the story, and Tommy hadn't offered to read out loud to her since Thanksgiving, either—something she attributed to their new schedule demands. But she definitely needed to find out where Tommy was on it.

Seated and blessed, Tommy dove into his medium-cooked steak with enthusiasm while Lilly bantered on about this year's Christmas festivities and the garden club's upcoming carol-historic-downtown—*why, it's tomorrow night already, and would June and Tommy like to join her this year?*

"Depends upon the temperature," Tommy said around his food.

Lilly glanced at June.

"That's true," June said. And to Walt, "What does your almanac say?"

"What's an almanac?" Tommy asked.

Walt's eyes sparkled. "That, my boy, is a bona fide book of magic."

"Really?"

"It might predict warmer weather tomorrow night," June finished.

And Lilly nodded her approval.

"It forecasts?" Tommy asked.

"Sort of like a magic eight ball," Walt answered.

Lilly agreed because she indubitably gardened by it.

"I'd like to see it." Tommy sawed away at his steak with his dinner knife.

"Here," Walt said, "Let me show you a trick."

Tommy slid his plate toward Walt.

"How do you like my new silverware?" Lilly asked June.

Tommy dropped, no—June thought, more like threw his fork, then his knife.

"Silver?" he exclaimed.

June braced herself. "That's why you have your starburst, Tommy. Remember?"

"That protects me at school," Tommy argued. He studied his palms, obviously looking for blisters.

Lilly opened her mouth, and June quickly placed one hand over hers. To Tommy, "You mean you went to all that trouble for selective

Falling Stars

protection?"

Tommy looked up at June, nose raised in thought. "Okay. I guess you're right. This time." He showed her his hands. "No harm done."

"Now, that's better." Lilly smiled at him.

And Walt proceeded to show Tommy proper cutting technique with Lilly's silver while June engaged in enough surface chatter to calm down her mother.

The real touchstone in the delicate family cha-cha, June knew, had origins in a unilateral move Lilly made before Tommy was born. Perhaps she feared for her daughter's sanity, or the even greater horror of losing public face—June never determined. When she pulled out of medical school the semester following her fiancé's death, Lilly got busy. She had connections, friends of friends who knew a director of adoption services in Springdale, and Lilly was the one who'd filled out an initial adoption petition and supplied additional file requests. When June came home the summer after she graduated medical school, Lilly took her to Mercy Hospital's obstetrics ward to show her a little fellow who could be her new baby, born June 7, only four days earlier—and June never questioned not taking home that bundle of joy, not once.

June couldn't turn down the opportunities for residency and a practice in Chicago, either—and Lilly didn't fight her. When she signed on the dotted line for Tommy, June swore all manner of allegiance that she could do this with professional help. She employed live-in nannies until Tommy turned seven and Molly part time for pre-K and kindergarten, full time on Zoom for his first two grades during the pandemic. Tommy even accelerated one grade level ahead during the first semester after his diagnosis. Because they'd managed so well for so long, just the two of them—asking for help now seemed . . . absurd. She had to imagine Tommy felt the same way. But how to ask?

"Would it be all right if Tommy spends the night with you tomorrow night?" June ventured. "I probably won't be home in time for caroling."

Tommy, on his last bite of steak, zeroed in too. This was different.

Lilly gave June a sly look. "Is someone going out?"

Tommy stopped chewing, blue eyes quizzing his mom.

June groaned, not intending to call this much attention.

"I don't think it's any of our business," Walt stepped in.

Lilly cut her eyes at him, an old argument.

Even if she'd felt bulletproof enough to share, June couldn't very well tell Lilly and keep her Christmas present a secret, could she? Better this way.

"Just someone from the office," June fibbed. "A working dinner, you know."

"What's a working dinner?" Tommy asked.

"One that works," Walt quipped.

"Oh, you quit that," Lilly fussed at him. June, feeling full ten minutes ago, ate the last bites of stew she really didn't need—anything to avoid answering more questions.

Prince Hairy was *one hella cool dude*, and Tommy wouldn't let him down, *no dice*, he was going to fix him up. Grandpa had loaned him a bucket of special tools (some disassembly required) and a take-home-with, he was all set to pull out Hairy's jigger box and take a look inside. Except—

"Did you name all the other one hundred seventy-four bears?" he asked June, who had just pointed their e-tron *home James,* all busy adjusting those seat heaters again. He'd reminded her before about a remote preconditioning feature on her smartphone's Audi app, *no-go computo.*

"Are there that many bears, really?" She sounded surprised.

"Yuppers."

"Well—most of them, yes, I think I did." she said. She was looking pretty fried, and he wouldn't be surprised if she called lights-out before ten.

But Hairy would take longer than that for sure. The box-thingy in his back was kinda dopey—sorta like the one in Delia's head. He was glad he didn't have one—although *hey, he had his own dippy-duh stuff, so shut the door, right?*

"If you name something, does it make it easier to fix?" He poked around until he found a tee-niney zipper.

Mom tapped the steering wheel like she did when she was braining it, yeah—and she finally said, "Sometimes. Yes, I suppose it does." But she sounded *elevendy-hundred-million* miles away.

Alzo—you can imagine his surprise when they got home and Mom went bee-straight to her room, no orders, zip. He settled in, FaceTime with martha_whoosis, she was all over Fan Expo, hyped about the latest buzz even he'd missed, well *hell yeah*—he was in school, after all. That writer dude Miles Cochran was paneling, she said, *yuh-huh, cool beans,* she was all over "Bad Blood," had read it even, and thought it was pretty sick too—especially since *lucky you, you live there and how cool is that.* Yup, good to know, he said, because he had some questions for old Miles, and they weren't easy-peasy. And that was pretty much it until they got a chance to hook up again, Eve Online.

Then the strangest thing, when he went headphones-silent to listen up for Mom. Two doors down he heard her Tonal, low-level Michael Jackson, with coaching.

What the squiz? It was past her bedtime for sure.

He did a twitch-switch into his pajamas, headed down the hallway, and *up periscope—*

Damn, she's on HIIT. Yup-yup, something's got her going. When she looked up, he ducked.

"Tommy," she said between sucking wind, "is everything all right?"

With me, yeah. He stuck his head through the doorway. "It's kinda late to beat yourself up, you know."

She grinned. "Tough day."

Nope, there's more and he knew it. "Are you going out with that painter guy?" *Def* not the most lit question in the whole freaking universe—

"Yes," she finally said. *No smile, no beefin'.* "But you can't tell Grandma. It's about her Christmas present."

"You're *buying* one of his paintings?"

"I am."

"Dinner too?"

Apparently, that was funny. When she finally stopped LMAOing she said, "Probably."

Then, "How'd you figure it out?"

Tommy shrugged. "He's like the only single dude around here, right?"

When she stopped laughing for the second time she told him he had to go lights-out and that it really wasn't a date.

"We'll see about that," he said, and headed back to his room. It still pissed him off, Masters saying he didn't paint Welsh ponies when

Tommy was *one-hundred-ten* he'd seen a couple in there, yuppers. He'd found Welsh pony pictures online, even some big-ass ones harness racing for the Welsh Pony & Cob Society of America, and he wanted one for his room. If he had Mom with, *well hell yeah* she'd get the real scoop out of Masters and he could probably get one too. In the darkness Tommy regarded the empty space on the wall where he wanted to put it and sighed.

Maybe next week. He still had Sister M.'s *for-real* assignment and a reread of *Philly's*, so he dared to put a lid on it quite literally, his casket's head panel.

He lay for a moment in the dark with the lid closed before switching on the overhead screen. Sister M., as it turned out, really wanted him to do an essay on the harmony of the worlds, she'd already decided, yep, his pitch for Tassemon was dead in the water. He could've snagged something more straight-up, yeah, like Gerard. *He* was going to tell everybody how the church gift shop roof became the local wishing well and demonstrate the chances of his dime staying up there on first throw.

But school wasn't all whips and chains. He was back by last Thursday, *no-wayzee* gonna miss the Christmas parade Friday. His Arkie amigos were pretty tight with him now that he'd returned from near death and he had a cool-o card of the Crab Nebula they'd all signed (including Sister M.) with BFF and stuff, wishing him health and *things going swimmingly, yada-yada.* He kept it in the side panel of his casket.

On the subject of celestial bodies—M. thought his star fever would convert him to the idea, and he tried really, really hard to get jazzed about her assignment. But if M. thought he'd just forget about Tassemon, she had another thing coming. The prompts she'd e-mailed him went like this: *musica universalis, or universal music, is a harmony of the planetary and gaseous spheres, an ancient philosophy that considers movements of celestial bodies in our galaxy as forms of music.* Tommy stopped reading. *That's like really snoring-boring.*

He bookmarked the page and swapped windows, for he had more important things to do, which included rereading "Bad Blood" Part Five.

Chapter Fourteen

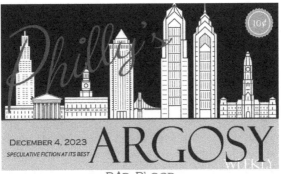

BAD BLOOD
THE CASE of Claudius Fallon
by Miles Cochran
Part V

7 May 1943

As war drags on it becomes unmistakably clear we must do something to flip the tables on all manner of military strategy we have employed so far. Our Lady remains the largest and fastest troopship in the water with her record load of 16,683 soldiers at a continuous speed of 30 knots. After those early runs transporting several thousand Aussies in '40 and '41, we settled into two years of six-day transatlantic shuttles running that many more American GIs to No Man's Land.

My ship logs reflect the rapid about-faces from tedium to terror while we zigzag the open seas, sailors scudding from long days on blanket duty playing Burn and Turn to those warning orders to *strap on your Mae West and sink your last anchor.*

Nearly two years ago Hitler placed a bounty on this transport ship, a whopping two hundred fifty grand and a German Iron Cross to any U-Boat captain who can sink her. We've sailed unscathed nearly three years to date save our own unfortunate miscalculation with HMS Curacoa.

Within months in fact after America entered the war effort, Our Lady was nommed the Grey Ghost, and thus far she's managed to outwit the combined military intelligences of the Axis. But The Allies are now onto what must be done to win this war. We are currently transporting British Prime Minister Churchill and his staff to New York where he will meet with FDR, and odds are they'll pound out another Operation Sledgehammer—an amphibious assault that's apparently not winning his cabinet's confidence at the moment. Churchill and his men are working around the clock, alternating Lapsang Souchong tea and Johnnie Walker Red like water. We also have 5,000 German POWs on board.

Many of us expected the war effort to end twenty-two months before it actually did. The seven-year, worldwide skirmish raged 792 battles, campaigns, or military invasions on virtually all soils and seas by the end of 1945. I will hearken to 1941, however, because that particular stretch brought on a series of pivotal events and fubar that forever changed my world.

Norman Baker was convicted on seven counts of mail fraud in federal court and booked at Leavenworth 16 April. Tassemon (who would've happily testified against him) was neither subpoenaed nor called in as a witness. And while at least some of us would've preferred giving Baker the hot squat, in the end we were left hoping the forty-page supreme court indictment (also evidencing his cancer cure as pure hoax) was sufficient to keep him from setting up shop elsewhere. Hitler's Luftwaffe bombed London for 57 days and nights straight in 1940, a blitz that stretched randomly into 1941 for another six months and five days until 11 May. After Cardiff was bombed in July, I wrangled with the Bank of England to grant probate of Fallon's estate—to release the boy's inheritance due—until the next July. Pearl Harbor was attacked 7 December. Mum wired news of Nonna's death on New Year's Eve.

Also mashed in the middle of our tour of service was our fateful collision with HMS Curacoa 2 October 1942. We departed 27 September from New York harbor once again bound for Britain, and five days later, we sank her. Bridge watch sighted the British cruiser off our bow near Scotland, notwithstanding at these coordinates we were under strict directives never to stop. The keel order didn't come soon enough, and we cut her in two. Of the one hundred one survivors was my dear old friend Dr. Dewey Langston.

We both agree I owe him a tall one.

Now we are rolling up our flaps and looking alert for our most notable wartime passenger, and the air is thick. Spud duty is cranking on the double to turn out courses like macaroni bolognaise, navarin of lamb, and corn ox tongue—all served on silver trays bearing the British prime minister's coat of arms with cocktails, cigars, and dinner mints. His entourage is housed in top-level staterooms that remain outfitted with Our Lady's trademark Cunard luxuries, but I've also marked the minutes of a rigorous schedule the Queen's officials are keeping while they orchestrate plans for *the* Allied invasion—amphibious, aerial, and ground.

It's clear Churchill wants his strategic options buttoned up before he meets with FDR this time, and any one of us "retreads" on board hopes he's a contender, for it's high time to put an end to this. But as much as we wanted to stop Hitler's regime, the fifteen-day conference in Washington codenamed Trident would ultimately decide to delay the invasion so critical for reclaiming German-occupied Europe for another year. Because of supply shortages, cross-channel offensive maneuvers to liberate France didn't take place until the following summer, a composite of plans Churchill had toiled over for *this battle forced upon us,* his words, mind you—and the successful campaign known as D-Day.

Germany surrendered 7 May 1945. We began removing our ship's armaments twenty-one days before, confident of war's end in sight. I would not return to New York until the end of summer with the last homebound troops to yet another ticker tape welcome, for Japan had finally surrendered 15 August.

I'm officially retiring again at captain's rank and must bid goodbye to the lady who has carried me safely home once more. Pop, showing his age these days, really needs me at the factory. I have one duty to carry out before joining those ranks full time, though. Pops is simpatico —I think he's only too happy his son made it home.

The viscount's voice sounds strong on the horn, and he gives me careful directions to his rental. Although Claudius inherited a goodly sum, he has wittingly chosen not to settle, and the clapboard shack he lets near town (like many in Eureka) all but hangs off the cliffside— roosting untidy enough to wash downriver with the first good thunderboomer, it looks like.

What concerns me more is the viscount himself. Though he certainly appears in good stead, he's still only a strapping eight or nine at the most—*uncommonly young*, for by his birthdate I'm certain he should be nearing twenty-two. He acquired an operator's license in anticipation of receiving the Woodie, which now sits catawampus on the driveway's three-quarter limestone gravel, its subgrade likely never properly prepared.

I don't see how the viscount can remain in these accommodations, although he's certainly been busy and currently uses his home as an atelier. It's a Gable Front, about 1,100 square feet, two stories, a large front room that cuts into a tiny kitchen—and indoor privies, I'm glad of. He says he sleeps upstairs where it's warmer although cold air blasts quite freely through the poorly insulated and warped pine that has long since shifted with the rock it clings to. The front room has an ample fireplace, no wood in the andirons because he says he needs to clean out the flu. The base flooring is bowed as well, the stairwell yawing outward a good six inches or so.

Finished and unfinished charcoal and pencil sketches are everywhere, many draped across what few sticks of furniture are in here. Some hang outright on the walls to help block the evening's northwest wind shear and others are still in the process of being framed.

Claudius assures me he will invest in a home elsewhere soon, that his art is selling well, and the butcher continues to employ him. For any working art commissioned outside of the county he's accomplished those trips over the past four years by hitchhiking. I am amazed by how unafraid he is, stepping into such squalor following a life in parliamentary luxury. I suggest he might consider making his home with us in Jersey at some point, and he assures me he would be happy working in our factory—but for now, he must continue meeting with Tassemon each month for a reassessment of his condition. This surprises me; I was under the impression his medicine trials were complete by the winter of '40. I ask him how much longer Tassemon must continue to monitor him, and he explains his care will probably end when he reaches biological puberty, that he will likely remain on medicine for life.

The viscount came through Jersey in the spring on his way to Cardiff, but he returned within the month, back to his artwork which he said sells like hotcakes Stateside. As years rolled past, he continued sending me postcards from all his travels and stopped by the factory whenever he was in New England on business.

It turns out Claudius was privately tutored alongside his sister in Cardiff's royal court and had already completed high school before we met. I don't think he found it necessary to pursue higher education because his talent was his skill set, and he found he could rely on it. I didn't visit him in Eureka Springs again, so I'm not clear how his art developed or where it sold—he could draw so many things quite well. I suppose he eventually landed on a specialty and made a home somewhere, but that wasn't the foremost topic of conversation whenever we visited. His life of solitude was.

I don't think the viscount chose a life of seclusion willingly—he was smarter than that. Keeping an ear to the ground about what is going on in the streets now and then can be a fellow's sole protection. Yet constant pressure to align to human protocols and social norms also renders clear thinking powerless. At the forefront of our postwar era came detriments from failing to distance ourselves from the world at large, but these couldn't hold a candle to the hardships of isolation, which may sire all manner of bizarre and misguided ideas. For the most part Claudius seemed to keep the two in check, but I worried about him from time to time.

In 1951, my concern grew once more because of new draft registration requirements and the war in Korea. At the time, the viscount still appeared no older than twelve or thirteen, twenty-nine according to his birth record—ages albeit that fell outside of those selective service requirements. For a brief period afterward, he was dizzy with a dame from Louisiana. I was sure he would marry, but he did not.

Claudius helped me pack my bags and return to the lady I loved in 1967. I sold my shares in the factory and moved in with my sister Clara, something I'd sworn I'd never do. All in all, it worked out okay because I leased the guest suite behind her home in Belmont Heights. In truth I moved out there for RMS Queen Mary, to care for her once again.

He was jet-setting in those days, theatrical consulting, he mentioned—and arrived in Jersey with two tickets to LA. War was revving up in Vietnam, and the Military Selective Service Act of 1967 had just extended the ages of conscription from eighteen to fifty-five. I was again ill at ease because he *looked* eighteen by then, documented as forty-five by his birth record—but he told me Tassemon had already fixed him up with medical disability papers.

Then he said something strange while we packed, broad strokes charting a scenario I could never unsee. *I come from a family of foot soldiers with certain advantages,* he said. *I don't suppose anyone could kill me that easily. Maybe if I stepped on a toe-popper but the ground tells me where those are. Or someone could try and fill me with thirty rounds, but the air tells me where those are. And trees everywhere are home to me; they will never see me coming.*

He flew out in 1972 to see Elvis on his 15-city MGM tour and had me book the stateroom he and his sister had occupied in 1939. RMS Queen Mary's first 150 rooms were open by November, and the viscount, one of our very first visitors.

Consulting or not, the "Seven Stallions" suite wasn't restored to the same standing or even on the same deck, for that matter. He didn't seem disappointed at all and insisted it was all right, that he would very much enjoy his stay regardless. As I remember it, he remained for nearly a week that time, and on more than one occasion I overheard him conversing with someone inside his quarters although I'm relatively certain he brought no one aboard but himself.

At one point his stateroom door had opened a crack when I was leaving out for the day, and I stopped to bid him goodbye. Piped in through the room's stereo sound system I could hear music—*Opus 39, No. 15*—as I approached. The viscount was biologically around twenty by then, taller than I. I stood at the doorway for a minute or so watching him waltz with something I couldn't quite make out, and by the height of his handhold, apparently much shorter than he. When he caught on, he admitted his sister was there, that she claimed she'd never left.

23 August 1988

The viscount continues to come out once a year for a visit, always a pleasure to see how he handles time as it goes by and he adapts (mostly in effort to blend in, I suppose) to current fashion trends. He sported the slicked back combover for a while and a '70s Beatle shag with mutton chops—thereafter, mostly undercuts. He went bewhiskered for a couple of years, then back to clean-shaven. We've spent many hours over hops poring about the affairs of this world and the extent of things, say, a hundred years from now. He'll more likely remain its witness long after I am gone, and I think he is okay with it.

Last stopover on Our Lady, Claudius admitted he continues to implore Agnetha each time to leave her ship's confines and return home with him. I'm sorry to say I'm no longer sure where *home* is since the eighties brought with them my own verge with needles—intrathecal injections to manage pain after back surgery and intra-arterial chemotherapy for the retinoblastoma which ultimately claimed my vision. The last two visits I could barely make him out because of my strabismus, and recent posts to an address I thought the viscount last occupied have all been returned, so I'll check again with him when he comes out in September.

The End

✯

Callan skimmed the fifth installment in *Philly's* a final time.

How I miss you, old friend.

True to the last, Gaye ultimately refused to explicitly reveal how Callan made his living or where he hung his hat.

Even while age and infirm were claiming Gaye, he'd worked smart and hadn't included information in his journals that could ultimately incriminate him as Claudius Fallon.

He was free to remain the myth he'd always been.

Locked away in the back office was a box of returned letters Clara had given him in '88, ones Gaye (in the last year he'd lived) had addressed to an incorrect zip code. Callan suspected his eyesight was the real issue, for Gaye was very much aware he still lived in the same shanty he'd originally rented. As years went by, he'd given the property a major overhaul, including an enclosed garage for the Woodie, treated timber that didn't shift, and an asphalt drive, but it was still the same place. Callan checked his watch.

Except—*fuck me, I had to go and ask her out.* Any recoil was all on him, he knew. Gaye would say *it's about time*, and Tobias—well. Callan was very much aware of what could happen, and *this was not good.*

He was banking on the chance she'd totally forget about dinner, but he also wanted to sell the painting and *oh hell enough already* he finally decided around five he'd better not be a sod and reserve a table if they hoped to get in anywhere tonight. That wasn't difficult because the maître de at Rogue's Manor had a standing agreement with him for any working dinners with investors who dropped by his studio. Holiday traffic moved at its usual Christmas crawl—feast or famine, and it looked like he could very well be out of here soon.

He stared at June Lucas's business card, his cell phone, back at the business card. And it occurred to him, *the thing about texts these days*—*yes,* that's how he could do it. He thumbed in her number and texted his best *techy-vague.*

Your painting, ready at six.

There. No such insinuation about dinner, and if she'd forgotten about buying the painting—*well, that was just that.*

She'd treat his anonymous text as smishing and walk out of his life forever.

He locked the front door, killed the lights, and went to the back office to take his blue juice. Phosphorescent light gleamed from two rows of 1 mL Luer syringes, sixteen left in the rack before he said adios to yet another retiring cook, always a bit of a hoo-ha if the next one hadn't been properly informed. For that, he had a thumb drive with its precise chemical construction in case somebody threw out the reactants. He mixed the Luer, uncapped it, and drank in the dark.

His phone pinged.

See you then.

Damn. He sucked his teeth. *She remembered.* Or at least it sounded like she remembered, and he'd set up this switchback by being shifty in the first place, didn't he? Now he was *figuring her out.*

He didn't reply.

Callan turned the shop's sign, put on the rear track lights, thought about it, and dimmed them.

No need to make a fuss here.

He walked to the back office for the "Knicks Go" he'd brought in from the cave last night to frame Alma-Tadema style because he was pretty sure Grandma lived in the Queen Anne down the road from Sheffield Dairy. This gave the smaller one some weight, too, the frame's deeply canted triangular sections painted with a run of gold dog's-tooth on a black background, gold lotus buds and water lilies along its polished ebonized rail. A perfect foil for this piece.

After he showed it to her, he'd wrap the painting in interleaving paper, help her store it in her car, and surely be on his way to dinner-for-one. He checked her text again, a last-ditch effort to read between the lines.

Damn.

The day had warmed off to the upper sixties, more indicative of the insane ups and downs with climate change or an upcoming rain than anything else, he guessed, so the Inverness was out. He'd brought along a full-zip windbreaker that didn't look too shabby against his standard business casual if he needed even that, and—he'd forgotten about shining his Oxfords. He went over them with a shoeshine sponge to keep himself busy until he saw her car pull into the same parking space as yesterday.

When she got out, his heart tanked.

This was dinner, no question about it.

She'd tucked her hair back in a narrow headband, but it was down —straight and silky past her shoulders. A polo pullover sundress, Breton—*no, nautical*—navy and white stripes with tailored white trim and a V-neck. Sleeveless to show off those shoulders, a casual cotton knit just form-fitting enough to matter. Swingy, not tight. Horizontal stripes that worked since she was slim and—*those legs.* Easy-going flat sandals.

Callan set the shoeshine box aside, swallowed, and went to the door to meet her.

She walked *clip-clip* up the sidewalk and hesitated, noting the shop sign.

"It's unlocked," he said through the glass and opened the door.

She smiled with a little less certainty this evening and stepped through the doorway.

"Can you believe this weather?"

"Only in Eureka." He smiled. He could see by her carotids she was nervous as a hairless cat in a barber shop, so it seemed best to keep things moving. "Come in, I have the painting over here and I can bring up the track lights if—"

"No, no worries." She was several steps ahead of him already. Callan shut the door and stood for a moment watching her admire the "Knicks" he'd propped against the south wall. "It's perfect." She ran

Falling Stars

her fingers along the edges. "This wonderful vintage frame."

"I don't normally frame before appraisal, but that one seemed to fit."

She stood back. "It does. Mom's going to love this."

She was prepared to pay using mobile or digital currency, but he told her a check was fine, for his own reasons. He wrapped the painting and placed it in her boot. Throughout the transaction *dinner* hadn't come up yet, and he wasn't about to mention it, *no siree*. He thanked her for her purchase instead.

She lowered the boot's lid remotely using her key fob and smiled up at him, calmer now. "And thank you for—" she tilted her head in search of the right words, "accommodating my budget."

He grinned. "Doctors have budgets?"

June narrowed her gaze. "Don't get me started." A blip of silence, about the time he thought she was out of there for sure—

"Where are we off to?"

He swallowed. "Rogue's Manor?" *Next time, cast a spell, numskull.* "I got a table there."

A flicker of disappointment in those blues (even through the smile) much like yesterday, carotids going again.

"I hope that's all right," he added.

"It's an elegant place," she said quickly. "I haven't been there in years."

He had a feeling there was a reason for that too—and he had ways to find out.

Since cell phones could do virtually everything except spot an errant clown these days, she decided her cell was enough to take along and left the small shoulder handbag locked in her car. He took his windbreaker and one of the umbrellas he'd bought at the hardware store.

June reminded herself during their five-minute stroll to Rogue's Manor she was happy where she was at this moment, especially when the hostess directed them toward *exactly* the same table by the box window her late fiancé had selected to propose to her ten Christmases ago. *No matter*, she warned herself, *yet another one of life's fabulous little ironies running amok in my world lately.*

She chose the other chair, though.

And Callan was on it. "Wouldn't you prefer to face the courtyard?" He slid the chair out for her, anyway.

"No, this is fine," she answered.

Rogue's Manor, one of downtown's iconic and fine-dining destinations for over twenty-five years, was originally a private home walled off between two cantankerous sisters. The two-story Victorian-Craftsman hybrid backed up to a cliff along Spring Street and sprawled around the bend toward Pine, *the* place for a white-linen dining experience by candlelight and a popular venue for wedding rehearsal dinners and receptions.

I'm here again but I'm not who I was, June repeated to herself.

He'd asked if he might carry her phone inside his windbreaker's flap pocket and had offered an arm while they walked, only kind and courteous things to do. She reminded herself she was safe, to *calm the hell down* and ask about his great collector's umbrella after they ordered.

"Do you need your phone?" he asked.

She chuckled. "I don't miss it one bit."

He nodded. "They don't make very good menus."

"Aren't you glad we're past all that?"

As if on cue, their waiter arrived with two leather-bound cartes du jour.

"Speaking of." Callan smiled, *an incredible set of teeth*, she noticed, *he whitens for sure.*

They stepped through the formalities of ordering without a hitch—almost. *Yes* to splitting a bottle of dry Lambrusco and the tarragon chicken for her but a blue-rare filet mignon for him.

"Um—" she couldn't help herself, "are you sure you wouldn't rather go with medium?"

"He orders it that way every time," the waiter cut in.

"I do," Callan agreed.

When the waiter had gone, she leaned across the table and lowered her voice. "Food-borne illnesses can be fatal, you know."

He leaned in as well. "I'm aware, yes."

She studied his face, trying to read him. "You've gotten sick before?"

He nodded. "At least five or six times that I can count. Listeriosis, mostly. Not from here, though."

She couldn't hide her shock. "And yet you—"

"I like to eat it that way," he said flatly. Funny, he seemed more refined and intelligent than that. June sat back, still trying to parse this one out. She'd promised herself she wouldn't bring up Tommy off the bat, either. "My son's going through a rare meat phase. At first I thought it was sort of like eating dirt, you know, but he agrees to have his steaks cooked medium."

Callan squinted at her. "I've never much hankered for dirt, myself."

June clapped her hand over her mouth to stifle a deep belly laugh or a snort, she wasn't sure which threatened to come first. "Oh, time-out," she said between giggles. "It's really not any of my business what you choose to sink your teeth into, is it?"

A glint of something in those black eyes of his she couldn't put her finger on. He shifted in his seat. "Tell me about your son."

⭒

After they toasted to June's new acquisition and (she insisted) his continued health considering his food choices, they dove into dinner while she told him about adopting her son, his cancer, and how they'd managed before moving back to Eureka Springs. If anything, Callan only admired her more—for PNH was a dicey disease, and Tommy seemed *so-so* on the compliance scale. Evidently he still hadn't told her what really happened after school that day, either—just some trumped-up story about bailing out of his casket during a video game that ended in an emergency room visit. Callan had to hand it to the kid for ingenuity, he was absolutely two steps ahead of everybody else.

He was also amazed by what had *and hadn't* changed in treating blood cancers, and quizzed June probably a little *too* much. She didn't seem put off by talking shop at dinner and shared some promising cutting-edge research like identifying genetic markers in certain cancers and repeatable remission quotas using stem-cell therapy. Early cancer detection using bioengineered DNA in recent Melbourne trials also looked promising, she said.

And she explained why she thought Tommy had developed his own diagnostic fantasy revolving around vampirism. At the onset of his disease, the possibility he had porphyria was considered, probably a more manageable disease but not necessarily a preferable one to PNH, she said. Tommy had read everything he could about it, of course, to discover the various porphyrias originated as blood disorders prevalent among nobility in Eastern Europe, the stuff of vampires. Porphyria too, was inherited, and one of the symptoms included sensitivity to sunlight. Sunburns often disfigured its sufferers, causing their gums to recede over time and expose their teeth. Those stricken with it were accused of drinking blood because their urine turned red. In the Middle Ages some physicians even recommended that their patients drink the blood of animals to compensate for an absence of heme in their own. The sulfuric content of garlic often led to acute attacks in porphyria victims, causing abdominal spasms, weakness, and vomiting.

PNH presented with similar complications, and Tommy had latched onto a handful of these ailments as card-carrying proof he was a Dracul, she concluded. Especially after recently reading a new fantasy series in an online pulp fiction magazine about a vampire with an inherited blood disorder Tommy believed was like his own.

"He thinks he's a descendant of Dracula?" Callan asked.

June considered the possibility for a moment. "No, I don't think so. If anything, he thinks he's somehow related to Claudius Fallon."

Callan nearly dropped his fork, a quick *hup-two* to cover that one. "I think my steak just moved," he said.

She chuckled. "Serves you right."

Careful, Viscount. Boy, did he have some work to do.

"This is from the story?" he asked.

She sipped her wine. "Yes, he's the vampire in the story with Li-Fraumeni."

Callan stifled a cough. *What the hey?*

"My opinion, the disease he and his sister inherited," she went on. "In the story."

"I see." He tried to focus on cutting his steak.

"It's a genetic mutation that makes children susceptible to a variety of cancers, among them leukemia."

Well, he had to ask. "So—was this vampire cured?"

"It seems he was. If you want, I think I can share the series with you," she went on. "Supposedly he was a street artist right here in Eureka Springs at one time."

Falling Stars

Callan pointed at her with his fork. "Written by a tourist."

She chuckled. "Oh, don't we know it?"

Callan followed her facial movements very carefully, trying to intercept just how much of the story she'd truly digested. Did she read it word for word, or did she skim? After all, doctors didn't really have that kind of time on their hands, did they? Which gave him another idea.

"Your son, he can't go outside much?"

Busy with her vegetables, she didn't look up. "When he does he usually wears sleeves and carries an umbrella. Which, by the way—" blues on his, lying on the sill, "he'd love yours."

Callan smiled. "I just happen to have another one like it with his name on it."

"Really?" Blue eyes transfixed on him.

"At the gallery. I'll give it to you."

"I can pay you for it."

"No can do." He looked at the lights outside the window. "Sweat or snow, it's almost Christmas. My gift."

She followed his gaze and her smile faltered. "You're very kind." And quickly, "And this meal, even better than I remember."

"My pleasure." He met her eyes. "But what happened here, really?"

She quickly looked down. "You mean—"

"Before, in this restaurant."

With every one of Callan's questions, June recognized *something* beckoning her toward a void yawning in her own consciousness that craved meaning and value—and its directive to *fill, fill*—to hold nothing back. She normally didn't divulge this much about herself or Tommy, things even Lilly and Walt didn't know—and when Callan also asked about her previous encounter at Rogue's Manor, June was busy rehashing all the personal details she'd dished out already, ones that ran up against her comfort level.

She frowned. "It's really off limits."

His eyes registered her sorrow. "Like how I order my steak?"

"Yes, like that." She didn't smile.

"We could've gone somewhere else. Anywhere," he said.

She held her ground. "Yes, we could've. That would've been easy."

"You prefer difficult?"

"I prefer—" she hesitated, "remaking memories when the opportunity presents."

"Is that what we're doing?" He topped off their wine glasses.

June's training kicked in again, an exam room code of conduct that recommended *never* jumping to conclusions. "For me, yes." She sipped her wine. "I can't speak for the room."

He chuckled. "No, I guess you can't." He raised his glass. "To memories, yours and mine."

Which still delivered no guarantees he wasn't already terribly bored with her, she thought, all neatly tucked under a polite and professional guise he used to basically entertain another investor.

And *drat,* she could fall for him so easily. She adored his curious, piercing stares that trusted her acumen concerning medical subjects unfamiliar to him, pitch-dark to the last detail. The way he precisely rolled up his shirtsleeves before he set out to eat or drink, revealing the chic, well-placed tattoo which truly *fit* the artist. Or how he switched out his fork and knife while he ate, ambidextrous applications he claimed spared his painting hand. She also noticed how nicely his masseters flared when he read, chewed, or countered something she said.

A question had pestered her since the first day she'd walked into his gallery, one June briefly considered asking Callan before she proceeded to tell him how Sawyer had proposed to her ten years ago at Rogue's Manor, and how he died.

Callan was working his way to his last bite of steak. He put down his fork. "You outlived him."

An odd and self-evident conclusion, but true. She nodded. "I did."

"I'm sorry."

June took a breath. "This will sound callous, but I'm not. Not anymore." Upon umpteenth review, she knew in her heart their relationship hadn't been a good one. She took a sip of wine and supposed she'd end up telling Callan about that sometime as well.

"You found Tommy instead," he said, black eyes fixed on her.

"I did." She smiled. "And I will probably outlive him too—but I'm glad for every single day I've been his mom. He's a wonderful person to share life with."

The conversation turned back on Callan, but he wasn't as apprehensive

Falling Stars

about exposure as before. Clearly he'd managed to make June Lucas forget his existence in Eureka Springs during her formative years. He could do it again.

Maybe. If he wanted to.

"You opened your gallery after I left for medical school, didn't you?" June asked. She'd finished her wine.

Good enough if you say so. "That sounds about right," he said. "It's a blur, really. I guess I haven't paid much attention."

During dinner he'd memorized the tiny crease that appeared at the bridge of her nose when she thought she was onto something, the way she set her shoulders when disagreeable ideas (like his bloody steak) came to mind. And he adored them both.

He also realized something else about his own jaundiced viewpoint and accumulative bitterness toward being the one left behind. Tobias was right—he'd put up a wall around his heart long enough to forget the singular, delightful ticks of the second hand, and he'd also begun to overlook an array of personal joys found in loving someone before time inevitably took them. June had just reminded him he could enjoy someone else's existence even briefly if that's what life offered.

They decided to split a piece of turtle cheesecake. Coffee for her, hot tea for him.

She noted his order for hot tea with those blues but didn't say anything.

"Coffee messes with my digestion," he offered. Which wasn't true —he'd grown up on tea with the rest of the Queen's customs—but he thought it might be enough of a conversation topic to avoid *the other questions.*

June cracked up, leaning her head against the wall.

Did he miss something? At least she wasn't asking too many specifics. Yet.

"Says Mr. five—no six times—Listeriosis." She giggled.

Think, Claudius. "Coffee helps that," he joked.

Which threw her into another fit of laughter.

Sure enough, after dinner while he saw the opportunity to escort her back to her car and tactfully part ways, he ended up suggesting they might window shop instead. He did enjoy her company and it had been a while since he'd had this much fun. If things went sour, he had ways to cut it off without hurting her. She'd go on with her busy life and struggles like she always had because her remade dinner memories would drop into the same abyss where he sent the others. She'd only recall acquiring the painting, and he could make her forget the studio called Fast Horses, forget him.

Shops clumped along Spring Street winding down toward Main were known for their bibelots and gimcracks—some to the tune of several thousand dollars—particularly around the holidays. Dressed to the nines in tinsel and spangle, the cobblestone shopping trail always soothed Callan by drawing him out of his own isolation into the imaginations of others—whether traditional, bohemian, or hillbilly funk. On this small-town stage he could relive his youth in the company of finely preserved Folk Victorian emporiums, even the charm of some outrageously glaring storefronts and murals. Dinnertime gastronomy had a history of thinning store traffic to a trickle and many of these shops were closed by eight. Save the bars and clubs, the town fell asleep.

As June scrutinized some of the more eloquently bizarre items through the store windows, he could see her carotids going again, and he wasn't sure why. Temperatures had dropped a few degrees, so he managed to convince her to let him wrap his windbreaker around her shoulders even while she insisted she wasn't *that* cold.

Here and there between shops she'd step out to the curb and point out a constellation, first Aquarius, then Pegasus before clouds began to interfere. They continued window shopping toward Main and he enjoyed watching her, not much else. At some point she caught onto his inattention to the objets d'art all around him and decided to check in.

"What do you think about these?" She pointed. He was an artist, after all.

Callan peered through the window over her shoulder. "Some ferlies, some havers."

June tilted her head, studying his reflection in the glass. "British?"

"Scottish."

"Wonders and rubbish, right?"

"You got it."

"Show me."

He put his arm around her and in that display window he pointed out all the ferlies.

A band at the same tavern that inspired him a couple of weeks ago struck up something Latin American. He left her for a moment and stepped out into the street. From there Callan could just see tops of sombreros over the second-story railing.

"Mariachi next door," he said, and executed a spot Volta followed by a drop-turn into a double step.

June blinked at him. "Did you train professionally?"

He continued a series of cross steps in the direction of the tavern, umbrella tucked under his arm. "Amateur. New York City."

"You are full of surprises." June walked along the sidewalk behind him, watching. "Salsa?"

"Samba." He continued down the street.

She adjusted the windbreaker around her arms. "Amateur, really? You're very—good."

"I've swot at it a bit," he said.

She chuckled. "Scottish?"

"Welsh." He spun to a stop. "Come here, I'll teach you."

She didn't budge. "My hips *do not* move that way."

"Says you."

June laughed. "Don't make any claims I didn't warn you."

He smiled at her shyness and offered his hand.

Probably not his usual investor entertaining, June surmised as she walked into the street. He parked their belongings on a limestone retaining wall that bordered a streetside paseo and rejoined her. Without the windbreaker, the night's chill crawled over her shoulders, but the heartrate monitor on her Garmin sports watch indicated she wouldn't feel that for long, either.

"Take a breath," he said, holding her hands in his. Funny, she thought, how easily he calms me down. *Nobody does that.*

"Let's start with a whisk." He placed one hand just above her right hip. "Lead in this way." He demonstrated what was essentially a step-ball-change executed sideways.

But the hips, June worried. Somehow, it never mattered.

"Press into my hand," he said, and by following his instructions, she was *actually doing it,* a snappy cha-cha using the same circular hip rotation he'd demonstrated. Callan seemed pleased with her progress.

She was primed to learn the box step when unannounced rain began pelting the streets like knives. His eyes returned her disappointment, and they ran hand-in-hand toward the nearest awning.

Pop-up thundershowers around Eureka Springs can generate some ruthless, incidental waterworks carved out by raw forces of nature and gravity-driven tributaries that cut down the cliffsides. Man-made structures designed to retain or redirect water—mains, runoffs, culverts, side ditches, underdrains, and levees—cannot fully manage the onslaught of rainwater at the speed it gathers when flash floods hurl down the slopes. Natives usually go downtown prepared for Eureka's little Niagara with galoshes, but she'd worn *sandals*.

They'd only gone a block or two huddled arm-in-arm under his umbrella, ducking where they could under shop awnings before water several inches deep sluiced the streets.

"Here," he said, handing over the umbrella. "Up you go." He scooped her off the sidewalk before June could factor his body mass index ratio against hers and whether or not he was safely lifting using his legs, let alone carrying her under these conditions. When she informed him this wasn't a certified safe-carry for his back, he laughed and performed a pair of flawless spot Voltas.

Chapter Fifteen

Tommy, *def* onto Plan B since, well—this morning, after Sister M. announced papers due Monday (he'd had a whole dogpile of inside scoop on Tassemon, but *no-o—no can do,* she said). By 9:00 p.m. he was dismantling his telescope on Grandma's porch because, no dice, it *would* have to rain tonight. He'd already located the seven other planets in the solar system, though, and one of Jupiter's moons, Ganymede, and a whole mess of Saturn's, plus the comet 144P/Kushida that happened to be screaming past the constellation Taurus. *Sure good-enough* he was all set to barf up something about *Harmonices Mundi,* even if the whole idea was stupid as shit.

Tommy wasn't thrilled by any stretch, so when he sat down to review the handout M. gave him about Kepler's book and the harmony of the worlds with its—*six*—known planets at the time, he was up to his eyeballs in disgust. And they *dared* allege Tassemon wasn't real, M. and Mom, they'd really ganged up on him, all because Tommy claimed the doctor was as ever-living real as her *not-a-date.* He couldn't explain it and *hell if he could prove it,* but in his heart Tommy knew he was right. He just *knew.* Evidently that wasn't good enough, though, and somehow this pile of paper published in 1619 was supposed to be more real than Tassemon *or* Fallon.

Donkey balls.

Tommy wondered how his mom and *the dreamboat, honest to God* (said Dawn, said Casey) were getting along, and if she'd remember this time to ask him if he painted Welsh ponies. Tommy hadn't exactly said he *wanted* a painting, *we're just racking up more research on Fallon, yuppers,* and Mom reminded him he needed to focus on his school assignment instead, that she'd been reading along about Fallon all on her own and they'd discuss him tomorrow. *Way cool* that she'd squeezed the story into her 24/7 but not so cool how she said she

Falling Stars

wanted to *discuss* it. Tommy saw where that was headed a mile off—*oh well*.

At least his telescope gave him a good running start, *hooyah*, it synced with his smartphone and did way-cool stuff like guided sky tours, star pattern recognition, and real-time calculations. All he had to do was point and record.

If only the rest was that easy.

Sister M. said it all started with an astronomy book Kepler wrote called *Mysterium,* his theory that musical intervals explain how celestial bodies orbit the Sun and each other. Since outer space has no atmosphere, hence zero sound, *no-duh*—Kepler declared planetary harmonics inaudible, heard only by the soul, he said, offering its listeners a certain degree of bliss. And Tommy wondered if that kind of *yee yee* was like the first atomic blip of silence on mornings he'd wake up without any homework and realize *it's a Saturday*. Before he whooped it up.

According to Kepler, connections between geometry, astronomy, and music formed an intelligent arrangement of all matter in the universe. He put the Sun in the center of the solar system, *thank you*, or Tommy would've been way too pissed to carry on. An illustration in *Harmonices* from 1806 *yes-way* somehow got the planets spaced apart at the right distances and the constellations proportionally correct. Tommy was impressed.

At that point he got *bleh*—more interested, even without really wanting to admit it, and started scoping out how he might pull this off without too much work. Because he had to talk about a whole shitload of stuff. Tommy raised his nose in thought.

I got this.

Grandpa stuck his head in the door now and then to check on *the situation*, and Tommy's answer was *now and forevermore* the same. Yup-yup, he was on it, mighty fine, *even if I have to handwrite this whole galactic pile of—*

Tommy squared up his stack of notebook paper on the rolltop desk, sharpened his No. 2, and began to write.

A yea verily long time ago a mysterious force of attraction called gravity drew celestial bodies toward each other in space. Some didn't end well—they wiped each other out, for real. Others did something like a disco bump and spun off in different directions. The ones that stayed on the dance floor continued slowing down and speeding up, slowing down and speeding up, sorta like prom night. Kepler hypothesized that each heavenly body dances to its own rhythm, music made by the way it spins, which for the most part can be harmonious if it keeps a (no touchy) appropriate distance from its partner at all times. He went to all kinds of trouble measuring six planets in what he then called the—ahem—galaxy, and developing algorithms to prove the Milky Way and everything spinning around inside was, ahem, divinely ordained. Stable systems that don't collide are in something that he called orbital resonance and will continue humming along pretty much to the same tune for ages. That seems kinda boring to me, I'd much rather watch a pair of celestial bodies alter each other into a near-collision course and self-correct at the very last second. Just sayin'.

    Holy crud, he barely had a full page and he needed two. M. said he also had to *discuss* a planet *without* orbital resonance, *dippy-do*. He could've filled up *ten* pages on Tassemon already, and he'd have to put in some elbow grease to crank out the rest of it, maybe some info about the galaxy's *Wreck it Ralph* a.k.a. Saturn's rings, *yada-yada*...

    But this could *def* wait until tomorrow, he'd only promised Mom he'd get started. High fives around to all the busted bears, he was outta there for one of Walt's super sundaes stacked with cherries.

From the waist up they both were dry, but their legs were soaked. Despite having the umbrella and making good time hugging the sidewalks, the downburst was clearly the chicken-dinner winner. June was laughing, however, as Callan finally set her down in front of his store. She shook out the umbrella and stood it next to the door to dry while he retrieved their smartphones from his windbreaker, the only items the rain had spared, for she'd clutched them in her lap all the way back.

    "I have some towels in the office," he said as he unlocked the door with his cell. He flipped on the rear track lights. "Come inside, I'll get them."

She'd stripped off her sandals to avoid making a mess in the gallery, and he decided to do the same, off with his Oxfords and socks while ignoring a little nudge that said *why stop there?*

When he located the pair of towels he was looking for and returned to the front, June was nowhere in sight. He tucked his cell phone in his shirt pocket and glanced around the studio before heading toward the door. Her Audi was still parked along the street. She wasn't in her car, either—her smartphone still lying on the sidewalk beside her sandals and his umbrella. Light but steady rainfall pecked at the streets from the same line of thunderstorms now moving southeast of downtown. A waning crescent moon had just pulled out of cloud cover.

If she's out there without a brolly—

Callan heard a soft chuckle a block away and walked to the end of the sidewalk in front of his gallery. His was one of the last units on Cushing before the walkway stepped off into a vacant, wooded lot. He could see her outline in the moonlight around the bend from German Alley where she stooped to retrieve something off the street before wading her way back, barefoot. Truly a native, he mused.

"I thought the general idea was staying dry," he called.

"It was, up to a point," she called back.

"What did you find?"

"Christmas." She stepped out of the shadows holding one of his shop spangles. "Floating down the street."

He realized then the one at the end above his head was missing.

She giggled and handed over the ornament. "I haven't had this much fun in a while."

"Clearly you haven't."

She was soaked, head to toe. Callan laid aside the wayward bauble he'd planned on replacing anyway and shook out one of the towels. He kept a pair of oversized bath sheets for somewhat such purposes, this one now the precisely timed cape of the corrida as he swirled it under and over, the figure-eight flourish of a verónica—and just enough to capture her attention as he wrapped her up in it and kissed her.

She didn't seem to mind being cocooned by surprise and kissed, her elbows loosely tucked between their hearts, hands pressing lightly on his chest. She did pull away briefly, just enough to singe the air between them with those blues.

"That was sneaky," she said, and went on kissing him.

Callan was glad for setting it up the way he did when his shoulders began coiling outward and the tips of his acromion processes protruded. *That*—was different. Though he'd loved Milja deeply, turning had never been an issue.

Blazes, he needed to scale this back or—

"I want to show you something," he whispered and drew her closer.

"But I must carry you one more time."

"Sure, let's go," she said cheerfully. She seemed content resting her head on his chest near her hands, which gave him enough cover to take a breath. *Hell's bells, this was bad.*

So before June had a chance to speculate whether he could tote her again without hurting his back, he scooped her up, sprang along the vacant hillside east of his gallery, and flew into the woods.

⭒

The foothills near Fast Horses have some remarkable rock formations Callan discovered seventy-eight years before, not long after he bought the gallery. Streams gushing down the cliffs during torrential rains swirl into eddies near the bases here and there, and river rocks become grinders, tooling away inside small sedimentary depressions developed downstream. The waters that flow there are turbulent enough to set up vortices along the banks, whirling that starts with a core of bubbling forces churning like ship props. Some increase in diameter rapidly, and when they collapse, it's loud, columns of mist shooting straight up from their centers right before they implode.

Cavitating waters have long since been one of the main elements in surface alteration around Eureka, forming enchanting erosions especially where stream waters run warm. Rainfall cavitation is responsible, therefore, for much of the rapid deepening of plunge pools, holes in stream beds, and waterfall recession.

The rock formation Callan found all those years ago was truly one of its kind, a stunning four-by-eight-foot basin trenched out by running water and polished as smooth as the inner shell of an abalone. It arched its way up the hillside, whorls of pearlized sediment gleaming even under the cover of night.

What Callan had counted on happened. By pushing his complication to full tilt, he could also quickly scrub it out of his system.

His last involuntary *transfiguratio* had occurred at Baker Hospital in 1939, no full-on turning since—for Tassemon had warned Callan, and he'd taken it to heart. Incomplete turns like the ones on the day he'd helped Tommy required some very strong intention—difficult to muster because his ersatz blood saw to that.

He was terrified on his first day at the hospital.

But what frightened him now?

Callan was still mentally chasing down the possibilities when he felt his bones countersink the wings into those human shoulders all his own, and he set June down. His teeth were back in order too.

"Expergiscimini," he whispered to her.

And she woke, surprised perhaps at first by their absence of shoes.

"Did I—?"

"You did," he said.

She studied his face. "How rude of me."

He smiled. "You have a lot on your plate."

"That moves." She yawned.

He chuckled. *If only she knew how much.* "Look behind you," he said.

As he'd expected, she adored the rock formation with her fingers much like the frame. She turned, bright blues wide-awake. "It's stunning," she said, and released the towel.

And he loved her there.

In that hour he memorized every tilt and whorl of her landscape as they traced a visionary company together called rapture. Slow and circular movements were inviting because these implored for more— forging gentle hand holds while fingers trail in for a quiet touch, the weight of them his only cue to the next surface. Into his incomplete world her halcyon eyes looked deeply, and how he cherished this, for years too long had claimed his own. He knew her truly then, first encounters beyond such secrecy—

Her hands in his, hijacked leaves weaving into shapes they discovered while coiled together, hearts pressed down, blood tides entrained.

She met him midway inside this dreamscape shored along a nacre basin near rainwashed rills—

And he was better for it.

Rainfall combed their backs, rise and fall, until skin on skin they glistened, air growing blonde between breaths, shadows lurking in pursuit. Her hair, sinuous serpents down her shoulders, his tongue among theirs. Mute shudders that could haunt him when in absentia he drank the dawn.

He followed droplets where they stippled and wept along her alabaster skin, singly wicking the strays, nothing unclaimed—
Who was this joy, whose flesh he moved upon?

On horizons past he'd met death's stare in slow survey, and now Lazarus, from her slope with sod and billow breaking, soil shifting and water astride, all bending to Coriolis outflow—

Never a straight line drawn north or south. How he knew this.

He held her life—her soul—beneath larger storms and forces of oceans ever-moving, all churning down into depths that resurface life-giving Neptune. The ground below surged with them, once formed in colossal meanders from creeping Rossby waves charting hot and cold in tandem. The perfect orbit of Venus—his only plumb line—placed her pitch alongside his in true, an intermittent resonance shared as they purled through deep space.

He didn't want her searching for this place, so he kissed her once more before whispering "Somnum," and put her to sleep again.

Timing the next half hour was critical, and Callan could not turn. After wrapping June in the towel again, he dressed himself, gathered her clothing, and carried her back to the gallery. He was pretty sure the thunderstorm earlier had driven everyone inside—but even on the slim chance of encountering wasted, disoriented tourists or community carolers feeling first dibs, he decided using the back door was a better option.

The second towel he'd left at the front was still dry, so he retrieved it with their belongings off the sidewalk before locking up this time—*not very swift of you, Viscount*—and scolded himself for his carelessness.

She was lying in the back hallway still in deep sleep; he draped the other towel and his Inverness coat over her. The temperature had dropped, and his clothes were sopping as well. He quickly changed into an extra pair of business slacks and a shirt he kept at the office and

Falling Stars

hunted for a pair of socks. He'd folded her dress, gathered her shoes and smartphone before noting he might not be able to get inside her car —let alone drive it.

When she'd briefly checked her cell after dinner, his eidetic recall supplied a possibility of numbers for her lock screen passcode, and voilà, he was correct. After searching the cell's home screen for the correct app, he tried the same pin to unlock her car, and he was *in*. Which made all the difference in his best-laid plans (*still on point, no walking this one back*) to take her home while she slept. He got in the driver's side and shut the door.

Well, shit.

This was a fucking spaceship.

Manufacturer defaults and custom presets were likely the most difficult to navigate, Callan reasoned, so he didn't touch anything, not yet. The instrumentation display behind the steering column was less complicated, essentially an odometer and speedometer. Her vehicle appeared to have 70 percent charge remaining, with a digital gas pump icon reading 165 miles to "empty," plus a score of other helpful details he didn't really need at the moment, including the date and time, and an indicator that the front passenger airbag was ON. An MPH dial on the right.

The real agglomeration of multimedia interface screens spanned the center console. Not that Callan wasn't screen-savvy or hadn't developed his acuity cheek by jowl with technology. He'd just never updated his own daily driver. The temptation was there, though, with each new retrofitted *gimbal-gizmo* imaginable coming out every year for as long as he could remember. He'd had the engine overhauled twice, but when it came to newer amenities, he flat-out refused to modify the Woodie from her original state.

For she was all that remained of Cardiff.

Sure, he'd fussed with driving airport rentals when traveling and had considered taking an EV for a test drive a time or two, but car dealerships annoyed him.

So here he sat, fully aware that aside from the endless colors, numbers, and menus in her car's virtual cockpit, he only needed to know how to turn it on and put it in gear. He'd ridden with a couple of investors who drove electric vehicles and recalled that most—if not all, used brake servo systems that had to be engaged on startup. He'd also learned that car keys were no longer *keys* by their original definition, not with the current silicon prestige of fobs, conversation AI, and mobile apps. All he had to do was find the ignition switch.

The button was located where ash trays used to be, simple enough, labeled with a standby symbol and bold letters START over STOP. Callan depressed the brake, took a breath, and pushed the button.

Music drummed out of the 3D sound system, something with robust bass that the scrolling bar identified as ambient pop from her most frequently played selections on Amazon Music. He went for the gear icon first and noticed the screen vibrated when he opened the settings. Haptic touch wasn't lost on him, but he also knew he'd need to be careful not to rearrange her screens. He found a little button with a speaker icon on the steering wheel that scrolled and lowered the volume.

The headlights were adaptive, and Callan didn't have to bother with those. The gear display behind the ignition switch had an apparatus that looked like a stick, and after a couple of tries he managed to toggle the shifter into drive. He drove around to the gallery's rear entrance, parked, and went inside to retrieve June.

He placed the rest of her items with the umbrella for Tommy in the passenger seat. She'd slept soundly save a small stir and flicker of those half-mast blues when he lifted her this time, a proviso that called for a brief cease and desist on his part. After a moment or two he carefully laid her in the back seat and pulled the Inverness around those fabulous legs to secure her for the ride.

The drive to June's house was a short one, Callan's only faux pas, adapting to the vehicle's responsive steering and accidently activating internal voice recognition with his thumb. The steering wheel kept vibrating when he changed lanes without using turn signals.

As he bore left onto Fairmount Street, he could see she'd left one lamp on in the great room. He didn't need light to navigate his way through the house and made a mental note to stay in the shadows, since neighboring homes had full view, particularly the extra nosy one next door. He was prepared to expand his search for a HomeLink icon, or a garage door remote tucked on the visor like his own, but the overhead door opened automatically.

Now that's something. She had some sort of proximity sensing technology in her garage. Maybe he ought to rethink adding that feature to his own garage, why not?

The last checkbox on Callan's list was the possibility June had armed her home security system. He found the app on her phone and amazingly enough, she hadn't. In the lane of luck, he'd already hit a four-bagger since she'd also mentioned over dinner that Tommy was staying the night at his grandparents. All Callan had to do was follow through with his original decision, and unfortunately, he knew what that might mean.

He was familiar enough with the general layout of the Brighton house to recall the large master suite was in back. Tommy, on the other hand, had uncontested sanctions to the front drawing room just like June had explained, and Callan spotted the casket through the doorway.

Rather creepy, he thought—*even if I must say so.* He continued carrying her down the adjoining hallway.

June's master suite was its own center of operations. A workstation and workout platform that rivaled her car seemed somewhat incongruent to her quaint Jenny Lind style queen, but he liked it. She'd stayed in deep sleep, which accommodated his plans nicely. He pulled back the covers, removed the Inverness, and tucked her in.

Hence came the most trying part of the evening.

Regretfully, June was smart enough to ferret out details, he knew that. Inconsistencies *would* matter, ones he wasn't prepared to answer for, and in this state of affairs, a false memory charm was best. June would only remember dinner and dancing up to the moment she'd waded out into the street to rescue his shop decor. From then on, he'd introduce a new reality: she'd slipped in mud, made a mess of herself, and decided to call it a night. Not the way he preferred she remember him—but benign.

And cruel.

He stood for a moment with the notion that he couldn't afford to have her drilling down to the last detail. That would never work.

Callan shifted his weight. *No.*

He couldn't do it.

His heart wanted June to remember their time together, those first moments loving each other in saturated 4-D. He couldn't take that away.

Damn. She'd have questions; he was certain of it. Date night manners kept her from pressuring him with too many mainstream topics at dinner, but he could see she had an insatiably curious mind. Much of that had softened now with unconsciousness. Free of the daily intensity during her showdown with a disease that invaded skin, bone, muscle, fat, and blood—June's delicate features amplified while she slept.

He really wanted to stay.

The previous owner of the Brighton place had an antique and frame shop in this room for twenty-five years, some of the best he'd ever found. She'd always complained that one of the bay windows in the master never latched properly, and Callan found it still didn't.

He climbed out that window, scaled down the oriel, and dropped to the ground. Across the way he could see the Purple Passion and a light on in the second story. He'd never liked the way the hairdresser ran her mouth around town, plus the night was beginning to wear thin on him. Cooler air steamed around him. He stepped back into the shadows, enraged by the possibility he was being watched.

"Oblivisci," he growled, hurling the spell toward the window. A thoughtless knee-jerk on his part—he hadn't used obliviation even on the classless-act hoods because it could do some real damage. For an instant it seemed his eyes had fooled him. Directly he saw movement, though—somebody taking cover behind the casement.

Just as well. He buttoned the cowl on his Inverness and walked across the street. *Teach them to mind their own business.*

In a small community like Eureka, he might have to make amends and undo it at some point, but he didn't really care at the moment. He missed June already, and it had taken every ounce of Spartan self-hatred to leave her.

This was bad.

His only recourse now was to do what he always did. Callan headed for his cave to paint.

✧

Casey, bored looney tunes on this *so lame* Friday night, lay face-first on her bed. *She* had to cook dinner, clean the oven, *and* finish all her homework modules before midnight. Grand squeeze: if she did all that, Dawn had *promised* she could play video games with Tommy on

Falling Stars

Sunday.

In his kick-ass fucking casket.

Casey was *so* on it, forever not wanting to miss her chances for *that* opportunity, especially after Tommy announced VR as *no problemo, bring it on.* She'd screamed through kitchen duty and was about to howl *hasta la vista* at pre-Algebra with minutes to spare before lights-out.

Because she had those three-some-odd minutes, Casey decided to check up on June. *She* was the *all-gorgeous goddess* with a real happening life, going out to dinner with that *drop-dead* painter guy. Tommy had told her on their way to school this morning.

Casey saw June's car pull into the garage. She kept *waiting* for all the other house lights to click on like they had for the past seventeen days, especially if June had *muahaha* and *lmao* brought company home for a sleepover.

When that didn't happen, *dadgum* Casey was peeved enough to take this downstairs for a closer look, she was. So *not-fair*, until she saw movement along one side of the house. *Shit, it's—uh, like somebody's rock-climbing, crawling down the side, OMG—it just flew down to the ground, and it* saw *me.*

Casey quick-stepped it to the side of her window but with that, even—the world she once knew faded to black.

June opened her eyes mid-morning Saturday, puzzled at first by the amount of sunlight pouring into her bedroom.

She hadn't slept this late since—

When she reached for her cell phone to determine how delinquent she was, it wasn't bedside. She sat up, aware all at once she didn't have on pajamas, either. The two bath sheets still shrouding her said everything.

Oh, shit. She looked down.

Yes, we did. She remembered that.

But how exactly did they get there?

She replayed dozing off and apologizing, no criticisms—just an incredible amount of loving attention in the great outdoors—somewhere. June crawled out of bed and went straight to the bathroom.

The mirror proved she was a muddy mess. She twisted a leaf out of

her hair, about as snarled as she'd ever seen it.
Wow. We really had a good time, didn't we?
She slowly turned her back to the mirror. *Yep.*

June also made a mental note she was nearly three years into her current IUD and needed to schedule a new patient visit with a local gynecologist. She smiled. The year-in, year-out precautions she'd taken on the single chance of *zigtataboom* since Sawyer, an occasion that had never—

To think she'd considered dropping contraception altogether at one point.

Still pretty sure she couldn't afford a pregnancy, not on top of everything else.

And just how did she get home?

I'm on call today.

All at once alert and terribly awake, June walked *very* quickly to the garage. Her e-tron was there, *not on the charger*, she noted—clothes neatly folded and placed on the front passenger seat alongside her shoes, purse, cell—the umbrella for Tommy, the painting still in back. June frowned. No figuring this one out in five minutes, let alone why she'd lost consciousness twice last night. She was here and now though, not as neatly buttoned up this morning by any stretch, but safe.

Except—how?

While she showered, scrubbed, and dressed, June thought about it. The hardcore Capricornian *must*-know had her primed to go back *immediately* to Fast Horses (yes, he was open most Saturdays, some Sundays, he'd said) for an iron man interrogation.

By the time June reinstated her clean, dry ponytail and fielded a couple of incoming calls from after-hours, she'd toned down her original plan. She had to go pick up Tommy before noon or the house on Grand Street would have way too many Spock brows, she knew.

As she ticked off last night's events, June could verify a handful of *had nots*.

Her drink had not been spiked.

She had not felt sleepy.

She had not felt afraid.

She had not driven herself home.

In residency June trained herself to fall asleep at the drop of a hat, or she didn't get much. But last night? *Too strange.* She'd known an intern who developed narcolepsy...

Could it—?

No way.

June really wasn't okay with any of those scenarios.

Yet—she could also count on one hand how many second dates got canned because of her own balls-to-the-wall inquisitiveness. When she came on *way too*—off they ran.

Arsy-varsy as it seemed, June understood she needed to post-chill if she ever hoped to go out again with Callan.

As long as she was safe, their roll in the hills had to develop on his terms, at least for the next date or two.

Assuming those would happen.

She and Tommy were busy enough until after Christmas—her plate ah-so naturally full of things that moved, including his first immunotherapy outside of Illinois.

On the other hand, she knew she wanted to see Callan again. That much was decided. Very likely not a cakewalk, though. June squared her shoulders.

I got this.

Chapter Sixteen

Jon Snow went *wakey-wakey* at first light to a cell alarm streaming something Billie Eilish, *don't know jack* except yeah, *is a gurl for a gurl* —also by the amount of hot pink they saw spilling out of the closet. The *flippy-do* wall letters spelling C-A-S-E-Y didn't necessarily certify they were a girl, but the taffeta ruffled miniskirts did.

Jon a.k.a. C-A-S-E-Y sat up (*let's get this straight*) cause *if I'm in some sorta deep space doo-doo, I don't get a whiff.* Jon looked down. They were still in yesterday's clothes—shorts and T, but the *ICEE* on the windowpane *def* said no pickings for those today. Jon shivered, got up, and made a low run for the closet. They weren't sure who might be watching, but it could happen, and they pulled out a pair of sweats and T—a bald-faced negotiation for anybody that might have oversight, they couldn't remember who.

Homework still looked like it was working on that side of the bed. Jon gazed at the numbers. *Holy fuck*, w*hat in the world was that?* They pressed three fingers to the forehead in a mystified attempt to figure this one.

Nothing came.

Downstairs, *Queen Bee* suddenly yelled up the stairwell, something about *getting your move on* and *late for muffins*. Jon recognized the voice as *Mom* (didn't know shit about muffins) and hoped that meant these were ready because they sure were hungry.

Walt and Lilly appeared unexpectedly upbeat after Tommy's first-ever overnighter without June, an adventure *as-successful-a-one I ever saw*, Walt told June on the sly—*though the rain nixed that downtown sing-along Lilly was raving about.* Tommy didn't mind, he added. *Quite a little man about it, did his homework until he hit the sack.*

And did y'all get wet?

June's quick face-off with her dad to cheerfully inform him he was fishing on thin ice was met with a goofball grin and a suggestion to get food truck tacos for lunch. A dragline of calls saved her from fielding anymore questions from Lilly, plus she'd already planned to make good on a past-due promise to take Tommy out to Odd Fellows Cemetery before temperatures dropped.

She needed to discuss *Philly's* with him too—no more putting that off.

Over tomato-loaded tacos June confirmed next week's after school pickup schedule with Walt and discussed some possibilities for Christmas Eve and Day meals with Lilly. Walt helped Tommy gather his paraphernalia and load it in the trunk while June tried the preconditioning feature to warm up the car—a tick ahead on Tommy's techy account.

Then they were on their way.

Did she ask Masters if he painted Welsh ponies?

Shit, she forgot. June took a breath. Tommy had clearly been holding onto that one since she'd arrived. They weren't even at the end of the driveway.

"Oh no, sweetie—I'm sorry." She knew she'd better come up with something good. "But I have to—go get some hanging hardware at his studio next week, you know, for Grandma's painting."

His eyes grew wide. "You really got it?"

June smiled. "I did." She only needed to return the towels, and yes, she'd decided to do that. Tommy seemed satisfied enough to wait on another unfulfilled promise, but June internally kicked herself once again for those things she didn't get around to, or in some way didn't pan out. No matter what, *those* charges became paramount—she saw it in his eyes. Adulting could get complicated, but why did adults do such things?

"Don't forget this time," he muttered.

"I won't."

Finding conversational middle ground was always a challenge, and how June knew it. If they discussed *Philly's* the way she'd planned, Tommy might ultimately concede that harvested Welsh ponies and Claudius Fallon were rightfully fabrications of someone's unchecked imagination, and she wouldn't need to ask Callan about Welsh ponies at all. On the flipside, June felt compelled to tread lightly even here, because taking away Tommy's license to dream could yield some unfavorable results.

The very reason she'd put off this tête-à-tête too long.

Eureka old-timers like Walt still referred to the burial ground—officially renamed Eureka Springs Cemetery decades ago—as Odd Fellows, after its founding order. June thought of the beautiful old graveyard as Odd Fellows herself because of the eclectic arrangement of headstones—a variety not common to community memorials.

Shortly after adopting Tommy, June found his birth mother here, under one of the flat grave markers near the back of the property. As she steered the car down the winding asphalt road that looped in with others, she fretted about what to say, for nothing sounded right in her head.

Tommy was all over it, June noticed, eyes peeled to headstones as they passed, *did you know them* and other questions, some to which she answered *yes* and others, *no*—for Walt and Lilly were acquainted with far more Odd Fellows residents, she explained. Stray gravel crackled under the tires the same way it had eight years ago, the funerary tract virtually unchanged.

June had barely clipped the car into park before Tommy popped off his seatbelt, out of the car in a flash. She watched him walk straight up to the headstone, yes, the correct one—yet another example of his *mystique confidential*.

He pointed. "Is this it?"

June walked around the car. "That one, yes."

"Syl—via Milford?"

"She was your birth mother." June stood for a moment before bending down to brush away leaves banked around the marker, as if that would solve anything, or help her plan what to say next.

Tommy studied the headstone quietly. "She was younger than you are," he finally said.

June straightened. "Yes, she was." She'd braced herself for the inevitable question about cause of death, but Tommy was gazing across the cemetery.

"I need to go look over there." He took off.

Steam curled from Tommy's bomber jacket as he trotted away, and June quick-checked the temperature on her cell phone. Warmth of noon-

Falling Stars

thirty sunshine would hold for another half hour, but a winter front had clearly come in late last night. While she probably should be driving him, on second thought June allowed him to walk. She was pretty sure he needed to process—*that's what he's bound to be doing*—without any interference. June tucked her cell phone inside her jacket and followed.

The plot Tommy headed toward lay along the east side, a longer hike than June anticipated. This area was much older, the usual assortment of markers jutting up from the bedrock—upright, slanted, obelisk—all neatly arranged near the property line.

Tommy fished out his cell, fixated on an above-ground companion crypt hewn primarily from unpolished white marble, one of two June counted in the cemetery. He walked around to one end and continued snapping photos of a well-weathered inscription. When he turned back toward her, his eyes shone with excitement.

"Come look at this," he called.

June jogged the last several yards toward the plot, trying to make out the faded inscription she was running toward.

Tommy pointed at the large letters in Tristram style—not easy to decipher until June stood a few feet away. She frowned.

"Don't you get it?" Tommy gestured. "From the story?"

June had to admit she'd scanned some parts, but there it was.

Scurlock.

And she certainly didn't want to have *the talk* out here in the cold.

Did you even read that part Tommy was asking. *Yes, yes*—she had. June looked down at an incoming text from after-hours on her phone.

"Let's get some more pictures and talk about it in the car," she said.

*M*om had nothing on him, *she* knew what Scurlock meant, even if she *deepfaked* she *didn't exactly remember* reading that part. Tommy took a couple more photos and checked the ground for tracks to see if anyone else had been out here recently, but *no dice*. Besides the groundskeeper it looked like no one had been out here in a real long time.

Mom was *infinity and beyond* finishing her text, all the way back to the car *for real*—and when they got inside, she didn't immediately drive off like usual. She jacked up the heat, glanced around the cemetery, and locked the doors instead.

"Okay," she began—and Tommy knew what *that* meant. *Okay* really meant things weren't okay, and it usually had something to do with him. "In the story—"

"The Scurlock crypt is where Fallon's sister is buried," he interrupted.

She nodded. "Right." She didn't look at him, though, because she was cooking up something big, he just knew it. He waited, *one coconut, two coconut...*

Finally, she sighed—didn't sound very *alrighty—*

"Hear me out?" she asked.

He wasn't real *hoody hoo* about that either, but it wasn't the time to disagree. "Sure," he said.

"People who write pulp fiction like—what's his name?"

"Miles Cochran."

"Right. Sometimes they visit the places they write about, and select certain features to use in their stories, even real buildings and locations." She glanced his way.

Tommy couldn't believe his ears. "Is that *all* you think he did?"

"Scurlock might even be one of his own relatives. He just added it into his story."

"You *absotively* don't think Fallon is real?"

Mom looked confused. "What's that?"

"Absolutely and positively."

She shook her head, still very sad. "It's—just a story, sweetie." Checked her texts again.

He stuck out his lip. *Then let her get a load of this.* "I saw the Woodie."

"The—what?"

"The Packard. In the story."

That got her attention. "You mean—the one that Gaye—"

"Drove across the country. Three times."

"Where did you see it?"

"Church parking lot."

"At school?"

"Yep. Grandpa saw it too. But he couldn't remember who owns it."

"Someone probably brought it here for a car show."

"On Thanksgiving?"

"It's possible."

Funny how something as unbelievable as *that* could be possible to her, he stewed. "I saw it another time *without* Grandpa." *Whoa, so—*he'd better *chillax* a bit. *Can't have Mom asking too muchy.*

"When was this?"

"First day of school."

"Did you ask Sister Madeline? It could belong to someone who goes to the church."

Also said the painter dude in Tommy's total recall. *What gives?*

"No. But I will," he replied.

"She'll probably know." Mom looked at him, her face still sad. "The story was incredible, Tommy, really. And yes, I'd like to know what ultimately happened to Dr. Tassemon, and especially Claudius Fallon."

"Then why won't you help me?" It came out louder than he'd *thunk, yuppers*, a little spit up there on the dash.

Mom put her phone down. "Tommy, we've been over this before. When you reach a certain stage, a bone marrow transplant will put your cancer in remission. The disease Claudius Fallon had in the story was untreatable. He didn't conjure some . . . spell—or take a magic potion to cure himself. Those things just don't exist, honey."

Tommy had told himself to suck it up like fifty times in the last five, no *wahface*, but he couldn't help it. When Mom reached for his hand, he pulled it away.

"Tommy," she said. "Tommy, look at me."

Like he had a choice. She wasn't all pissy, though—just *yes-way* sad. *Level 80.*

"You *are* going to get over this." She grabbed his other hand before it got away this time. "It really doesn't make any difference *how* this started. The treatment and the outcome remain the same, and you've got a very good chance at living a normal life."

"But I *like* being a sick vampire."

A sorta *tough-guy* hand squeeze, but she was smiling now. "That's just it, don't you see? You don't have to be sick to be a vampire. And you don't have to be a vampire because you're sick."

"I can be a *well* vampire?"

"You certainly can."

He looked down, Mom's hand *smushing* his. She had it all figured out. *She* had so much hope.

"But he was just like me."

"That's what good stories do."

"You really finished it?"

"I really did."

"Can I still read the rest to you when we have time?" For he was reasonably sure she'd skimmed, and he *yessiree* had more questions.

"Of course."

Tommy clocked in on the new arrival lying at their front door before June saw it, out of the car instantly. June worried at first the delivery might be one of his Christmas presents, but it wasn't. He came down from the porch lugging a dozen red roses in a vase nearly as big as himself.

"They're for you," he said.

The drive home from the cemetery was tough, June second-guessing every word said or unsaid. Tommy had played a game on his cell phone, seeming no worse for wear, while June detested herself, guilt calling her out with demands to undo countless false steps against the race called Time. When on Capricornian impulse she misspoke, she longed for do-overs even while questioning what difference they might make.

For Time was an unforgiving tyrant.

"Here, let me take those." June checked the card, *yes deliverable to her*—and carried the flowers inside to the kitchen counter, Tommy in lockstep with her.

"Looks like it was a success," he said.

"What are you talking about, Tommy?" June eyed him and opened the card.

"Your *not-a-date*," he answered.

June turned away so he couldn't see blood creeping into her face. "I imagine it's just a standard thank you." She glanced at the enclosed card and quickly tucked it away. "For making such a large purchase."

Tommy didn't budge.

"For Grandma."

"Where is it?" he asked.

"In the living room." Callan had suggested she leave the painting in the interleaving paper before adding her own gift wrap. She'd carefully leaned it against the wall.

Tommy knelt by the painting and peered through the clear wrapper, his hands planted on the floor. He really was a good kid, June thought.

"I'll need to gift wrap it sometime today and put it in the closet, in case Mom drops by," she said. "Want to help?"

"Sure." Tommy straightened. "And I think you should go out and suck face with the painter guy again too."

"I—what?"

Tommy glanced toward the roses in the kitchen.

Hands on her hips. *"Tommy* Lucas."

"My vote. Just sayin'." He grinned and took off for his room.

June stood for a moment, trying to emotionally digest Tommy's confidence that making out and beyond with Callan Masters was somehow good for her. He didn't seem jealous at all. In the kitchen, she reopened the card and read it again, searching for the right interpretation.

Thank you for a lovely evening.

It hung in the air in all its simplicity with a terminal touché. No, she decided, there's no *let's do it again* in that sentence. June picked up her cell phone, sighed, and thumbed in an equally conclusive text.

Thank you for the lovely roses.

Underneath it, she sent Callan the link to "Bad Blood."

On Monday the weather held its vise grip on winter, so June drove Tommy and Casey to school. Tommy was under no uncertain terms still rankled at Dawn for preempting their video game knock-out planned for Sunday, *something about Casey's noncompliance*, he'd griped, which June interpreted as delinquency in chores for the B&B.

June had seen Casey only once, on the day they moved in—and therefore questioned whether she truly picked up on something *off*. Casey's conversational overtones seemed more bombastic, and she was dressed in something trans trending this morning that walked right up to the line. She wasn't wearing a coat, either. June drove slowly to give the two a chance to chat about the next possible time to hook up and play, maybe even this weekend—or over winter break.

June agreed either was fine with her; she felt sorry for Casey and some of the responsibilities Dawn demanded. After dropping off Tommy, June drove Casey to her bus stop and tried engaging her in small talk, but the kid seemed troubled. Before she bolted out of the car, June handed her one of her business cards.

"Call me if you need anything, okay?"

Casey gave June *not like her* two thumbs up. Just very odd; June thought about it. Trying on new identities was a timeworn tween practice, true. Something else disturbed her about Casey, however—and as much as she preferred avoiding Dawn, June knew she ought to check in. She'd also better ask Tommy about it.

Lunch break was ample time to return the towels to Fast Horses since June was working televisits from home. Downtown traffic on a Monday could have potential spillovers from weekend tourism, she knew, a potential parking shortage she was prepared to face. She squeezed the huge bath sheets she'd washed over the weekend into a giant paper shopping bag and went scrubs over thermal, ponytail casual.

Sure, this could've waited several days, but that didn't feel right, either. June circled back for a parking space that eventually came open a block down from Fast Horses, not at all surprised to see the studio buzzing with customers. She was set to wait in line and peruse some paintings, and should she be so lucky to identify a Welsh pony champion in one of them, it would mean one less question to ask. She pulled out her cell to do her own research.

Callan hadn't trusted his own resolve to proceed cautiously *in favor of reply* and therefore didn't engage in a texting match with June on Saturday. In truth, he hadn't answered her at all. So when she walked into his gallery a little after one on Monday, he mentally warned himself about sending her mixed messages. He did need to make up his mind.

But there she was, as beautiful as ever.

She didn't seem in a hurry to return to wherever she was working, probably a good thing, for he spent several minutes fielding questions and sending two groups of customers away with lithograph prints. When the gallery was finally empty, he walked over where June stood scrutinizing the east wall's selections against her own cell phone data. A large shopping bag sat at her feet; he could see the bath sheets inside.

Falling Stars

She didn't seem aware he was standing right behind her.

"Are you looking for something in particular?" he asked, feeling like a chump already.

"Is Bonanza Boy the only Welsh champion you've painted?" She'd been scrutinizing that painting, the stud's second consecutive success in the 1989 Welsh Grand National. A loaded question coming straight from the kid that he'd need to sidestep for now.

"He is," Callan answered. In all honesty he hadn't had much interest in returning to Cardiff for the races then and had painted this one from a photograph.

She seemed relieved, all at once pocketing her cell phone and handing over the huge shopping bag, blues at last skirting his. Carotids going gangbusters. *Maybe he ought to step in.*

"You didn't have to return these," he offered.

"I know," she replied, eyes locked on. "But they come back to you with a question."

Shit. Callan steadied himself.

"Will we have a chance to use them again?"

Pitching woo? Surely, she's not—

June looked down at the floor and giggled. "That didn't exactly come out right." Blues big and bright on him again. "Dinner sometime? My treat?"

The following Monday, Callan loaded a delivery into the Woodie's wayback and drove to Bentonville. The trip was a twofer—hang a painting in a client's home and a stop by Nexis Bioworks, the medical food processing plant he'd used since Tassemon scrawled out his original prescription. The company name and location had changed a few times, but in review Callan had been lucky. He'd never gone without, even when components in his blue juice had to be temporarily outsourced. From cook to cook the formula remained the same, some chemists questioning its efficacy more than others, but none refusing the money that bought it. For this too, Callan had one hard and fast rule: he always met the new distributor in person. If they stayed with the company long enough, he had to use his talisman.

The drive gave Callan time to clear his head and review his second date with June. The awkward exchange over the towels in the gallery last Monday hadn't convinced him to turn her down, *nothing* had convinced him to turn her down. She'd suggested meeting at the studio once again and he'd constrained himself to a courtly hand-kiss, which got her carotids going again.

They'd dined on Saturday evening at the stately Grand Central Hotel on Main, white linen ensconced in lovely Victorian shades of red and dark walnut, Billie Holiday and crooner music streaming—a venue too wistful for him to dine alone, for it took him all the way back to his first days in Eureka Springs.

June brought her exquisite levity to the table with claims she could only eat here a couple of times a year because their hospitality bread was *just that good*. She didn't comment about his blue-rare that night, either. While he'd steeled himself for a cross-examination over dinner, it simply didn't happen. She did ask if the *Philly's* link she'd sent was functional, and he claimed he hadn't had a chance to look at it yet. He also felt safe enough to share some of his travel plans to upcoming races in the spring, *maybe she might come along with?* He couldn't believe his own mouth, but there it was. He'd also tried to intercept the check, but she stood her ground that she was buying.

Tommy was overnight with his grandparents for a second time, her hint it was okay to love her without the towels in a more conventional setting—her own Jenny Lind—and he did not turn. Callan knew then he was no longer afraid, that he had a firm handle on the whole shebang whenever he so unfortunately should have to make her forget. For the time being it seemed she was enjoying his company as much as he, hers. Sometime in the wee hours she invited him to Christmas Day dinner, to which he stupidly said yes. It felt right, though. He could advise Lilly Lucas where to display her "Knicks Go", June suggested, and he already imagined the old house with a full-on clutter of heirlooms and ferlies. The only uneasy topic of conversation the entire evening involved June's concerns about Tommy's friend and next-door neighbor. She'd been acting strangely all week and had come home from school with a black eye on Wednesday, June said.

Something he'd need to correct. He knew it at once.

After the delivery Callan stopped at Nexis Bioworks, parked, and walked inside. A facility less than ten years old, it architecturally trended toward a new design model that supported open or closed labs and technology against environmental sustainability. The lobby alone stood an imposing five stories high, glass on steel with a large central atrium. A security guard at the information booth ushered him into a small cubicle where he was told to wait.

The take-home: *chem grads Stanford cranks out these days aren't exactly what they used to be.* Or perhaps the replacement had falsified his vita. The new pharma who eventually arrived to meet him was an overfed, constitutional mess in a lab coat, probably a basement dweller or couch surfer apparently more interested in his smartphone than anything else. Impressive, Callan thought, if this one lasted six months.

You mean you've been taking this shit for nearly ten years? To which Callan simply said yes and handed him the plastic. The less anyone knew, the better. That never changed.

Tassemon had remained a teetotaler, remarried, and continued his practice in Springdale until the midseventies, his continued supervision of Callan's formula something he insisted on until his death. A cardiac arrest in 1978 took him suddenly, probably not as much to his own surprise as was generally speculated, for he'd confided to Callan during their last dinner together—whispering aside from the wife—*make sure you always take it slow on the spirits, Viscount, and don't let them clobber you more than your ticker can take.*

The more challenging part of Callan's day was locating Casey Wenner. He'd seen her walking home from school a couple of times when picking up deliveries from his cave, but he also knew that the spell might have her doing things differently. After considering the possibilities, he decided he'd take his chances on arriving at the rectory after four. He could always detour to the cave or try again on another day. Then again from what June had described, he needed to handle this straightaway.

Around half past four he saw her, or someone he presumed was her hailing the trashed-up baggy jeans look, hair stuffed under a ball cap. He knew the effect of obliviation by other indices—the eyes, the gait— and this one had it. Callan waited until she'd turned off Magnolia Path, a pedestrian crossway through the ravine up to Crescent Drive, before stepping out of his car. He followed her on foot until they crested the hill.

"Casey," he called after her.

No marvel she didn't look back. Obliviation had a way of turning the mind on itself, not pretty.

He clicked off five seconds before she spun around, scowling.

"Vicissim," he said as he twisted his hand behind his back, a cantrip to blow off her ball cap.

Casey blinked at him, the thousand-yard stare his mother had warned him about which accompanied such spells.

He picked up her cap and held it out toward her. "You dropped this," he said.

With the return of Casey Wenner came a tempered, crestfallen observation that she was not clothed in her norm, plus the confusion and inhibition she felt while actually *talking* to the Instagram-famous art guy in their little town.

"Oh—*sorry*, um—that's not mine," she said. "But thanks, anyway."

She turned and ran off.

✯

On New Year's Day, June woke to two inches' snow and a portrait miniature of herself on the pillow next to hers, where Callan had been. No larger than a business card, he'd rendered it in oil and framed the tiny painting in a gold cast floral oval. June examined it under the pale rays of the first light.

This was—*a very old custom*.

He'd left hours ago to catch up on some painting and run a couple of deliveries, he said. Still more questions she must file away until—well, the time was right. Her bedroom felt drafty this morning, so she tugged on a pair of sweats and opened the search bar on her cell phone.

Apparently the practice of painting portrait miniatures (also called limning) dated back to the fifteenth century— customarily rendered in oil, watercolor, or etched on stretched vellum, copper—sometimes even playing cards. June continued reading—*intimate gifts, usually given among family in the course of someone's absence during war, immigration, marriage, or death*. They were also exchanged, the article said, *by hopeful suitors during courtship*. Some even had space for a lock of hair underneath, or the same could be displayed on the back of the frame in a decorative weave. The replication of her features was stunning. But what was Callan trying to say? Sooner or later she was going to have to ask.

Falling Stars

They'd rung in 2024 last night over dinner downtown, the fourth in a string of weekly encounters, dates that now fell into a generic understanding they would see each other again. June didn't know much more about Callan at all, something she fought down like a bad case of acid reflux. She didn't even know what kind of car he drove.

He did mention over Christmas that he walked to work much of the time because he lived on Spring Street. Meeting at his studio downtown at the close of his day had worked for both their schedules, and they'd continued in the same manner. They cut a rug in the streets to holiday music, June still fretting about the hips while Callan reassured her she was getting the hang of it. He'd also found out about her upcoming birthday and wanted to treat her on Saturday. When she dared to ask about his, he'd told her he was a bullish thirteenth.

Opinions around the room: Lilly, beside herself with amusement; Tommy, glibly calling them hookups (without a richer understanding of what that really meant, June was pretty sure); and Walt, simply tossing out *it's clear they're getting on pretty thick*. June's main worry was Tommy, should he start feeling left out. And she still wasn't comfortable imposing on her parents as much, either.

"Knicks Go" was a hit on Christmas Day, and in the company of the artist himself, Lilly mangled her standard banter more than once. Even Tommy had cut his eyes his grandma's way a couple of times over dinner, all June could do to suppress a snicker. Finding a gift for Callan was the real hustle. She'd noticed his interest in her sports watch, but for his fashion style she decided on a Withings with its classic Swiss-made timepiece, fine calf leather strap, and analog style clockface. With it he could track his steps, analyze his sleep, and set alarms. He'd given her a bottle of Lambrusco, a clever way of presenting a delicate aquamarine pendant lashed around its neck. The silver bail holding the gemstone was a caduceus.

Tommy had fawned over his umbrella probably longer than necessary and kept giving Callan curious glances whenever he switched his fork hand during dinner, she'd noticed.

When they'd returned home to Tommy's new blackout shades and the casket recently outfitted with snow and fog, he was over the moon with wonder. It didn't take much convincing for Callan to give the 4-D gaming platform a test drive, either. June was reasonably sure she hadn't imagined the glint of delight she saw in those pitch-black eyes when Callan climbed out.

He also sifted through the sound box hardware Tommy had wrenched out of Prince Hairy, pointing out where its turntable was worn. He knew a tinker in town who could replace it, he said, if he couldn't do so himself. Tommy seemed okay with Callan taking the toy with him when he left.

June checked the time. She'd barely managed to convince Dawn to allow Casey over for video games today, and she needed to go pick up Tommy. Such a gift from Callan deserved a phone call later, June decided. She stowed the miniature portrait in her bedside table for the time being.

Tommy had mentioned that Casey was *far less uncool* the previous week, so June agreed she'd see for herself before involving Dawn. When Casey arrived, however, she announced her mom would be over with margarita mix *in a few, after the last guests checked out of the B&B.*

June pulled a margarita machine out of storage and washed it while the kids set up way more electronics than they'd get around to, in Tommy's room. Before long they were yucking it up loud enough to send any sensible adult outside, so June turned on a propane patio heater for ritas on the porch.

Midday sunlight melting the snow-laden ground drew up a mist between their houses, and sheets of ice that formed on the roof overnight randomly had released their grip all morning, *flash and whomp* skidding to the ground below.

June observed the beauty around her and internally announced that even a visit with Dawn Wenner didn't have to be dreadful.

Twenty minutes later, June and Dawn were bundled in blankets on patio loungers in a hearty forty-one-degree high noon drinking frozen margaritas, double shots for Dawn. She pulled a small vape pen out of her coat.

"You mind?"

June shook her head and sipped her drink. *These weren't too bad, really.*

Dawn powered on the pen and took a slow drag, *a faint whiff of peanut butter, yes*—and June noticed she made a point to hold the vapor in her mouth for a moment, a cloud chaser technique that obviously gave her the throat hit she craved.

"It's been a week." Dawn pressed her fingers to the bridge of her nose.

"Is Casey all right?" June asked.

"*Now* she would be. Little shit." Dawn sniggered and took another drag. "Four—no *five* sets of guests, *the* Christmas rush, and she just—forgets everything."

"Everything?"

"Total amnesia, I'm telling you. She comes home with F's and picks fights at school, then *open sesame,* she's back. I don't know what to think."

"An FSH panel might be helpful."

Dawn regarded her blankly.

"Hormone levels. With her doctor," June added.

Dawn slowly nodded, eyes like a stunned mullet. "Why—you know, that could be. I had female problems when I was her age." She released a monster cloud. "You really think that's it?"

"Certainly worth checking," June said.

Dawn switched to her margarita. "Well, praise God and Jesus. That certainly makes sense."

"She's a good kid," June said.

Dawn coughed. "Yeah, but it still pisses me off. She'll be the rest of the semester getting her grades up."

That again. Surely Casey was good for it, all things considered. "I'm glad you let her come over to play video games with Tommy today."

Dawn's eyes narrowed. "Does he really have a casket in his room?"

No hiding it now. "It's his video game console."

"Aside from being god-awful bizarre, I bet that cost you a chunk of change, huh?"

June smiled. "Worth every single penny."

Dawn sighed. "*Jesus,* you're a good mom, you know?"

"That's very kind."

"Nope. I really mean it." Smoke all around Dawn. "Then again before it gets too cozy out here, I think you need to know something," she went on.

Okay—

Dawn frittered with the swizzle stick in her drink for a moment, some sort of twisted melodramatic pause before dishing out small-town dirt, June figured. She sipped her own margarita and waited.

"I think Casey might be Tommy's half sister."

An ice dam chose to underscore the news with a screeching nosedive to the ground, and June's right calf knotted up. She fumbled her drink aside and swung her feet to the porch.

"Cramps?" Dawn regarded her smugly.

"Didn't see that one coming," June muttered.

Dawn gave her a moment before continuing. "Tommy's mother is Sylvia Milford, right? The one six feet under?"

It figures Tommy told Casey about their cemetery visit, June gathered that much.

"Yes." She flexed her foot before deciding she'd have to walk it out. She stood.

Dawn glanced toward the patio door and lowered her voice. "She's the one my ex was still married to while he was banging me."

June turned, uncertain what to say. "You're sure about that?"

"Garrison?" Dawn upended her margarita and drained it.

All June could think about were dozens of dead-ended leads. "Any idea where he might be?"

"Nope, and I don't want to know."

This could go both ways, June realized. "You're certain Casey—you and Garrison—"

Dawn regarded June through eyes narrowed to slits, about as close to open contempt as it came. "*I* was exclusive with the sumbitch, if that's what you're implying."

June swallowed. "Pretty much, yeah." While every ounce of personal fortitude warned her about forging any alliances with Dawn, June couldn't ignore the niggle that this relationship might be lifesaving for Tommy. *But how to do it?* She suspected Dawn's opportunistic agenda could also easily ignore Casey's wellbeing.

"If Casey really is his half-sibling, there's a good chance she could be a donor," June said.

Dawn didn't follow.

"Tommy's going to need a bone marrow transplant sometime in the

Falling Stars

next two or three years," June went on. "The closest genetic match is usually parents or siblings, sometimes half-siblings."

"You mean—she can donate—this . . ."

"Bone marrow. It's a similar procedure to donating blood platelets."

Dawn took a drag. "Can she get money for that?"

Not surprised, June thought. She'd need to steer this carefully.

"She can if she's a match." The raw statistics, a 1-in-500 chance Casey would be, June knew. For that reason, bone marrow donations usually failed as money-making propositions. The Wenners might get a small amount for registering Casey as a donor with a national blood bank, but if she was a match to Tommy, the real payoff for donating her marrow would come out of June's pocket.

June therefore promised herself she wouldn't go there, even while she did so. "It's a bit of a process. Casey would have to agree to it."

"Does it involve needles? Casey hates needles," Dawn clicked off.

"It does, unfortunately. One in each arm." Current donation methods using stem-cell apheresis, while far less intrusive than surgical harvesting, still involved pumping blood out of one arm and back into the other—a setup much like donating blood—that lasted six to eight hours. Plus five days of filgrastim injections prior to donation. And possible side effects afterward like back pain, fatigue, headaches or bruising. Those could last for weeks.

"How much money?" Dawn asked.

"Last I checked, the going rate was ten thousand."

Dawn stiffened. "Oh, I think I can definitely talk her into that."

June's calf had recovered, so she sat down. "We can only do this with Casey's informed consent. First, we check to see if she's an HLA match using a cheek swab."

Dawn was clicking off the boxes. "Consider it done."

"Sometimes secondary verification requires having blood drawn," June continued.

"Okay."

"If she's not a match, we can't go any farther." *Disappointing and no dinero no matter how they sliced it.*

"I see." Dawn studied June's face.

"Another one?" June pointed to her glass.

"In a minute," Dawn said, turning off her vape pen. "So what I really want to know is—are you seeing that god who paints horses?"

Careful, June. Lilly had her nails done last week, and the cat was out. "A couple of times, yes," June said.

Dawn chuffed. "Erm—just twice? So he's not gay, then."

"Where did you hear that?"

"Well—I don't know. Pearl, maybe."

This could just as easily fish both ways, June supposed. "Do you remember how long his studio's been here?"

"Oh. Well—five, six years?" Dawn held out her margarita glass. "You know how things come and go downtown."

Raiding the fridge, *absotively woot-woot* protocol after any leveling up, had Tommy scoping out Red Bulls and Cheetos in the kitchen until Casey picked up on some *adulting* going on outside, and curiosity won out. Sure, he was maybe sorta still getting used to the idea she was his older neighborly halfway sister gamer, and not necessarily in that order, and that *her* mom was out there delivering those goods to *his* mom, as Casey so casually pointed out.

He watched Mom pacing like she always did when she was *braining* it, and he showed Casey a little recess near the porch where they could sit and listen in. When Mom started talking about blood and needles, though, Casey's eyes got *real* big, and she ran back to his room. It took him the better part of fifteen minutes to set things straight, that he didn't need a donor because he was going to the Fan Expo convention in St. Louis, *he* would find out where Claudius Fallon fell off the grid, subpoena him, and 3-D print a formula exactly like his.

Which somehow made Casey even more uptight, and all he wanted her to know was, she was off the hook. Then he asked if she could come with, but she told him there was *no way in God's fucking hell* her mom would let her go now, not after the grades she brought home last week.

And Tommy told her he'd check with Sister M., but he was pretty sure God did a quit-claim on hell a long time ago.

The birthday gift Callan presented June the next Saturday evening brought her to tears; she couldn't help it. For he gave her yet another portrait miniature—Tommy's.

My sincerest apologies, he'd stammered, not having seen this side of her. Training kicked in and she somehow pulled herself together enough to enjoy the rest of the evening. The timing of everything was bearing down on them, and the next Friday—just two weeks before Fan Expo—she was comparing Tommy's numbers one screen to another at her home workstation and fighting back tears again.

She'd learned a long time ago not to gauge her son's morbidity based upon pallor or energy levels. Symptoms themselves weren't reliable markers for the degrees of cascading oncologists looked for, and infusions had never completely arrested his anemia or fatigue. Like 70 percent of other PNH patients, Tommy lived with those. Up to now they'd only dealt with intravascular hemolysis, no breakdown in Tommy's liver or spleen.

Friday's blood tests showed something terribly and awfully different, higher bilirubin and lactate dehydrogenase levels indicating those organs had gone adrift together into a spastic cha-cha. Both intravascular and extravascular hemolysis were now happening simultaneously in Tommy's body, a process where proteins set up a chain of events prompting the immune system to attack organs. His little accident with his casket hadn't done him any favors, either. A hardcore visit with his new consulting oncologist laid the groundwork.

Here's the numbers, no more waiting.

You're looking at a transplant in six months.

He can finish the school semester, but I encourage you to take all the appropriate measures and precautions.

Post-treatment came with the usual drags and nausea, and Tommy stepped through the sweat-downs during and after the four-hour infusion in fits and starts. They'd switched arms after the first site blew, so he came home with a compression bandage around his left elbow, all forgiven when the nurse allowed him to pick black cling gauze.

June couldn't help but speculate that the heightened stressors during their move and Tommy's accident were integral with those changes, although his treating oncologist didn't agree. They'd gone home with more oral anticoagulants, folate, and antibiotics.

Casey had consented to a cheek swab, the initial results an HLA match. Secondary verification was still a stretch for her, however. June swallowed hard, told Dawn that could wait, and re-upped Tommy's records on the national donor databases instead.

In his stepped-up environment Tommy was more determined than ever to prove he was well enough to go to Fan Expo; he'd pulled himself together over the weekend and gone back to school on Monday. As the countdown to the convention began, June watched Tommy's efforts to bounce back with both admiration and sorrow.

About a week before the convention Walt brought up something else, a topic June thought they'd put in the rearview mirror. Upon reconsideration she couldn't be alarmed or angered by it, for this was yet another of many coping strategies Tommy employed in the face of receiving awful news.

After carefully reading the online summary of name change procedures in Arkansas for minors, he'd evidently downloaded a petition to change his name. In an attempt to bypass June's consent he'd asked Walt if he could use their estate attorney to file the form in circuit court.

Tommy wanted to change his name to Lucas Fallon.

When her cell phone rang the Monday before Fan Expo, she thought at first it might be Walt, or even the school, but her caller ID said Fast Horses—the first time he'd actually called her. He said he was checking in on Tommy, a bit precocious, he acknowledged, since they'd only just seen each other over the weekend. Then he admitted he was missing her already. And it seemed only natural to answer his question with another one, June decided, a bit stumped about why it hadn't occurred to her already.

"Would you like to go with us to the Wiz Convention on Friday?"

Chapter Seventeen

Callan understood he'd probably just leapt from the proverbial frying pan into the fire, but he also saw attending Fan Expo as an opportunity to shut down Miles Cochran for good. He barely knew Clara and her immediate relations beyond cursory introductions, let alone progeny—but if falling *not too far from the tree* was an inevitable genetic consequence, her husband had been a real horse's ass.

The smell carrying over to Cushing Street this week was dreadful, and under no uncertain terms could Callan ignore it; Tommy was bucking up against some rapidly accelerating cellular decay. He also expected Tommy would likely play his cards close to the vest because of his determination to attend the convention.

While he'd wanted to blow the whistle several times already about the schoolyard punch-up, Callan felt such a confession would encourage too many questions, including what he was doing in the neighborhood in the first place. Apparently Tommy hadn't told June about it, either. She'd just admitted over the phone that the best they could do going forward was to prevent any further physical or emotional trauma from acting as catalysts in the mix, and that she was trying very hard not to hover. In so many words she'd said she needed Callan as her wingman on this trip to help rein in Tommy's impulsivity, and had finagled an extra entry ticket, upgraded their hotel room near the convention center to a suite—all set to go with the usual efficiency he'd grown to love. And Callan didn't want to pass the weekend without seeing her.

Tommy would attend school for a half day on Thursday. Then they would be on their way, the five-hour drive to St. Louis. The only contingency this time of year was the possibility of a winter storm, and that wasn't forecast until the first week in February.

The gallery would be closed over the weekend but that was also a nonissue, for he usually took time off in January to handle paperwork and charitable contributions from home. Callan tried putting his mind back on track as he sifted through a pile of invoices and an undrawn check spread before him on a card table he'd pulled out of the broom closet. The check he hadn't yet deposited was June's—having decided not to do so until she determined the costs of curing Tommy.

And since when had a loaf of bread gone from twenty-two cents to two-fifty?

He switched his pen to the other hand. Sometimes it felt like just yesterday, as if no time had passed at all. He'd watched the monster called Inflation come back for dinner four times since his arrival in this country, largely due to the inevitable task of war and its consequential supply chain interruptions. He'd adjusted for surging costs at the end of WWII while he struggled to finish the gallery, and again in 1974 after Watergate, and during the 1980 recession following the energy crisis. Then came the politico-public health unpreparedness for the pandemic in 2020, and the beast fed once more. Callan didn't have to crunch the numbers on the rising costs of dry goods to see it already; he needed to recalculate his donation to the food pantry.

On Wednesday, June determined that a jog around the neighborhood during lunch break would do her soul some good, so she changed into trail leggings and a storm jacket and hit the streets. The Crescent Drive winder that fed into Spring Street and looped back to Fairmount gave her a mile's worth, so she set out with the intention of making two laps before clocking in again at her home workstation. The air today was good for it—just dry and cold enough to cast off steam without freezing up her hands and feet. June hadn't planned on snooping per se, but when she turned on the downhill stretch on Spring, she realized this was exactly what she was doing.

Chances were she could verify Callan's house by the name on the mailbox, but she didn't even get that far.

Green Packard at my two backing out of a garage. June ducked behind the fence line and waited. The neighboring home had some reconstruction underway with lumber and multicolored bins stacked up by the curb. June skirted the fence and crouched behind the bins where she could watch the Packard as it rolled to a stop beside the Gable Front she'd guessed was his—and Callan got out.

June stifled a cough. *It's him, all right.*

He went inside and reappeared in all of ten seconds with a large black binder under one arm, pausing for a moment by the driver's door for a quick survey of the street, nostrils flaring. June hunkered behind the bins until well after the Packard had backed out of the drive and turned downtown, trying to get a mental handhold on this new development.

Could it—?

Her diaphragm hung in knots, hamstrings drawn up, and June was suddenly sweating bullets.

I saw the Woodie.

Words raced by at light speed, and her throat closed.

Don't you get it? From the story?

She bent over, hands on thighs. Hard breaths.

Grandpa saw it too. So—was this vampire cured?

She needed to backtrack the half-mile she'd just made, sort this one out. June straightened as the city trolley rumbled by—and she took off, dread dogging her heels.

You absotively don't think Fallon is real? He orders it that way every time. Oh. Well—five, six years?

At the next intersection, June jogged in place. She couldn't go home, not yet. She needed to think. June continued up Spring toward Dairy Hollow.

People who write pulp fiction, sometimes they visit the places they write about, and the clapboard shack he lets near downtown all but hangs off the cliffside, so what I really want to know is—are you seeing that god who paints horses? He gave me those eyes and made me all fiddly, I tell you that's what good stories do, but I like *being a sick vampire, I've swot at it a bit.*

June ran faster on the fat chance she could outrun it.

You prefer difficult?

At Ellis Grade she finally stopped, Darth breathing. When she crossed her front yard four miles and forty minutes later, she'd worn down the voices and the panic into a dithering pool of sweat.

I'm being ridiculous, she thought. This unforeseen situation with Callan wasn't about to undo her no-nonsense grip, *no sirree.*

It's just a story, sweetie.

June had come toe-to-toe with human drama frequently enough to know better; in the exam room, she *could not, would not* pile on any of her own. A big part of managing any biological dilemma was determining what factored in as a crisis and what did not. When the chips were down, her strength as a physician came by examining whatever presented at face value. The *why me* and its accompanying emotional undercurrents were second down the line and not critical to her first assessment.

Unnecessary, and necessary.

A lousy way to talk herself down but here she was.

She couldn't let herself get caught up in the daily fight club and hope to win the war, because—

June sighed, scudding her running shoes along the sidewalk to knock off the road dirt.

Because suffering is essentially unstable. Upticks were equally cruel as downturns, both temporary states in a somewhat longer process called mortality. *All fucking day long* she saw the same biological impermanence. It hid itself well in the busyness of daily living and particularly inside a digital convenience culture, albeit one that still longed for permanence somehow.

A durability never ours in the first place.

So what if he drives a Packard, she argued. One former owner of Basin Park Hotel had a fleet of limos during the Cold War years, a Packard among them. Before it was used as a limo to transport dignitaries, politicians, and soldiers on furlough to Eureka's hopping nightlife, it was a hearse. Her hometown, rich with conversions and castoffs from its varied history, beginning with the first souls who came to Basin Park to bathe in medicinal waters, enjoy pure air and sunshine, and die by the hundreds each day—prompting the town's need for nine crematoriums.

June hit the shower. If compartmentalizing was what it took to get Tommy past Fan Expo and forestall her own *need to know exactly* who she was dating, she was good for it. Callan had been nothing but kind so far. And he'd just offered to help her manage the ins and outs of taking a sick child to a mass event.

Secrets aside, he was everything she wanted in a companion, she'd realized. On the drive home from Fan Expo she'd ask, in all likelihood before they left St. Louis city limits, *hell yeah*—but then. That's how she'd handle this.

The TikTok link martha_whoosis had just texted him was *cool beans*, an Expo promotional for *the* CGI holographic collation of recorded interviews with Frid and live chat with Darrow. *Yes-way* this was tomorrow at sixteen-thirty with a rewatch party afterward, she said. Tommy was *on it, hit me back, meet up with me and Molly at the gate?* Friday's events started at ten. *Was she there?*

And Chelsea replied *I'm game, good for it.*

Mom and the painter dude were into adulting about something political, *snoring-boring if anybody's asking*—so Tommy continued his backseat dive into all things Expo on his tablet. Mom had said everyone needed to start addressing the art guy by his real name so, *sigh*— *Callan*—had brought his own tablet just in case he got the chance to take a look at "Bad Blood," he said. That was before he'd gotten sidetracked with Mom and weather and politics. Tommy had just told him twenty minutes ago *for the second time* he'd better hop to it, because St. Louis wasn't that far, *it's a pretty long story*, the reason they were going to the convention, *anyhoo,* and it would really blow his mind. Then Callan mentioned he was having trouble connecting up his new sports watch with his phone app, and Tommy struck a deal: *read "Bad Blood" and I'll fix your watch.*

So—for an art dude, he didn't have that many apps on his cell, *for real*—and while Tommy dove into all things Withings, Callan read, and Mom listened to music. The sports watch app looked pretty much in order already, sorta like he didn't really understand it because he was probably close to Mom's age for sure, but *holy crud* it said he'd averaged 19,495 steps a day this week and got only two hours' sleep last night. Tommy changed some settings and hoped that would straighten him out.

Then it was time to stop for dinner, and Mom had gotten fashion masks to go over their N-95's, way-cool white fangs for him, girl fangs for her, and Callan said he was okeydokey wearing plain Jane black. Tommy also wanted to drag the mall at the convention center whenever they arrived (it was open, he checked), but Mom *that's the breaks* was being a real hard-ass and told him *no*.

Falling Stars

After dinner Tommy stretched out and slept for the rest of the trip. When his small snores dropped into a steady rhythm from the back seat, Callan powered off his tablet.

"I can see how Tommy relates to the boy in the story," he said.

June glanced over his way. "How far along are you?"

She certainly seemed on edge, but he'd already chalked that up to Tommy's condition. "I just finished Part Two." He swallowed. "It seems rather complex for his age, though. Do you think he understands it?"

"Yes, he read most of it to me."

"Really?"

"Just some questions here and there."

"Wow. He's one smart kid."

She nodded. "Who also still thinks those things in the story actually happened."

"Oh. Well. I can see why you're concerned, then."

She smiled. "I guess we'll find out more at the *Philly's Argosy* autograph party tomorrow, won't we?"

Not if I can help it, Callan thought. He really needed to change the subject. "Have you read anything else written by Miles Cochran?"

When June pulled her car into the parking lot at America's Center Convention Complex at nine o'clock, Tommy was wide awake again. At the end closest to their hotel they could see lights blazing from the center's lobby, pre-function areas, and second-floor atrium—and Tommy was whining about wanting to cruise the halls again.

After locating the EV charging stations and completing check-in, June managed to get him into pajamas, but he was face-to-window, looking longingly at the massive convention center when Callan knocked on their adjoining door.

"There's a great in-room cocktail kit, and I'd really enjoy a nightcap," June said to Callan between her teeth, "but I can't get him to settle down." Everything considered *he really needed to settle down*, she fumed. And Callan—*so* calm, regarding her with eyes she could drown in.

"May I try?"

"Knock yourself out," June muttered. "I need to go find some ice, anyway."

Callan crossed the room and stood beside Tommy, where he was comparing a virtual tour of tomorrow's program schedule on his tablet to the monster complex just outside the window.

"See that?" He pointed.

Callan tried following his finger. "Which part of *that* am I looking at?"

"The dome, right over there."

One massive, covered sports arena he hadn't yet visited. "Yes, I see it."

"We have to walk *all the way around*, back to the plaza entrance to meet my friends in the morning."

"We'll need to get a head start, then."

"Yuppers. Everybody lines up in the courtyard, and you go inside where the rotunda is."

"The atrium?"

"Yeah." Tommy swiped to the next picture. "There's this *big-ass* staircase inside, or you can take the escalators if your knees hurt."

Callan smiled. "My knees are okay, I think."

"There's some pre-function areas by the ballroom up front where you and Mom can hang out if you get tired."

"Good to know."

Tommy pointed. "The annex is mostly used for breakouts and staging for the dome shows."

"What kinds of shows?"

"Professional cosplay, live-action roleplay like jousting and sword fighting, you know, *Game of Thrones* and Hell House from *Supernatural*, TWD, stadium stuff. A few old movie cars like the Ecto-1, the DeLorean, the Batmobile, things like that."

"Sounds like the place to be."

"Eh, not so much. The halls are where most of the people go for celebrity signing, merchandise, photo-ops, comics, free stuff if they have any."

"*Philly's?*"

"They're in there. The 'Bad Blood' panel is in one of the meeting rooms, though. That's at four."

"I see."

"Then I have to step on it if I want to catch the CGI interviews with Chelsea, cause they're at four-thirty in the Ferrara Theatre, over here. Photo-ops with Darrow in the lobby."

"Sounds like a full day."

"Yeah, you and Mom ought to get some sleep."

Callan actually felt a yawn coming on. "Well, you got me there."

Tommy was back on his tablet. "It's part of my skill set."

Callan watched Tommy scroll down to the last of tomorrow's events on his tablet before stepping closer and whispering in his ear. Then quickly, "ambulante," to keep him upright. He caught the tablet as Tommy's arms dangled and took him by the hand.

June arrived with a bucket of ice minutes later to find Tommy tucked in and fast asleep, Callan sitting bedside looking over the convention schedule on Tommy's tablet. Her big, expressive blues registered a shock and awe he'd adored from day one.

"How did you—?"

Callan smiled. "I guess he was a little more whipped than we supposed."

⭐

And he thought he saw nonessential hype at the races. Callan smiled. If the line outside America's Center was any indication the next morning, they were about to step off-world. The temperature was brisk, so June had decided to drive them to the plaza entrance, park, and catch up. She'd wrangled Tommy into a black duster, one he could remove as soon as he graced the door, she promised. He'd have plenty of time to sport his cape, yessir.

Whenever that might happen, Callan thought, for this was *some* line leading to the security checkpoint. He was glad he'd brought along his Inverness because the wind here wasted no time cutting through his standard shirt and slacks.

About 90 percent of the fans waiting to enter the building were in cosplay—costumes from every imaginable comic book, TV, or movie series since the '40s—yes, Dorothy from Oz, Anime, zombies, wrestlers, action figures, and vampires. He could see why Fan Expo was advertised as the ultimate playground for sci-fi, fantasy, horror, daytime and nighttime soaps, forensics TV, wrestling, ninja, and video gaming. And they weren't even inside yet.

Tommy wasn't alone in his effort to mask up, either—probably a good thing on several levels. Over the past four years Callan had come to accept wearing a mask as the new norm with the rest of the world—especially when traveling during flu season, or from heightened levels of awareness about outbreaks and good public health practices in general. Masking up also offered him another option for maintaining anonymity in mass gatherings like this one—especially important *here, today*.

They'd only held their places in the lineup for a minute or two before Tommy suddenly broke away and ran toward the plaza lobby. Callan was on it with quick, long strides toward a young woman in an Ahsoka Tano costume from Star Wars who Tommy was hugging. She'd done hers right—a faux leather skirt and leggings, Beskar armor, and a headdress with the true-blue montrals of the Togruta species.

"You must be Molly," Callan said, and extended his hand. She had a vigorous handshake with a quick *such an honor to meet you*, he noticed. *Someone* had been talking, and as much as he hated subsisting with the same obligatory hypervigilance year after year about word on the street, Callan rarely lowered his guard around any hearsay or theresay.

Although this seems harmless enough. When he saw June heading their way, he worried even less. With her, all the nasty little details felt better somehow.

They'd just cleared the turnstiles at the entrance when another friend of Tommy's tagged them from the back of the line.

"Hey, you guys!" She'd pinged Tommy's phone to locate them, she said. Her skin was griffe, Callan noticed—

And he recognized her carotids.

She wore the understated Martha Jones apparel from *Dr. Who* like Tommy said she would—a maroon leather jacket with flared jeans—although she'd obviously gone to some trouble stacking up those cornrows into a braided bun.

Their little group converged with noisy introductions, handshakes, and hugs. Callan thought he managed himself well enough—excepting the struggle to avert his attention from martha_whoosis's neck and how the blood flowed into it. He was pretty certain his eyes were a dead giveaway when he learned her surname was Dumont as well—but June

Falling Stars

didn't seem to notice.

For the girls took a moment to mask up for Tommy and dropped into a cheerful banter about each other's necklaces. June had on her aquamarine caduceus today, and Chelsea . . . *an Art Deco engagement pendant just like the one he'd given Milja in 1968.*

A good thing he didn't need to contribute much to the discussion at the moment because the teen Creole who came to the party *was* the party, a string of chatter that rivaled Milja's even on a good day. He also noticed the way she stood pigeon-toed—an ancestral trait that had never impaired Milja's dancing as much as she'd believed.

Her voice was bright and shiny, several ticks louder than everyone else's. She oozed the confidence and refined defiance he'd often wanted for his former lover. And her profile—*well*. Callan looked away.

They'd fought about the pendant, but Milja finally consented to add the one item with her belongings she wouldn't remember, nor the suitor she'd received it from. No one had ever come around asking about it, either.

Now Chelsea was explaining how the necklace that once belonged to her great-aunt Milja (who didn't end up with any girls of her own) had passed down through her dad's side to her. And June was holding Callan's hand as she mentioned he'd given her the aquamarine for Christmas. Behind the mask his masseters flared, and he knew it didn't really matter if they assumed he was simply feeling self-conscious when he looked down. Truth was, life had a brutal way of circling back on him, and in these moments it felt *too damn long.*

A few years before when Wiz had announced past events and convention celebrity banners as new arrivals to its online vault, June had purchased an autographed Jonathan Frid for Tommy. He'd pulled it out of a moving box just last week, still *braining* where to hang it, he said. Now Jack Darrow's booth also displayed one from his first season starring in the newly resurrected *Dark Shadows*, she noticed—but she was standing in line for a signed copy of Elise Anderson's *Starscape*. Tommy would want one, if they didn't sell out before she got over there.

Two rows right of her, Tommy and Callan waited in line to ask Miles Cochran one free question or thirty seconds' Q&A, whichever came first. As fans crowded into the exhibit halls, their group had agreed after stashing their coats in lockers to divide and conquer. Tommy had *two* questions and didn't want to wait for a kiosk to purchase chat time, so June got in line with Tommy's other question, and Molly and Chelsea opted to cruise the dome to find the cosplay costume contest. Molly would text the details, and they'd all meet up at the professional cosplay seminar beforehand.

Philly's booth first appeared three years ago, June remembered, in a section with other artists and exhibitors who advertised year-round merchandise in Wiz's online vaults. This year they'd leveled up with a bigger step-and-repeat backdrop in proximity to the celebrity tables. They'd also rolled out half-a-dozen of *Philly's* top contributing writers, and a "Bad Blood" banner was stanchioned behind Cochran's table.

Because the COVID-19 hiatus had isolated fans to at-home video chats, Q&A Twitch, YouTube, or Facebook Meetup for nearly three years, this experience was unofficially endorsed to be *bigger* and *bolder* and in living color, all within arm's reach. The restlessness was palpable.

Fan Expo was *back*. St. Louis, come on down! *Geek out.*

June glanced around the exhibit hall at fans crowding in to meet celebrities, the usual suspects who frequented the docket and some of Hollywood's same bankable has-beens they'd seen in Chicago five years ago before Tommy got sick.

Falling stars, June realized. Prey to age and decline like the rest of us, under the harsh cast of society's limelight.

Darrow and the up-and-comers were more strategically placed near the exits around the dome.

Surrounded by a sea of selfies, June snatched a glimmer of frenzy-driven joy that her son was somehow well enough today to participate. For some, this event offered chance-of-a-lifetime opportunities. For Tommy, the possibility of being *rockin' out and strange and that's okay* for several hours in a world where normal couldn't fly. The real challenge was helping him prioritize his wish-list this morning, for Expo was packed with family-oriented attractions, coupons, and perks, and *way* too many options came at no additional charge with admission. Those freebies included autographs on virtually anything up for sale or grabs, including limited edition comic books, artwork, costumes, or bring-along personal items.

Falling Stars

As June studied the glossy roster she'd picked up at the entrance (also good for celebrity signatures), she could see that everything in Tommy's promotional material and sneak peaks over the past weeks proved accurate. This year, Expo had trotted out entertainers, exhibits, and events by the dozens: true-crime and comic book authors, podcasters, illustrators, ghost hunters, mediums, wrestlers, free-to-play gaming and tournaments, auctions, panels, hands-on workshops, and multiple screening room presentations.

Retailers easily topped several hundred, selling items like rare comic books, custom artwork, limited edition prints, graphic novels, film memorabilia, Blu-Rays, videos, games, toys, and T-shirts. In Artist Alley, Expo fans could meet up with their favorite pencillers and inkers for original art and sketches, something June anticipated Callan would want to check out after they switched off with Tommy.

Which might be longer than we estimated. June caught a glimpse of Callan between the bodies lined up two rows over; theirs had barely crept forward. She couldn't help wondering at what point Tommy's adrenaline rush would crash in his race against time, or if they could possibly complete all the items on his agenda today.

No way they'd get to the cosplay seminar *or* the costume contest on time if this writer dude didn't get a move on, Tommy grumped. And all for one question. *It's a Shaquille, though, and I gotta ask.* He rocked up on his toes until his sneakers squeaked High C and tried to see over the fans in front of him. The only thing he could figure was, all fifteen people ahead in line had purchased more chat time, or the big dummy was ignoring his timer.

Twice already the CEO, a *skinny dipper* pigging out on licorice Twizzlers, had stepped in and told him off, *no joke.* All the online ads for the upcoming panel showed a writer's quill instead of Cochran's author photo, and now Tommy could see how come: the guy was an old fart. *Yes-way* maybe he wrote a cool story, but Grandpa would say he was a real pud in person, *yay-uh.* Especially if he made them late for cosplay.

At last, their turn, and *yeah, we wish—that this guy keeps his ass in the chair and doesn't all of a sudden decide he needs a potty break.* He didn't look very healthy at all, sorta like a snowballed Jabba with big gobs of sweat rolling down his cheeks. Every now and then he'd pull out a roll of paper towels to mop his face and slurp on a Super Big Gulp he kept under the table.

Since *Philly's* was primarily *no-duh* digital, they'd cranked out a big stack of "Bad Blood" comic books, the whole series for fifteen bucks each, or—in the absence of bringing your own stuff, a smaller stack of trading cards with their e-zine logo that Cochran would sign for free.

"Another card?" He picked up one off the deck and twirled it between his fingers.

"Nice trick," Tommy muttered. Behind him, Callan came up with fifteen in cash, *nope, I did not ask*.

"Let's get you a copy," Callan said, and laid his money on the table. Which evidently was the *right-o* thing to do, and at least one of the reasons the CEO was reaming Cochran's ass: he wasn't making very many print sales.

"Smart man," Cochran gushed, handing over a copy. "This one's already signed." And to Tommy, "Love the mask, it works." He coughed, a wet one that brought out more paper towels.

When Tommy opened his copy, he saw what Cochran meant—a pre-printed autograph. *Sorta sub-personal if anyone's asking.*

"Gives my shaker a break," Cochran went on, the old drooler trying to look friendly.

"But I still have a question," Tommy said, a little louder.

Cochran cut his eyes at the timer, the one he'd forgotten to set. He popped it on.

"Make it quick, we're on the clock," he shot back.

So, let's do this. "Does Claudius Fallon still live in Eureka Springs?"

Cochran pursed his lips. "I get some version of that one all the time."

I betcha do since you started it. Tommy glanced at the timer.

Cochran leaned over the table and mumbled. "Let's just say . . . I had a whole lot more about Claudius Fallon that ended up on *Philly's* cutting room floor."

Aces. "So you're saying it's possible?"

Cochran sat back, *a little too happy with himself,* Tommy decided.

"Anything's possible," he quacked.

Like that's a stunner. The timer went off. Tommy checked his cell phone. "That was a fast thirty."

Falling Stars

"As they can go." Cochran snickered.

Tommy scowled at him. *He really didn't have anything else, did he?*

"I'd like an autographed card," Callan cut in.

Cochran sighed, *not even trying* to hide his beef with *that kind of hassle*, Tommy noticed. He rubbed his maw, fumbled for a pen, and slouched over the table—sorta like Gru. "Name?"

Then Callan leaned *wa-a-ay* over, Tommy noticed—closer to Cochran than *he'd* ever want to get, *yes indeedy*. Tommy tuned in with his amplified hearing, a bit of a challenge at the moment because everything around him was *so freakin' loud,* and his ears were tired already.

"An old friend," he overheard Callan say.

June completed her free chat time with Elise Anderson well before the line toward Cochran had advanced at all, so she walked quickly over to Darrow's booth to see if she could purchase a 2022 celebrity banner. Since following Elise's column with Tommy, June had grown to admire this young entrepreneur. Anderson had an exquisite eye for detail and wrote like someone who had it all together, who knew how to call the stops in a competitive industry. Today she'd applied fuchsia and blue wash-out hair wax to her natural blonde shag to match the Helix Nebula on her trading card.

Even her standard signature across NGC 7293, the great cosmic eye of Sauron, was efficiently cursive with a suitable amount of attention to detail. June tucked the card inside her hip pocket as she stepped up to the *Dark Shadows'* merchandise booth. When she'd explained the dilemma of Tommy's unanswered fan mail, Elise seemed genuinely upset. She added their home address to the back of the business card June gave her to *investigate this right away, guaranteed*. And June knew she could count on Elise to do just that.

Pleased with herself for snagging a hot ticket item for Tommy, June turned to see those two finally headed her direction along the gangway, and an incoming text on her cell from Molly announced the cosplay seminar started at the dome's south end in eight minutes.

Tommy, steamed about *no effin' way* getting his full thirty seconds *(pee-*

ode, more like it), was still trying to figure how an old fart like Cochran didn't know diddly about running a kitchen timer, *analog stuff*—when Callan stepped in and did his thingy—and *one coconut, two coconut* Cochran stumbled out of his chair puking, just like that.

Yuppers, Tommy knew the drill. When you *vurp*, there's nowhere to go fast enough. The old guy tried to, though—*donkey balls* right through Philly's ginormous wall banner, a cowboy trot for the nearest fart-and-hurl. *OMG*. The line behind them disintegrated, *poof*—everybody onto the next guy over, and Callan—*cooler than ice*—watched Cochran for *one coconut, two coconut* before he turned to go.

"What did you *do* to him?" Tommy shoved his way in front of Callan. *Something gnarly was up, he knew it.*

"He did it to himself," Callan answered.

Tommy didn't budge. "Really? Just like that?" *Nobody nohow* had given him a straight answer about *shit* today, and the art guy was *so freakin' calm.* Tommy waved his arms.

"*Hello.* Maybe you can tell me why we're still standing here, then. After all that waiting, he didn't even answer my question."

"He couldn't."

"Why not?"

"He didn't write the story."

"Really? How do you know that?"

"He didn't know the answer to your question."

Masks always made it so *flippin'* hard, but the dude was dead serious, not a smile in there anywhere. *He really did have iffy eyes sometimes,* surely Mom had noticed. "Well—who wrote it, then?"

"I'm going to find out."

"How?"

"At the panel."

"You better, because this is serious stuff."

"I know."

The conversation between Tommy and Callan appeared strained as June approached. *Fine,* she heard Tommy say, and he darted past her toward the stadium.

"What gives?" she asked Callan.

"Cochran was a bust." He followed Tommy with his eyes.

June studied Callan for a moment; he was genuinely concerned. "He'll calm down," she said, and turned to watch Tommy disappear into the crowd. "It's a shame, though. I think I had better luck than you two all the way around." She unrolled part of the banner she'd just purchased, Jack Darrow baring fangs.

Callan obviously wasn't as impressed as she expected he'd be. "We'd better catch up with Tommy," he said.

★

The pro-cosplay seminar, cosplay competition, and break for lunch at Fan Expo's mega-concessions did a world of good for what disappointments ailed Tommy after they'd sandbagged *Philly's* main event at the autograph table, Callan observed. His little spirit bounced back for an afternoon of unplanned exhibit encounters and purchases June agreed to before the scheduled "Bad Blood" panel. But when they saw a notice on the assigned event door that Cochran's appearance had also been canceled, it quickly became clear Tommy was wearing down. He had little interest in what Elise Anderson, Cochran's stand-in and editor, had to say about crafting the story.

Callan suggested he take the panel while June and Tommy join Molly and Chelsea in Ferrara Theatre for the CGI event, where seats were going fast. How he hated missing the chance to see Frid in action again—and the much-talked-about holographic simulation—but Callan had appearances to keep.

He also had to come up with the right answer to Tommy's question.

★

Forty minutes later, Callan ducked out of the *Philly's* panel in progress, partly because he was convinced Elise Anderson was the author-in-fact who chose to sub certain elements from the journals Cochran had provided—and the stench was overwhelming. Questions about the possibility of an ongoing "Bad Blood" series was met with an editorial filibuster between Anderson and McWatters, *fine by him*, for the two all but admitted they hadn't planned for the series to take off like it did, or for a new contributor like Cochran "to produce such compelling material." Midway through the Q&A, Callan realized Cochran probably didn't have all the journals in his possession, for Clara *was just bitch enough to squirrel them away* . . .

That's what happened, he decided. *Philly's* could try all they wanted, but Cochran wasn't going to be mentally fit enough to obtain or option any more intellectual material anytime soon.

The panels were staged in meeting rooms a good city block's walk from Ferrara Theatre, its rear west entrance accessible from the first-floor gallery. He'd just crossed the central breakout section by the plaza lobby when he saw the paramedics filing into the theater.

For an art guy he was *yes-way* ripped, *uh-huh*, going up, up the glammed-out stainless steel that some window washer probably had orders to wax to the max—no slips or gronks, just a steady edge and smear, *hup-hup*, scaling America's tallest man-made monument with Tommy riding on his back.

Just like he knew Claudius Fallon could do, on Jesus of the Ozarks or whatever. They were still in the Lou, though, winds whipping around them *purdy darn* good. Except—

Holy moly, this really *was* the art guy in the same clothes he had on this morning, but *dayyum now he has these big-ass wings stuck on me*, super gluey ones like the bats he'd seen at Lincoln Park Zoo.

In case I decide to let go, Tommy figured as much.

He didn't want to interfere, but Tommy really needed to know *why* they were climbing the Gateway Arch tonight in the first place—and all sixty-three stories, looked like. From the top they'd be able to see thirty miles of city lights all around (he knew that already) and 630 feet below to the concrete. *Donkey balls.*

He decided right then he better not look down, even if it obviously hadn't occurred to a vampire who could possibly fly that there were tram tours *on the inside* of the arch every hour on the hour to the observation deck on top (also inside).

A little less risky, doncha think?

But this was *way cool*. Literally. He supposed the art guy had already left holes where he stabbed into the walls with those *yay-ho* freaky talons, *yuppers*, hands where his shoulders ought to go. *Gnarly.* Good thing he had a firm grip on it because the wind had picked up *again*, and this big-ass concrete *loop-de-loop*, all 43,000 tons of it— was swaying at max tolerance, *yessiree—le-e-eft*, then *ri-i-ight* . . .

Jeepers, what a *pitch and ro-o-oll*—

"Tommy," he heard Mom say.

Nope, his mom didn't belong anywhere in this fabric of the universe, but here she is, in my face. Tommy blinked his way back into a world where he didn't belong with Mom standing over him, *N-ninety-fived* and all serious-like. He was in the hospital. Again.

The goose juice they were giving him numbed-out the *donkey balls,* but he felt like glazed-over shit.

"I have to step outside for a minute, sweetie—but Callan's right here, okay?"

No he's not, Tommy wanted to say, but the words wouldn't come out.

⭒

Tommy drifted back under before Callan had the chance to join June at bedside and confirm his presence. He pulled up a chair and sat.

"Go ahead, I've got you covered," he told her. ICU was a cell-free zone, and June needed to contact Dawn. So she reluctantly left ICU for the first time since Tommy was admitted. In the central hallway where cell phone signal boosters brought reception up to four bars, she'd make one last-ditch pitch to Casey that they were running out of time.

Through the observation window in Tommy's room Callan could see beyond the nurses station into a lobby where Molly waited tearfully, and Chelsea paced. June stopped, updating them, and he noticed Chelsea followed her out. When they returned he'd need to step outside and give Tommy's friends a chance to tell him goodbye.

Until then, he needed to continue where he left off. Perhaps there was something in it for Tommy, for the old arbor's legend still hailed him when Callan closed his eyes, its entrance into a paseo that bought him time.

Balm of Life.

He wasn't the first desperate soul drawn to Eureka, and he wouldn't be the last—as long as humans or derivatives of flesh and blood like himself came broken and seeking.

Baker's wasn't the first show on the block, either. Remedies hit the streets fifty years before his arrival, most of them coming out of a spring unpretentiously named Basin. Situated on a cirque that Osage warriors introduced to the world and white men clearcut, the healing waters running off nearby Miles Mountain at one time turned downtown into mud.

Doctors who came to the springs and cured themselves were the most passionate. The mud didn't bother them; the deaths didn't stop them. The cure for many ills was already sworn in, and Eureka became *a most peculiar place with an apparent disregard for any order or arrangement...*

A city of springs, stairs, and stories.

Glorious words full of hope and illusion. Little curio advertisements collected in passing turned out to be today's gruesome amusement. He remembered every single one of them, the desperation behind every bit of hokum trotted out to bypass human mortality.

The first sanatorium, The Perry House.

Here invalids can sit or walk, enjoy pure air, sunshine, and the nearby spring. The dining room, a model of elegance and comfort, has a table second to none. Guests unable to leave the building have full advantage of pleasant company for amusement or pleasure, and from these galleries an ever-passing throng to and from the springs may be studied. A scrupulous concern is shown for those unable to leave their rooms from any cause. Weekly rate, $10-15.

Dr. D. H. Himes and his Twin Wonders of Eureka, whose office happened to be located opposite Basin Spring.

For thousands of years the scientific world has searched in vain among mineral substances for the cure for Cancer. It was of good fortune for suffering humanity that Dr. Himes, in compounding vegetables, which he first used on old sores, discovered the balm would cure Cancer and eradicate it. When he learned of the curative waters of Eureka Springs, he condensed the water of these famous springs, used it in conjunction with his Vegetable Eradican, and after testing it in hundreds of cases, has found that the New Remedy, wondrous to all, is a Dead Shot on every case of Cancer, Tumor, Ulcer, Fever Sore, Milk Leg, Bone Erysipelas, and Kindred Diseases. No cure, no pay! He is certain, hence the offer. Come and see the cures he has affected.

And why not Tommy? Callan opened his eyes and surveyed the boy's tiny body with lines and hoses hooked up everywhere. This might keep him alive for a day or two if it didn't kill him first, *but what do I know?* Just four hours ago, his spunky little friend was still holding out that Fallon's biological product could cure him—and now they would never find out, would they?

"Good news," June said from behind. She'd quietly slipped in and stood watching Callan watch Tommy. He turned.

Her eyes told him everything at once, that a new hope more rock-solid than her usual was afoot. She smiled. "That Chelsea. Clinical ethics aside, I really ought to hire her."

"That so? Why?"

"She talked Casey into donating."

Callan sat back. "You're kidding me."

"I am not. A couple hours' at Fan Expo while her labs process, a Martha Jones jacket, and a year's shipments of super gummy worms from Archway."

Callan smiled. "That is quite a haul."

"Dad's driving her in tomorrow morning." June walked around to the other side of the bed and checked the PICC in Tommy's right arm again. "We may have to switch to a central line."

And he really did need to get on with some other things she couldn't know about, either. Callan shifted. "Do you still plan on spending the night here?"

She was onto examining something else. "Yes, I have to."

Callan studied her face for any hint about what she really prognosed for Tommy but saw only dogged determination. Her carotids were steady. He glanced out the observation window. The girls were gone.

"Molly and Chelsea will be back to visit tomorrow," June said.

So she was counting on Tommy to pull through even this. Callan nodded.

They decided he'd stay while June fetched her suitcase from the hotel and some takeout for their dinner. He'd noticed the ICU nurses rounded every hour for a full assessment on Tommy, and June waited until the next rotation before she left.

Less than fifteen seconds after the ICU nurse finished recording vitals and June said goodbye, Tommy's eyes popped open, and he started squirming around.

Callan reached for the bed's intercom button to call back the nurse. "Are you uncomfortable?"

"Nope," Tommy said, trying to sit up.

Callan stopped, hand mid-air.

"No nurse?"

"*No way.*"

"Go easy there, then. I think they want you to rest."

"I'm not sleepy."

Yes, he was a bit *Hang on Sloopy*, but far more alert than Callan had counted on. "You weren't asleep?"

"Nope, I was faking it."

"The whole time?"

Tommy raised his nose. "Didn't we just climb the Gateway Arch?"

Callan smiled. *Yep, we did and I grok you.* Maybe not to June, but he'd known he'd ultimately have to tell Tommy who he was somehow. Hence, the dream.

"That was *trippin'*." Tommy's half-mast eyes took in the room and his situation. "You didn't drop me, did you?"

"No, we got down okay."

"Yeah, you—*flew.*"

Callan nodded.

"You're *him.*"

"I am."

Then Tommy was trying to turn his head so he could see the bag on the IV pole. "Are they giving me the same stuff you got?"

"No, unfortunately, it only works for me. Casey's coming in tomorrow for your transplant."

Tommy looked at him crossly and rolled his head from side to side. "No. No can do. She hates needles."

"It's the only way you'll get better."

"No, it's not. I just thought of another way."

Callan didn't like the direction their talk was going. In fact, he'd ultimately had in mind making things easier for June by persuading Tommy to greenlight receiving the bone marrow transplant, though he could tell already by Tommy's flagging carotids that tomorrow's procedure was likely a long shot—that his secret could very well go to this little boy's grave with him.

"Maybe you should get some sleep. We can talk about it later."

"No can do. We only have one chance to get this right."

If Tommy was about to negotiate for Callan to share his sanguinary talents with June, he wasn't ready to do that yet. He couldn't imagine what else the little guy could've drummed up, either.

Tommy cut his eyes toward the observation window and his voice dropped to a whisper. "You've got to turn me."

"Pardon?"

"You heard me. You need to bite me. Your vampire subclass lives longer than mine, obviously." Callan studied the tips of his Oxfords, unsure how to answer that. The concept, while brilliant, wouldn't fly for one minute, he knew. His bite hadn't turned Gunner all those years ago, or anyone else, for that matter.

"It won't work," Callan said. "You'll just run more of a risk for infection."

But Tommy was already peeling the dressing off his left elbow. "No one will see it here, and there's a good artery too." He held out his arm, his joint laxity exposing weeks-old discoloration in his cubital fossa, and a perfect plateau for biting.

Callan swallowed. "It won't help you, Tommy."

Tommy stretched his arm out farther. "Maybe it will." *And of course he would think so.* Callan stared at Tommy's battered arm for a moment, wondering how he'd basically come upon a soul more convincing and stubborn than he was. Callan stood.

He's going to die, anyway.

"This won't be pretty, you know. I'll need to put you to sleep."

"No, you don't. Just do it."

"First things first," Callan said as he turned toward the observation window. The nurses at the central station were a couple of hours from a shift change, duties that required more screentime as they stepped through EHR protocols. They shouldn't be in for half an hour at least. He rotated the Mini-Blinds by degrees to three-quarters' shut and pulled down his mask.

With Gunner he'd been both annoyed and hungry, but the strategy was the same—a quick in and out, a flash-rip that tears down to subdermal layers just deep enough to bleed the brachial vein. As he transformed, his head grazed the ceiling of the tiny cubicle, so he stooped and coiled into a snap-to across the room, teeth in and out of Tommy's arm before his face registered the pain.

"Somnum," he snarled, with more inalienable malevolence than he'd ever wanted Tommy to remember, but that was that. He caught the blood drips with one hand and went to the sink to wash out his mouth.

June's ten-minute drive from St. Louis Children's Hospital to the convention complex still racked up over an hour while she picked out overnights, made extended-stay arrangements with the hotel, and stopped for takeout. She checked her watch for the five-hundredth time if she checked it fifty—as if *that* would somehow make the duration of her absence from Tommy any less.

When June walked back into ICU, she was at first relieved to see Tommy was resting quietly. But Callan, still holding vigilance bedside, looked drained. She hadn't seen him this tired before.

Let's go out here for a bit," she said, holding up a super-size shopping bag of Chinese takeout, the *Lucas and food in there somewhere* tradition, ever a noteworthy thing. He smiled then, happy but weary creases around those black ones.

She also noticed he picked at his Hunan beef steak although she'd requested it medium-rare, and he seemed rather listless in general. So after dinner in the lobby she began laying out her things on the sleeper cot in Tommy's cubicle and strongly suggested Callan take her car back to the hotel and try to get some rest.

When she had made all her arrangements to go lights-out and it looked he wasn't going to budge, she sat down on the cot and talked to him some more, mid-sentence about ordering a rental for him to return home if he needed to get back and such, when the room went black.

Callan had only wept over five women in his lifetime—his sister Anya, his mother, Nonna, Milja, and now, June. For being an inextricably messy part in their lives, he'd tried to clean up as best he knew how.

Hell's Bells and buckets of blood he'd thankfully managed to miss Tommy's artery, or the mop-up agenda on that one would still be under hospital review. As it turned out, the wound cleaned up nicely with some sterile gauze and the original dressing adhered to the right location precisely enough. He'd reinstated the Mini-Blinds to broadside open after his shoulders were back in order, and June had arrived half an hour later.

Even in the midst of all this she remained the resilient, cheerful June who considerately looked out for everyone else. For that reason she couldn't know the part he'd contributed to any of this mess, ever.

When she'd finally settled down on the sleeper cot to try to help him address whatever predicament of his own she knew nothing about, he caught her mid-sentence with *Somnum* again and laid her gently back on the cot. For as much as he'd tried, he couldn't see any other way around this. Tears were free-falling then, sloppy ones he didn't try to stanch. He held her hand and cast the spell.

No longer in your heart and head, be gone after all is said.
I decree it best. I have loved you, and I release you. So be it.

Chapter Eighteen

In days gone by—before Callan arrived in Eureka Springs—a snarl of underground tunnels connected *ab urbe condita* most of buildings or businesses downtown. Little by little, individual merchants bricked up and closed off much of what went on under the streets, because by 1929, their real problems weren't hooking or bootlegging, but pilfering.

Shafts located on the foot walls originally snaked alongside each building's substructure in one direction or another for miles. Today, they dead-end into solid brick walls at each adjacent property.

All but a handful, and Callan knew where they were.

When mining, it's assumed the bedding plane is practically vertical, but Eureka's is not. Some shafts, therefore, were sunk vertically, and others inclined—whatever the topography called for. And since the original base of downtown Eureka was once a mud bowl that could hardly be called flat, the tunnels also varied—drifting off on several levels, intersections dependent solely on a questionable accuracy of any available surveys in the day. The shafts sunk near foot walls had less problems with dislocation over time, for the bedrock held them steady enough.

Most were barely large enough for an average-size fellow to pass through, rectangular constructs with the longer sides transverse and timbered to cleavages and spurs of bedrock where they passed, which slowed the rate of slabbing. At one time or another some encased openings had to be propped up by cross bars or buntons spiked into their cribs, others hanging on by stringing planks warping downhill, gaps just large enough to crawl through after nearly a century.

Callan knew where those were as well. He'd mapped out every alley, rat run, or ravine downtown including the undersides of staircases or emissaries—way back when he worked for the butcher.

He did it because he knew one day he might be hunted.

This he feared more than laboratory examination or hypodermic needles—the possibility of a public volte-face. Just one commiserable event coupled with the arrival of a critical mass was all it would take. Whether by backstairs tub-thumping or a shiner from digital media—he realized chances were the day would come when he'd no longer be able to lull the town into forgetfulness, and a local vigilante group could single out the diablo in their midst.

After Tommy succumbed to his illness, they didn't come after him with pitchforks and torches. These guys carried assault rifles and cell phones, and they were in a footrace with the local police. He'd stopped by the gallery on his way in from St. Louis for his regular rotation of blue juice, and as he closed up, in they came.

Callan wasn't yet aware Tommy was gone; his own cell phone had redlined at 2 percent hours ago. He dodged the coup well enough, but a quicker cowboy with something that looked like a livestock syringe managed to soak the back of his shirt with sulfuric acid before he got out the back door, into the night.

Tommy's death was on him, and this hippie-town posse planned to put him on a stake or a rope, he didn't know which. His wings couldn't come in now, either—so he ran.

They'd try to catch him in the middle of town where he heard the hammering, something going up near Basin Park, a fitting place for a lynching if he must say so. Callan ran first to Leatherwood Creek and jumped in, willing the sub-zero water to wash away what scorched him, then out again, shuddering—tossing his wet Oxfords as he skirted downwind toward sublevel streets near Montgomery. The hunt could become endless if he kept to the lower parts outdoors, and the tunnels were his last resort.

A safer option was probably his cave, but how to get back to it . . . for he could hear them bushwhacking on the south side of Cliff Street a hundred yards away. He knew then they were fanning out their operation, that they'd probably already tossed his house and absconded with his only method of transportation out of here. Not a chance of blending in with window shoppers or holding out in one of the longer tunnels west of town—not now.

The cliffside boardwalk off Montgomery wasn't a great choice either, he knew, so he hopped over the staircase railing and swung to the frost-rimed ground underneath the deck and waited. They might have scotopic equipment, but he still had distinct advantages at night. With his hyperacusis, however, what he hadn't counted on was how *annoying* the gallows raising could be, or the grass-roots smarts behind a relentless pounding that threw off his acuity . . .

Callan jerked into the realm of the living on a rose-carved Empire sofa, the one for all the guests he'd never entertained in the front room of his house. *Sunlight, way too much.* He pulled a pillow over his face.

Damn roller shade he forgot about and they're trying to take out the front door with a battering ram. The room spun when he sat.

Come and get it, yahoos.

He wasn't in any shape to walk to the door, let alone fight them off. After—five days, *aye, sounds about right*—they'd finally found him. The confusing part was remembering how he got from *there* to here. Callan sat spread-eagle and propped his elbows on his knees.

That's better. He might be able to remain upright this time, he was *hell-yeah* awake and frosty enough. Somewhere in that eyesore of bottles on the coffee table he had a chaser of potato vodka—or maybe he'd cashed it in already, on the floor. He found it under the couch on the second pass, several ounces shy from nearly enough as far as he was concerned, *fuck those pistol-packing hillbillies,* the banging was driving him nuts.

"Enough already," he yelled. *Silence.* Precious, precious silence. It didn't last long, though. The brass door fitting he never locked was bouncing now, and he watched it dully for a moment or two, wondering when it could've possibly worked that loose. He was about to follow up with a more vulgar remark when the door swung open to full mast, some *skinny little fucker* over there blooming in way too much *tejas*. Callan guarded his face. *Goddamn,* even his eyeballs hurt.

His sight for the most part was piss-poor in broad daylight and at this rate he'd never see what got him, anyway—but he recognized the footfalls.

June.

With the local posse?

When he tried to stand, he went back down just as quickly. He couldn't see them yet, but he could *feel* those Bunsen burner blues taking in everything, and *yessir,* she was annoyed.

Falling Stars

But so was he.

She wasn't supposed to be here. Ever again. *What the fuck?*

The door closed behind her, a graciously gentle click-to. *By herself, then.*

But—*why?*

"Where do you keep the garbage bags?" she was asking. It took a moment to register, and by that time she was opening and shutting drawers in the kitchen.

Oh hell, no. Callan slumped back on the couch. Of all the things she should be doing after losing her son and—*he'd cast her a ninth level, why didn't it take?*

Then she was slinging pots and pans and he heard water running. Nice of her to do the dishes but *he really couldn't abide that ruckus, either.* Come to think of it, he hadn't done much of anything this week except drink, pass out, and run from the imaginary posse in an alcohol-fed stupor. He had on—the same clothes he wore to Fan Expo. Callan closed his eyes.

Ting ware on wood, the kinds Nonna used to serve in the thick of a card game. He recalled that sound with fondness, but that wasn't exactly what was going on here. It *did* wake him up again. His stash was gone, and he was staring down a pitcher of water and a mug of something highly acerbic—two, three, five tea bags he counted.

"Drink up. Then we'll talk."

"I don't drink it that way," he argued.

"You do now." He could see her face a little better this time, and she was dead serious.

He picked up the mug. "This could really punch it the other way, you know," he went on.

Silence. She hadn't yet removed her duffle coat, the one she wore when temps fell into the teens, arms crossed in front of her.

"Just saying." He strangled down a sip, calculating how long he might be able to hold down this bilious belly-wash.

"It's freezing in here. Where's the thermostat?"

"Down the hallway." He thumbed in the general direction.

While she was gone, he poured a generous amount of the five-alarm tea into a barf bucket he kept under the table, and he heard the heat kick on.

After texting and calling Callan for five days with no response, June was steamed. Then she began to worry. His shop had gone dark too. After the second drive-by before a winter storm was due, she decided she had to try—to determine whether Callan really *did* walk out on her and Tommy, or if she needed to report him missing. At least that was the logic she'd repeated all the way down the mountain to his front door.

But here he sat, Brahms and Liszt, drunk as a boiled owl.

The sheer volume of firewater he'd managed to tank up on while somehow evading ethyl alcohol poisoning was alarming. He blacked out during the larger part of her cleanup, probably a good thing since he did seem to have an attitude.

Here and there she'd pause to watch the seams of his shirt rise and fall, proof he was still breathing. *If those are the same clothes he wore in St. Louis*, she noted, there's yet another reason he could use a shower and a shave right now.

The insight she gained while bagging up his red-eye collection also began to answer—well, some things. Not everything.

While he dozed she snooped. He had Prince Hairy bottoms-up on a card table next to an unopened shipping box from Build-a-Bear. Helter-skelter around the front room were sketches, some of a child that looked like her—yet not her. These pieces were dated September and October, a month before they met.

In 1939.

June gulped down her surprise and studied them more closely, carefully turning the friable paper flipside for anything else he'd written. Five below in a pile of sketches on a nearby chair she found another one, the same young girl. Inscribed—

Agnetha.

June stiffened, the Ping-Pong analysis in her head serving a sidespin, how it both *could* and *couldn't* be. In something that looked like a keepsake box on the kitchen counter, she picked through an assortment of old scraps of paper, business and trading cards—*very old ones*, some dating as far back as 1922. She examined them long enough to determine they weren't vintage reproductions. A collector, perhaps?

She held onto that idea until she found a check-size envelope with two place cards for first-class dining. Both were imprinted with the authentic Cunard Steamship logo, the crowned golden lion dancing with a world globe. When she read the names, her hands shook. She quickly put the envelope back inside and shut the box.

Time to wake him up.

✯

Well, she wasn't buying his disappearing tea act. June replaced the mug with one of his straight-sided water glasses and pushed the pitcher at him. *Now you're talking*, he mused, *but I'm really not too keen for anything that's not liquid sunshine, either.*

"Do this often?" she asked.

On second thought, he really could use some H_2O—but no, this whole development had been unequivocally and purposely a one-shot deal aimed at punishing himself for getting involved with her in the first place. And Tommy—*well*. No luck for that little puddle hopper from day one, he'd known it. Elbows propped on his knees again, Callan could only look down, his back bowed with frustration and exhaustion.

She poured the water then, and he noticed she'd also unearthed his cell phone. "Where's your charger?" she asked.

"The kitchen, I ken," he mumbled, and picked up the glass with both hands. *Thirstier than he thought.* He gulped down half of it and listened. More rummaging, items being moved about in the kitchen. He just couldn't figure, though, why she'd even be here doing this after he'd precisely cast her just like the rest. She should be burying her son on this day—*unless*—he nearly dropped the glass then, a flummox between his knees, the floor, and the coffee table right in front of him. *Fuck*, this was bad. *Unless*—the spell had removed her memory *to Tommy instead.*

Callan managed to aright the glass on the table and sat back.

"You didn't get any of my texts or calls?" she asked. *Still moving things around in the kitchen.*

In truth he hadn't charged his phone all week because *I killed him, didn't I?* he really wanted to ask. "I think it needs a new battery," he lied.

From the kitchen, "Really? It seems to be charging just fine." She was back, looking him over once more. "You need a shower. Come on."

She let him flounder his way after her to a three-quarter bathroom just off the kitchen where he showered in the summer, the bath upstairs reserved for deep winter and any available heat that rose up to greet.

He'd refurbished the one downstairs a while back with a tiled-in shower and corner seat, though—it was nice. He thought it wouldn't strike her as too shabby while he watched her adjust the showerhead as if she'd done it a hundred times before and he also noticed she turned *only* the right faucet. When he started looking for the buttons on his shirt, she stopped him.

"In you go, all of you," she ordered. "We need more tonic alertness and then we'll talk." She shoved him inside—shirt, pants, socks, and all—and shut the shower door behind him.

That got him going.

Fuck, this is freezing. He reached for the left knob.

"Oh no, you don't," he heard her say from behind. "Sit down and take it like a big boy."

He groused under his breath but did as she asked, teeth clacking already, snot dripping from his nose. "I'm awake now," he grumbled.

She had her own cell phone out and put it aside on the counter where he could see a timer running. "Two minutes," she said.

He shivered and glared at her, realizing his worst didn't have the same clout it once had even just days ago. She pulled up a stool nearby and sat. When the timer pinged and the water torture was done, she opened the door, turned off the shower, and tossed a bath sheet at him.

She definitely had on some kind of black athleisure for snowshoeing, he decided, plus her coat, her hair armed into a slick, high ponytail—and boy, was she pissed. He could see it in all the solipsism and small movements, little backfists and purls he' never noticed before. All-business, ready to deck him if she didn't drown him first. He shook out the towel and clutched it to his chest, no verónica today, *no ma'am,* all he could muster to keep from circling the drain. He thought about trying to stand, but she had an answer for that as well.

"You stay put." She sat back down on the stool four-some-odd feet away, close enough. Her carotids were popping, and he could feel the heat, *blessed* heat.

"I'm going to ask you a question," she said.

He'd expected as much; when they were done with hers, he had some of his own. "Okay."

"And you *are* going to tell me the truth."

Yes, that. He washed his front teeth with his tongue and waited for

Falling Stars

número uno.

"When did you move into this house?"

A roundabout way of asking, perhaps she really didn't want to know as much as she'd imagined, but he thought he could humor her. They'd cart him off to some laboratory and stick tubes up his ass when she was done with him, anyhow. He didn't give a rip; he was done for.

"Nineteen forty," he said.

Oh *shit, shit, shit.* Callan didn't dodge an inch, black eyes fixed on her. His answer brought up *so much more*, and June could clearly see he was in no shape to get through her entire pick list. He was dehydrated and ketotic, eyes red-rimmed and sunken, as wan as Tommy had once been.

But she had to know.

She got up, deliberating the best way to get at this. "I don't believe you," she said.

Callan slumped against the shower wall and groaned. "Then *why* did you ask?"

June could feel the chill from where she stood. "The truth, please," she repeated.

He leaned his head against the shower wall and shut his eyes. "I just told you."

"No, you didn't," June snapped, resorting to what she usually employed to get past upsets like this one, pacing the room and sounding off as conclusions arrived, her eyes downcast in thought. "You haven't told me *how* you could occupy a house before you obviously were born. You haven't told me *why* you drive a 1937 Packard. You haven't told me how it is that no one can seem to remember *when* your gallery opened. You haven't—"

June couldn't be sure what tipped her off first. She looked up mid-sentence and stopped cold.

The thing standing in the shower wasn't human.

It roared at her then, *canines flared, sawbill fangs*—

June, eyes locked on its teeth, commanded herself to think, *think*. Her go-to, it turned out, was the same autocratic reflex that had served her during many a clinical scrap-to, very little thinking involved. "You —" she held up a finger, "put those up."

Callan collapsed against the shower wall and slid down to the seat. Tassemon had warned him about the ramifications of turning, pretty much what he'd been doing lately and then some. Maybe, he thought, *just maybe*—this was the last proof anybody would ever need.

After his bones sank into something more identifiably sapiens, he opened his eyes, surprised to see June kneeling on the floor in front of him.

"You didn't hear yet, did you?" she began, searching his face for the answer.

And he waited for her to tell him the awful news.

"For all you have suffered, you saved my son."

Callan blinked at her. *Tommy's alive?*

She smiled at him through tears. "When he showed me his infusion site and the marks, I didn't believe him. Then all his labs came back normal." June backhanded the tears off her cheeks. "No one knows what to make of it."

He wasn't sure how that happened, either. "Did he get the transplant?"

"No need. He's fine." She picked up the wet bath sheet off the shower floor and stood, busy finding another one. "Casey made out like a bandit and baked enough gummy muffins to ruin all our teeth."

Callan smiled. *After just witnessing the genuine article, probably a good thing she could take it down a notch.*

"Tommy told me about the fight at school." She opened the linens cabinet.

Yes, that. Which brought them back to why she ever came over in the first place.

"You were supposed to forget me," Callan said.

June returned with a dry towel for him, unfolded this time. She stopped, eyes narrowed. "So that's how you do it."

"It is," he waited, unsure how she would take such news.

She draped the towel over his shoulders and began tucking in the sides. "It didn't work."

"I didn't want it to," he said, following her tending with his eyes.

She cupped one hand over his cheek, the same tender mercy he'd admired on the first day they'd met. "I'm glad," she said. "I never want to forget you."

He would've kissed her then, but the back of his teeth had a buildup of something crusty that didn't belong there.

"So—this other thing you do," she went on. "It'll be our secret, okay?"

"You won't study me?"

She grinned. "Oh, I'll be scoping you out regularly, just not that way."

He was pretty sure she hadn't thought through what his potential lifespan might ultimately mean for their relationship. "I'll outlive you," he said.

Then again, maybe she had. "At the rate you're going," she countered, "I wouldn't be so sure."

He managed a simper at her gallows humor, too weary to laugh. *Hungry too.* "How do we do this?" he asked instead.

"We'll start with something bland," June said, helping him stand.

"That's not what I meant."

She looked up at him, the little crease between her eyes already informing him that those finer points could wait. "If there's one thing you should realize by now, Viscount—I can deal with you."

"I never doubted it for a minute."

"You need to deposit that check I wrote you, by the way."

She was right. Dating her wasn't cheap.

June continued talking to him while she laid out his toothbrush and shaving kit in neat little rows. A gentle reminder for him—yes, how often she dealt with these very same dilemmas: the frailty of human existence, and at times, the unfair resilience of life.

Casualties were hard.

Surviving was harder.

She also reminded him he was a wonderful person to share life with, and that love, however lengthy or brief, goes far beyond measuring the time we have left. Then she was off to the kitchen in search of something bland. But not for long. He was working his way through some fossilized dental plaque with his toothbrush when she leaned through the doorway.

"So, just curious. What's your vaccination status?"

He spat in the sink. "Cholera, typhoid, polio."

She thought about it. "The oral ones, okay. Nothing else?"

"I don't like needles."

She smiled. "Obviously. And how old did you say you were again?"

That's sly, all right. "I didn't." He rinsed and spat in the sink one more time while she waited. "One hundred one," he said.

Her eyes registered genuine shock and awe. *This might be more fun than he originally thought.*

"Wow. Dental work?"

"Nope."

"*Amazing.* Yearly exam? Prostate check?"

"*No.*"

Totally rad, Casey texted, *no school* Friday for her, either—all because it happened to snow a shitstorm the night before. Since she didn't get to cut school for the whole almost-transplant-Expo gong show, she was super jazzed, cool for building a Yeti snowman and two levels of *Rockin' A* because the B&B was empty and Dawn didn't need her, anyhow.

Life was good in general since he and Mom got back Monday, just normal stuff like he used to do and back to school on Wednesday. Mom patched things up with the *art guy* who was really the vampire guy *but no tellin'*, Mom said, *dem's dee rules*, she made Tommy swear on a stack of Bibles.

Otherwise things were really pretty *chillaxed* since Fan Expo, *no problemo*. Except, he had to admit, that *rip-torn* Kodak moment really didn't turn out to be a turning, anyway. He was still the same vampire he'd always been, minus the PNH. Fallon had warned him—and sure enough, the outcome spoke for itself. He *really, really* couldn't turn anyone.

But Tommy felt alive again. *Better* than alive. Curfew was super-duper hard because he didn't get sleepy anymore. He was rocking out with "Drac's Got Plaque" this morning and had planned on returning to the sink to spit straight—when he noticed something ...

Odd.

The same old toothbrush he'd used, like, for donkeys' ages, didn't *buzz on* like usual, and when Tommy glanced in the bathroom mirror—*holy Godzilla*, for *one coconut, two coconut, three coconut* he was looking at a piranha-jaw remodel like something streaming on Marvel.

Yeet, waz iz? Hold the freakin' speed dial.

He felt it in his shoulders also. Then *brain freeze*, he was back, *just me*, yuppers. *And what the frig was all that,* he supposed, his heart racing. *Donkey Balls.*

Epilogue

All of us are fabricated from stardust and we have fallen here. Some time ago I boiled down life to this ad hoc element inside the working day shove-and-deliver, even before Gram dusted the base of the Black Mountains and made it a point to follow me more closely than my personal comfort zone allowed at times.

In the weeks following Fan Expo when both Percy and I verged on burnout, I was practically tripping over her on my way to the mail bag at the end of my workstation. Perhaps I'd outgrown Gram somewhere along the way with current worldly concerns, but I wasn't about to let her go. Although "Bad Blood" had run its course, inquiries kept us busy for several months, and in those months I needed her.

As for the fan mail, McWatters naturally elected that *me and thee* should handle the rest and the residue since his sixth-removed had obviously bailed on us. Some low-volume conversations I happened upon here and there might've been Percy's hugger-muggered and altruistic efforts to reconnect, I don't know. Last I officially heard, Cochran had settled somewhere down in bayou country. After his peptic flameout at Fan Expo, he apparently lost interest in producing any more material for optioning or pursuing a writing career with us.

When I got around to answering the fan letter I'd forgotten in my briefcase, we'd just taken *Philly's* into redesign, vying for a 70 percent renewal rate in our perpetually insane undertaking. The reply I finally wrote, therefore, felt canned and dated no matter how many runs I made at it.

Dear Tommy, I typed. *The crew at* Philly's Argosy *wants to thank you for your continued readership. We make every effort to answer our fan mail in a timely manner and in the order it is received.*

So, yes, that was a grand fudge, and Gram was in on it. I did my best to explain my mealy-mouthed attempt at sticking to industry standards in low whispers to her—head down, moving on.

It's our goal to serve our readers with the best in speculative fiction, and we hold our contributors to the highest of standards.

After putzing around with Cochran, I was reasonably sure we'd need to reinvent our mission statement. I'd demand it, in fact. But Gram had one finger raised, warning me to tidy up, that I needed to get going with the task at hand.

While in all accounts the role of Claudius Fallon as written in the "Bad Blood" series remains a work of fiction, we can neither confirm nor deny the existence of such a person living in Eureka Springs today. We would encourage you to check with your local voter registration office or the department of motor vehicles. Other public records you might inquire into are birth or death certificates, marriage or divorce licenses, military records, or contracts relating to property rights. Beyond that you might also consider naturalization records.

I signed and dated this banalized reply—one that smacked of the inner workings and groupthink of a flummoxed market focus group—and addressed the envelope. Once I got a stiff nod from Gram, I stuffed it, and after that one joined the others in our mail drop, she vanished.

I was left behind and alone then, onto the next tale, forever *that one* —for the pile in my inbox somehow isn't getting any smaller. Perhaps we all are myopic to some degree, shackled by the very same time and space that compels us to run toward *the next thing*. And somewhere in that endeavor could be the truth we're longing for.

Acknowledgments

He's still not sure if I want to thank him or not, the better half who happens to be my husband, because he understands that the process of reading aloud *anything* first off is always painful. The fact is, his ears were the only ones in-the-know and forced to wait yet another month between most first-draft chapters—for fourteen months. Thanks, Dear, for your abiding enthusiasm.

Thank you too, Bill Grabowski, for editing this one with such professionalism and care. And to thirty-five beta readers, eleven whom I call my wordies: Nan Davis, Becky Hoag, Jane Derden, Doedi Meyer, Rebecca Flynt, Lois DiMari, Monica Wacker, Cheryl Swanson, Diana Throckmorton, Debra Brown, and Misha Lee.

Also by Julie Rogers

Happy Tails: How Pets Can Help You Survive Divorce

Simeon: A Greater Reality

Seven Shorts

Hootie

When Pigs Fly Over The Moon

Letters: Sidereal Insight for a 21st Century Mystic (with Seth Rogers)